Desert Sons

Mark Kendrick

Writers Club Press

New York   Lincoln   Shanghai

Desert Sons

Writers Club Press
an imprint of iUniverse, Inc.

For information address:
iUniverse
2021 Pine Lake Road, Suite 100
Lincoln, NE 68512
www.iuniverse.com

This story is not a dramatization, although some
real place names are used throughout.
All characters are figments of my imagination and do not reflect actual
people who live or have lived in Southern California's Morongo Basin.

ISBN: 0-595-19130-4

Printed in the United States of America

"Sometimes, I feel the fear of,
Uncertainty stinging clear.
And I can't help but ask myself
How much I let the fear
Take the wheel and steer…

…It's driven me before,
And it seems to be the way that
Everyone else gets around.
But lately I'm, beginning to find
When I drive myself my light is found."

Incubus, **Make Yourself**, *Drive*

"Let me be the one you call.
If you jump I'll break your fall.
Lift you up and fly away
With you into the night."

Savage Garden, **Affirmation**, *Crash and Burn*

PREFACE

Just some of what people have said about this bestseller:

"This first novel by Mark Kendrick hints at a maturity of style rare in many first novels. The characters are well conceived and presented in depth. There is real growth of character here presented in unabashedly erotic and emotional scenes."
    —Ron Donaghe, author of *Common Sons*

"In reading Mark Kendrick's first novel, I often forgot about the plot, not because it didn't interest me, but because Kendrick succeeds so incredibly at bringing readers deep into the minds and hearts of his two main characters: Ryan and Scott."
    —Duane Simolke, author of *The Acorn Stories*

"It really is a tender love story…and the evidence of familial support is heartening. Also, the wonderful settings (desert and coastline) make this read like a mini-vacation. This, Mark Kendrick's first effort, is impressive; his attention to detail is remarkable. A job well done."
    —a reader from New Jersey

"Amazing is the only way to describe this book. It is rare to find a gay-themed coming out book that is worth the paper it is written on, which is why this book is such a find. The characters are very real and believ-

able. The situations ring with truth as do the conversations. The author is so skilled with his descriptions of the people and places that at times you will feel the heat of the desert or the coolness of the rain washing over you. I found myself relating to both main characters in a way that other books could only dream of doing."
—a reader from Georgia

"The characters in this book were so real to me that in a way I felt that I am Ryan. This book provides a positive, truthful, realistic perspective on young life, and is well worth the time to read. It proves how important friendship and love are for people, gay or straight."
—another reader from New Jersey

"The author does a very good job at making the story come to life. It was also a nice change to read a book that shows a young gay couple committed to each other. I wish I had read this book when I was a little younger. I think everyone, especially gay teens, could benefit from reading this. It is much more then your typical coming-out book."
—a reader from Pennsylvania

"This is a very-well crafted coming-out book. The author has a fine ear for teenage dialogue and writes with a style that owes no apology to the best 'literary' gay novels. Kendrick makes the reader care very much about his two young protagonists, even though one of them (Ryan) is a "troubled" youth. His boyfriend, Scott, is the most likeable character I've ever encountered in fiction. Kendrick also works in a number of very explicitly erotic scenes that never feel gratuitous. I've read many gay coming-out books; this is one of the very best."
—a reader from California

Thank you all!

Mark Kendrick

To Glenn, who puts up with a writer.

CHAPTER 1

Seventeen-year old Ryan St. Charles woke up with a terrible headache. He then became painfully aware of his nose, his upper lip, and his left elbow. *It's true,* he thought as he opened his eyes, *I'm still alive.*

Only half-conscious in the ambulance as he was being driven to the hospital, he nonetheless recalled seeing two EMTs hovering over him. He remembered blood being all over the steering wheel and his hands. The last thing he recalled was being stretched out on a gurney which was going down a hallway before he went unconscious again. Now he recalled blood being all over his favorite pair of jeans and, in the semi-dark hospital room, he realized he no longer had them on. He was sure they didn't save them or the nice shirt Crawford bought him last month. Knowing that made him curiously sad and angry at the same time. Yet, try as he might, he couldn't remember exactly what happened to him.

The stark hospital room was quiet in the middle of the night. The silence was as annoying as the pain. He moved his left arm and found it in a sling. Judging that since it wasn't in a cast, he figured there were no broken bones. With his free hand, he touched his forehead at the hairline. As he felt around, he found that a wide area had been shaved down to the scalp. There was some sort of bandage covering it. Although his head hurt like hell, he had to get up and see what he knew were stitches underneath.

He pushed the sheets away and slowly moved his legs over the side. As he rose upright his head hurt even more. He stayed put for a moment. Outside the window to his right, it was dark. He glanced at a clock on the wall next to the window. It read two thirty-three. The floor was cold as he rested his bare feet on the linoleum and headed for the bathroom. Wearing nothing but a standard green hospital gown, he felt a little embarrassed, but the other patient in the room was fast asleep, so his embarrassment was short-lived.

He took a peek at the old man who lay in the bed nearer the door behind a semi-parted curtain. A tiny lamp clamped to a metal rack next to his bed cast a feeble light across his right side. His sparse white hair was in disarray and it looked like he hadn't shaved in a couple of days. Two IVs hung next to the bed. One of the lines trailed conspicuously to tape at the crook of his elbow. It silently testified that the man was worse off than he was just now. The yellowish-brown bruises beneath the translucent tape stood out at him and made him woozy as he looked away and continued to the bathroom. He was glad his injuries only made him feel as if he'd been in a fight and nothing more. He slowly shut the door behind him in the harsh, sterile bathroom and flipped on the light. It hurt his eyes, and as they adjusted, he looked in the mirror. What he saw did little to help soothe his feelings of cold and isolation.

Ryan had medium length, layered, almost jet-black hair parted on one side. Although the crowd he hung out with wore their hair decidedly longer, he preferred his shorter. Now a large patch of it above his left eyebrow was shaved down to his pale white scalp. He inspected the bandage covering part of his forehead and slowly peeled away one side of it to reveal ten neatly-spaced stitches along a slightly curved gash. Surprisingly it didn't hurt too much when he touched them. He carefully pressed the tape back into place.

He tilted his head back to look at his nose. It was swollen and flecks of dried blood fell into the sink as he ventured a finger to one nostril. He touched his lip and winced as he pressed. Even his gums hurt. Luckily, all his teeth were intact.

Ryan's dark brown eyes, deep set, with long black lashes, were a stark contrast to his pale skin. The mostly cloudy climate of his home, here in Crescent City on the northern California coast, wasn't conducive to a tan. Now his face was even paler, except for the shiner now prominent around his left eye. That explained why he could barely open it, he now realized.

The ill-fitting hospital gown did him no justice. At five-foot ten inches and 160 pounds, he was of medium build, but wasn't particularly muscular. Regardless, he had wide shoulders and well-defined chest and abs, due to only minor body fat. He would normally have felt horny examining his virtually naked body in front of the mirror. Yet, now, he couldn't feel anything but despair and stupidity.

It was beginning to come to him now. Horniness was what had started the whole mess in the first place. In an attempt to get back at Crawford Grant, the man he'd been seeing his entire senior year, and end his continuous desperation about their secret relationship, he had wrecked his prized vintage Chevelle. He had hoped he would be killed in the wreck. Unfortunately, he was still alive and now had to face what he had done. And Muh, his grandmother, was surely going to throw him out now. She had warned him enough times about all the tickets he had gotten over the last year. Now that he had wrecked his car she was sure to be extra angry. And what did he have to show for his rash decision? Stitches, bruises, his elbow, a black eye, a swollen lip, no car, and now a sinking feeling that he had lost everything. It was the awful feelings he was trying to escape in the first place and now he not only had managed to compound them, but also was still right in the middle of them all.

The quandary he had lived through these last nine or so months just wouldn't end, he thought. To make it even worse, he had wrecked the car on purpose. He had gunned the engine just enough to miss a hairpin curve coming back from Frank Gaviota's house, a man he considered his friend, but still couldn't trust with his secret, damn it! He was angry that he was too scared to tell Frank what had been going on between he and Crawford, how the fights with his grandmother had become more frequent, how he had alienated his brother, and how his so-called girlfriend wanted more than he was willing to deliver. He had wanted to tell Frank everything, but just couldn't. It was a huge, jumbled mess, and every step of the way he had gotten more entangled in it. If he hadn't been so scared or stupid he wouldn't be looking at his bruised and cut body now. The mixture of sadness and anger swirled inside him making him sway as he stood. He gripped the edge of the sink to keep his balance. His headache was growing more intense.

It was all so disgusting. He couldn't even commit suicide properly. The thought of having tried it for the third time, and failing once again, weighed on him. He had been good at keeping his emotions in check but now found himself getting teary-eyed. Things just had to change, God damn it!

Graduation from high school was only a month away and despite an almost failing grade in Composition and two C-averages in other classes, he knew he could pull through. He wasn't dumb, it was just that Composition was his last class of the day. He usually didn't do the homework and occasionally just skipped the class altogether so he'd have time to see Crawford. He looked at his wrists as he thought about him. The abrasions had started to fade but were still noticeable. *I'm sure the EMTs saw them*, he thought. *I wonder if they could tell they were from handcuffs?* Crawford's handcuffs. Crawford the handsome, Crawford the sex god, Crawford the blackmailer.

He opened the bathroom door, flipped off the light, and slowly shuffled back to his bed. His chart was hanging on the end of it from a peg.

He pulled it off with his good hand, rested it on the mattress, and flipped open the top. He hazarded a look down the sheet trying to make out what he could. He had no idea what it all meant. The only two words he could make out were 'observation' and 'concussion'. Well, that explained his headache. He flipped the top back down and slowly replaced it on the peg. He sat on the edge of the bed for a moment. His throat was dry and felt sore. A small blue plastic jug of water sat on a stainless steel wall-hung table next to the bed and he reached for it. A folded piece of paper with his name on it in his grandmother's handwriting sat conspicuously upright next to it. He looked at it from the corner of his open eye as he drank. Afraid to read it, he hesitated, knowing what it would say. It could only be one thing. He knew he shouldn't have, given how he felt, but he opened it and read anyway. It said exactly what he expected:

Ryan—

The police report was clear. You were going too fast again and they're taking your license this time. I've talked with your Uncle Howard about coming to get you after the court date. It's best if you live with him now. We'll talk about this later.

Love, Muh.

Her handwriting was crimped and smaller than normal, giving away her tenseness. At least she said '*Love, Muh,*' he thought.

His chin trembled and he forcibly made it stop as he read it again. In a way, it was perfect. Howard was his convenient way out. But his uncle lived in the desert way down in southern California. Surrounding Yucca Valley was nothing except endless sand and rocks. He had seen the photos and heard him describe it before. Yet, it seemed the only way to escape from Crawford, end the girlfriend lie he had gotten himself into, and remove himself from the endless confrontations he had had with Muh.

He crumpled the note and tossed it into a small waste can to his right. He eased himself back onto bed and rested his head on the pillow. He grasped the call button at the end of the black cord near his pillow and pressed firmly with his thumb. Maybe a nurse would have something for his aching head.

CHAPTER 2

Sixteen-year old Scott Faraday watched the green, black-spotted lizard scuttle past and into the crack of the copper-colored rock to his right. He continued up the remaining several feet and surveyed the top of the high rocky mount where he was perched. His dark rust-colored hair blew in the steady warm winds of the high desert this late afternoon. Standing now at the summit of Inauguration Peak, a mere one hundred-fifty feet above the desert floor, he welcomed the short time he'd have to play his flute.

The dry windswept landscape of the high rocky desert surrounding Yucca Valley yielded an emptiness that Scott interpreted not as desolate, as would some, but as compelling, even though he had lived here for more than half of his nearly seventeen years. This was where he found solace and the unusual quiet not available anywhere else. And there was no other place this close to the house with a view like this.

He raised his hand up to his forehead. An observer would have immediately noticed the dark reddish eyebrows and eyelashes, which contrasted quite handsomely with the bright green eyes he shaded from the sun. Wearing only shorts and hiking boots, Scott stood 5' 8". At 148 pounds, his stocky yet lean frame revealed why he was one of Yucca Valley's varsity runners for the last two years. He inspected his shoulder only briefly. No need to worry about a burn with all the sunscreen he had on. And he already had an even base tan despite being light-skinned.

He dusted his hands off on his shorts and reached back to pull a faded blue and white bandanna from one of his back pockets. He briefly wiped his armpits of the salt that had accumulated there, then stuffed it back into his pocket. His canteen dug into his bare shoulder and he pulled it off, letting it drop to the flat stone surface. Next to it he set down the metal instrument case he had been holding.

He spied his tiered circle of flat rocks off to the right and reached them just as his Black Lab, Shakaiyo, bounded her way to the top with him. At two and a half years old, she was his constant companion on most of his varied activities. She immediately wagged her tail upon see-ing him but declined to lick his outstretched hand as she panted.

From beneath the capstone of the tight circle, which he moved aside, he retrieved a translucent 35mm film case that held a rolled-up piece of paper and a stubby pencil. Carefully unrolling it as if examining an important document, he inspected the writing. His initials and dates were written down the paper of his most recent treks up here. Now oth-ers read *BAO* and *MJJ*. There was also a short message that simply said: *"We're watching you!"*

"What the…" he said aloud as he looked up and scanned the area. Who could have possibly found his scroll? He placed his initials and the date beneath the others while pondering, then replaced the film case in the opening. Then it dawned on him. It took a moment to figure it out because he never used their middle names. Of course, the initials were from drummer Bryce Owens and Mitch Jenner, the bass guitarist from Centauri, the band he did sound for. How did they just happen to find his film case? They weren't the type to go scrambling around these rocky hills.

He stepped back to the instrument case and opened it. Inside was his flute. He put the sections together with a quick twist. There was a dent at the end of the last section, and the nickel was flecked away in several places, but it produced a beautiful sound. Being in band in junior high and as a freshman in high school had taught him most of the technical things he needed to know about how to play. But he was beginning to find that he had his own special way with it nowadays. Being with in rock band this last year had accelerated his need to find his own way of playing it. Months earlier, Colleen, the lead singer of the band, taught him an unusual tremolo that he had never thought of before. He had finally gotten the hang of it. He sat cross-legged in the shade of a high overhang with his back against a vertical surface. Shakaiyo, seeing that he had decided to sit, came and sat with him, too.

Scott licked his lips and raised the flute to them. As he did so, he surveyed the vista below him. From 'his' peak, at the foot of the Little San Bernardino Mountains he could see most of town through the light haze. He could even see their family's restaurant on the highway way off. Much closer below him was the short cul-de-sac street where three homes lay on quarter-acre plots, one of which was his. The Faraday home was the last one right at the end of the cul-de-sac, with its rock and cactus garden in front, doublewide carport to the side, and a covered walkway connecting it to the house. He could barely see his converted guesthouse-turned-bedroom at the end of the backyard behind the fence, all tiny from this distance. Just beyond, the high desert plunged downward into the low desert past Morongo Valley. From the four-lane highway cutting through town, Yucca Valley was the vanguard town greeting everyone on their way to the interior of the Mojave.

Music in the open desert, surrounded by warm breezes, wasn't at all like the darkened audiences he had grown to know this last year. Many a time he had come here to have the sky, the rocks, and the sand—this huge open expanse below him—absorb the voice of his haunting notes.

He closed his eyes for a moment, waiting for something to come to him. Starting with a single note, he let it go to be lost with the thousand others he had given away over the years. Beginning the tune, he changed and altered it as he went, inserting notes here and there and stretching it out in parts. When he was done, one would have thought he was cold in the ninety-degree heat from the goose bumps on his arms. It always happened that way when he let the tunes come to him. It was happening more and more as the months went by. He never told anyone this, but he called it 'natural magic'.

Many minutes later the last note disappeared and he lowered the silvery instrument onto his lap. School had been out for only a week and he was anticipating his seventeenth birthday later in July. Then senior year would finally be here. Last year he had done quite well on the track team, but the band was taking up more and more time, especially valuable weekend time, which he didn't mind at all. He figured he'd probably not return to the team, despite his excellent record. He wondered how he'd be able to tell his best friend Doug Sandefur, who was also a teammate, much less Coach Wilkins. Doug was Yucca Valley Regional High's star runner and had been so for two years now. *He's phenomenal, that's for sure,* Scott thought. He'd miss practice with Doug. But Doug liked girls, which was a growing issue for him as well.

He thought about his interest in music in general and the conflict that seemed to present to his parents. His father, Ralph, wanted him to go into their restaurant business and be his partner at some point. But Scott knew he couldn't work there all his life. At some point, he'd have to tell his dad that he had little interest in it, but how to do so was a problem. Ever since his older brother had opted out of the business, Ralph had been coaxing Scott for the position. Being a host at the restaurant was fun since he had gotten to meet quite a few people from town, was somewhat popular in school because of the high profile it afforded him, and it had given him an opportunity to even meet some celebrities as well.

Shakaiyo whined a little and nudged the canteen. He leaned over to retrieve it and poured some water into his cupped hand while she lapped it up. She nuzzled it again. He poured more out and she lapped it dry, and sat down again, beating her tail against the rock as she looked out over the wide valley with him.

He glanced at his watch. It had been over an hour since he left. Since it was close to 5 p.m. already, he started down.

"C'mon, girl." Shakaiyo was on her way as he crab-walked down the treacherous first ten feet.

Scheduled to be at the restaurant at 6:30 p.m. he was a good twenty minutes away from the house. Once there, it would take almost that much time to get ready.

Finally at the backyard, he opened the gate, went up the short cement sidewalk and slid open the sliding-glass door to the kitchen. He reached into the refrigerator for a soda and popped the top. His mother Elaine called from the master bedroom. "Your uniform is hanging on the back of the chair in the dining room, honey."

He inspected the freshly pressed black outfit. "Thanks Mom." He grabbed the hanger and headed across the fenced-in backyard to his room. Before the Faradays had bought the house, the unattached guest room had been converted into a full bedroom complete with a built-in closet and full bathroom. It was small, but private. His brother, who was eight years older than he, had had the room before he left home, but now it was his haven.

He showered and changed, and ran to the car after making sure Shakaiyo was secure in the yard. Elaine had already started the engine and was putting boxes of clean linen in the back of the station wagon.

He approached her in his mock western sheriff persona. "Hey, gal, need some hep?" Elaine usually thought it humorous that her son would assume at least one new role a week. His sheriff accent was a familiar one though. This time she was too much in a hurry and didn't respond in her usual style. She frowned instead. "We're gonna be late unless you get that last box."

He retrieved the remaining one from the steps of the side door and deposited it into the back of the vehicle. "Don't worry, ma'am, I'll drive!" He took her keys and escorted her to the passenger side. She couldn't help it and a smile finally ran across her face. *She's always in a hurry,* he thought.

Elaine buckled her seat belt while he pulled out of the drive. *He's a good driver,* she thought. *No doubt his father will buy him that Jeep after all.* She pulled down the visor and adjusted her reddish hair one last time in the tiny illuminated mirror. It was starting to show some touches of white here and there and she decided it was time to visit the beauty parlor to make it disappear again.

She looked at her son. His window was rolled halfway down. His hair, with its weight line about three-quarters of the way down from the top—quite in fashion—blew back in the breeze as they headed for the highway. Except for the dark red hair color, which he got from her, he looked more like his father than did his brother Steve. Scott had his father's thick hair and the same green eyes. That's one of the many things that made her fall in love with Ralph all those years ago, his beautiful green eyes. Scott was shorter than he, though, and had a more stocky athletic build, a little different from Ralph's growing paunch. She knew her husband was proud of his second son, even though she couldn't remember the last time he told Scott directly.

That day last summer flashed into her mind. The day he came back from Parker, Arizona after having been at her sister Cinnamon's place for most of the summer. That was the day he told her he was gay. How could he possibly have known something like that? After all, he had only been sixteen for a month. She was sure he was making it up. But he insisted he wasn't. She made a phone call that night; sure she was going to give her sister a piece of her mind. The phone call was extraordinarily long. And it was she who did most of the listening. She found out things she never knew about her son. Cin had always been the more perceptive one though, and Elaine knew her son related well to her. When she found out that her sister knew first, and not her, it made her feel slighted and a little jealous. Cin seemed to have quite a bit of influence on him as well. And she hadn't put those thoughts in his head. He had told her. Even though Elaine had cried about the revelation for days afterward, she had never let her husband know what her son had revealed. When Scott had told her they talked about not telling his father until the timing was better. In fact, she had been keeping it a well-guarded secret. And neither she nor he had told him yet. She still secretly hoped it wasn't true after all, that he would grow out of it. After all, who could anyone possibly know one was gay at his age? *Thank God we don't live in Los Angeles*, she thought, *where the urban influence of gay life could turn him into who knows what?* She deliberately stopped her train of thought. She realized she was obsessing again.

They turned the corner and she reached over to muss her son's hair. He looked at her and frowned. Still in character, he tried his John Wayne imitation. "Here we are, ma'am."

"Come on, son. Enough of that now."

They parked by the back door and Carmen, the head waitress, helped unload the boxes of linen. Once done, Scott immediately went in and used the lint brush on his uniform, then re-combed his hair. From the corner of his eye, he saw Clark pass by and glance at him briefly. Clark was the headwaiter. Scott knew him to be about thirty-two or so. He was the only person he even remotely thought was gay. Clark wasn't married, lived by himself, and never talked about women. Although Clark was friendly, Scott noticed that he kept his distance. He wasn't exactly sure why that was, but it only added to his suspicions. He just couldn't tell since his radar was seriously underdeveloped. He had asked his mother about him once, but she had said she didn't know. None of the other wait staff had ever made any remarks about him either. He could have asked Clark directly, he knew, but somehow had never been able to broach the subject with him. He wasn't sure why something as simple as that question couldn't come out of his mouth.

The restaurant had been Faraday's for nine years now. For almost as long as Scott could remember it had been Ralph's focus. Being an astute businessman, he had gotten a good deal in the purchase of the building, had renovated it, and soon afterward had a thriving three-star restaurant. It was one of the very few nice restaurants for a good seventy-mile radius. In fact, it was said to be perhaps the best restaurant in the entire high desert—at least one local newspaper article said so. Scott was proud when, last year, he clandestinely added an ingredient to the then nearly famous Faraday's Shrimp Sauce. That put it over the top. When Ralph found out what had happened, he was at first not too pleased with the secret change of the recipe. He relented though, and was sure his son would eventually be a fine partner.

This evening, like most evenings, his father was at the helm, as he liked to call it. It usually meant he was supervising, helping cook and generally making sure the kitchen area was well run. Scott didn't mind working with his dad, it was just that they never spent time together away from the restaurant. And their contact with each other rarely strayed from the tasks at hand. It wasn't that they didn't get along. Ralph just took a few too many things for granted. Real communication with Scott was one of them. Working more than eighty hours a week, he rarely seemed to connect with Scott's other interests, such as with Scouting several years back. The gap in communication extended to his other interests as well, such as rappelling, track (although he came to two meets last year), and his newest endeavor with the band. His father had missed being drafted in the last war but was still too young to be in the generation of Scott's retired military acquaintances at the VFW. It used to be a source of confusion to him. He knew people on a first name basis that were older than his dad, but his dad didn't quite relate to him. Ralph didn't seem to like Scott's ability to shift characters, nor his funny accents. Ralph liked things he was sure of, like business, money, and customers. He was a proud man who didn't like things he considered a waste of 'precious time'. Scott was sure that if his dad would just get a sense of humor things would be completely different.

Elaine put her things down in the storage room.

Ralph glanced up at her. "Elaine, did you pick up the deposit slips?"

"Yes, dear. I got them earlier. They're in the bin on the filing cabinet, where I always put them."

Scott overheard the last part of the short exchange on his way to take his place at the host station up front. It really seemed that his dad was all business twenty-four hours a day. He wondered if it was so he could avoid any exchange with his mom that others might construe as love. *Parents are so strange*, he thought.

Beth was his favorite swing-shift waitress and she was on tonight. She was a Marine Lieutenant's wife from the nearby Twentynine Palms Marine Base and worked too much as well. She passed him on her way as she placed salt and pepper containers on some of the tables. She loved the way he so fluidly was able to change personalities, most of which were humorous, in a moment's notice. Because of that she found him to be the most interesting teenager she had ever met. He was obviously more talented than a mere host should be. She recalled how other places were dull, boring, you name it, she'd been there. Whenever Scott was around, she always felt more cheerful.

"So, Scott," she eyed him up and down in his handsome black and white outfit, not quite casual, and not quite a tux, "who are you tonight?"

"I'm the famous gigolo. You know, Scott *'Hot-To-Trot'* Faraday."

She grinned. "Darn. If I weren't married, *and* you weren't jailbait." She whirled past in a flash and was gone.

He grinned now. He loved teasing her.

They traded good-humored insults most of the night. Elaine even joined in with some humor of her own, which surprised them both. It was almost 9 p.m., closing time, and the crowd finally dwindled down to one couple. Carmen came back to the kitchen to tell Scott that a late arrival was up front. "Tell him we're about to close," she said in her heavily accented English.

Elaine overheard the exchange and followed Scott up front. "Oh, hello Howard. It's closing time, but we may be able to seat you at the bar."

"Oh, no Elaine. I just came back from the airport in Ontario and stopped by to say hello before we got home."

AeroSun, the industrial design consortium in Desert Hot Springs in the low desert, had recently opened and Howard St. Charles was a senior project manager for the company. Howard and several of his colleagues had been regulars for lunch or dinner at Faraday's for months now. Lunch was very popular at Faraday's since they had much better prices during the day. Since his crowd of white-collar co-workers was friendly, and he was such a lively person to talk to, Elaine, and the rest of the crew quickly warmed up to him.

Howard was identifiable by the thin line of a scar that led from the corner of his right eye to his ear. It was from a hang-gliding mishap from his youth, but he had long since given up such pursuits. It gave him a rugged look, which contrasted with his otherwise conservative style. Tall, and in his mid-thirties, he stayed trim with regular workouts and eating right, despite his frequent meals at Faraday's. They usually saw him wearing neatly pressed trousers, a white shirt, and a tie. Tonight the tie was missing.

The two remaining patrons got up to leave. A busboy cleared the table, and with a wide smile, Beth escorted the couple out the door. She spotted a teenager who was stuffing a windbreaker into a bag in Howard's car trunk. He shut the trunk and came toward her. Passing the leaving patrons, he eyed her briefly and said hello as he came through the door.

"Hello?" she asked, a bit puzzled.

"I'm Ryan."

Howard turned around as he heard Ryan's voice. "There you are. I thought you got lost." He turned to Elaine. "This is my nephew Ryan. Ryan, these are some of the friends I told you about."

"Hi," he said cheerfully.

Whoa, who is this, Scott wondered. The previously unannounced nephew immediately took him. He sized Ryan up. His dark hair seemed to be perfectly sculpted to his head, except for a patch along his forehead, which was cut almost to the scalp. He squinted to look more closely. *Is that a scar? Must run in the family*, he thought. His deep-set dark eyes, accented with long black lashes, made him look incredibly cute as well as mysterious. His dark hair contrasted with his pale, yet also dark complexion. *Is that the remains of a black eye*, he wondered. *He must have been in a fight.* He noted the shorts, the bulge in front that invited him to stare, and the nice curve of his rear. Slightly broader in build and a little taller than he, Scott figured Ryan was about his age.

Ryan knew about Scott only from the brief sketch Howard gave him of the people he was going to meet. Now he was standing in front of that very same guy. Ryan checked Scott out as well, mentally making detailed notes. Scott was stocky, yet muscular. He was a little shorter than himself. He wore his dark rusty-colored hair short and had a totally in-style cut. His full pouty lips and fleshy cheeks, with a touch of white peach fuzz, were as cute as he could remember on anyone. He could see that Scott's eyes sparkled green. God was that hot. And that body! He might be a jock, he figured. His firm thighs and calves as well as his curved hard butt were noticeable even in his formal attire. As he stole a look at Scott's crotch, his heart pounded. He wondered what Scott looked like in shorts, or better yet, in nothing.

As quickly as he looked, he quelled his thoughts. This was how he ended up being with Crawford. *Never again*, he thought.

Howard introduced Ryan to everyone, and lastly to Scott. It was fleeting, almost imperceptible, but Scott knew Ryan looked at his crotch several times. Guys don't look at other guys' crotches, Scott knew. Especially not three times in a row. He wondered for a second what that was all about, but felt embarrassed about his own attraction to him while his mom was standing next to him.

Elaine smiled, "So, this is Ryan."

Scott was puzzled. *How does she know about this kid,* he wondered. *Then again, I don't know Howard nearly as well as my parents do.*

Ryan explained that he had flown down from Crescent City to live with Howard for the time being. He had just graduated from high school and was going to enroll in college later on. He also explained that for the last several years he'd been living with his grandmother and younger brother. The black eye? A car accident, which he didn't go into any detail about. Scott noticed that his parents were conspicuously missing from his background summary and neither Howard nor Ryan seemed to explain that.

Now that he had heard Ryan talk some, Scott felt a sense of false bravado oozing from him. Sure, he was in new surroundings and perhaps felt awkward, but it was more than that. He scrutinized Ryan's carefully chosen veneer, picking up the little details of his speech. He's hiding something, Scott surmised. It's not just that he doesn't know us and he's holding back, it's something more. It seemed he was too puffed up for his own good. Acting. Deliberate, careful acting. That was what came to mind. *I can do that too, ya know,* he thought.

Ralph came up front from the back office to see what all the laughing was about. Howard introduced him to Ryan. Ralph said hello but little else. In his usual businesslike manner, bordering on rudeness, he went back into the kitchen almost as abruptly as he came out. After all, it was it was a long day and the restaurant was closed.

Ryan rapidly became the center of attention. Scott could tell he loved it. *Am I jealous?* Scott thought. *No, I get my share of laughs. Yet my laughs come from my chosen characters, or me, not some fake attitude that I pretend is real. Am I the only one who sees this?*

An important part of Scott's life for his entire junior year was his discovery that he was gay. It was no secret to him, but it wasn't something he went around announcing to just anyone. Survival in high school depended on it. He remembered how embarrassed he felt when he first told his aunt. But he trusted her like no one else. He had told her how being on the track team was what clinched it for him; how he was attracted to some of the other guys, *that* way, but wouldn't dare say so to anyone. He explained how he had a girlfriend and how he was aware that he wasn't at all interested in her like he was 'supposed' to be.

He remembered how warm he felt when his aunt held him as he let the tears out, then laughed once he was over his embarrassment at telling her his story.

"I knew, you know," she said when they finally stopped laughing.

"But how? I've never, uh, you know…"

"Intuition. And there are other clues that are kinda obvious. Like your active disinterest in Jeanine." She was referring to their neighbor's daughter who was a year older than he and had been interested in him all that summer. He had been actively keeping his distance from her the whole time.

"No wonder Mom's afraid of you," he had told her. "You see things she doesn't."

"Your mom is a wonderful woman. Remember, she's seven years older than I am. That makes her from another generation almost, at least to me. She never worked with young people to the extent I did. But her heart's in the right place and that's what counts. Besides, look at you. You turned out all right."

They had talked well into the night about how hard it was being different in high school, where the social code demanded conformity. She had said it had been that way for a long time. He wasn't telling her anything she didn't already know. He had bared his soul to her until there was only him and her left. No ego, no barriers, just their love for one another. He had literally transformed that night. It was the first time he had ever had that deep a conversation with anyone. That experience never left him. And what was once a huge problem became something to embrace and rejoice about, even if others didn't understand it. Nonetheless, he knew that discretion was still the watchword.

A powerful urge to get even more connected had gotten stronger after that. It was the purge of false facades that had dared him during his junior year to act in two plays. Granted, they were just Humanities class roles, nothing like the real Thespians in school, but they were, nonetheless, acting roles. What an exhilarating feeling it was to pretend and not cling to the part. Somehow, facades and personalities were easily sorted out on stage. All his funny accents and imitations started to really take shape then. Being able to see the difference between pretending a part, then dropping it, and pretending for the sake of a facade soon became clear to him. Ironic how his non-acting classmates couldn't see its simplicity. Perhaps it was because they hadn't experienced a powerful transformation as had he.

Yet, his greatest fear was still with him. He had felt that if he came out to his peers they'd immediately drop him. Or worse. He might end up with bruises, or broken bones, maybe even stranded out in the middle of the desert because of someone's hatred. That really haunted him. He was all too familiar with the ignorant cruelty that was a frequent part of being a high schooler. He didn't pretend he wasn't gay. He never needed to since he blended in with no problem.

He had made being a jock an excuse, of sorts, for having dropped his girlfriend back in September. It had been difficult not having a girlfriend during his junior year and not be noticed because of it. There were only about four hundred fifty kids in his class and he knew just about everyone, at least by sight. All of his other close friends were either dating regularly or had a girlfriend. He was the odd man out.

Scott listened as Ryan talked about the '69 Chevelle SS he'd owned. An unfortunate trek down a winding road in the mountains back home had totaled it. There would never be another one like it and now it was wrecked. Scott noted he was the driver when he had had the accident. *Stuck*, Scott thought. *Stuck in his role as hot rod owner. He's the same as the rest of the guys.*

Several weeks back his dad told that he would help him purchase a used vehicle for his birthday later that summer. Scott had found an ad in the paper just three days ago for a Jeep Wrangler. From the brief description, it sounded like the perfect vehicle to him. Ralph had clipped out the ad, but had seemed uninterested in an early birthday present.

Howard yawned and tried to casually look at his watch. Everyone saw him do it though, and Elaine checked hers. Now that it was a little after ten it was time everyone went home. The rest of the crew had finished cleaning up and were about to leave as well. Elaine wrote something on a piece of paper and gave it to Howard just before he left with his nephew. Scott escorted Beth to her car in his guise of '*Hot-To-Trot*' and she drove home to her apartment outside Twentynine Palms up the highway.

Ralph had his own car and usually left later than everyone else when he worked a late shift. Elaine started her car, and Scott jumped in, now as himself.

"How did you know about that kid, Mom?"

"Howard told me about him some time ago. I didn't mention it because at the time he wasn't sure he was coming down."

Images of cute Ryan still swirled in his mind. "Oh."

"Howard says that Ryan'll be working with him until he starts college."

She was quiet for a moment as she watched his hand sticking out the window. He absentmindedly let the wind move it up and down as he banked it left and right.

"He doesn't know anyone around here, of course. I hope you boys become friends."

He pulled his arm back in and thought about the remark. Friends? He was the one who picked his friends. And his friends were those who were crazy enough to know when not to be serious. Like his bandmates in Centauri. They were the only bunch of guys he knew who were crazy

or not serious at the right times. What good was a friend who only had
one role to play?

"Son?"

"Yeah?"

"I said I hope you boys become friends. He's going to need someone
to show him around. Howard works so much, and I'm sure he'll be
bored just working all the time."

"Huh?" *Is she serious*, he wondered.

"Are you listening?"

"Yes."

"He's your age. And I'm sure you can show him things to do around
here."

There was a lot to do at that. He knew his desert home better than
most. The book *Dune* came to his mind. He'd even read it twice; his
copy was carefully placed on a bookshelf back in his bedroom. In a way,
it was a reflection of how he thought of his environment. The Fremen,
the natives of the planet in the story, were in tune with the desert. It was
their friend, not their enemy. He even secretly imagined himself as one
of them from time to time.

"Sure, Mom," he said offhandedly. "I hope he likes rappelling, and
music."

She was very much aware of her son's love of the outdoors and his
penchant for rappelling, which she considered a little extreme. "Can't
you show him something a little less dangerous?"

He tried to imitate the dry tone of Sergeant Friday from the old
Dragnet reruns. "I haven't fallen yet, Mom. And under my supervision,
if he decides to accept the mission, he won't fall either, ma'am."

She let out a sigh. Someday she would just have to get used to his
climbing all over the rocks in the Monument.

After Elaine pulled the station wagon into the carport, he headed for
his room in the backyard. Shakaiyo stood in the yard between him and

the bedroom door trying to get his attention. She had been taught not to bark unless there was good reason and just wiggled and whined instead. Her profuse tail wagging thumped steadily against the door until he opened it.

Inside, on the bookcase against the far wall, was his stereo equipment. In another second, LEDs and fluorescent meters illuminated previously darkened faceplates as he clicked on the master switch. He pressed play on a tape deck. With music in all four corners of the room he was able to experience exquisite concert quality sound, especially when he really needed the volume.

Shakaiyo jumped up onto the foot of the bed and sat there, her tail swishing back and forth along the hand-loomed woolen blanket he had bought in Mexico last fall. He checked on Legs, his tarantula, which was motionless. It had a cricket backed into a corner of the terrarium.

"Hey, girl." Shakaiyo's tail still wagged like a metronome. He shed his clothes down to his underwear, dove onto the bed, and gave her a long and fulfilling belly rub.

The tape faded, the deck clicked and started playing the other side. In the short silence, he hung his clothes up, and turned on the overhead fan. He started the shower in his tiny bathroom. As usual, Shakaiyo tried to follow him, but was snubbed by a closed glass door.

Later, once dry, he shut off his stereo, and lay on top of the covers. He crossed his legs and rested his head on his clasped palms on top of the pillow. All was quiet except for the sound of the overhead fan and Shakaiyo's breathing. With one hand he reached down to absent-mindedly pull on the red-blonde hairs, what little there were, that grew just below his navel.

This Ryan guy, he thought. *It can't hurt to give him a chance. Who knows?* Hanging on a nail just above his head was the white 141-gram World Class Frisbee faintly glowing phosphorescent green. *I hope he's seen a Frisbee before.* He smiled, remembering the prize money and ribbon he won in a Frisbee contest just before the trip to Mexico. He had spent all the money bartering for different things, including the blanket.

He switched on the bedside light, got up to open the trunk at the foot of the bed, and inspected his prized rappelling gear. Costing quite a lot, he had saved the money to purchase the finest equipment. Coiled up neatly were two long multicolored nylon ropes. One was one-half inch thick and the other was a five-eighths inch diameter rope. Along with them were two harnesses, two pairs of gloves, his hardhat, climbing shoes, carabiners, slip-chocks, and other miscellaneous equipment. He closed the trunk lid and a brief high-pitched whine came from the hinges. Shakaiyo emitted a short whine at almost the same pitch as she yawned.

He got back in bed and lay under the sheet. He fondled his penis as it grew in hardness. Ryan had come to mind again. What a cute face he had. He especially remembered the curve of his butt and that thick jet-black hair. Diego Garza at school had that same thick black hair, which he always found sexy.

It didn't take long before the summoning up of all the detail made him fully erect. No doubt about it, Ryan was indeed good-looking. He wondered what the guy looked like with his shirt off. He gripped himself harder, creating fantasy images of him in his head.

As usual, he had masturbated before he got out of bed that morning. Scott's ritual was usually twice a day at minimum. He was overdue for his second time. He pulled the sheet to the side, and lazily stroked as he imagined Ryan in more and more detail. It didn't take long before he was breathing hard and enjoying the feeling of a sense-engulfing orgasm. He didn't sit up until it started to run down the side of his abdomen. He slid open the drawer of the nightstand, wiped himself up with a small golf towel, then stuffed it back into the drawer. He pulled the sheet back up to his waist and turned over onto his stomach. He stuffed his longer pillow lengthwise to his side under the sheet, and grasped it with his left arm. He laid his head on the smaller of his two pillows. The mattress and pillow were cool against his warm skin. That was the last thing he remembered before sleep took him away.

CHAPTER 3

The clock showed 7:13 a.m. when the intercom buzzed. Shakaiyo jerked her head up and dropped to the floor from the foot of the bed. Scott was on his stomach, his face half buried in the pillow. He opened one eye, reached over, and touched the red button. "Yeah?"

"Howard called a few minutes ago. He wants you to call him at work today. I left his number in the kitchen."

"OK, Mom," he said at the end of a yawn. He turned over onto his back and stretched before pulling out the golf rag from the drawer again. When he was done, he wiped himself up and tossed it in the hamper. He pulled a fresh folded one from his clothes drawer, tossed it into the nightstand drawer, and slid it shut.

He let Shakaiyo out, then examined his face in the bathroom mirror. As usual, only the small patch around his chin and a little just in front of his ears needed to be shaved.

Later, after showering and dressing, he entered the house. It was quiet since his dad, as usual, had gone to the restaurant early. In the kitchen, the small blackboard over the phone indicated that his mother was out running errands. Only last year his parents had managed to cut back drastically on their work hours. The swing shift manager closed for them three nights a week now. Many times, they were both home by nine or ten in the evening but sometimes much earlier. It used to not be that way at all. Nonetheless, his father still worked around eighty hours a week.

Howard's work phone was written underneath her note. Beneath the phone number was the message: "*S—, please water plants on front porch.*" He had wondered why the empty pitcher was in the kitchen on the countertop. Now he knew why.

Outside, Shakaiyo scratched on the sliding glass door and he let her in. She went for her bowl and he poured her some fresh water.

He showed her the pitcher. "You wanna do this?"

She looked up, but didn't quit slurping, her tail wagging as usual.

"I didn't think so." He filled the pitcher and got about fifteen of the African violets on the windowsills when he heard the toaster pop up. The fichus in the corner and the remaining plants would have to wait.

He spread jam and butter on the toast and put them on a saucer. Sitting at the counter, he called Howard.

"AeroSun, may I help you?" answered the receptionist.

"Hi, Howard St. Charles, please."

"One minute." Scott munched on his toast.

The phone rang twice at the other end before it was picked up. "This is Howard."

A dry portion of toast got stuck in his throat as Scott swallowed. It made his voice go up an octave as he tried to speak. "Hi, Mr. St. Charles," he squeaked before he regained his voice. "This is Scott." It was embarrassing.

Howard chuckled. "Hi, Scott. Too early for you?"

He took a sip of milk. "I was trying to swallow my toast," he said after a couple of short coughs.

"Oh. Scott, thanks for calling. You met my nephew, of course."

"Yeah." He didn't mention that he had even had sex with him in his mind last night.

"I think you guys might have something in common. He expressed an interest in what the Monument has to offer."

"Yeah, the Monument is awesome," was all he could say.

"I was also hoping you might be able to introduce him to some people around here. He won't be starting college for at least another year and I'm afraid all the people I work with are quite a bit older than he is. He won't have a lot of time to meet people his own age at home if he's working so much."

"I guess I could."

"I'm sorry if I'm imposing, but really, you're my only contact with people your age. I hope you understand."

"Yeah, no problem."

"I appreciate it. I talked to your mother earlier. We'll be there tonight around six-thirty."

"Oh?"

The notepad caught his eye. It read: *BBQ tonite.* A couple of his parent's friends last name was jotted down along with Howard and Ryan's name. The time was written through several times in pencil as well: *7:30.*

"Yeah, we're having a barbeque with you guys?"

"See you later tonight?"

"Sure." *Jeez, everyone is trying to get me to like this guy*, he thought as he hung up the phone. Maybe I can introduce him to some people and get rid of him in a couple of weeks.

Scott didn't have to work today so most of the day he spent at the VFW talking with employees and patrons. Ever since working on a community service merit badge, while in Scouting several years before, he had attracted the attention of a few of the old veterans. That led him to still participate in events at the hall on occasion, including hoisting the American flag on the fifteen flagpoles out front of the hall at various times during the year. He was surprised at how interesting some of the guys were for old geezers. And it sometimes seemed that they couldn't get enough of him. Sure, he heard stories about Korea and Vietnam, but it was actually quite rare. Talk about problems associated with the

Persian Gulf was beginning to take up more conversation time now. It was something he was completely uninterested in. For the most part, though, the old guys wanted to party. It was the camaraderie he liked the most among them. Of course, he never told the veterans he was gay. He thought it was funny they never suspected.

The couple that owned the furniture store across the street from Faraday's, Floyd and Edna Briar, arrived early that evening. His parents had known them through the Chamber of Commerce for years. Scott was quite familiar with them. They were older than his parents, and always nice enough to him, but he found them somewhat boring.

Howard and Ryan pulled up at the house around 7 p.m. He found himself nervous about his attraction to Ryan with both his mom and dad there, so he fought off an inclination to mentally peel his clothes off.

After the introductions, the adults sat on lawn chairs in the backyard while Scott led Ryan into his room.

Scott eyed him as they took a seat on the carpeted floor. "So, how do you like Yucca Valley?" It was trite to be sure, but he couldn't think of anything else to ask. Nonetheless, he was expecting the same pretentious manner as last night.

"It's really hot here. I guess I'll get used to it though. And I can actually get a tan." He stretched out his arm to show him his un-tanned skin.

Scott noted the well-proportioned forearm. *Mouthwatering, even,* he thought. "What'll you be doing at AeroSun? What do they do anyway?"

"They're an engineering group. You know, alternative energy projects and other stuff that has to do with wind, sun and geothermal. I'll be making blueprints mostly. Not like actually drafting 'em, but copying 'em, sorting 'em, and keeping track of 'em."

"Oh," Scott acknowledged. He noticed that Ryan seemed to be avoiding his eyes. It made him seem nervous. But he figured Ryan couldn't be nearly as uncomfortable as *he* felt.

"So what kind of stuff do *you* do here?"

"Now that schools out I'm working a lot more, but on weekends I do sound for Centauri."

"What's Centauri?"

"It's the band I'm in. I handle the soundboard, do their tapes and mixes, run cables, and keep up with the equipment. And when Mitch or Barry, who're guys in the band, run dry, I help write some lyrics for our original tunes."

"Really?" Ryan's eyes grew wide and he became noticeably more interested. "What kind of band?"

"Mostly 80s stuff. But we do everything really, except country. No, I take that back, we do a Marshall Tucker tune by request every once in a while, can ya believe?" The original tunes really drove them and actually made them somewhat locally popular.

"Marshall who?

"Tucker. They were popular in the 70s. Not so much nowadays. I'm sure you've heard them. What kind of music do you like?"

"80s. Rock. The typical stuff. Can I, uh, I'd like to check out the band sometime."

"I don't know. The guys are kinda touchy about people watching us practice."

Ryan's look of excitement immediately died, as if he'd been told to go away. Scott felt awkward about having been so abrupt. "They, uh, might make an exception," he offered. *Why did I say that*, he wondered.

Ryan took another sip from his soda can and studied Scott's face, trying to discern how true that might be.

Scott thought about how Howard had asked him to introduce him to other people, but he thought it might be better to keep him from his band friends at this point. He continued trying to find something in common with him. "Ever done any rappelling?"

"No. The mountains near Crescent City are pretty much wooded. It's not so…barren, like around here."

Scott was taken somewhat aback at his tone. It was one of disgust. *This character needs to see how excellent the desert really is,* he thought. The area was stark, that was true. Nonetheless, what the desert offered was adventure. Plus, there was nothing like the beauty of the Joshua Tree National Monument. That might change his mind. He poured the rest of his soda into a glass. *I'll show* him. "Well, let me show you how bitchin' it is."

Ryan stood, then sat on the bed as Scott put a Centauri tape in the player. Shakaiyo turned around several times then plopped down on a pile of several pairs of Scott's shoes which were in a jumble by the bookcase. He opened his gear chest and explained what the equipment was for as he pulled each piece out. He handed an item to him. "…and the harness keeps you completely safe during a descent."

Ryan held the harness out, trying to figure it out. "How do you put this thing on?"

Scott took it. "It hooks in the middle like this." He demonstrated, then gave it back to him. He watched as Ryan strapped it around his loins. What a turn-on it was to watch him tighten the straps. He felt a little embarrassed as he turned Ryan around to see if he'd cinched it correctly. It was difficult to keep his eyes diverted as he checked out how tight it was around his buttocks. Ryan's legs were covered with profuse short dark hair and it was difficult to keep from staring at them now that he was this close to his butt. He was already busy fantasizing about how hairy it must be as well.

Ryan checked himself out in the full-length mirror on the bathroom door, observing his rear. He caught Scott looking at him. His buttocks were perfectly framed by the straps. The silence of the moment was overwhelming.

Adrenaline zoomed through Scott's body. He diverted his eyes and repacked the ropes in the trunk as Ryan un-cinched the harness. Shakaiyo nuzzled Ryan in the crotch and he jerked back a little. Scott reached over and scratched behind her ears.

"Sorry, she does that to everybody. She, uh, saved my life once."

"Serious?" he asked as he gave the harness back.

Scott took it and placed it back in the box. "I had tied a rope to a scrub pine at the top of this escarpment," he began. Shakaiyo wagged her tail as if she knew she was being talked about. "It was near Big Bear. You can see it northwest of here when we go outside. I had just finished tying the rope off and the rest was coiled up next to the trunk. I stepped back, somehow slid on some loose rocks, and ended up sliding down the cliff. I still can't figure out how I didn't just fall backward and land on my head at the bottom. Luckily, there was a ledge about eight feet down. I landed flat-footed right on it and was able to grab on to some roots sticking out before I fell backwards. She nudged the rope far enough for it to fall down the cliff face. It wasn't exactly near me, but it was close enough to grab and pull myself up. I was so freaked out that I cried right there."

"Whoa," Ryan responded. "No one was around to save my car last month," he added somewhat absent-mindedly, as he looked out into space. "I had the coolest Chevelle in Crescent City. It had glass packs, chrome wheels, and a posi-traction rear end. It was a beast!" He unconsciously touched his scalp where the hair had already grown back and rubbed the scar. Only a tiny bit of it was noticeable now.

Scott shook his head ever so slightly as he closed the lid on the box. Everyone he knew since starting high school who had been in a car accident was drunk when it happened. It was their own fault, and he knew four examples in just the last three years to prove it. He was sure Ryan had just left that part out.

"Now all that's left are some scarred trees on Prieto Canyon Road," Ryan said.

"Prieto Canyon," Scott repeated. "Nice place?" He wasn't focusing his attention on Ryan just this second. He was still thinking of sheer cliffs and rappelling. He sat back on the bed and leaned against the wall.

Ryan sat next to him. His eyes lit up. "Yeah, it is. It's this neighborhood up in the mountains by a branch of the river that goes by our place. My friend Frank Gaviota lives there."

Scott saw the look in his eyes. It was different. His vocal tone had changed, too. It was fleeting, but there was authenticity in his voice for the first time.

Now Ryan lied. "Anyway, he pissed me off and I left. I was too much in a hurry, I guess. Ran it right off the road just past the 'Steep Grade' sign. I was lucky I wasn't killed since it totaled the car. The cops took my license and I won't get it back until I'm eighteen. Too many tickets."

He stopped there and bent over to retie his loose left shoelace. He had played that version of the story so many times in his head he felt he was beginning to believe it now. He finished retying the shoelace and added, "Howie says one of his neighbors has a broken down scooter he's trying to sell and that I should buy it. I can't 'officially' ride it since I don't have a license, so Howie said he'd handle the registration for me. And he told me he'd put it on his insurance until I get my license back."

"Why buy it if it doesn't run?"

"A scooter? It'd be easy to fix. I did most of the work on my car anyway."

"You work on cars?"

"Sure. They're a pain in the ass sometimes, but they're not that hard to fix if you have the tools, and money, of course. You have a car?"

"Not anymore."

Ryan snorted. "You wreck yours, too?"

"No. It died last month. It was my brother's and was it old. It had a lot of miles on it, so it was gonna go soon. Pissed me off, too."

"I bet. Is he in the military?" Ryan was aware at this point that a Marine Corps base was nearby.

"Military?"

"Your brother."

"Oh. No, he runs a business in Singapore."

"Singapore. Isn't that in Japan or something?"

"More like by Malaysia," Scott answered, leaving it at that.

The tune on the tape deck ended while both of them thought about their respective cars.

Scott spoke up now. "My dad said he's going in halves with me. I found a Jeep I want in the paper but it'll be sold by the time he's ready to help out."

Ryan raised his brow. "A Jeep? What model?"

"A Wrangler. He said he's not coughing up his half 'til my birthday."

"When's that?"

"July twenty-seventh."

Ryan mentally counted off the weeks. "That's a month and a half away." He thought about the lack of transportation for both of them. "Damn." Then he added, "Hey, mine's a week later. You gonna be eighteen?"

"Seventeen."

"Hmm. You seem older."

"Not. So, you're eighteen?"

Ryan nodded. "Gonna be."

From outside, Ralph called out to them. "Hey, you guys, food's on." They left the bedroom with Shakaiyo bolting out between them. They were almost done eating when Elaine changed the topic. "Scott, we've got some good news for you."

He wondered why she and Howard had given each other that look for the last five minutes or so. And his dad seemed to be avoiding some unknown subject while everyone was talking. Scott's mouth was full and he stopped chewing for a second as he saw all eyes on him. Even Howard was beaming. Elaine looked at Ralph as he made the announcement with his usual succinct style. "This coming weekend we're going to the bank, then out to get your Jeep."

Hadn't he just talked about this with Ryan? *Boy, can things change fast when you're out of earshot,* he thought. He couldn't swallow and spit out the last bite onto his plate. "Totally!" he blurted with a big smile.

Elaine continued, "We decided that it would be better, especially now since Ryan's here. You're going to need some transportation so you boys can do things."

He studied her face. *Did she say 'you boys', like I'm gonna be hauling him around or something,* he thought. *Like he could instantly be my friend, just like that? It sure is assuming I want to hang around with him.*

He glanced over at Ryan. Ryan's face expressed a mix of jealousy and excitement. Scott visualized the Jeep for sale way out of town. The summer was going to be better than he thought. Finally, he'd have a vehicle again. And it was one *he* wanted this time.

CHAPTER 4

Scott sat on one of the high-backed bar stools at the counter in the kitchen. Ralph finalized the addition to the contract with his insurance agent over the phone and hung up. He was on the phone again after sifting through several pieces of paper from his wallet. Out came the ad. Scott quietly ventured for more orange juice as his dad waited for an answer from the other end.

"Jim? Ralph. Yes, hello. My boy and I will be over in a couple of hours to purchase the Jeep. Yes, yes. Good-bye." Short and to the point. It was the Ralph way.

The next hour seemed like all day but procedures were procedures at the bank. Scott wasn't too happy about the fate of his savings account, but it was for a good cause. Finally, though, they were on the road to see Sergeant Beck, a retired Marine who settled with his wife in a house quite a ways from town.

The unpopulated, desiccated land along the two-lane road was in stark contrast to the relative metropolis of Yucca Valley. Soon enough though, homes and other structures became increasingly spread out until only an occasional building was visible from the road. Scott had to endure AM talk radio the whole way, and hoped his new vehicle would at least have FM. Nonetheless, he enjoyed the time with his dad away from the restaurant. When was the last time just the two of them had driven together to do anything? At least four months ago.

Two German Shepherds barked furiously at them from the driveway as they pulled up to a ranch style home at the end of a quarter-mile long driveway off the main road. Sergeant Beck came out and made the dogs go into the garage where they stayed.

"Hello there, Mr. Faraday," Sergeant Beck said as he came up to the car.

"Hello yourself, Sergeant Beck.... This is my boy, " he said as they both got out of the car.

"The birthday boy!" the old man said with enthusiasm.

"Well, not yet. That's still a ways away," Scott said.

"It's never too early to get a birthday present, son."

He took in the old man's visage, wondering why he never frequented the VFW. He thought he knew or knew of most veterans who had settled in the area—but not everyone wanted to hang out with all those old guys. *Maybe he has better things to do,* he thought.

Sergeant Beck motioned them around the house to the back. Flat and well-rounded boulders of various sizes marked the corners of the backyard in a haphazard square. At the end of the undefined stretch of driveway was a wooden-framed garage badly in need of a fresh coat of paint. The Sergeant unlocked the hasp and swung back the double doors to reveal a dark blue Jeep. Scott could smell the aroma of freshly blackened 70-series tires. The light streaming in revealed a bright finish and a red and white pinstripe along the sides. *I should have known it'd be red, white, and blue,* he thought. Despite the patriotic look of it, he decided right then that it was flawless. Caressing the hood briefly, he tugged on the latches holding it down, then inspected the spare tire hanging on the back. The roll bar was neatly taped with wide black tape. And yes, there was an FM radio. He quickly spied the speakers mounted under each side of the dash hoping they worked. The Sergeant produced a key and stepped in to start it.

"I changed the oil last month, and I've been running it every once in a while to keep the battery charged, otherwise there's only eleven more miles on it than the day you stopped by, Mr. Faraday." The Sergeant motioned to Ralph to observe the odometer as he stepped out. Scott's ears perked up. 'Stopped by', Sergeant Beck had said? So, his dad had been thinking about him after all.

Scott jumped in, now quite excited. The hundred dollar bills in the envelope in his back pocket made a crinkling sound as he turned to observe the back seat. He pulled the envelope out and handed it to his dad.

"Go ahead, let it out of the garage," Sergeant Beck said.

"No problem!" He started it up, put it in first, and slowly brought it into the blazing sunlight.

"Take it around, son," Ralph said.

He tested the clutch and brakes before stopping at the end of the drive. From the rearview mirror, he saw his father hand Sergeant Beck a check, then count out bills into the Sergeant's outstretched hand. He then took off toward a crossroads about a half-mile away.

He punched the buttons on the radio and quickly zeroed in on his station. He was in ecstasy. The wind blowing across the top of his head and the feel of the purring engine completed the feeling. When he was sure he was out of range of the house he let out a loud "Yeah!" He wound through the gears and quickly shifted to fourth. He was already thinking of the impression he'd make when school started at the end of August.

He didn't go too much farther, but rather pulled over to the shoulder, made a U-turn, and headed back in five minutes. Soon he was back at the house and headed up the drive. Ralph and the Sergeant were shading their eyes as the older man pointed to his new roof. Knowing his dad's body language, he saw he was visibly irritated at the Sergeant's drawn out discussion that was probably taking place.

"Dad, it's great! I can't wait to take it to the Monument."

"Great…. Are you ready to go?"

Sergeant Beck took the cue. "The wife and I are planning on comin' into town this weekend. Maybe we'll make a reservation."

Scott reached over to adjust the right mirror as his dad smiled politely and said he should eat out more often. Scott felt like shrinking into the upholstery from the way he said it and hoped the Sergeant didn't notice his tone. He looked up at the old man, seeing him still smiling and waving. *Maybe I'm the only one who notices his gruffness*, he thought.

On the drive back Scott was in character again. He was on his way to a mining expedition in the ghost town of Calico several hours away into the Mojave. His imaginary prospecting gear was stowed in back and there was a sack of gold nuggets in the passenger seat. He was on his way to the assayer's office to get his hard-earned cash. Days spent under the hot desert sun had left him grimy and sweaty.

The scene started to run away from him. He felt an erection come on like he hadn't felt in—only a couple of hours really. He was sure that after long weeks in the desert by himself he was ready to do it with anyone. Ryan, the new guy, came to mind. Ryan was also grimy from spending weeks in the desert and needed a hot shower with Scott. The fantasy made him hard in an instant. Somehow, though, his attention shifted back to reality despite how interesting it was getting. The Jeep was his and now the summer was his, too!

And that Ryan. For some reason, he wanted to drive straight to Howard's to show him.

The vehicle already renewed the sense of freedom and maturity he felt he had lost when his old car had died. Now hanging out with the guy wasn't such a worrisome prospect. If he observed him being stuck inside his one-role personality, he could just change the scenery, with or without him.

He followed behind Ralph all the way home and pulled up behind him in the driveway. He left the car running and told him he would be going to Howard's to find Ryan after all. In no time, he was back down the street to the highway that ran through town. The way to Howard's led him by the hotel and convention center where Colleen, their lead singer, worked. He wasn't sure she was there at that time or not, but stopped anyway. In fact, as he pulled up, he wondered why he had thought about Ryan before the members of the band. He was far closer to them, despite all of them being older than he was by a couple of years.

Colleen Fitzsimon worked behind the front desk of the Grande Pointe Hotel. It was the only hotel in Yucca Valley with conference facilities and was the most modern one in the area. Just off the main highway, one of the larger craggy hills loomed up behind the building making it look smaller than it really was. It was a stupendous backdrop for the new facility and the beautifully landscaped grounds.

He pulled up under the marquee and stopped. Two women and one man were behind the huge marble counter when he went inside. He recognized only one of them.

"Sheila, is Colleen on?"

She eyed his sparse attire—only a t-shirt and shorts with tennis shoes. "Hi Scott. No, she went home about a half hour ago."

"That's okay, I'll catch her later."

"Bye," she said as he left in a hurry. He felt disappointed for a moment, then hopped back in his vehicle and continued down the highway.

Howard's ranch style home was one of five in a newer housing development outside the city limits. The single street was laid out near several huge green circles of soybeans. Situated on a half-acre each, the homes were built on a parcel of the farmland that had been sold off a couple of years back. The huge circular fields still dominated the area, though, and were one of the few green areas near the city. What an anomaly it seemed having acres of green vegetation carpeting the brown desert. It also set apart the house from the surrounding hills and isolated the subdivision from any entry except the main road. No off-roading in this area for sure, he observed.

Howard's expensive cherry red sports car was in the drive. Scott honked the horn and Howard appeared shortly from around the back of the house. He turned his head and said something Scott couldn't hear. Ryan appeared next, clad only in shorts and sandals. His skin was shiny from sunscreen. Scott drew a sharp breath as he watched him approach. Ryan's shoulders, chest, and tight stomach glistened, begging him to stare. Images of the locker room back in school shuttled through his mind and he wondered if Ryan was wearing a jock strap under his shorts. How was he going to hang out with this guy if he was so attracted to his hot body?

"Awesome, you got it!" Ryan exclaimed.

Scott shut off the engine and jumped out. "Bitchin', isn't it?"

Ryan briefly rested a hand on the hood and approached the driver's side. "Good choice."

He stood so close Scott could hear him breathing. Scott stopped making any movement so he could hear it better. *Jeez, he's only breathing,* Scott thought. *Why does stuff like that get me so horny?*

Howard appeared now and checked it out with them. He stood with his hands on his hips smiling at the excitement the two boys shared. Scott felt a little nervous about his intense attraction to Ryan, especially with Howard there.

Scott dug into his pocket for his keys. "Mr. St. Charles, wanna go with us to town?" Ryan recognized the invitation, and his eyes showed it.

"I don't think so. You guys go right along. It's time I cleaned up the dishes in the kitchen anyway."

"I'll get a shirt. Back in a second," Ryan said. He followed Howard inside and was back in a flash, now sporting a white tank top. He'd changed out of his swim trunks and had slipped on some regular shorts as well. Tennis shoes in hand, and out of breath, he jumped in the passenger side and slid the shoes on. "This is great. You got wheels!" He quickly changed the subject. "Hey, know anybody who can buy us some beer?"

Scott eyed him a moment, then backed the Jeep down the drive. "Yeah," he said slowly.

"Well?"

"Two of the band members are over twenty-one, but I'd have to track 'em down. But I don't think they'd help me buy alcohol. I got a different idea though. Like the drive-in on Tower Road. It's quite the hang-out."

It certainly wasn't as if he had never drunk beer before, but it was still daylight and he barely knew Ryan. The idea of just up and going to a liquor store seemed a bit odd.

Ryan cocked his head a little, trying to decide if he was serious, then resigned himself to the fact that there would be no alcohol. Scott wondered if it was such a good idea to come over right away after all. His initial impression of him wasn't the best. Now Ryan was trying to scam beer. He knew he should have just gone to see Bryce, Mitch, or someone else in the band. But Scott knew the reason he came to see him. Ryan was better looking than any of the band members. *Fuck it*, he thought.

They drove in silence for a moment while Scott tried to find something to say. Anything he said was going to come out wrong since he felt so attracted to him, so he tried for the innocuous angle. "So what are you gonna major in? I don't remember what you had said."

"Engineering."

"Oh, yeah. What kind?"

"Don't know yet. I don't have to know right away. I might just major in partyin', actually."

No doubt, Scott thought. "How did your uncle get you that job so quickly?"

"Physics."

"Physics?"

"I did best in my physics class, but that was the only thing I did well. I like mechanics and engineering seems a good fit for me. Plus, my uncle says I'm the right type for that kind of work. At least he thinks so. AeroSun had a summer internship open in his department, and I got the job. And since he's a project manager, he has some clout. Howie told me they don't make you wear a pocket protector though, so I'm safe."

Well, he has a sense of humor after all, Scott thought. "You're lucky to have an uncle so close to L.A."

Ryan spied the hills in the distance and the mountains even further away. *L.A. may as well be a million miles away,* he thought. "Yeah, I guess. But I'm not really into big cities."

Scott glanced at the wind rippling over Ryan's dark leg hairs. His legs weren't tanned yet but they were cute nonetheless. *Nothing like hot, tanned legs,* Scott thought, *with cute dark hairs all over them.* He quickly looked down at his own thighs. The wind rippled his rust-blond hairs. His skin was already as dark as it was going to get which was decent. At least he had a tan line despite his fair complexion. "So, which side of the family is he from?"

"Howie?"

Scott nodded.

"He's my dad's little brother."

"How'd he end up here?"

"He used to live near Indio, but got a divorce, and lucked out with this job, so moved here. He's been with the company since it started. Personally, I think he wanted to put some distance between him and his ex."

They pulled up to a stoplight and waited for it to change. "What about your parents?" Scott asked. He was still curious about that missing piece of information from the other night.

The quiet Jeep engine was the only sound now. Ryan was too quiet and there was something odd in his eyes. "They're dead," he said in a monotone.

They. As in both of them. It was clearly the scariest thing Scott had ever heard as his eyes got wide. Never in his short life had he known anyone whose parents had died. That made Ryan an orphan. Maybe that was what caused the false bravado, the haughty attitude, and the demeanor of 'I don't care'. The realization of what it must be like for Ryan suddenly made Scott feel extremely uncomfortable. What went through his mind was waking up one morning and finding out he was an orphan, too. He quickly decided on something else to talk about.

"Uh, so tell me about Crescent City."

Ryan's inflection shifted completely. "I lived in the last homestead in the *Jedediah Smith Redwoods State Park*."

"In a park? That's weird. I thought nobody lived in parks."

"Normally you can't," he answered.

Scott looked at him. "Well?"

He started like he was reading a brochure. "Our family has owned the five and a half acres on Del Norte Pass Road for like eighty-five years. About twelve or thirteen years ago, the State bought up the area surrounding the property to expand the existing park. It's gonna include our land when Muh—she's my grandma—passes away. It's on some kind of lease plan or something. I don't understand most of it. What it means is that neither me nor my brother get the place when she dies. Instead, we get the cash."

Scott listened while pieces of Ryan's personality filtered through. It was weird. It was like he was just being cold about everything. Sure, the exuberance rang in his voice and there was certain intelligence in his words. But there was that fake feeling he felt coming from him even now. Obviously, Ryan wasn't going to reveal everything about himself, but still, Scott was trying his best to be friendly. He let his thoughts sit still, just to be with it all. His Aunt Cin had taught him how to do that. *"Don't try to figure things out when the going gets weird, just let the answer come,"* she had said. It was an odd way to find answers, different from what he learned in high school, but it worked just as well. He pulled the Jeep over at a convenience store and they jumped out.

"Got any quarters?" Scott asked.

Ryan reached into his pocket and pulled out some change. "Just three."

"That's good enough." Scott raised an eyebrow. "I'd cream you even if you had ten."

"I doubt it. Name the game."

"Empire Destroyer II."

Ryan snorted. "You're on."

Scott waved briefly to the girl behind the counter as they went in. She waved back with a wide smile as they strode to the row of video games along one wall. Ryan inspected the screen when the winner's initials flashed on. The top five were Y.E.A. He wondered if they might be Scott's.

"Y.E.A?"

"Commander Faraday. Who'd you think?"

"But Y.E.A.?"

"I woulda put in an 'H', but you can't add a fourth letter."

Ryan stood with arms akimbo. "Prove it's you." Scott inspected his stance. He couldn't help but look him up and down for a brief instant as he again wondered what Ryan's legs looked like all the way up to his crotch.

They played three games and Scott beat him soundly each time. When Scott pushed the last two sets of initials off the list at the end of the last game, Ryan's wound up at the bottom.

The girl behind the counter called to them. "Am I gonna have to reset the machine again, Scott?"

"Wait 'til I *completely* fill the winner's screen this time," he said, then grinned at Ryan.

They stepped outside the doors and hesitated on the sidewalk in front. It was covered with flattened, dark gum spots. The ice machine behind them kicked on with an angry sound.

Ryan spat on the hot cement. "Asshole."

"Mellow out. No one's beaten Commander Faraday yet."

"Don't be so sure someone won't," he said visibly irritated.

As they got back into the Jeep Scott felt somewhat amused. Ryan's response was odd. He hadn't seen anyone take the game as seriously as that.

"You know," Scott began, "I went in there a couple of months ago and someone's initials were in second place. I didn't recognize them. I found out that it was some kid who didn't even live here. That girl in there, the one behind the counter, she told me he was with some family of campers on their way to the Monument." Scott hoped he would mellow a little at that tidbit. He still looked mad anyway.

The way to the drive-in on Tower Road was only a half-mile further on. They pulled up under a covered stall and he stopped the Jeep.

A longbed pick-up with bright chrome tailpipes and wheels was idling in the parking lot across from them. Joe Engle again, observed Scott. Joe was the only one in his class who gave him any real grief. Somehow it seemed Joe was suspicious about him not being exactly straight. The only thing he could figure out was that Joe must have known Alan from Scouts several years back. There was some tentative sexual experimentation in Alan's garage one weekend, which had led to nothing, much to Scott's disappointment. Alan's father was transferred out of state before the next school year began. Alan left his life and their brief experimentation was part of the past, or so he thought. It was shortly after that that Joe taunted him every once in a while. Alan may have been his friend or something, he figured. Perhaps it was mere coincidence. He wasn't sure. Oddly enough, Joe had never taunted him when his friends were around. It was only when no one else was in earshot. The last time it happened Joe had asked him if he wanted to visit the bleachers at the high school stadium with him. At night. Joe's body language had given him away though. It had seemed like a come on, but had the wrong tone, like a bashing was in the offing. He had declined the invitation. It was just a little too weird. Scott's radar just wasn't hooked up properly at all yet.

Ryan broke his reverie. "Looks like some nice tanned bods to me."

Scott followed his eyes to see what he was talking about. Walking toward Joe's pick-up were two girls wearing shorts, halter-tops and sandals. They spoke to him briefly, then Joe gunned the engine and screeched out of the lot. They waved to him as he left.

"My, my," exclaimed Ryan as he sized them up.

Scott was busy watching Joe's truck speed away. He scowled and went into character. This time feigning a Russian accent. "Mister Engle, vee need to test dis dewice. Please stand here vis dis blasting cap."

Ryan's eyes had been following the girls as they entered the restaurant, then he looked at Scott. "What?"

Scott leaned over a little toward him. "Mister Engle you're not doink dis correctly. Dis iz a critical test und conditions must be met as told."

Ryan knitted his brow. "Who's Mister Engle? And what the hell are you talking about?"

Scott flailed his arms and yelled. "BOOM! Wery good. Test complete." Not saying a word, he stared at Ryan.

Ryan broke out in laughter. The fake accent, the flailing of Scott's arms as he yelled, then the deadpan shift that happened so quickly, were quite the comic relief.

"What was that all about?" Ryan asked.

Scott pointed with his chin. "That was for Joe Cool who just sped off." He wondered if Ryan had spun donuts in parking lots with his Chevelle and other such antics as did Joe. *Probably*, he thought. "The shorter girl is Brenda, his girlfriend. The other one's her cousin."

"Well, what are we waiting for? Let's pursue the cousin."

Scott knew he wasn't going to like it. He hadn't really considered how he might react if Ryan wanted to pursue girls. All he wanted right now was just to be with him. Nonetheless, he didn't resist just yet. He turned to admire his vehicle as they walked in the front entrance and excitement welled up in him again about it. He stepped over a cement parking block and followed Ryan inside. Scott watched him as he moved. He seemed so sexy. Ryan might just be the best-looking guy in all of Yucca Valley, he thought. *The* best-looking? Start getting over him, he told himself.

They ordered at the counter then sat in one of the booths, waiting for their number to be called. Ryan eyed the two girls who had taken a seat three booths behind him by the exit door. Brenda's cousin appeared preoccupied and kept glancing out the window into the parking lot. It could have been worse. Joe could have told Brenda, or anyone else, what he suspected of Scott. He could have started out with one lie about him to her and she could have spread all kinds of rumors. Nothing like that had ever happened though. He wondered if his reputation at Faraday's had anything to do with it. Maybe it was something else. He couldn't be sure.

Their numbers were called and he went to pick up both trays. Ryan stuffed his face with fries and spoke as he chewed. "So, what do you know about those girls?"

Now Scott was faced with questions he hoped he might avoid. Since he already knew Brenda, he told Ryan what he knew.

"She's okay. She's gonna be a junior. She's all over Joe Cool."

"What about the other foxy one?"

"She's Katie, She's gonna be a senior, but we've only had two classes together. I don't know her as well."

"So, you never dated either one of them?"

On the spot again, thought Scott. "No."

Ryan looked up only briefly, taking in the single word, but seemingly searching for more. "You should see if you can fix me up with her."

It was always like this. *Everyone likes girls that way. Every guy I know,* he thought. "Maybe."

"Later, of course," Ryan added.

That was strange, Scott thought. *He dropped the subject just like that.* Scott was sure he would have pursued the topic until he had had the girl's phone number.

Scott shifted characters again, sounding dead serious this time. "She was almost killed once in a ballooning accident." Ryan stopped chewing and watched him. "She had only two minutes of fuel left and was about to hit the Tower Road Drive-In. Luckily, Scott Faraday was in the next balloon and tossed a canister of propane to her...."

He didn't get to finish his sentence as Ryan interrupted him. "Suddenly our hero was there. He cut the ballast and she managed to avoid certain death. She was carried off by him only to be found days later, exhausted by the sex-crazed maniac."

Scott nearly dropped his French fry as his heart leaped. Ryan had taken his lead and played his mind game with him—his favorite game. No one ever did that. To say the least, he wasn't prepared for this kind of connection with him. The ensuing silence lasted only a second or so, then both started laughing. The two girls heard them and glanced their way.

So far, Brenda had only paid them incidental attention. Now she and her cousin took turns looking at them and giggling.

Ryan casually looked back and raised his voice. "Seems like those girls need us, Scott."

Scott ducked his head involuntarily, sure that they heard him.

Ryan leaned back and stretched out his legs across the length of the bench seat. Scott looked down at the dark hairs that trailed down and stopped at Ryan's sockless ankles. He studied the contour of his tennis shoe for a second. "Seems like *real* men are what they need," Ryan continued.

Scott rolled his eyes and sighed. "Keep it down. I don't need Joe on my butt."

Ryan glanced down at his crotch then over to Scott. In the same loud voice he said "Keep *what* down?" He didn't seem to care about the social repercussions Scott would receive.

Scott whispered, raising his eyebrows as he showed his concern. "Shut up, fuckhead. I *know* them."

Ryan quit for the moment and the girls stopped their giggling. They started to collect their purses as a car pulled up by the side entrance. Brenda waved briefly to the driver. Ryan looked out the window at the guy driving. He happened to be watching the boys as Ryan jerked his thumb back. "I guess I'm too late to save Katie anyway."

Once in the car Scott watched as Katie got in the middle and Brenda slid in beside her. The boy, who Scott recognized as Brenda's brother, and Katie, talked for a moment while he kept both hands fixed on the steering wheel. He put the car in park and got out. Scott didn't like the look on his face.

"Uh, oh," he announced as the kid walked toward the exit door.

"What?"

"Shit." He heard the car's motor still rumbling outside as the door opened. At least that told him it wasn't going to be a lengthy confrontation.

"You," the boy said from the doorway as he looked toward Ryan.

What irony, Scott thought. He was sure to be blamed for the incident since he knew them. And what was worse, he didn't want anything to do with them in the first place. Now his supposed friend was going to get him in trouble.

Ryan stood up from the bench seat and straightened his shirt. Brenda's brother was bigger than either of them and sounded formidable enough as he strode over. "You got something to tell me?"

As the boy stood in front of him, Ryan readied to fend off the verbal attack. Ryan looked calm despite what Scott was sure was going to happen next. In the most apologetic voice Ryan could feign, he spoke. "I'm terribly sorry. If the girls thought I was being rude I must apologize." That left the kid speechless. Ryan had disarmed him with just the right tone of voice.

"Don't be saying shit to my sister." With that, he glared at Scott, turned around, and left. Ryan took a few steps toward the door, but stopped short of following him out.

Brenda looked back at Scott as they drove off. He tried his best to show her he wasn't to blame by shrugging his shoulders and rolling his eyes.

Acting like nothing happened, Ryan slid back into the booth. He took another fry from the now almost empty greasy paper in the basket.

Scott was flabbergasted. "Do you do that all the time?"

"Do what all the time?"

"Act like an asshole?"

"He started it."

"No, you did with all those comments."

"I don't think so."

"Well, that's just fucking fine," Scott slapped the tabletop. "Joe just added another year to my fucking sentence." Ryan didn't ask what that meant.

Scott looked at the situation. It was brief by all accounts. Yet, he didn't hang out with people who acted that way. His friends weren't assholes. Luckily, Ryan hadn't heated up the confrontation or the manager might have kicked them both out. But there was something more going on here. What it was exactly, Scott couldn't tell. *It's too bad Ryan's a butthole*, he thought, *he's so fucking cute*. Somehow that mere fact allowed Scott to let it slide for the moment. He knew he wasn't the only one who had that tendency: to let good-looking guys do or say anything they wanted.

A few moments later Scott spied three members of Centauri pull up outside. They were Sparks, Bryce, and Darryl. Sparks, who did the lights, regularly wore an inch wide red piece of cloth tied around his pant leg, just above the knee. A bandanna was too big. Tonight he had two strips, one above the other. They came in and Scott hailed them.

"Who're they?" Ryan asked.

"Guys from the band."

Up to this point Ryan wasn't sure whether Scott had been kidding or not about the band. But when the group saw Scott they lit up and immediately came over.

"Sound Dude!" they yelled almost in unison. Suddenly Scott was faced with having to introduce Ryan. *What the fuck*, he thought, *he'll eventually leave the picture anyway.*

Ryan checked them out one by one as Scott introduced him. "Ryan St. Charles, this is Marty, but we call him Sparks. He does lights." They shook hands. "Bryce Owens is on the drums and Darryl Osterhaus is the wicked dude with the keys."

Bryce nodded. Darryl stuck his hands up and wiggled his fingers in the air on an imaginary keyboard.

"Hey," Scott said to get their attention. "I got the vehicle."

"No shit! Let's see it," Sparks said. They went outside to inspect it. Everyone commented on how nice it looked and how much of their equipment it would hold. He had to let each of them drive around the parking lot at least once. Finally, he got them to leave it alone and they went back in to sit at the booth.

As all five squeezed onto the short benches Scott noticed right away that Ryan looked uncomfortable. And he was sure it was more than just the cramped space making him that way.

"Where's Mitch?" Scott asked, referring to their bass guitarist.

"He's with Barry," Darryl said. "They're working out the main licks for the tunes we're doin' tomorrow. We don't have to 'cause we already have 'em down." Scott and Sparks laughed as they all agreed.

Bryce tried to sound mysterious. "Scott, have you been to the Peak lately?"

Scott raised an eyebrow. "Does it have anything to do with my Sacred Film Case?"

"Shit. Mitch said you'd figure it out."

"Mitch has my brain."

Sparks answered before anyone else had a chance. "See, I told you he had shit for brains, too."

Scott laughed with them. "So, Sparks, why two ribbons?" he asked.

Sparks straightened an imaginary tie. "Can you say score?"

Ryan's ears perked up. "As in pussy?"

"I wasn't talking about football."

Ryan seemed annoyed. "Just checking."

Scott lowered his voice. "Your girlfriend's finally puttin' out?"

Bryce chimed in facetiously. "I personally sniffed his dick to make sure."

Sparks answered Scott. "It was about time, too. I almost had to beat off for the first time in my life."

Darryl looked at him. "Shit, dude, you're in the World Records book."

Everyone laughed, but Scott was sure *he* personally held the record. Ryan was unable to see the humor and wasn't laughing.

Scott noticed that Ryan was noncommittal now. Was it the comment about masturbating that did it? Was it the whole conversation about sex? Scott wasn't sure.

Darryl looked at his watch and all of three of his band mates removed themselves from the bench. "Where're you guys headed?"

"Carla's house. She made her radical brownies and said to stop by before we went cruising. But don't worry. We'll be back in time for practice tomorrow," Darryl replied.

"Weird Carla? Count me out."

Bryce answered. "I know you don't like Carla or I'd 've invited you. See you at the Royal Garage tomorrow."

"Like clockwork," Scott replied.

The guys departed and Ryan and Scott were left in the silence. It was as if a whirlwind had died.

"Weird Carla? Royal Garage?" Ryan asked.

"Weird Carla's this friend of Barry's who did too many drugs way back. Her brain's fried and she's weird. They only go there 'cause she's got the hots for Bryce, and she makes these killer brownies, the kind *without* pot in them.

"Most of the egg cartons nailed to the walls in Colleen's garage for sound deadening, are made from purple colored paperboard. So, we called the place the Royal Garage. Colleen's the lead singer."

Ryan thought for a second. "What's that about Bryce sniffing Sparks' dick?"

Scott looked up at the couple that just sat down in the next booth, hoping they didn't hear his question. "He was kidding." Scott looked at him for a moment. He was sure he wouldn't be coming out to him.

At Ryan's insistence, they played video games there and next door at another convenience store. Scott knew them all and had an amazing dexterity Ryan lacked. That left Ryan even more frustrated. He became so annoying that Scott finally felt compelled to get rid of him. "I've had it. Ready to go?"

Ryan agreed. "Let's get the fuck outta here."

In the Jeep, he was quiet while Scott mused over his odd question earlier. Of course Bryce was kidding. It was purely a joke. Although Scott hadn't ever had sex with anyone yet he was sure Sparks was having plenty way before his double-ribbon symbolism started. Among the things Scott admired Sparks for was the smooth talking he did with girls. Scott was sure that if he told him he was gay it would probably put an end to their friendship, and of course, him doing sound for the band. After all, he was only sixteen and the rest of the band was nineteen or older. He had always figured they could easily replace him.

The night air was still quite warm as he let Ryan out at Howard's house. "Hey, I'll be leaving for practice about eight-thirty. Will you be up then?" Scott didn't know exactly why he extended his invitation after having his fill of Ryan today. *Must have been the cute butt that did it*, he thought.

"Yeah."

"I could stop by and pick you up."

"Yeah," he replied with great enthusiasm.

Why am I bothering, Scott wondered again. *Oh yeah, he's cuter than hell.*

Baseline Drive was the main cruising road at the edge of town. Running east-west along the base of a hilly rise that effectively was the north end of town, it afforded the place everyone needed to cruise in their vehicles in the evening on the weekends. If one didn't cruise Baseline Drive, one wasn't part of the in-crowd. He didn't intend to race his new vehicle. He merely wanted to join the crowd there to show off his new possession. As the evening progressed, the guys finally showed up from Carla's place. As much as Scott liked being around them, and despite the annoyance of his new acquaintance, somehow he felt a little empty now that Ryan wasn't around.

Hours later, as he headed home, the tires on the pavement hummed with a distinct E-flat, he noticed. The afternoon spent with Ryan came back to mind. The guy was such a bizarre mixture of bad attitude and incredibly cute body. Despite the attitude, Scott noticed that little of it was directed toward him. Ryan's antagonism earlier with the video game issue was more of a self-defeating attitude than an attack on himself, Scott realized. And, if Ryan didn't have the good looks going for him, he was sure the guy would have been history this very evening.

Once home, he undressed and dropped his clothes on his desk chair. He stood at the window before peeling off his underwear. From the dark of his room, he looked out at the Jeep parked under the carport. His Jeep, his very own Jeep, he thought. Everyone else cruising Baseline Drive loved it, too. Finally, he had his very own vehicle, the freedom he needed, and it was just in time for summer. Shakaiyo's tail swished across the carpet as she sat, watching him lay down in the bed. She laid down with her jowls on her outstretched paws.

Sparks' dick. Sparks had the tightest leather pants, which he wore during concerts. Guess what was quite noticeable when he wore them? Scott wondered what Spark's dick smelled like just pulled out of them

and hard as a rock. He didn't think Spark's was particularly good-looking, but he had fantasized about that noticeable dick on occasion. It
didn't take long for him to get hard. He stroked himself casually, wanting to build it up then slow down. He went too far too fast and ended up
finishing himself off more quickly than he wanted. That happened
often. When he was done, he wiped up with the golf rag, pulled the
sheet up, and quickly fell asleep.

CHAPTER 5

Scott was starting to enjoy not having to get up early ever since school ended the first week of June. Still, he was up by eight most days anyway because of work, or band practice on the weekends, and today was no exception.

By 8:30 a.m., he and Shakaiyo were headed to Howard's house. As he pulled into the driveway, he wondered how he should explain to Ryan to be a little mellower than he seemed to be yesterday. He was reluctant to be there now that he had had a taste of his quirky manner. But he had promised to take him along and somehow he couldn't say no to that cute face. Ryan's uncle must be gone, he surmised, since the garage was open and his car wasn't there.

He rang the bell at the front door, then told Shakaiyo to stay put.

Ryan answered and let him in. Scott sat in the large dining room with him while Ryan finished his breakfast. In the living room, music videos played loudly through the stereo while the accompanying video played on a large projection-screen TV. Scattered all over the long, wooden, and expensive-looking dining room table were trade journals on accounting, engineering and industrial topics he had no clue about. Next to them were stacks of various memos and other papers. Blank letterhead with the AeroSun logo was in another stack, while a half-dozen envelopes lay next to it. A neatly folded Wall Street Journal was wedged into an empty acrylic napkin holder. A brand new laptop computer lay next to it, with its lid open. Its screen was dark. Scott placed his fingers on the keys and pretended it was one of Darryl's keyboards as he danced his fingers across them briefly. His attention then went to the last of Ryan's cereal floating in the milk. Nondescript shapes clung to the spoon; the rest was hidden beneath the opaque meniscus.

Ryan raised his voice over the music. "Is your band video quality?" He squinted to see the title of the video that just ended.

Scott looked on, too, and shouted back. "Ask the jarheads on the Marine base. We do gigs there every once in a while. And some of our friends have seen us at the VFW auditorium outside town." He didn't mention the rest of the gigs they were still trying to get at bars in other nearby towns. He also didn't say that at the gig about four months ago the sound was awful, and that at the last one only about fifty people showed up. The sound problems had been solved with the new sound-board, and now, with Sparks doing lights, they had been promoting themselves as the much improved Centauri.

Ryan heard him, not sure what to think. He finished his cereal, then stapled a check to a form and folded it. He turned a large manila envelope over and stuffed the papers inside. The cover of the envelope was preprinted with the address: *Office of Admissions, UCLA.*

Scott watched him lick it, the address staring at him. "UCLA? I thought you had to be smart to go there."

"Duh," Ryan answered.

Scott cracked a smile. He picked up the college catalog that lay on the table and turned to the dog-eared chapter labeled *College of Engineering.* On the first page was a line drawing map of the various buildings. The Engineering school buildings were highlighted in a light brown color. "The catalog for the school here in town isn't nearly as big as this one," he commented.

"Where's it at?"

"Out by the freeway. It's just a little way past the hotel where Colleen, our lead singer, works. My dad says that if I do well there he'll send me to a real college for business."

"Cool."

"I don't know though. Business seems kinda boring to me. But you can make some bucks in it if you got the right job," Scott said trying to convince himself.

"At least *you* don't have to worry about where you're working after school. You got it easy," remarked Ryan. "Just graduate and you're, what, a partner or something?"

Scott looked away, feeling forlorn, yet not knowing why. "Yeah, that's what they want." He thumbed through the required first year courses. The next page had course numbers circled, some in pen, and others in pencil. One of the courses was struck out with a big X. He read the fine print. "It says here you have to take English."

"Yeah, I know. I just didn't erase the X."

"How'd you do on the SAT?"

"I took the ACT."

"Oh."

"I did decent though. Made top ten percent in the country on the math part. What about you?"

"Decent, too. I did better on the verbal part." Scott wasn't big on math.

Ryan pulled two stamps off a sheet that was in a small plastic basket on the table and carefully applied them. The basket contained items that would normally be in a desk drawer. He seemed downcast as he put them on the envelope, then placed it into the letter bin marked "Out."

Scott noticed the look on his face. "I thought you were hyped up about going to college."

"I thought I was, too, 'til Howie started talking about it."

Scott laid the catalog back down. "Huh?"

Ryan paused for a moment, watching the computer graphics of a tennis shoe commercial on the TV, then at Scott. "I didn't know anyone when I first got here. And I won't know anyone again in L.A. when I go there, either."

Scott didn't get his point. "I don't know why anyone wants to live where you need a gas mask just to breathe."

"Well, I don't plan to live there all my life."

"You could think of it as a vacation."

Ryan sounded far away. "Yeah. I guess."

"Are you finished? We're gonna be late. And I'm the soundman, remember?"

"Yeah, yeah." Ryan quickly donned tennis shoes, then turned off the stereo and TV with a flip of a switch. The room was completely quiet, a totally different place now.

"Howie's a cool uncle. He's got the best stereo stuff," he stated.

Scott had already noticed every piece of equipment and had determined that it was only so-so. He couldn't help but grin at Ryan's assessment. "Wait till you hear the bitchin'est band in town."

They headed out the door and into the Jeep. Ryan scratched behind Shakaiyo's ears as they pulled out of the driveway. She put a paw in his hand to try to make him continue…which he did.

He turned down the winding road onto the main highway and sped up. There was a lot of traffic today and the other end of town was ten minutes away.

Ryan glanced over at Scott. "So how did you get into this band?"

"Darryl. You know, keyboards?"

"Yeah."

"He used to live down my street. I met him the day we moved in. That was back when I was in seventh grade. He's played keys since he was fourteen. He's nineteen now. He's one of the original members of Centauri. They used to have another guy who did sound, but he was pretty much a goof. He asked me one day last year if I wanted to take over and I said yes. I made him promise to write a keyboard score to my tune as part of the deal."

"Your tune?"

"For my flute. It's a song I wrote called *"Out of Breath."* I might even play it for you later."

"It seems kinda funny for a guy to play the flute."

Scott was annoyed by the comment. "You obviously haven't ever listened to anyone play a flute outside of, like, high school, have you?"

"Well, no."

"Well, get over it." Now he remembered why he didn't want to have Ryan along and started regretting having picked him up.

Ryan mulled it over. He seemed to be programmed to repel anything that smacked of being effeminate. A guy playing a flute seemed that way to him. Scott was right though. He'd never seen an orchestra except on TV. Most of the flutists were men. And Scott didn't seem in the least effeminate. He wasn't back home, damn it. *None of my friends can dictate how I'm supposed to think anymore,* he thought.

Ryan changed the subject. "This Colleen. You like her?"

"She's probably the coolest girl, uh, woman I know."

"How old is she?"

"Twenty-three."

"Married?"

"No. And she lives with her parents. There's this guy that comes in every other week who leads some sort of seminars at the hotel where she works. They've gone out a lot, but he lives in Pomona. It's quite the long distance thing, and doomed to fail, if you ask me."

"But she's gettin' some. She must be good-looking, huh?"

"You think I, Scott Faraday, would hang out in a band that has an ugly girl in it?"

"Twenty-three, huh?"

He feigned the usual interest. "You like older women?"

"Just checking."

Scott glanced briefly at Ryan. Why was he so interested, then not?

They arrived late and pulled up behind a Nissan sedan. Musical instrument stickers were plastered all over the bumper and back window. There were four other cars parked in the driveway, too. One was a mid-1960s VW van parked to the side, sporting a shiny paint job. Ryan noted that it was quite the artifact and mentioned that to Scott. The Fitzsimon's house was a tidy doublewide trailer on a cement slab. A well-shaded wide front porch had lawn furniture in a circle at one end of it. A gently sloping hill around back led to huge copper-colored boulders that effectively fenced in the backyard on three sides. At the bottom of the slope was a large off-green corrugated garage that looked like a machine shop. They heard music emanating from it. A concrete sidewalk wound down from the back porch to it. The rest of the property was relatively barren except for the buildings and a huge majestic oak tree that partially shaded the garage.

Shakaiyo jumped out and followed the boys as they walked down the back sidewalk. Ryan listened as they walked. They could already hear Barry's guitar and Darryl warming up on his keyboards. "Doesn't sound all that hot to me."

"That's just practice."

As they approached the entrance Bryce was about to sit at the drum set. "Sound Dude's here!"

Inside Ryan heard the echoes of other guys yell "Sound Dude!" as loud as they could. "Why are they yelling like that?"

"Standard greeting."

For some reason, Shakaiyo liked Colleen's backyard. Perhaps the yard had certain smells she liked because she always roamed around the perimeter and sniffed at everything before she ever entered the garage. From inside the garage the sliding doors perfectly framed the largest of the boulders in the backyard. For all one knew, one was in the middle of nowhere from the view they had.

Colleen was just plugging a mike into the soundboard when they came in. She quickly tied back her hair with a burette and smiled as she saw Scott. Ryan noticed that true to what Scott told him, there were two-foot square egg cartons stapled to the pegboard walls and along the ceiling joists. All had been stamped out of various shades of purple-colored paperboard. They stepped over several cables and Ryan surveyed the guys. All were dressed in shorts, tank tops, and tennis shoes. Mitch was wiping his black bass guitar with a handkerchief, which he then stuffed into a back pocket. Ryan was impressed with Darryl's keyboard setup. His A-frame stand held three different ones. Two were long and a shorter one sat on the top rung of the frame. Scott stopped at the soundboard, picked up his headphones, and slipped them around his neck as he looked at Colleen. She smiled at Ryan this time.

"And who is this, Scott?"

With an impish grin on his face, Scott answered her. "No. His name's Ryan."

"There was a comma in that sentence." She tugged on the mike cable. "You just missed it."

He looked into the air as if trying to find something out of his reach. "Oh, I see it now. Ryan St. Charles, this is Colleen. He just moved here from up north."

"From Crescent City," Ryan chimed in, as he shook her hand.

Barry heard him and did a mean slide on his guitar. "The redwoods?"

Ryan's eyebrows rose up as he looked over at him. "You've been there?"

He tried to make it sound official. "Yeah. I've partied on the Smith River."

At least one of them knows where my hometown is, he thought.

After Scott formally introduced him to the rest of the band, Ryan took to them rather quickly. They showed him their equipment and while Bryce tapped on his drums, Ryan and Barry talked about the redwoods and, of course, cars.

Scott thought it odd that Ryan was so interested in Colleen at first, and then seemed to just forget she was there. *Maybe she's not as good looking as he imagined.*

Scott talked with Colleen as Ryan talked with the rest of the guys. "Sorry I brought him, but he's new in town and doesn't know anybody yet. And I had to come over today, with practice, and all."

Colleen looked amused at his trying to excuse himself. "Don't worry about that. Guess what?"

"What?"

"We got the agreement to do three more gigs at the base."

Scott's eyes grew wide. "Totally! When?"

"The last two weekends in September and the first one in October. That gives us a couple of months to get it together."

"Shit, and I'll have school, too."

"You have to give up a lot to be with the best."

"Well, I still have to go to school. But I'll do the gigs."

"And now that we have a real soundboard and more hot tunes, this could be the break we're looking for. But what it really means is we have to *practice.*"

Scott swept an arm out in front of himself. "Today Twentynine Palms, tomorrow, L.A."

"Not so fast. We've got quite a ways to go."

"The Sound Dude knows. By the way, where's Sparks?"

"One of the guys called in sick at the store and he had to go in."

"I'd hate to stock groceries on a Sunday." He noticed Colleen had bags under her eyes. "You look half asleep."

She didn't look directly at him. "By the time I got home this morning it was pushing the hell out of dawn, so it's caffeine awareness day for me."

"I thought you didn't like coffee."

She pointed to an empty cola can, a tall glass of ice, and still-bubbling soda.

"I see. Jim again?"

Colleen just smiled modestly.

"What do you see in that guy anyway? He's only here every other week,"

"Let's say he's quite a charmer." She told him. "And last night we were, well, nuclear."

Scott flicked his fingers in front of her face, his eyes wide. "Meltdown alert! Meltdown alert!"

Colleen stepped slightly closer and lowered her voice. "So, Scott, tell me about your friend. He's quite cute. You gonna make the move on him?" Even though they rarely spoke about it, Scott had come out to her about six months ago. Every once in a while she'd say something like this, trying to embarrass him. Luckily, not around the guys, though. So far, it was their secret until he decided to say something to them.

Ryan was still talking to the guys as Colleen and Scott talked.

"He's not my type," he lied. What was true was that Ryan was perfectly his type, but his attitude was definitely not.

"Stuck up."

"Give me a break. He's straight. And I can do without a bloody nose."

She crossed her arms and checked out Ryan's rear end. "Oh, well…he'd be quite the catch," she whispered.

Scott copied her stance and briefly looked at him with her. "Well, yeah. He would be."

Mitch broke up the guys and picked up his guitar again. He pointed to Colleen and Scott. "Hey you two. Time to start. For real."

Ryan sat on a stool next to Scott as they went through the first tune. They stopped and started several times as they found out which rhythm would carry them through. The soundboard was a maze to Ryan. Still, he sat and marveled at the adeptness with which Scott varied the sound. He seemed to know which combinations to use to get just the right sound they were looking for. Scott kept notes on some of the levels for future reference in a small notebook.

About an hour and a half later, the sky grew darker than normal for this time of the day. Ryan looked at the clouds, feeling a little melancholy. He was already missing the familiar leaden skies of Crescent City.

Barry called for a break and he, Mitch and Darryl went into the house. One of Bryce's sticks rolled on the snare making a racket before it fell to the cement floor.

Colleen went outside to look at the sky. "Wow. Is it gonna rain?"

Ryan looked exasperated as he checked out the clouds. "It'll evaporate before it hits the ground."

"As usual."

Shakaiyo, who usually roamed around during practice, zigzagged her way across the backyard sniffing invisible trails and digging little holes. She looked up once and, upon seeing Scott, wagged her tail. She ran over to the hose coiled to the side of the house and nudged it with her nose. He turned it on for her and let the hot water run out. She tried to bite the stream as she drank, wagging her tail the whole time. Once she had had enough, she was off again.

The boys came back with Darryl holding a section of the paper. He folded it and put it on the soundboard. Scott scanned it and finally saw the ad.

"*Rocky Horror*'s back, just like I said."

"Totally. When are we going?"

"Tonight, of course."

Scott looked at Ryan who took the paper. "*Rocky Horror Picture Show*," Ryan read aloud. "What's that?"

Colleen looked incredulous. "You don't know what *Rocky Horror* is?"

"Never heard of it."

Bryce spoke up, sounding melodramatic. "Someone who hasn't heard of *Rocky Horror*? How can that be?"

"You forget. He's from a dinky town," Scott told him.

Ryan was instantly on the defensive. "It's not dinky."

Mitch let him know. "It's dinky if *Rocky Horror* hasn't played there."

Ryan sounded irritated. "Well, what is it?"

"Take him with us," Darryl said.

Bryce looked at Ryan. "You'll love it. It's so weird. Plus, you can sing with us."

"Sing? I don't sing."

Scott was getting extremely annoyed with the whole interaction. Having him tag along was definitely not a good idea. It was turning out now that he couldn't seem to get rid of him.

Darryl and Bryce put their arms on each other's shoulders and started on an impromptu version of the *Time Warp* as they attempted to dance. Colleen broke them off. "We have to practice, remember? The movie doesn't start until this evening."

"Okay, mother," they said almost in unison.

Finally everyone assembled behind their instruments. Ryan listened as they ran through more of the tunes. Their music wasn't at all bad, he decided. He was surprised they did so many original tunes as well as a few he'd heard on the radio, too.

Colleen announced the next song as if doing so for a real audience. "Here's another original tune. *Cradle Fall.*"

Bryce started with a melodic drumbeat, joined in by Mitch with his signature bass guitar sound. Scott was equalizing the two when Barry yelled. "Hold it. Hold it." They stopped and all eyes were on Barry. "Scott, that's *too* much bass."

Scott dropped his headphones down to his neck and listened as Mitch plucked a string. Darryl looked back at Barry. "You have to have a *reasonable* sense of impending doom," he said in a perfectly serious tone.

Ryan whispered to Scott. "Doom?"

He whispered back. "Listen to the lyrics. This is where the guys harmonize and sound like a Gregorian chant. Then Colleen joins in."

"A what chant?"

"Those droning songs monks sing."

Ryan raised a corner of his lip. "Sounds weird."

"That's the idea," he said as he replaced his headphones. *Sheesh.*

He adjusted the potentiometers before they began this time. When they were done with the first take Barry took a moment to retune his guitar.

Colleen sipped her soda. Ryan's eyes were wide. "Wow. That was excellent. How'd you do that?"

She pulled on one of her earlobes and laughed. "Talent. And the fact that I shave the edge off my vocal tone so I won't drown the guys."

They did the tune again. This time Scott taped it so they could hear the full range of sounds. Later they all stood in front of the large speakers and criticized their work.

Despite the constant fans they had blowing, it was still growing hotter, which lead Bryce to pull off his shirt. Now he was wearing just shorts and his tennis shoes. Ryan tried not to stare, although his crazy antics at the drums were quite compelling. All the while he was making faces and twirling the stick he wasn't using at the moment—which served to draw more attention to him. Before they knew it, four more hours had passed.

When they stopped for the day and turned off everything, Scott ran outside and immediately started the hose until the hot water was drained out again. He doused his arms and face with it then proceeded to turn it on Mitch. In no time, Mitch had the hose away and on Scott who raised his arms up in a show of strength as the water splashed against him and ran down his chest. Both stood there soaked—hair, shorts and shoes. Ryan wanted to join in but found their intense camaraderie somewhat disturbing. It was playful and yet too homoerotic for him. It was the homoerotic part he was trying to avoid. It felt too much like being around Crawford. He sighed, feeling alone, despite being surrounded by all these fun people.

Darryl leaned against the shaded side of the garage, watching them until Colleen shut off the water. "It's almost maximum craziness time. Less than an hour before the movie starts," he announced.

Barry and Colleen, the oldest members of the band, bowed out. They'd seen the movie about a dozen times anyway, almost more than the rest of them had seen it put together. In the heat, they all dried off quickly and soon Scott's clothes were only damp. The guys squeezed into his Jeep, and they stopped briefly by his house. Scott let Shakaiyo into the backyard, raced into his bedroom, and changed clothes.

In the huge parking lot at the mall, all the light poles were bolted on top of huge truncated concrete cones. One of them had a jagged chunk knocked out of the top and along one side where black paint remained from someone brushing too closely to it at one time. Long ago, they had decided that was their spot and always parked there.

The line in front of the theater was long and Scott wondered if they should have shown up earlier. Ryan observed that at least ten people in line were dressed for what seemed like Halloween.

"What's the deal with the costumes," he asked as they crossed the parking lot.

The rest of the group exchanged knowing glances. Bryce answered. "Audience participation."

Darryl pulled a small plastic bag from his pocket. "Rice. Courtesy of Colleen's pantry. And the weapon of choice." He produced a small water pistol.

Ryan looked at the small translucent green water pistol and was sure he was being left out of some huge joke. Where Darryl had been hiding it, he couldn't figure.

Bryce waited for Ryan to take his ticket and pulled him to the side as they walked into the lobby.

"Hum," he said as he pointed to his nose.

"Hum?"

"Yeah, hum."

"For what?"

"The movie, of course," he said matter-of-factly.

"Okay," he answered slowly, not knowing what he was up to. He hummed and the rest of the gang hummed in different octaves, changing pitch until they were a cacophony of crazy sounds. They laughed at their collective foolishness.

Mitch turned to Ryan. "You're about to see what it's really like in Ohio."

Ohio, Ryan wondered. "Come on. Is this really a horror movie?"

"Better." Darryl tried to sound serious, "It's an exploration of sex at its finest. They say California has their kooks. But we know better."

"Yeah," said Bryce, now trying to sound like Larry of *The Three Stooges*.

"Yeah," Scott feigned the accent after him, a little higher in pitch. In a second, they were all doing it and laughing again.

Ryan gave up. He would just have to wait until the movie started to figure it out. The energy he felt from the crowd made him look forward to whatever it was about anyway.

They passed a tall poster hung on the wall that featured the movie. Ryan thought it odd that the black-haired character with the white make-up had on woman's clothing and lipstick, but didn't think much of it at first.

Soon enough the movie started and no one in the audience would sit down. After the opening scene started, Darryl took out his bag of rice and poured some in Ryan's palm. Soon they all had some as well.

"Throw it when I say," Scott instructed.

Finally, it seemed obvious what was going on. Ryan started to feel that it was one of the best movies he'd seen in a long time. Until Janet and Brad reached the castle.

Now Ryan knew what Darryl was talking about when he said it was 'an exploration of sex at its finest'. He was talking about the main character dressed in drag. As it became clear who this Frank-N-Furter character was, Ryan became uncomfortable. It was difficult to follow the story line because of the amount of noise around him. There were dances and lyrics he didn't know. He felt it odd that the guys he'd hung around with all afternoon were getting a kick out of some transvestite wanting to create a monster.

When he saw that the monster turned out to be a blonde guy named Rocky he wanted to sink into the floor. Here he was standing on the arms of the seat with everyone else, watching people dance crazily in the aisles, and no one cared that the main character was essentially gay. In fact, it seemed like some sort of bizarre celebration of the very thing he was trying so hard to forget. His eyes were riveted, nonetheless, to the screen as Rocky paraded around in nothing but his tight shiny golden shorts.

At the scene where Dr. Frank-N-Furter seduced Brad, Ryan couldn't believe what he was watching. He sneaked a peek at Scott; his eyes were closed. What was he thinking? Was he visualizing the same thing he was? Or was he trying not to see any of it?

Finally, at the closing scenes, Brad was dressed in drag, too. It was too much. Except at the end where Rocky picked up Dr. Frank-N-Furter and he got another eye full of Rocky's hot body again.

At this point Darryl had emptied his water pistol from firing it all over the place. Ryan was wet from having been targeted by others with their pistols. As the movie ended, he likened it to a huge indoor carnival. Or like he'd seen a porn video without any sex.

Standing outside in the lobby Scott couldn't wait to ask him what he thought.

"Too weird. You like seeing guys dressed up like women?"

"It was good clean fun," Mitch said. "But that's about all the clean fun I can stand for one day." Then to Scott. "Home, Brad."

Scott answered and pointed across the parking lot. "Didn't we pass a castle down the road a few miles? I can drop you off."

Darryl, standing behind him, grabbed him by the shoulders and steered him toward the Jeep. They crossed the parking lot, dodging cars. Several knots of rowdy Marines from the nearby base whooped, hollered, and sang some of the songs Ryan heard in the movie. How many songs were there? Ten, fifteen? He couldn't believe the audience knew them all.

The rest of the band obviously had a good time. Ryan squeezed into the backseat, lost in thought. He had an eerie feeling that the joke was on him. He'd just watched the weirdest movie he'd ever seen and everyone liked it except him. It was disturbing to watch Brad be seduced and transformed just like that. Similar to what he felt Crawford did to him, only neither of them ever wore women's clothing. Images of Crawford swam in his head now and actually made him feel homesick. Crawford was familiar, Crawford was sexy. But he was also an asshole. Now images of Rocky and the reason Dr. Frank-N-Furter made him wouldn't leave his mind. The transvestite made the 'monster' purely for sexual reasons and no one seemed to get it. He wrestled with it until they reached Colleen's parent's house again, where everyone's cars were.

Scott tapped his foot on the driveway until they agreed on the time for next practice. It was a negotiation process that ended in more joking and kidding around. Finally, everyone took off.

Scott was on the highway before he asked Ryan. "You seem kinda weirded out. "

"You guys saw that movie before. I didn't know shit about it."

"It was cool, though, don't you think?"

"No."

Scott was greatly surprised. "No?"

"I'm not into transvestites."

"Neither am I. I prefer guys who want to be guys." Scott couldn't believe he'd said it, but in his present mood, it just came right out. Besides, it was actually a harmless statement. He didn't think Ryan would take it the way he really meant it. Yet he waited for a response that didn't come.

Ryan carefully avoided looking at Scott. He could have taken Scott's statement two ways. The movie had brought up so many thoughts and feelings about Crawford that he didn't dare say anything in return. Whereas he thought Scott was just making an innocent comment, it was true for him. He preferred guys who wanted to be guys, and who wanted to be *with* guys. That way. Crawford flashed into his thoughts again. He was the most masculine guy he'd ever known. He sighed. It seemed it was going to be a long time before it all faded from his mind after all.

"Let's make a detour before I take you home," Scott said, half-asking, half-stating.

"Why?"

"I wanna play my tune *No Restrictions.* I think you'll like it. I have a key to the auditorium at the VFW. My flute sounds really bitchin' there."

"No one's there?"

"It's after midnight, dude."

Ryan looked at his watch. "I guess."

They pulled up in Scott's driveway and both got out. Scott let Shakaiyo in his bedroom before they entered. He put his flute case on the bed and went into the bathroom. As he shut the door Ryan checked out the tarantula in the twenty-gallon aquarium. He looked around the room for a moment, sat on the bed, looking at the intercom, the phone, and the Frisbee hanging on the wall. Something caught his eye. It was a towel or rag. Part of it stuck out from the slightly opened nightstand drawer. It begged his attention. He knew what it was right away. He listened for Scott to start peeing, then slid open the drawer. Pulling the corner up, he inspected it, and sure enough, it was encrusted as he expected. He wanted to take it with him, so he could fantasize about Scott and use it himself. Yet, part of him wanted to pretend he hadn't seen it at all. He wanted to pretend Scott wasn't sexual, so he wouldn't feel so attracted to him. It was getting disturbing now. The more he tried to keep himself from thinking about guys, and especially Scott, the stronger it seemed. And Scott, being so incredibly cute, wasn't helping matters at all.

An incident from his sophomore year came back vividly to mind. While waiting for a buddy in the yearbook staff room, he had checked through a long open file drawer stuffed with old photos from past photographers. Once he started looking, he couldn't stop. He came across at least a dozen picture of shirtless guys. Guys in odd compromising positions: bent over, or with someone play-humping someone's rear. One where a guy was standing in an empty hallway in school wearing nothing but a towel around his waist.

It was a spur of the moment impulse. It was a simple matter to take some of them home. He had slid them into his bookbag before anyone noticed. How many times did he jerk off to them, fantasizing to those boys with their cute smiles, frozen in time? Enough to completely encrust a rag about the same size as Scott's. That was just one weekend.

That was the first time he knew for sure he was different.

Ryan's heart pounded as he quickly stuffed the rag back in and quietly slid the drawer shut before Scott came back out. Scott took the flute, oblivious to Ryan's discovery. He pointed to a boombox that lay on the floor by the stereo. "Get that." He pulled out a tape from one of his tape boxes.

"Onward," he said. Then, "Come on, girl, we're gone again." Shakaiyo followed them out and he left her in the backyard.

They drove out of town and soon enough they arrived at the VFW auditorium some three miles away. Scott pulled in to the big empty crushed-rock parking lot. Not a single car was parked in the lot.

The three-story building seemed out of place sitting out in the middle of nowhere. But the large auditorium was next to a football field and served its purpose. Two sets of bleachers out back, on either side of the field, were half-hidden from their vantage point until they rounded the back of the building. A baseball diamond was adjacent to the field further on.

Scott took the boombox from the floorboard behind him and offered it to him. On the ground, below an oversized window air conditioner was a cinder block that caught the condensation when it was in use. Ryan kicked at it as he followed Scott to a short wooden ramp that led to an awning-covered door.

Scott deftly inserted the key. He pushed, then pulled on the knob; jiggling the key a little, as if he was working a combination. The door opened to a dark foyer. The air smelled like old dry wood and leather, and it was hotter than outside.

"This is the back way in." Scott told him. They stepped in and darkness surrounded them. He felt along the wall and flipped on a light switch. They walked to the end of the hallway and came to another door.

"Hang on just a minute." He walked up a couple of steps in the dark.

"Where are you going? This is like a maze."

"Lights."

Ryan heard some switches click after Scott reached the electrical box. The hallway and part of the side stage became illuminated.

He came back swinging his flute case. "Come on up." They walked up onto the stage. "You can sit anywhere you want."

Ryan's eyes adjusted quickly to the dim illumination as he looked out over about fifty rows of seats.

Scott took the boombox from him and set it on the wooden stage floor. Ryan walked to the edge of it, shading his eyes from the lights shining down on them from above.

"Any seat." Scott repeated as he set his instrument case on the floor.

Ryan jumped the several feet from the stage and walked down the middle aisle. Most of the seats looked old and uncomfortable.

Nonetheless, they were all solidly bolted to the cement floor and looked quite sturdy.

He chose a place seven rows back and pulled the seat down. It creaked with a heavy wooden sound. He stayed there for only a few seconds then decided on a seat further back in the dark where he finally sat and waited.

Scott placed a folding chair in the middle of the stage, then went behind the curtain. In another minute, the lights dimmed and only one light illuminated him at center stage.

He sat down on the chair. He leaned down, opened the case, and put the flute together with a quick twist. He started the tape and the click of the button echoed in the dark silent expanse. Ryan heard the hiss of the tape before the music started. Several LEDs shone from the box and his attention focused on them as they jumped. Barry's soothing acoustic guitar gained in volume, reverberated throughout the room, and became quite melodic. Darryl's keyboards set the tone in the background and after another few measures he heard a flute. "I mixed a couple of tracks of the flute into this. But the main track I always do live."

Ryan leaned forward, placed his arms on the back of the seat in front of him and rested his chin on the back of his hand. What a contrast from just a half hour ago. Now they were alone in a theater with Scott being the only actor. At least he was properly on stage. Not like before where everyone was in the aisles, throwing rice, squirting water and mimicking that transvestite, he thought.

"My tune doesn't have any lyrics, but if it did, this is what they'd be." While the intro played Scott slowly spoke into the darkness, so his words would properly echo.

"Straining,
but the struggle
has you up against a wall.
You know there's someone out there—
no one answers all the calls."

His voice trailed off, the last syllables echoing in the cavernous auditorium as Scott put the flute up to his lips and began. Ryan slowly
leaned back now. Those first couple of lines of lyrics grabbed his attention right away. Scott seemed to be trying to sound mysterious and was
doing a good job at it.

Scott joined in with his flute now. Louder than the volume of the
tape player, it filled the auditorium with rich tones that echoed back
and forth with the recorded tracks. Ryan immediately felt a chill as Scott
continued for a few more bars, then slowly let down the flute. He spoke
out again, sounding deliberate and quite bold.

"Don't be frightened
hear the desert
as she brings to you this song.
Can you feel it
as it courses through your heart—
it's been so long."

Ryan sat transfixed; the lyrics were haunting. Scott raised the flute to
play again, and Ryan leaned back to rub his triceps, trying to rid himself
of the goose bumps. Scott and the tape continued. The melody was
haunting and soothing at the same time. Ryan had never felt this way
before about a tune. Granted, he had never been privately serenaded
before either. There had been other times where this kind of feeling had
swept him. They were rare, and being so overwhelming, he had pushed
it aside when it had happened. Somehow, though, being near Scott, he
felt safe about it. In fact, it was surprising that he was the one who was
making him feel this way. That reminded him of how cute he thought
Scott was, which flooded his mind with images of Crawford again. It
only made him melancholy.

Scott didn't care if Ryan liked the tune or not. It was something he'd
created and he liked it just fine. Oddly enough, he had never insisted on

playing it for anyone else like this. Granted, an audience for his unique style of music was limited—but he felt an almost annoying attraction to Ryan, despite his initial impression. He played for a moment more and let the tape continue as he finished reciting stanzas.

> *"Don't cry into the night*
> *'bout how you feel, so true.*
> *For your waiting now is over—*
> *I am here.*
> *Take my hand,*
> *hear my laughter,*
> *share your secrets now with me.*
> *Coming home, coming home,*
> *you are home."*

No way, Ryan thought. *Share my secrets? Is he kidding?* Scott played for a few more minutes while Ryan tried to quell the feeling the tune was still bringing up in him. He was sure the smarting he felt in his eyes was making them red and he hoped it wouldn't be obvious.

When the tape ended, Scott pressed the off button and the auditorium was quiet. Ryan sniffled, and took a moment before he got up.

He approached the stage, placed his hands on it, then hoisting himself up. He walked up to the still-seated Scott. "That was amazing. Who wrote those words?"

"Lyrics. The *Mother of the Desert* wrote them for me one night. She sends me some from time to time."

"Right."

Scott could see that his Muse wasn't something Ryan could relate to. He stood and put the case on the chair. "Seriously, I wrote it about seven or eight months ago."

Ryan placed a hand on the back of the chair and watched as Scott pulled apart the flute and placed the pieces into the case. "You ever thought about being a professional musician? Or maybe work in a recording studio, or something?"

The conversation Scott had with his parents last winter came to mind. He told them he wanted to get more serious about music and maybe even major in it in college. That was just after he got serious about being with Centauri.

They had carefully explained that a business major would ensure his future financial security if their restaurant business ever fell through. Though he had gone along with them at the time, the feeling of being stifled hadn't left yet. More and more, he was discovering music to be a growing passion. Yet, he kept the real fire of his passion hidden from both of them because he didn't want to disappoint them. Realizing that they had agreed to pay his way completely through college, he dropped the subject. Anxiety sped through his body for a second as he considered the idea again. He answered with a lie. "No. It would never happen."

"You should think about it."

Scott wanted to change the subject. "Let's get outta here." He dug for his keys and they jingled as they came out of his pocket. "Get the boombox." Ryan picked it up as Scott deposited the chair offstage, and hit the lights.

They were on the highway five minutes later. Scott talked randomly about the gigs at Twentynine Palms. "We've got some real gigs coming up. If you wanna watch us I'll have to figure out a way. They don't let non-band members on base. We've got a lotta practice ahead of us beforehand though…And we need some flyers, or posters or something. Hopefully we can find some place to do 'em cheap."

Ryan was thinking about the incredible feeling Scott dragged out of him back in the auditorium. More stirring than the movie, it was a powerful emotion. Now he felt glad it was Scott who prompted it, too. "I could do a poster for you guys."

"Huh?"

"Yeah. I draw all kinds of stuff. I could even do something to hand out."

"You're an artist?"

"I dabble. You should see my bedroom door at home. I mean, in Crescent City. Serious. I could make the bitchin'est promo poster you've ever seen. I can see it now: a series of Centaurs, each with a bow firing an arrow at a big star above their heads. I could make something to hand out. You'd just need a copier. Whadda ya think?"

Scott visualized the graphic for a moment. "Hey, that's not bad." He had no idea Ryan could draw, much less want to do something for the band. "I'll talk to the guys about it."

Scott dropped off Ryan at Howard's house. As he backed down the driveway, then looked ahead again, he saw that Ryan must have stopped because he hadn't reached the house yet. Just at that minute Ryan turned and rounded the corner to the back entrance.

It was as if Ryan was watching, staring at him.

Ryan watched Scott pull away. He thought about the rag that lay under the bed in his bedroom, just like the one Scott had. He'd have to use it tonight. Because of Scott. *I can't seem to keep him out of my head,* he thought. *At least when I think of him I smile, unlike when I think about Crawford.*

Hmm, Scott thought as he pulled away and down the road. *Wonder what was on his mind?*

CHAPTER 6

Scott seated himself in the small cubicle his dad used as an office, and was successfully disguising his voice as he spoke on the telephone. "Ryan?"

"Yeah?"

"How would you like to go with Scott Faraday to the Joshua Tree Monument next weekend?" His accent was a success.

"Who is this?"

Scott made up something fast. "Ranger Rick."

Ryan responded almost immediately. Anger resonated in his voice. "What the fuck!?"

Beth leaned against the doorframe listening to him. This wasn't the first time she had heard Scott try to fake someone out. "Who are you messing with this time?"

Scott quickly held his hand over the mouthpiece. "Shhh!"

"Is this Scott?"

Scott tried to sound gruff. "I said it's Ranger Rick...."

There was a click and the line went dead. Scott had a surprised look on his face as he looked at the handset then to Beth. "He hung up."

"Who was that?"

"That new kid, Ryan. I was trying to invite him to go rappelling."

"I guess he told *you*," she answered as she left. As Scott tried to figure out Ryan's unexpected response, his father passed by and asked him what he was doing just sitting at the desk. He didn't know what to say exactly so he got back up and went to the host station. People were starting to come in at a steady pace now and he focused his attention on them. A few minutes later, the phone at the front counter rang. Elaine answered it, chatting for a minute before she handed the phone to her son.

"It's Ryan."

"Ryan?"

"Howard's nephew?"

"Yeah, I know. Why would he call the front desk?"

Elaine handed him the phone, then surveyed the reservation book and the awaiting guests. "Be brief."

He took the phone and turned around so as not to be heard by the people standing at the station. Elaine seated the next group of people.

"Ryan?"

Ryan launched in immediately. "What's this Ranger Rick shit?"

"Just a joke, dude. Why'd ya freak?"

Ryan's tone changed to a friendlier one. "It was too weird."

"Whadda ya mean?"

"There's this ranger who works at a station just off our property up in Crescent City. His name's Rick Simmons. My brother and I call him Ranger Rick. He's a real asshole. I thought he called me or something."

"That *is* weird."

"So what's this about the Monument?"

"Just wanted to see if you wanted to take a trip with me to go rappelling. And get ready for an intense day. We can even camp overnight. If you want."

"Bitchin'. Wait. I don't know how to rappel. And I don't have any camping equipment."

"Not to worry. I'll show you everything you need to know. I got a tent and all the gear, you just need a sheet, blanket and a pillow—and whatever else you want to bring. You know, food and stuff."

"Well…I guess."

"So, Saturday. Say eight o'clock?"

"In the morning?"

"Of course."

"That early? How are you gonna get out of band practice?"

"Believe me, you have to get there early to beat the rest of the climbers. And the band doesn't practice every weekend."

"Oh."

"See ya on Saturday?"

Ryan was astonished at how fast his weekend was shaping up. "Yeah. Bitchin'."

Scott didn't see or hear from Ryan until Thursday when he and Howard stopped by the restaurant for take-out. Ryan, at first, looked depressed but his demeanor changed when he got a chance to talk to him. It was brief, but the short time together made him feel refreshingly good the entire next day. He was happy that simply being around Scott put him in a good mood and wondered if he would be able see him more often after the weekend was over.

✷   ✷   ✷

Shakaiyo's tongue hung out to one side. The brightly colored, Aztec-pattern bandanna tied around her neck flapped furiously as she leaned into the wind from the back seat. The three of them rode at the speed limit toward the west entrance of the Monument. The sun had been up for hours and the evening's relative coolness was well behind them now.

Scott told the ranger that they would be camping, and after asking for a yearly sticker, paid at the entrance. He stopped briefly in the parking lot to affix the sticker to his windshield. He came here often and would so even more now that he had his new vehicle. The yearly fee was worth it.

It was steady driving for almost a dozen more miles before they reached the main rock climbing area.

"What?" Ryan yelled over the wind in his ears.

Scott yelled back. "I said, we're heading for Hidden Rocks," he pointed to the sign.

"What's Hidden Rocks?"

Scott knitted his brow. "It's the best rappelling and climbing area."

Scott checked out Ryan's legs again. Despite the sunscreen, his legs were darkening already. Soon enough he'd be darker than Scott. "You must be laying out."

Ryan lifted the hem of his tank top to reveal his tight abdominal muscles, and patted his stomach. "Yeah, most days now. I never knew I'd get a tan."

"I figured you'd get one right away."

"Why?"

Scott held his arm out next to Ryan's. "Your skin's way darker than mine."

From just that simple action, Scott felt the blood rush in his temples. He wanted to caress Ryan's arm, run his fingers down its short hairs, and clasp Ryan's fingers in his. Of course, kissing him would also be on the agenda. Funny how that incident back at the drive-in had quickly become past history. He had Ryan figured out all wrong. He seemed all right after all. And, despite being a year older, at times Ryan seemed younger than him.

Ryan looked back to inspect the gear stowed away in back. Shakaiyo was on top of his blanket and sprawled across the rest of Scott's gear. Next to her, the bag of ice shifted back and forth in the maroon and white cooler. A bag of dried dog food, its top rolled down, was stuffed just below it next to the wheel well. He lifted the cooler top and grabbed a piece of ice from the open bag. Biting it in half, in a second the other half was down the front of Scott's tank top.

"What the fuck!"

Ryan slurped on the ice. "You looked like you needed to get a little cooler."

Scott pointed a thumb to himself. "Like I'm not already?"

"Humph," Ryan responded, but had no snappy retort to offer.

As the cube melted, a wet trail ran down the middle of his chest. The melting chunk rested just below his navel spreading a wet spot along the top of his shorts. The thought of the ice making the nylon of his running shorts become translucent was something of a turn on. Ryan noticed he wasn't bothering to get rid of it.

"Aren't you getting a little…cold down there?"

"I was just going to ask you to get it out for me, I'm driving, you know." Scott couldn't believe he said that, but couldn't resist.

The weight of Ryan's imagination made itself present. He sucked in a long breath. How it ached to feel this way, he thought. To want to do exactly what he couldn't bring himself to do. He wanted Scott to keep taunting him, to egg him on, to force him to try to get the piece of ice. It would be an innocent reach, completely innocent. But he knew he was nothing of the sort. Innocence was in his past—taken long ago by Crawford.

Now the road gently sloped upward and soon they reached its zenith. The valley that spread out below was huge. Joshua Trees in all shapes and sizes grew everywhere. Huge outcroppings of weatherworn rock rose from the gravelly feldspar and reached into the shimmering desert air.

Scott turned off the main road and went down a trail marked by a large sign that said *Hidden Rocks*. The conspicuous sign mentioned something about the area being reserved for rock climbers and rappellers. What at first looked small soon loomed large as they got closer. Ryan eyed the huge wall of rocks suspiciously.

He jumped out after the Jeep came to a halt. Intense silence surrounded them and he strained to hear something. Shakaiyo was out a moment later, looking for something to track.

Scott watched his reaction. "Neat, huh?" He noticed that he saw only a couple of the normally ubiquitous climbers.

"I've never seen anything like this before."

Scott was already psyching himself up for the descent. "That rock face there," he pointed, "knows me very well."

Ryan still stood perfectly still. "It's really quiet out here."

"If you listen hard enough, the desert will talk to you." He didn't mean to sound cryptic, but to him the desert had a language all its own.

Ryan grunted at him. "Right."

Scott looked at him, wondering if anyone other than him ever did hear the desert, or rather what his insides told him when he was in its silence. He went around to the back of the vehicle and pulled up his pack from the pile. From it he retrieved his leather gloves, then moved it aside to haul out the ropes. He put one of the coils over his shoulder and gave the other to Ryan.

Ryan shaded his eyes, surveying the summit. Scott stood still then whispered loudly. "Shhh! Don't move."

He cocked his head, trying to hear what Scott appeared to be listening to. "What is it?" he whispered back. Scott didn't respond.

Looking puzzled, he checked out the situation. Shakaiyo didn't appear to have heard anything, and she wasn't what Scott's attention seemed focused on. He ventured a question, again in a loud whisper. "What did you hear?" The wind was in his ears now and he suspected Scott heard something he hadn't.

"A worm."

Ryan surveyed the ground ahead of him looking for earthworms, furrowing his brow. "A worm?"

Scott looked quite serious. "A worm. Big ones have been sighted in this area before. The natives of this planet warned me about them."

At first he thought Scott was using some sort of sexual innuendo. Then he figured he was in some sort of character again and decided to play along. There was that book, he remembered, in Scott's bedroom that had a gigantic snakelike creature on the cover. It had a one-word title, *Dune*. That was it. He remembered the lone figure of a person on the cover with the gigantic openmouthed creature in the background. Scott crouched low and rested his hand on the gravely surface of the desert floor. Some of the carabiners rattled as he crouched. Ryan raised an eyebrow, not exactly sure of the scenario he was playing out. "Do they eat people?"

"Do they! They've been known to eat entire parties of rock climbers. Luckily, I have my magic carabiner." Scott unsnapped one from the bandoleer. Ryan moved a little closer, so close his leg hairs brushed against Scott's leg. He looked at Ryan's firm leg, then to his face. Another surge of adrenaline passed through his body at the simple touch. Ryan still looked puzzled. *Good*, Scott thought, *he has no idea what I'm doing.*

He offered the carabiner to Ryan, then whispered to him. "Here, toss it."

Scott actually had him going at first but now he decided to play along. He couldn't believe he was really playing this silly game. If it had been anyone else, he would have instantly started making fun of him. Somehow, it was amusing enough for him to hold back from doing so. Scott seemed a master at his funny character game and he even found it endearing. Ryan tossed the carabiner ahead of him. Scott nodded his head and quickly rose. Immediately he was back in his own personality. "Should be safe now."

A broad grin now stretched across Ryan's face at the odd antic. Scott took the rest of the gear needed for the descent and handed him a two-liter bottle of water before claiming his. Shakaiyo was ready for them. Already anticipating their trek to the top she took off ahead of them to find her own way up.

Twenty minutes later they reached the summit. From their new height, the wind was constant, but gentle. High cirrus clouds had started to form; yet, the sun was already particularly hot. Ryan was glad he had a hat on and plenty of sunscreen. When they got to the top they dropped the gear and Scott showed him how to don his harness again. It was all he could do to avoid staring at Ryan's perfectly framed butt in it. He secured a rope to an old gnarled tree twisting its way through a crack.

"Hey you. Get hold of this," he directed.

Ryan turned around and took the proffered rope. "Now the idea is this…" he began. The next few moments Ryan found out how to hold the rope properly, how to let go of it only a foot at a time, how to bend at the waist just right, and how to push away so his descent would be smooth and easy. Ryan was both fascinated and decidedly anxious. Finally, Scott hooked the ropes around his harness for him.

Once over the edge he was "standing" horizontally with his back to the ground. He looked first up at Scott, then behind him to the ground some ninety feet below. Scott noticed an almost invisible trace of fear cross his face.

"It's easy. Just go for it like I showed you."

Ryan's words gave away his nervousness. "You've done it before."

He wanted to say, 'Done what before?' and lead Ryan on. Instead, he shifted character again and pointed down below.

"He's down at the bottom, Roy. I hear 'im yellin'. Sounds like he's in mighty bad pain."

"What?"

"Quit yer yappin', Roy. Just grab 'im and bring 'im back up. I'll hold off the Injuns best as I can from here."

Ryan hesitated, wondering why he was sounding so stupid.

"Now git."

Ryan attempted an accent, which turned out to be a bad Texas drawl. "Sure, Slim." It seemed ridiculous to play Scott's character game under this kind of pressure, but he mustered up the resolve despite his anxiety. His biceps tightened at the weight of his body leaning back. Slowly he let the rope out. Two feet. Three feet. He stopped.

Scott was laying prone. Only his head was visible over the edge of the precipice. Ryan looked down at the fifty feet of space below him. His face was filled with anguish as he looked back up.

"Are you waiting for a good luck kiss, or what?" Scott asked him.

He narrowed his eyes at Scott then descended, jumping back periodically as he let out the rope.

Scott was surprised that none of the remarks he'd shot at Ryan had had any comebacks. Not a single one. That was making him mildly suspicious.

Cute Ryan. Will I ever get to actually kiss him, he wondered.

CHAPTER 7

Ryan touched the ground only moments later, hollering to Scott as he disconnected himself from the rope. Scott unhitched his harness, put it on backward, and reconnected the rope. He hoisted it over his shoulder and proceeded to go down the side of the escarpment face down. In just a few seconds, he had run literally down the side and was at the bottom.

"Holy fuck! Face down?"

"Aussie style. I won't show you how to do that today though. Takes nerves of steel."

Ryan rolled his eyes briefly. "Like I don't have any, huh?"

Uh oh, thought Scott. Don't start on him. He might revert to that fucked up attitude of his.

Ryan wondered if Scott was going to show him up on everything.

"How long did you say you've done this?"

"Since I was thirteen. The trick is to find the highest face you can find and still be able to bring enough rope. I end up having to stick to relatively safe heights since these aren't all that long." He disconnected it from his carabiner. "They're expensive as hell, too."

Ryan looked up where they'd been moments before. "That's high enough for me."

They descended several more times, progressing more slowly as the day got hotter. Luckily, the cirrus clouds that had formed earlier were becoming unusually dense, and were covering a good portion of the sky, reducing the temperature to a much lower level than normal. Nonetheless, they still went through quite a bit of water Scott had brought.

Ryan gained noticeable confidence at the new endeavor but expressed his disinterest in making it a full-time hobby. Scott was a little disappointed, but felt it was to be expected. Still, he was amazed at how Ryan's spirits lifted considerably as the day progressed. They stopped at the bottom several hours later and finished off the rest of the water bottle.

Far overhead a jet broke the sound barrier. Its sonic boom resounded through the quiet desert. They heard two echoes, so maybe it was another jet, Ryan didn't know. How different the desert was from his familiar home in the north woods, he thought.

Finally, they untied the ropes from the top of the cliff and stowed all the gear back in the Jeep. Scott drove them to another rock escarpment about two miles away. Several climbers were there so they chose a spot well away from them. They gnawed on some beef jerky before starting up again. They only descended twice before Ryan had had enough.

"Hey, ready to do it?"

Ryan took his eyes from the horizon and the heat waves that seemed all around them. "Do it?"

"Eat. And we need to make camp."

Ryan took one of the ropes and started to coil it up. "Sure."

Now shirtless, they found an easy route down to the Jeep. Scott tossed the ropes and other gear in the back and took the Frisbee out.

"Here, catch," he said to Ryan without warning. Ryan's eyes grew wide as he caught it.

"I'm pretty good," Ryan warned.

Scott figured it was another empty boast, but despite his better judgment, decided to test him. "Try me," Scott said as walked backward a ways.

They tossed it back and forth, moving further and further apart with each toss. Scott was the one surprised this time. Ryan was bopping the Frisbee with two or three fingers, and was able to snatch it from the air with a quick motion. He even let it roll up one arm, across his chest, and down the other arm before catching it one occasion. Scott couldn't believe he had found another worthy Frisbee partner.

Scott caught it a final time. "Wow. You *are* pretty good."

"We used to throw one around in the school parking lot. It was the thing to do between classes." Ryan didn't mention how many he just skipped altogether. Nor did he mention that he barely graduated at all.

The short dark hairs that spread across the middle of Ryan's pecs were matted down from salt. Dried perspiration also stained his sides around his armpits. Scott tried to keep his eyes off Ryan's bare chest as it rose and fell in a rhythmic pattern as they both caught their breath.

"We'll have to do this more often. There's hardly anyone I know that's as good as you. The guys in the band just mess around with it."

Ryan had a grin on his face. "Good. It makes up for the thrashing you gave me on all those video games. So, where to now?"

"Back to the main road, then to those two big piles of rocks we saw back a ways. There's a pond nearby. We can pitch a tent there. It's not a designated campground, but no one'll catch us. There are hardly any rangers around here." He had long ago figured out how get around the requirement to indicate the exact campground he would be staying at.

Ryan recalled the two piles of huge boulders. Some of the oldest structures in the Monument, they used to be hills. Thousands of years of being blasted with sand from the high winds had scoured them of softer material. Scott elaborated as he drove. "All that's left are, like, these mazes inside the boulders. They're like tunnels, only better, since they're not manmade."

As they drove around a curve they saw the two, almost twin mounds, off in the distance. The trail was barely visible as they went and there were wicked ruts, with steep inclines and declines to navigate. The going was slow most of the way. The huge mounds loomed larger and larger until they nearly filled the sky ahead of them.

"They're huge!" exclaimed Ryan.

"The Devil's Rockpiles," Scott announced.

One of the mounds was slightly taller than the other and separated by a stretch of flat ground. Scott took the Jeep through the passage into the shadow of the larger mound. Behind it was a small pond. He stopped the Jeep short of a tall sprawling Joshua Tree and parked in the shade of the tall rocks.

After they came to a stop Ryan hopped out to survey the pond. It was a narrow, shallow, clear watering hole. Water bugs scurried around the surface. Around most of its perimeter were short bushes and reeds. He didn't see so much as a minnow anywhere below the surface. He swirled his hand in it. It felt like it was at body temperature.

"I think it's fed by an underground spring. But it's not drinkable," Scott warned.

They unloaded the Jeep and leaned everything next to it. Shakaiyo bounded around for a while, found a trail to sniff, and was off. Scott opened up his two-burner stove and poured some water into a pot to boil. The frozen chicken breasts in the cooler had completely defrosted, he observed, as he sniffed the package, then put it on the closed lid.

Scott handed him a half stick of butter. "Here, smear this around in the skillet, but don't let it burn."

It was an innocuous comment, but Ryan took it as an insult. "When was the last time you saw me burn butter?"

"Last night, *dear.*"

"Hey, I'm the guy on this campout."

"You may have to prove it." No rebuttal again, he noticed. It was becoming fun to talk to him like that and not get the slightest rebuttal.

Once the skillet was hot, Scott started cooking the chicken. Ryan added a box of macaroni to the water in the pot and, once it started boiling, watched the little elbows tumble around for a moment. A little while later Scott announced all was ready. He dished out the macaroni and cheese, and the chicken, then poured Shakaiyo some food into a bowl. She ate hungrily and when she was done she watched them eat, but didn't once beg for food.

Ryan looked at Shakaiyo as she eyed his plate. "She knows better," Scott said. She wagged her tail as she stared at Scott.

As the sun started getting a little lower, shadows formed from the twin mounds covering their camp spot. There had been no one in sight even after they put all the refuse in a trash bag and put everything away. Ryan stood at the bottom of the larger mound, looking up into the boulders. Sand surrounded three sides of both rock piles and his tracks broke up the undulating ripples.

Scott started toward him. "I love this place. You can go in down here and take twists and turns all through these passages. You eventually end up on the outside again no matter where you go."

Ryan looked in a dark passage and put a hand on the little Mag light that was clipped to his belt loop. "Race ya to the top!" In a moment, he was swallowed by the dark.

"You're on." Shakaiyo followed him as he turned. Instead of following Ryan he ran to the other side of the hill.

Ryan was sure scorpions and snakes could be anywhere, but figured they most likely would be at the lowest level. With his flashlight, he carefully surveyed the dark corridors for them as he tried to find a quick route to the top. Each passage through the boulders was unique. He could take a left or a right in some places. In others, after he had climbed upward a way, he had to go back downward to be able to go up another story or so. In other places, he had to walk along the outside of the pile to progress any higher up. He assumed that the honeycombing was consistent throughout the entire structure. A few minutes later, his assumption was wrong as he found himself in a tall narrow chamber with a wide hole opening directly up to the sky. The only way out was the way he came.

Scott happened to be right above him when he arrived. He squatted, looking down at him. "What are you doing down there?"

"How'd you get up so fast?" Shakaiyo's head appeared above Scott now. She was panting heavily.

Scott sat down and dangled his legs into the hole as he looked down at him. He looked back over his shoulder, "Should I tell him?" He waited a second. "Okay, but he won't like the answer." He sounded convincing.

"Who the hell are you talking to?" Ryan asked as he played his flashlight all around him looking for a quick way out.

"I can't tell *you*. You're being executed in the morning."

"Like fuck I am."

The exhilaration of the game was with Scott as he thought about the statement. *Like fuck. I'd like you to fuck me, Ryan. Ryan, let's fuck. Have a fuck, Ryan? Maybe two? I'm good for it. I can do it three times in a row. Well, okay, that's by myself.* He wanted to drop down into the narrow chamber on him so badly. As he sat there he felt himself get hard just thinking about it.

Ryan decided to get out of his confined space. "I'm outta here."

Scott stood up; dug into his pocket to adjust himself, then lay on his back catching the last rays of the late afternoon sun. Moments later, and now out of breath, Ryan finally appeared at the top. Scott peered at him out of one eye.

Scott stood and pointed. "What's that?"

Ryan turned around to look.

"Gotcha!" he yelled as he lunged and grabbed both of Ryan's legs. He gasped, then realized he was being securely held. But, caught off guard, he teetered momentarily. Scott's cheek was nuzzled against his buttocks.

What I would do to just lick his leg right now, Scott thought. So he did. He licked ever so briefly.

"Did you just lick my leg?"

Scott spat. "Sorry, I couldn't help it." He ended up with more dust than salt on his tongue. It wasn't at all as pleasant as he thought it would be.

Ryan wiped the spot with his thumb. He should have hauled off and punched him, but he held back. No one else saw him do it so he was safe. He wasn't sure if Scott had assumed another personality again. "I'm going back down if you're gonna be the mercenary."

"Aw, shut up, wimp."

Immediately, Ryan clammed up.

Scott noticed his reaction as he shaded his eyes. "We should be gettin' off this heap, Slim. It'll be gettin' dark soon and the rattlers might be stirring in their nests down below." He led the way down and they were back on the sand at the bottom again a moment later.

Shakaiyo, her tongue still hanging out, ran up to them and followed close behind as they returned to the camp.

Scott walked the area, surveying the ground for a level spot for the tent. Ryan inspected a rock overhang near the pond. "How about right there? We'd have the pond to our right. We could even stash the gear under this ledge and not have to keep it in the tent.

Scott looked out to the water. "Animals."

"Animals?"

"Yeah, we shouldn't put the tent right next to the water. I don't want any animals getting near it. They'll be using the pond at night."

"Fuck. What kind of animals?"

"Skunks, coyotes, mice, you know, the usual kind."

Ryan let Scott choose a spot a little further away from the water.

The quiet desert evening was broken only by their rustling about, unfurling the tent and the occasional wind that whistled through the branches of the nearby Joshua Tree.

"What's that?" Ryan asked as Scott pulled out a bag from his pack.

Scott held up the bag. "Trail mix. Tons of it."

"Who eats trail mix?" Ryan had used a tone he instantly regretted.

"Well, I like it. If you don't, that's too fucking bad."

Ryan thought for a moment. It was as if he was programmed to say just the wrong thing. Usually, he didn't care how he came across but with Scott, it was different. Somehow, just being around him made him notice what he was doing and how he said things. He sat down on the thin, shiny surface of the fire blanket Scott had put in front of the tent door. Maybe Scott would forget his outburst.

He was right. Scott wasn't really going to hold out on the trail mix, and soon they were both downing handfuls until the bag was almost empty. He patted his bare stomach as Ryan watched. Part of Scott wanted to say it right now, that he was gay, and just get over it. If he did, he would be the first guy he'd ever told. Well, the second actually, but his Uncle Greg didn't count. He wasn't his age. Another part of him said no though. Why start now? Yet, once school started he would most likely never see Ryan again. So what harm could it do? He debated the question with himself for only a few minutes more before he let it go.

Ryan looked away, appearing distracted. It was difficult to wrest his gaze from Scott's body. After all, he was wearing next to nothing. "How about a real dessert?" He started to rummage through his pack.

"Whadda ya got?"

Ryan pulled a canteen from it and poured some of the contents into his soda can, and then Scott's.

He sniffed it, "Bourbon?"

"Jim Beam, to be exact."

Scott's eyes lit up. "Bitchin'."

Ryan held up his can. "A toast to Howie's well-stocked liquor cabinet. He has quite the stash."

They touched cans and sipped the mixture. "Ahh, now *that's* a soda," Scott said.

Twilight started to turn the sky darker and the breeze picked up a lot more than before. Scott pulled two containers of cut strawberries from the cooler and they ate every one of them with great ceremony. As night descended, the clouds never strayed from the horizon. The sky was perfectly clear overhead as it changed from a magnificent indigo to a majestic black, broken only by a myriad of brilliant stars.

The bourbon was hitting the spot now as Scott looked out into the dark desert. He watched as Ryan poured the contents of a full cola can into the canteen of bourbon. "Let's go for a walk," Scott said.

Ryan swirled the mixture around, then briefly sipped the contents of the canteen. "A walk? We're partyin'."

"No. I mean a *walk*. It's a different place here at night. It completely changes."

Ryan looked around, then straight up at the stars. Heat waves made them shimmer like mad. Scott was unlike anyone he knew back home, and he found himself quite attracted to his unusual sense of adventure. The more buzzed he felt, the more another thing was becoming more evident. He finally admitted to himself that Scott was the cutest guy he had ever known.

"Well, all right."

Scott was surprised at the abrupt shift, but was glad Ryan gave in. He retrieved his flashlight from the tent and tested the beam by aiming it upwards from under his chin. He grimaced and referred to the movie they saw last week. "Ready to go, Brad?"

"Yes, Janet." With that, he threw Scott's windbreaker at him. It landed on his head, covering up the beam. By the time Scott had the jacket off he was confronted by Ryan's flashlight directly in his eyes.

He feigned an authoritative voice. "Hold it! You're under arrest!"

"Like hell!" Scott tossed the windbreaker away and took off into the dark as fast as he could. Ryan's stunt with the flashlight had blinded him briefly, but he knew where he was headed. Shakaiyo bounded right behind at first, but slowed down as something caught her nose. The moment it took Ryan to adjust the canteen over his shoulder was Scott's advantage. He aimed his flashlight ahead to get a general lay of the area as his eyes adjusted once again to the dark. He felt buzzed now from the drink, but still had his wits.

Once he was at the nearby dry wash, he snapped the light off. He slowed when he reached the bottom of the sandy gully and walked backwards in an attempt to see Ryan's light. The open desert night sky just barely concealed his shape. Still, Ryan wouldn't find him now unless he yelled out or panned the area with his flashlight.

A tall, outstretched Joshua Tree lay just ahead. Several branches of the spiny cactus were twisted into grotesque shapes and hung quite low, some at ground level. Its shadow loomed in front of him from the sky glow. Underneath and slightly in front of the tree trunk was a cluster of short creosote bushes. He went behind the cluster and crouched down, waiting for Ryan to walk down the wash. With the low Joshua Tree branches behind him and the bushes in front of him, he was perfectly concealed.

Ryan was coming his way, but not as fast as he expected. He turned off his flashlight and walked down the wash in Scott's general direction. He stopped to listen but the breeze was steady, making it hard to hear anything else.

Holding his breath, Scott waited just until he passed. He leaned to his left as he extracted himself from behind the bushes. As he moved, then attempted to raise up to a standing position, his foot caught on a rock. With nothing to hold on to, he fell slightly backward before he caught himself. His abrupt movement caused him to be jabbed by one of the close Joshua Tree spines.

"Owww!" Scott yelped as he jumped forward. He held his side at his waist and moved out into the open. By this time Ryan was aiming his flashlight around the bushes. Since the branches were thick, Scott was a completely out of view. Scott waited a moment more, watching Ryan's flashlight playing through the branches, then took a mad dash around the tree toward him. With tremolo in his voice, he yelled a loud "Ooooaaaah."

Ryan whirled and aimed his light. "Shit!"

Scott clicked his light on to look at the red pinhole in his side. "That's what I said."

"What happened?"

Scott aimed his flashlight. "That Joshua Tree attacked me." Although his attention was focused on his side again, he could tell that Ryan was eyeing him with great attention. Just like back at camp earlier. What is going on here, he asked himself? Damn, I wish I could tell what he's thinking! Subconsciously, his radar was beginning to explain to him everything he needed to know. Consciously, he had little idea what information he was receiving.

The shallow puncture hadn't drawn any blood but it hurt like hell. Ryan inspected his side, running his finger over it. It made goose bumps rise on Scott's skin.

"Well, Lieutenant, it's only a flesh wound." He burped loudly. "The enemy can't hit the broad side of a barn."

Scott aimed his flashlight at him, surprised that he initiated the shift of character this time. Ryan had a grin on his face. He drew out the game. "Hey, douse the light. Article Six: no lights while in the war zone…dude."

Scott caught on and added, "I'm delirious, Captain." *Burp*! "I think I have Joshua Tree fever."

"You need a swig of my battlefield medicine." Ryan offered his canteen as they continued to walk down the wash in the dark. Scott took a swig of the still chilled mixture.

Behind the facade of the character he was playing, Ryan still had his attention on Scott's half-naked body. It was different now. Back when it was daylight, he eyed him every once in a while, drinking in Scott's body with his eyes. Now though, with the dark and them being alone he wanted to touch him, to caress him, to…. He looked away, trying to shake his desire. Scott was different from anyone he'd ever known. If he took a chance with him, it probably wouldn't faze him. Or would it?

Still it was better to be safe. He rubbed his wrists; remembering the distress Crawford had created for him, now well over a month ago. He took the canteen from him and took a swig. Another couple of swallows and the sting of the memory would be well numbed.

Soon they came to a string of tall granite boulders lying in their path. It appeared that they diverted water at one time since the wash branched off from them in a distinct Y shape. Scott could feel more of his inhibitions leaving him.

They climbed one of the boulders and sat quietly, side-by-side, just listening to the night. From their vantage point, only one lone spot of light, probably from a motor home off in the far distance, was visible at the horizon. A branch of a short Joshua Tree overhung one edge of the boulder, playing a dark shadow across part of it. Scott edged a little further away from it.

The night air was just starting to become a bit cooler and he could feel the heat from Ryan's body as he sat so close. He closed his eyes and felt a light breeze caress his face as he felt his nose becoming numb from the alcohol. "Isn't it just awesome out here?"

Ryan didn't know how to answer. The stark wilderness was so open it was almost scary. It wasn't at all like the protective, enclosed surroundings of the forest back home. He took another swallow from the canteen, hoping his buzz would let him speak more freely.

"They say the Joshuas are praying," Scott stated as he looked to his side. "They have emotions, too, so they can feel the beauty of the desert." He looked over to Ryan, leaned back, and laid supine on the boulder with his knees drawn up.

Ryan turned his head and studied Scott's dark profile, but still said nothing. The slow, steady breeze blew his hair all around. Scott's words sounded eerie, just like back at the VFW, and it was giving him goose bumps again. Scott didn't have to look to know that Ryan was trying to figure it out.

"Whatcha thinkin'?" Scott asked.

Ryan looked down as Scott turned his head. He couldn't just tell
Scott that he was intensely attracted to him. Despite that secret, which
he felt he must keep at all costs, he still felt a sense of trust developing. It
must have been the alcohol, he thought; as he decided to truthfully tell
him what else was on his mind. "A-about my parents."

Scott raised an eyebrow. Ryan had only mentioned his parents once.
"Yeah…?"

"They're dead."

That much he knew. "Yeah?"

Ryan broke the quiet and yelled, half to himself, half to Scott. "Well,
damn it. They're fucking gone!"

It was just a rhetorical question, but Scott had been answered with an
unexpected outburst. Now he wondered if he should take Ryan in his
arms, which his body said to do, or should he hold back? He compro-
mised. He put his hand across the back of Ryan's neck and rubbed.
There was salt all over it. Ryan felt as if an electric charge shot through
his body from his touch. He didn't want Scott to let go, and luckily, he
held on for a few moments. He was amazed he even brought the subject
up. He'd been drinking with his friends plenty of times before and not
once did he ever feel the need to say anything about them. The feeling of
trust that Scott elicited from him was alarming. If he didn't watch out,
he might even tell him about Crawford. Then his past would be common knowledge and his tenuous friendship with him would be all over.
He was sure of it.

Scott rose up and slipped down to the ground. The drop was only
four feet but he nearly lost his balance. The alcohol was really working
on him now. He looked around and found a sharp-edged rock, which
he used to draw a circle in the sand of the dry wash.

Ryan looked on as he drew. "What the fuck are you doing?"

"Shhh," Scott said as he completed his six-foot diameter circle. He
then placed the rock at a point between them inside the circle. He found
a long hollow limb of a dead Cholla cactus and stepped back into the

circle. With his eyes closed, and a hand on each end of it, he raised it above his head.

A sliver of moon was just starting to rise above the clouds along the horizon, casting a new and eerie glow all around them. In a monotone, he ad-libbed. "Oh, Gods of the Desert. Gods of Wind, and Sun, and Eons of Time. I ask that you take this human, Ryan St. Charles, and make him one of Us!" With that, he opened his eyes and looked up into the starry sky. He searched the blackness for shooting stars, hoping to see at least one, then looked up at Ryan still sitting on the boulder. Ryan's attention was riveted to the impromptu performance.

"Now, you stand up, too," Scott whispered.

Ryan slid the canteen off his lap and placed it to his side. He stood up, trying to keep his balance in the dark. He had to steady himself while looking up in the sky, too. It was weird—the not-quite-straight branch silhouetted Scott's arms and his body against the glow of the sky.

He ventured to know what was going on. "Who are you supposed to be?" He was afraid to say it too loudly, so had whispered, afraid he might spoil the mood.

Scott's voice was still monotone. "I'm the One you've been looking for…"

Ryan tottered back and forth a bit. The One I've been looking for? He crouched down, trying to steady his balance, then stood up again.

"Stand still…" Scott whispered. Then aloud, "I proclaim you cousin to the Night Sky, kin to the Desert Owl, and a brother to the Centauri star riders."

The most remarkable feeling swept over Ryan. A shiver crawled up his spine and shook him, almost with violence. Scott's eloquence had left him breathless.

As suddenly as the feeling rushed his head, he heard a whooshing directly in front of him up in the sky. Scott lowered the branch and whirled around. Something was coming directly at them and it was growing closer, its rhythmic whooshing sound growing louder. Scott quickly knelt to the ground, not knowing what was happening.

Ryan jumped to the ground. He knelt while pressing his back against the boulder as the sound passed directly overhead. Both of them were almost paralyzed with fear. Then, they heard a familiar call and the flap of wings above them. It was a flock of crows! The flock of perhaps half a dozen birds quickly flew beyond the boulder and the desert was quiet again. The crickets hadn't missed a chirrup.

Ryan lightly slapped his cheek. "Holy fuck!"

"Fuck!" Scott yelled as he threw the branch in their direction. Ryan rounded the boulder, trying to peer into the sky toward them but they were already out of view. "Jeez, I know I'm buzzed but I thought you called up the devil or something!"

Scott's heart was still racing. He'd been in the desert at night plenty of times, but this was a first. He jumped up and reached for the canteen that rested precariously on the slope of the boulder. His finger hit the bottom of it and it slid down to land in his arms. He wondered where Shakaiyo was, and whistled for her.

"Here, you need this," Scott said as he twisted off the cap and offered it to him. "No, I need it first," he said as he withdrew it. He took a little swallow then handed it over.

Ryan took a swig and wiped his mouth with the back of his hand. "I didn't know there were crows in the desert."

"I didn't know they flew around at *night!*"

"Speaking of a rush, I…I had this weird feeling while you were doing that. It was like…," he paused trying to find the right words. It was exactly like the time when Scott played his flute in the VFW hall. The same sort of rush, and this time it was okay to tell Scott about it. "…I'd heard you do that before. Like a magic ceremony or something…" Ryan took another swig, trying to get drunker. The cola had lost most of its fizz now, but the bourbon made up for the flat taste. If he got a little more buzzed, whatever he might say would not be him anymore and he could absolve himself of it in the morning.

Even from his buzzed state, Scott noticed how Ryan felt. *So Ryan has feelings after all*, he thought. He circled around him while Ryan turned with him.

"Darkness and the desert. It purifies."

"It what?"

"You felt it. That ceremony was no joke. The desert is *magical*." He whispered the rest. "And she spoke to *you*."

"You're wasted."

"Maybe. But it's true. It talked to us." He started climbing the boulder again. "That was no coincidence," he said as he looked back. Once to the top, he yelled down. "She's talking now. Open up your heart. Your heart knows the truth!"

He wasn't saying it for Ryan. He was saying it for himself. He really wanted to somehow make a better connection with him, but all he could do was say things that sounded mysterious, and he was sure, ridiculous. He was indeed buzzed. Perhaps in the morning he would be a little more coherent. Yet Ryan did seem disconnected. What if I *am* the One to show him how to get connected, he mused? He shook his head and the thought passed.

Ryan wanted to say something but couldn't. How could Scott possibly know what it was like being him? Maybe his heart knew the truth, but he couldn't tell anymore. He didn't want to hurt. About his parents. About his confused feelings regarding Crawford. About everything really. But how could he change any of it? He shook his head and tried to push the thoughts away. He just wanted the anguish to leave.

Scott checked the glow of his watch and read a little past 10:30 p.m. When he looked back to the ground Ryan was nowhere to be seen. "*Hey*…where *are* you?" He looked all around, but saw no movement. His side was tender now as he touched the puncture with a finger but the alcohol seemed to be numbing most of the sting. He jumped down, knowing Ryan must be nearby. But in his present condition he wasn't exactly sure where.

"Yaaah!" Ryan yelled as he jumped up from behind one of the nearby boulders.

"Jeez!" Scott was genuinely startled.

"That'll teach ya."

"Truce?"

"Truce," Ryan agreed.

Ryan looked up in the sky again as they started back. "Hey, I was thinkin'. If I had to take anyone up to show them my place, it'd be you."

"How much does it rain up there?"

"*Way* more than here, of course. We should see if we can both go up there. I'd love to show you where I live. Before it disappears."

"Disappears. Why? Earthquakes?"

"No, I told you. It's gonna eventually be parkland when Muh dies."

"I could go for it."

"We could go up later this summer."

"You think so?"

"Sure. We could go up and visit. Maybe after my birthday in August or something."

"How would you get time off? And how would we get there?"

Ryan looked at him as if he were stupid. "What's parked back at the tent?"

"It's what...*eight hundred miles* to Crescent City?"

"So? I know the way. You showed me this cool place. It's my turn to show you the rainforest."

"Rainforest? Sound like Brazil or something."

"Maybe it's a little colder than Brazil." With that, a shiver passed through his body.

Scott had never considered driving eight hundred miles before tonight. And now he was thinking of going to some place that may as well be in a different country. "But it would be excellent."

Ryan was in high gear now, planning the whole thing. "Howie could help me arrange it. I could take a week off, I'm sure." Scott felt Ryan's excitement. If they were going on such a free-spirited journey, should he tell Ryan he was gay after all? Like right now? Or should he still let it go? He continued to feel torn between his enthusiasm and the fear of what would happen to their fragile friendship. Nonetheless, he was sure that friendships based on a drunken night in the desert didn't mean anything. *One thing at a time*, he thought.

"What's today?" Scott asked.

"June twenty-third."

"Maybe we could go before August."

"Hey, wait. We could combine our birthdays into one party. At my, uh, at Howie's place. Plus, his yard is way better for having people over than yours."

It was true. Howard's back deck was spacious, whereas they had no deck at all. Their house was large enough, but the kitchen was small. Howard's had a much larger kitchen and everyone usually hung out in a kitchen or a back deck whenever there were a lot of people over.

"Yeah, that'd be cool. A double birthday party."

Ryan belched loudly, sending an echo through the dark. "And it'll be radical. Tell your folks and I'll tell Howie. *Then* we could drive up and have *another* party up in Crescent City. Nobody up there has to know we already had a party so we could keep the partyin' going for, like, the whole week!"

Scott extended his hand in agreement. Ryan took it and they shook on it. They continued their trek back to camp, kicking at small rocks, while avoiding the clumps of Cholla cactus along the sides of the gully. Ryan put the canteen strap over his head and pushed it around to his back. The almost demised contents of the canteen sloshed back and forth while he walked.

Scott wondered about Ryan's outburst earlier. It seemed frightening to know that Ryan had no parents. *I wonder if that's his problem*, he thought.

CHAPTER 8

Shakaiyo was waiting for them back at camp. She must have been back for quite some time since she wasn't panting at all.

Although Scott knew all the wood in the Monument was protected, he nonetheless decided to make a small fire from surrounding brush and dead Joshua Tree branches. It wasn't going to be anything elaborate as there was ample heat that evening. Nevertheless, a campsite just didn't seem complete without at least a little one. At least he wasn't going to shoot up all the live vegetation with firearms, as he'd seen done in years past.

The bourbon had made him quite dizzy. By the time he was done collecting the meager wood pickings he felt even dizzier. Ryan gave in to his tired body and leaned back on his daypack, an arm over his eyes. Scott glanced at him as he sat. Ryan was this burning enigma. He was so cute and he wanted to reach out to him somehow. At the same time, it seemed odd that he wanted to reach out to someone who was, well, lost.

"Ryan?"

"Huh?"

"Wasted?"

"Just mellowed out. I can't see."

"Your arm's over your face, stupid."

"Just testing you." He slowly moved it down and held his stomach. "Hey, Scott?"

Scott stared into the fire, watching the flames lick upward and disappear. "Yeah?"

"You're a cool dude."

Scott turned his head, surprised at what he heard.

"I can't believe you're so easy to get along with."

Scott ate up the compliment.

"And you're so easy to talk to. Even when I don't know who the hell you're gonna be the next minute. It's cool how you do that. I've never met anyone like you before. Friends?"

"Sure. Friends." The fire crackled while Scott poked at the red embers. *Great*, he thought. *I sure don't need to be friends with someone who's fucked up. And here I am saying, okay, let's be friends. What for? So I can continue hiding from him, too? And agreeing with him to go to Crescent City might have been jumping the gun.*

"Scott?"

"Yeah."

"D'ya have a girlfriend?"

"No. Just sophomore year."

"What was her name?"

"Karen." He thought for a moment about the question. He didn't bother to mention that they went out the entire year only as "good friends." In fact, he wasn't even sure why he was supposed to have a girlfriend at the time, except that half of his friends had one, so he thought that was what one was supposed to do. It wasn't until his sophomore year that he realized that having a girlfriend had a specific sexual connotation. He only learned that from constant observation of his peers. Late that summer at his aunt's place everything changed. Despite his newfound discovery of himself, he occasionally dated during junior year, but he knew it was only for show. The times when he double-dated weren't bad when they went parking. He went through the motions of necking and feeling up his dates, if they let him, with no problem. At first, it was a game, but it quickly became a scam. Yet it was just another role in the many roles he learned to play for real and for laughs. By the time Junior Prom came up, he was almost a pro at that kind of pretending.

In the distance, an owl hooted several times. Scott shivered as the wind picked up around them briefly, sounding ghostly in the labyrinth of hollow passages around them. *The desert does purify, or it scares you,* he thought.

Ryan raised himself up to his elbows and gazed at Scott. Scott was sure he saw tears. Maybe it was just the feeble flames of his little fire reflecting off his eyes. There was a look of puzzlement on Ryan's face.

"What's wrong?"

Ryan stood and cocked his head to listen. "Nuthin." He shuffled into the dark toward the pond. "I gotta wash this salt off me," he said wiping his chest with the palm of his hand.

Scott followed him to the water's edge and immediately started shedding his shoes. He didn't stop with just his shoes and quickly was naked.

"What the…?" Ryan asked.

"I'm gonna wash off too, dude." Scott started wading into the water and stopped when it got up to his knees.

Ryan stood there, not sure what to think. He was barely able to make out Scott's naked body in the dark. Scott started to splash the warm water all over himself.

Scott saw his dark outline at the bank. "What are ya waiting for?"

Ryan pulled off his tennis shoes and peeled his shorts down to his feet. Now naked as well, he gingerly stepped out, until the water was up to mid-shin, and started to splash water all over himself. While he splashed his face, Scott checked out Ryan's body. There was just enough starlight to make out every curve of muscle and the dark patch of hair at his crotch. He could see a good three inches of his flaccid penis even in this light since it contrasted quite a bit with his dark pubes. Despite his buzz, he felt himself getting aroused. By the time Ryan was done with his face, Scott was fully tumescent, but not quite erect. Ryan saw it immediately, but before he knew it, Scott was splashing him. Ryan splashed back, but couldn't move much from his spot. The bottom of the pond was rocky and a bit slimy, and he was barefoot. He decided to keep his ground since he didn't know how deep the water was further out. Soon they were both dripping wet from the antics. Exhilaration was now pulsing through Ryan's body when they stopped. The only sound was the breeze in his ears and the dripping of water from their naked bodies.

Scott opened his mouth. He desperately wanted to say something, but couldn't bring himself to say that he felt that Ryan was perhaps the cutest boy he had ever met.

"Scott," Ryan started. Before he could finish Scott let loose with another large splash with his leg. It crashed into him and drowned the rest of his sentence out. The next thing he saw was that Scott was right in front of him. He reached out and slicked back Ryan's hair with his hand, smiling at him. Ryan froze, wanting Scott to continue. He did, and brought his hand down to the back of Ryan's neck. What he thought was going to be something sexual turned out to be quite the opposite. Scott pushed hard, sending Ryan sprawling to his right and nearly falling into the water on his side. He regained his balance at just the last moment. Scott just stood there while Ryan noisily waded back to the water's edge. Reaching down, he gathered up his clothes, and dashed back to the camp. Scott grabbed his shorts and shoes up as well and followed a moment later.

The fire was only a glow of barely visible red embers covered in gray and white ash when they returned. Ryan laid his shorts on the fire blanket, found some clean underwear from his pack, slipped them on, and sat down cross-legged. He would be completely dry in no time in the warm air. Scott plopped himself down directly across from him. He stirred the fire a bit with a stick and a few feeble flames along with some sparks spiraled their way up. The glow perfectly illuminated his wet body as Ryan gazed in awed silence.

Scott whipped his head back and forth to shake the last drops of water from his hair. A few drops landed in the embers and sizzled briefly. His heart pounding like mad, he took a chance.

"I gotta beating off, do you?"

"Huh?"

"I really need to badly." He did. He wasn't used to missing even a day. Having seen Ryan naked in the water, and now mostly naked across from him, were the visual cues that reminded him why he had a penis.

"Well, *you* can."

Ryan dropped his hands over his crotch as he became tumescent in a matter of seconds. *He must really be buzzed if he announced that he's gonna beat off.*

"You don't care if I do?"

He's actually gonna beat off in front of me? Ryan glanced at Scott's penis. It was already at attention. "Do you do this all the time?"

"What? Beat off?"

"Duh. With guys."

"No, I never have before, but I figured you wouldn't mind."

In fact, Scott was sure he had perfectly figured Ryan out now. He leaned back against his pack and took his fully hard penis in hand. Ryan watched in mute fascination for only another moment as he thought about it, then slowly he brought his hand to his waist. Perhaps it was the alcohol, perhaps it was because he felt comfortable with Scott's lack of inhibition just now. He wasn't exactly sure. This was perhaps the most horny he had felt in months as he watched Scott.

"What the hell."

He raised his hips up enough to be able to slide his underwear down to his knees. He stopped as Scott glanced his way. Ryan quickly pushed his underwear down to his ankles. He flipped one of his feet out slightly and they landed at his toes. He was fully at attention by the time they were off. He sat cross-legged and started beating off as well.

Most of Scott's mind was focused below his waist just now, but another part was particularly focused on Ryan. It was just dark enough for it to not be too weird. But there was sufficient ambient illumination for the event to lend itself to the best fantasy he'd ever dreamed up.

In just a few more moments, Scott's prize landed on his abdomen and pubic hair. Grunting still, the rest oozed down his fingers. He held on until it completely stopped flowing out. Once the contractions finally subsided, he slung the sticky globs from his hand. He scooped the rest of it off his pubes and flung it into the sand next to him.

That was all Ryan needed to see. He straightened his legs out, leaned back on one elbow, and let out a long moan as it he splashed his abdomen. Scott thought he was in heaven. This was the first time he'd ever watched anyone besides himself do this and it was more incredible than he ever imagined. Ryan continued to moan as his toes curled. Scott watched as three short white streaks lined up almost in parallel across Ryan's navel, saw his abs tense and relax several times as Ryan held his head back, saw his thighs tense and relax, tense again, then finally relax completely as he finally stopped moaning.

Scott grinned when it was all over. He watched Ryan sit up. It wasn't quite embarrassment, it was more like a sense of awkwardness that overcame him as he looked Scott's way and observed him looking at him.

"I'm covered with jizz," was all Ryan could find to say.

He stood, looking for something to wipe himself wipe off with. Scott was checking him out even more so now and Ryan was acutely aware that Scott was staring. Despite Ryan's feeling of awkwardness, this wasn't the first, second or even the third time he'd done this with someone else. He and Crawford had done it together and to each other plenty of times. Of course Scott didn't know anything about that.

Scott was still incredulous. Ryan was clearly not the typical guy he'd ever hung out with. He had made no move to tell Scott that he should stop or anything. In fact, when he realized that Ryan was indeed going to go for it as well, everything he'd suspected about Ryan was in place. Ryan didn't seem embarrassed either. Wasn't he now standing in front of him, fully erect, a sticky mess plastered all over him? How many guys from school would have done that with him? Exactly none.

Scott pretended like it had been nothing out of the ordinary, which it was for him, of course. Indeed, part of him still couldn't believe he had actually done it, but most of his inhibitions had long since disappeared because of the alcohol. "Where's that canteen?"

Ryan pulled a paper towel off a roll that was in the back of the jeep. "Huh?"

"The canteen."

Ryan couldn't remember where he had dropped it. He started wiping himself up. "I don't know."

Scott rose to his feet and looked around. Ryan watched him as he searched. The red glow from the coals outlined his completely naked body. Scott was still hard and it pulsed noticeably, as he searched.

He finally spied the canteen near where Ryan's had been sitting and picked it up.

Ryan had finished wiping himself off and stepped over to retrieve his underwear. Scott's right heel was on a corner of it. Ryan was only just now beginning to lose firmness and the already awkward moment was heightened, as they stood next to each other, still completely naked. "You're standing on my underwear."

Actually, Scott didn't realize he was. He looked down, first at his own penis, still mostly at attention, then to his foot. He made no attempt to pick them up for him, but rather just moved his foot aside. Ryan bent over and quickly picked them up. Scott drank in the moment. He saw the back of Ryan's head, his wide shoulders, and his lats as he reached down. Ryan quickly slid one foot in the underwear, then the next. He pulled them up to his waist and sat down.

Scott opened the top of the canteen and took a swig. Ryan looked up at Scott, still not believing he had done it. But it had felt so good, being out in the middle of nowhere with no one around. He sorely missed the feeling. He had had sex outside with Crawford at least a half dozen times. It was usually on top of the wide fir stump way up from Crawford's house in the middle of his property. The stump was covered with a thick layer of soft moss. It was also completely private, yet afforded one hell of a view of the surrounding valley.

Scott put the cap back on and dropped the canteen onto the blanket. It landed with a decided thump. He rubbed the remaining moisture from his abdomen, then rummaged around in his pack. He found some underwear, which he slowly put on with what Ryan could only describe to himself as a decided tease. He watched Scott's every move, deciding it was the most erotic thing he had ever witnessed. Scott's penis was still perfectly visible, half-erect, as he sat back down on the blanket.

Scott was intensely aware that Ryan was not able to keep his eyes off him. His mind went a mile a minute. *All* the clues were in now. Somehow, despite the final measure, which he just took, Ryan was still pretending that he wasn't interested in taking the event even further. All the glances, the staring, not one word of rebuttal to anything he said all afternoon, the antics in the pond a few minutes before, and then the finale. It all added up, but Ryan wasn't solving the equation for him. *Maybe he's just not out to himself,* Scott thought. *That must be it!* And the excitement of finally figuring it all out, that Ryan must be gay, but not yet out, was truly exciting. Finally, he knew someone else his own age that was, too. Sure, somewhere straight guys might jack off together, but it was more than just that act that brought this particular revelation to mind. It was everything that had led up to that moment.

Silence ensued while Scott mulled over everything. As if on cue, they crawled into the tent at almost the same time. Scott smoothed out his blanket and lay on top of it. Shakaiyo found her spot at his feet and lay down. Ryan lay on top of Howard's sleeping bag with the sheet bunched up to his side.

The pale green tent was shaped like a long cylinder cut in half with an entrance fly across one end. It opened with a single zipper in the shape of a wide frown. Two mesh windows spanned the top and draped down the sides. They were also semi-circular and opened with zippers. The wind kept up its light blowing and rustled the partially zipped up entrance flap. The windows were positioned in such a way that the breeze easily found its way inside. Both of their heads swam as they lay there. A moment later Scott sat up and zipped the flap up all the way.

It's a good thing I'm on my back, Ryan thought, *or I'd probably be heaving.* He was having some awful bed spins. He wished he'd brought his Walkman to drown out the jumbled thoughts that swirled in his head, but he had left it back at the house. The voice of his ex-girlfriend rang in his mind. She was considered one of the best-looking girls in his senior class. He even liked the fact that the guys thought he was cool for going out with one of the more popular girls, yet she was just cover. To this day, he couldn't figure out how no one, not even her, had ever discovered that he'd been with Crawford all that time. And she had wanted more than he was willing to deliver. "You're not a fag, are you, Ryan?" she had once said. How many times that had echoed in his head since she had said it, he couldn't count.

He had spent so much time denying that he was gay that he still couldn't explain how he had been Crawford's boy toy for so long. He still didn't have the right word for his relationship with him. Boyfriend just wasn't it. It was more like Crawford was a mentor of sorts. Ryan was always learning something. How to lick just right. How to suck just right. How to loosen up to accommodate Crawford. He wouldn't dare use the word queer to describe himself, despite how Crawford used it to keep him under his thumb. Yet, now that he had met Scott, it was virtually impossible to deny it. His attraction to Crawford wasn't an anomaly. He still couldn't say it to himself. The truth was just at arms reach. *I can't stand this,* he thought. His eyes stung as tears welled up. That was happening a lot lately. Ever since he had met Scott. It made him feel more out of control than he usually did. Despite himself, he was sorely attracted to Scott, but that kind of attraction led him to Crawford and created the worst year of his life. He didn't want that to happen again. How could he like Scott the way he liked Crawford? They were so different. Here he was, alone in a tent with the cutest guy he'd ever been friends with, and could do nothing but ache. "Scott?" he blurted from his chaotic thoughts.

Scott turned and faced him, but it was too dark to make out anything.

"I, uh, I…" He couldn't go on. He almost said it anyway. He almost told him about Crawford, but again was too freaked about what that would reveal about him. He tried, but just couldn't say it. Just like with Frank. He couldn't tell his friend Frank either. "Never mind," was all he could muster. It was as if he was being tortured. No, it was he who was torturing himself. He knew it. He didn't like the feeling, but he was used to it. After all, he'd been at it for a couple of years now.

Scott pursed his lips, wondering what that had been about. Soon he heard Ryan's regular breathing, an occasional soft snort, and he fell asleep, too.

Ryan awoke with a start. The illuminated dial on his watch showed just after 1:30 a.m. He felt his crotch. It *was* wet. *Holy shit*, he thought. He hadn't had a wet dream in months. He felt around for his two-liter bottle, the one with plain water in it, and took it in hand, careful not to slosh it too much and make a lot of noise. Shakaiyo was at their feet and right at the entrance of the tent. He slowly unzipped the tent flap, still trying to be as quiet as he could. He hesitated for a moment as her tail thumped on the ground cloth a couple of times, then he continued to crawl out of the tent. Scott hadn't moved.

The lingering images of the wet dream had a familiar theme. He was fucking Scott. In that pond. That was something he'd never done before because Crawford had always been the top. *Fuck Crawford*, he thought. The last time he remembered a dream, which was last weekend, he was sucking Scott's dick. It seemed that lately he was only remembering sexual dreams, and the only other person he could remember in any of them was Scott.

He picked his way carefully over the now cool gravely desert floor in his bare feet. He still felt a bit drunk and weaved considerably. His erratic steps struck a rock with the side of his foot and it clacked against another one. He ignored it.

The sharp sound woke Scott up. The entrance flap was open and he figured Ryan went out to pee. Thinking it would be a turn-on to watch, he looked out and saw Ryan rummaging in his pack. The moon was up quite a ways now, providing ample illumination to the otherwise dark night. He watched with sleepy, still tipsy eyes.

Scott watched with astonishment as Ryan proceeded to strip his underwear off. Scott's dick immediately went to attention. He continued watching as Ryan poured water onto his underwear and wiped around his waistline just below his navel. It was obvious now what was going on. Ryan had had a wet dream and he was wiping himself up! *Wow*, Scott thought, *how cool*. He remembered only having a single wet dream in his whole life and that was several years ago. He was sure it was because he never let anything build up for any length of time.

As uncomfortable and excited as Ryan had felt about the dream, he felt equally comfortable standing in the quiet desert night. The now cool breezes that caressed his body not only felt soothing, but also had already made him somewhat hard again. The rubbing to get the last of the sticky fluid out of his pubic hair made him fully erect. It wasn't unusual for him to do it twice in a row. In fact, he recalled a few times in the recent past where he woke up less than an hour after masturbating to get to sleep and jerking off all over again. Yet, a wet dream was unusual nowadays.

Ryan dropped the soiled pair on top of the pack. He reached in to retrieve fresh underwear, and leaned against the back of the Jeep. He briefly caressed his face with the soft cotton fabric, breathing in the fresh scent. He quickly stepped into them.

Scott could hardly catch his breath as he watched. He could still perfectly make out Ryan's erection through his underwear in the moonlight. Ryan headed away from the Jeep. Scott figured Ryan had gone to pee at this point for sure. He turned over, facing his side of the tent.

The clues were even more solidly in now. *Ryan has no girlfriend*, he thought. *He never really talks about girls like the rest of the guys do, we beat off together, and he even invited me up north. And if I'm not mistaken, he had a wet dream! None of that necessarily makes him gay*, he thought, *but if the wet dream was the result of what we did earlier, then it certainly is another clue.* Finally, though, Scott decided. *If he's not gay, then neither am I. If it's true, he needs even more hints about me.*

This was the first time he'd ever known someone anywhere near his age that he suspected wasn't straight. There wasn't even a single person in school he had any clue about either. Sure, there were the boys others thought were sissies or were called pussies, but they weren't what he considered 'gay'. How was it possible that that very same person he suspected was also so good-looking? His thoughts continued to race. *Maybe if he were to figure me out, he'll come out to me*, he thought. *It could save me the trouble of being sure. Wouldn't that be too outrageous?* Still, Scott was at a loss at knowing what his best course of action should be. As decisive as he was on virtually everything, this was the one issue he couldn't quite figure out.

Ryan eventually made his way back to the tent. Scott pretended Ryan had woken him. As he stirred, Ryan froze at the entrance.

Scott tried to sound like he'd been woken up. "Hey, what 're you doing?"

"I, uh, took a leak." Ryan crawled in as quickly as he could, laid down, and pulled the sheet over him.

"Good idea," Scott whispered as he pulled himself out of the tent. He could tell that he was still feeling the effects of the evening's drinking since his equilibrium was a little off. Nonetheless, he headed out and went around the overhanging boulder out of visual range. Ryan hadn't seen it, but Scott had been fully erect. He stepped out of his underwear, grasped himself, and started all over again. Soon enough his knuckles were streaked with come. He had to grit his teeth to stifle his moans as he nearly doubled over. It was always intense when he did it again so soon. Really needing to pee now, the stream arched high at first, then straight out in front of him as he finished. In only a few minutes, he was back in the tent.

You are so stupid, Scott, he thought as he settled down. *Why don't you just ask him?* Somehow, though, he knew the direct approach would get him nowhere. *No, Ryan wouldn't tell me the truth even if his life depended on it.* After thinking about it for a few more minutes, he finally fell asleep with an exhausted smile on his face.

Early the next morning, they were still in the shadow of the granite monoliths. The sun had been up for well over an hour and already the temperature was creeping up. A gust of wind knocked something over outside the tent. Its noise woke Scott up. His rustling made Shakaiyo stir and she motioned to be let out of the tent. He unzipped the flap and she stepped out.

As usual, Scott's morning erection was about to club him to death. It was his first opportunity of the day to give Ryan some clues of his own. He sat up, checking how his head felt. He was surprised that he was really only a little dizzy. He sat cross-legged, facing Ryan. If Ryan were to look now, his face would be right at crotch level. His dick was straight up now and the idea he had in mind kept it that way.

Soon enough Ryan stirred. "My head," he croaked as he pulled the thin wadded up blanket from his face and opened his eyes. It was just as Scott planned. Ryan's gaze didn't stray from his crotch for a few seconds.

He launched the first salvo. "Like it?"

Ryan didn't know how to answer. Already he was growing hard and having Scott pose the question before even saying good morning threw him. Luckily, part of the sheet was over his lower body and Scott couldn't tell what was happening down there. "Jeez, dude!" he exclaimed. He covered his eyes with the crook of his arm.

"Maybe you need another look."

Ryan pretended to be calm, although he was worried that the situation was already out of control. *Why is he taunting me like this*, he wondered. *It has to be another one of his weird personalities.*

Scott tugged downward on his waistband in front, allowing the head to peek out. Ryan couldn't help it and looked. His heart pounded with excitement. He wanted Scott to stop, knowing he was enticing him. At the same time he wanted him to keep going and pull the underwear all the way off, like last night. He feigned sleepiness and closed his eyes again. Perhaps if he just held out he wouldn't have to decide what to do.

While Ryan's eyes were closed, Scott rubbed his erection through the white cotton with an open palm. Ryan reopened his eyes again as he heard the rubbing sound.

Scott saw he was mesmerizing Ryan. He was reacting just as Scott expected. He decided that his suspicions were correct. Hell, Ryan wasn't asking him what he was doing or why or even telling him to stop, just like last night. He wondered just how far he could go with his little game. He pulled the waistband away again and looked down. There was a crusty fleck still clinging to the side of the shaft.

"I'm ready for another round. Wanna help me out this time?" He let go of the elastic, which caused a noticeable snapping sound. He shouldn't have done that, he thought. It stung.

"No, I can't..." was all he could say.

"What about last night?" Scott asked as he rubbed again.

The ensuing seconds seemed like hours. Ryan's erection was straining his underwear and he could barely catch his breath. He came up with the perfect rebuttal. "There weren't any babes around." With that, he faced away from him and unfurled the sheet over the rest of his body.

What the fuck did that mean, Scott wondered. *He's lying for sure.* Nonetheless, he ended his little game. He had enough clues anyway. "Yeah, you're right. It's just a piss hard-on anyway." Like nothing had happened he changed the subject. "I'll start breakfast." He left the tent and took a leak. He pulled some shorts in his pack and pulled them on over his underwear.

That's seals it, Scott decided. *I just know he is now!* While he thought about it, he looked for Ryan's soiled underwear in his pack. Luck! They were right on top. He pulled them out and checked them. The fabric was conspicuously stuck together in places and most of it was on the inside. The unmistakable sign of a wet dream. He stuffed them back in as a wide grin crossed his face. He quickly started making breakfast.

For many minutes, Ryan wrestled with what Scott had done. *He was just playing with my mind*, he thought. Yet, he debated it with himself. *I thought I was the horny one. Maybe he's just horny all the time. I guess I don't blame him with a body like that. I don't get it, though. But what is he trying to prove? That he's gay?* He *was* just playing, Ryan decided. *He's definitely not queer. There's no way. He was on the track team. They wouldn't let fags on the track team, I'm sure. Or maybe he was acting again. Plus, guys mess with each other's minds all the time. That has to be it. Maybe he's trying to be funny because of last night.* The anxiety of not knowing had made him completely lose his erection and he realized he had to pee badly. He sat up. Immediately his head hurt.

He pulled himself out of the tent, pulled some running shorts and a badly wrinkled t-shirt from his pack. He quickly donned both items. He didn't bother with socks and pulled his untied tennis shoes onto his feet. He avoided Scott and peed out of his view.

Standing made his head pound even more. The nasty taste in his mouth just about made him retch. He needed water and he'd left the plastic water bottle somewhere by the Jeep. That would mean he'd have to go by Scott right away, he realized as he returned.

Scott pretended he didn't notice Ryan behind him as he saw him gulp the rest of the contents of the bottle. When he was finished, he started filling it again from one of the larger water containers.

"My head hurts like shit," he announced as he inspected the food Scott was preparing.

Scott pointed. "I got some aspirin in that green bag."

He was annoyed at Scott's cheerful tone. "How'd you think of that?"

"Be prepared, ya know."

Ryan realized he hadn't been preparing for much of anything, least of which was last night. He looked in Scott's kit bag and found a small tin. All the tabs in it were crumbled into powder. He poured some of it into a cup and poured some water over it. The grains made him cough as it went down.

"I think you drank too much last night," Scott said as he heard the coughing.

"Don't worry about how much *I* drank. You *definitely* drank too much."

Scott didn't like his tone, but couldn't help but feel bad for him. *He must really be hurting*, he thought.

Ryan went back into the tent, rolled up his blanket and the sleeping bag, and wadded the sheet up. Finally, he reappeared outside. "What 're ya makin'?" he asked now a little more friendly.

"Scrambled scorpion tails with mashed rattlesnake eyes. There's peanut butter, and garlic soap if you want that instead."

Ryan felt his face go flush. "I'm gonna hurl."

Scott grinned as he looked at Ryan's face. Ryan avoided looking directly at him. "This is really gonna be scrambled eggs," Scott said. "But the only way to have any bacon is if I get some help."

"My head's pounding," Ryan complained as he turned the bacon.

"Kinda like what I did last night? You know, pounding my head?" Ryan ignored his comment. Scott tallied another one. The checklist was growing.

Ryan's headache finally became more manageable after he downed some more of the aspirin powder and they ate in acute silence. Ryan still wouldn't look at him. Scott could feel the embarrassment oozing from Ryan. He wondered if Ryan was straight after all. If that were the case then the only thing he had going for him was his choice hair color, his dark brown eyes, and his just-about-flawless body. He ventured a glance again at the basket Ryan was packing in his orange nylon shorts. *Oh, yeah,* he thought, *and his cute dick. Which I absolutely have to see up close and in the light of day, preferably with my mouth near it at some point.*

Scott now thought about what Ryan said about them going up north to Crescent City. It still seemed like a good idea now that it was morning. If he went it may give him a chance to mess around with him at some point. *It's a stretch,* he thought, *but maybe it could happen.* He looked at the Jeep. What if the vehicle broke down on the way? He finally articulated his concern. "You know, I'm kinda worried about driving all that far. You know, to Crescent City?"

Ryan looked him in the eye for the first time that morning. "What are you worried about? Your Jeep runs fine. And we could share the driving," he added, visibly perking up. "All you probably need to do is make sure all the fluids are okay before the long haul. Don't forget, I know engines."

Scott stacked the scant dishes after scraping the remains for Shakaiyo. "I don't know."

Ryan heard his reaction. He knew Scott was his only ticket up north and he had to sell the idea to him. "With me along you'll be safe. The Jeep's only a couple of years old. Most of the tread's still there on all the tires. I already checked that out," he said, and left it at that.

As Scott took the dishes and walked to the serene pond, all he could think of was Ryan wrecking his car. He didn't want him to do that with his Jeep. He rubbed a bit of wet sand around in the dishes to clean them out, then rinsed them in the water. He continued to mull over the trip, especially thinking about how he might be napping while Ryan was driving. *Gross, to die in my sleep.* He looked up at the vehicle with a protective eye.

After they stowed the gear and took down the tent, Scott made sure the campsite was spotless. Neither a scrap of wrapping nor a chicken bone remained when he was finished inspecting. While he finalized the strap down of the gear with bungi cords, Ryan glanced back at the pond. He remembered last night's antics when they were splashing each other in the water. For a fleeting instant, he smiled. Last night's dream flickered in his mind. *Fucking Scott right here.* His smile went away as the weight of what he felt about Scott came back.

"Hey, you in la-la land," Scott called out. He was done and it was time to leave. He jumped in and Scott started the engine. "Let's go back to Hidden Rocks while it's still not too hot," he said, shifting into gear.

"Sure." Ryan felt that a little stretching of his sore muscles would keep his mind off his obsessive thinking.

A few minutes later, they arrived at the main trail leading to the sheer rocks. Two other vehicles were already parked there when they arrived. A cloud of dust overtook them as they stopped.

Ryan coughed a few times, pulling the neck of his t-shirt up to cover his mouth and nose. Shakaiyo looked back, then sneezed.

"You need a top for this thing, you know. And if we're going up north you should get one."

Scott shook his hair out. "I was just thinking about that."

They strode toward the rock face. "Hey, that's Kyle and Lisa. He's a climber I see here a lot."

Kyle and his wife Lisa were standing in the shade talking to two other guys. "Hey, Scott. What's up?" Kyle said.

"Just showing my buddy the ropes. The real ones."

"Cool."

Kyle pointed first to Scott then to Ryan. "Scott and…"

"Ryan," he said as he stuck out his hand.

"Kyle and Lisa," Kyle said as he pointed to his wife.

"This is Nick…and Terry." They all shook hands.

Nick addressed the boys. "You guys do much climbing?"

Scott and Kyle gave each other knowing smiles. Kyle was well aware of Scott's experiences at Hidden Rocks, mostly with rappelling.

Ryan spoke up despite feeling quite inept around the well-heeled guys and woman. "I taught Scott everything he knows," he said boast-fully.

Scott rolled his eyes. "Right."

Nick spoke of various technical climbs with friends in the Sierras and at Red Rock Canyon in Nevada. Terry asked Ryan if he had been to any of those "good" spots.

"No," he said, sounding dejected.

The three men continued to exchange more technical details about various climbs, and how they were going to tackle this particular one. Ryan looked on, wishing they would shut up, or disperse, or something, so they could get on with rappelling.

Lisa, seeing his obvious exasperated look, pulled him aside as the guys continued to talk.

"You're lucky to be Scott's friend," she said casually, as they walked toward the rocks and out of earshot. She took off her pack and dropped it by one of the tires of her vehicle.

"Why's that?"

"He's learns fast and he's dedicated to the sport." They walked a few more paces. "And he's funny. And cute, too," she said flippantly. She looked down at Ryan's tanned legs, noting that he was cute as well. She laughed mischievously as she touched his shoulder. "You two make a cute couple."

It was a completely innocent statement, an intended joke, but it seemed now that he was getting it from all sides. He squinted as he looked at her, trying to discern her meaning. *Am I wearing a badge that says 'I'm a big fucking fag'*, he wondered.

He quickly changed the subject. "So what do you guys do? I mean for money. You couldn't climb around here all the time."

"My husband and I are psychologists. We have separate practices in San Bernardino."

"So, you're shrinks?"

"Sure are."

Uh, oh, he thought. As far as he was concerned she was about to get inside his head. Back home, his friend Frank had a way of doing that, although he wasn't a psychologist, and it unnerved him that she might do the same. He spied the wedding ring on her finger and changed the subject again. "Uh, how long have you been married?"

She instantly had the answer. "Three years and eight months. We were in college together and got married about a month after we graduated."

They walked for a few paces more before Ryan stopped. He had to ask her. "What did you mean when you said we make a cute couple?"

She put a hand to her mouth. "I'm sorry, I shouldn't have said that. I didn't mean to embarrass you."

Before she could elaborate, Scott yelled from behind them. "Yo, Ryan!"

Ryan turned around. "What?"

"Come on. We're gone."

Ryan felt stupid now. She simply thought he was cute. Well, that was okay. But this thing about Scott and him, and to his face, was one step too close.

When they got back to the rest of the guys Ryan deliberately avoided eye contact with Scott. He was afraid Lisa would glean something simply by the way he interacted with him. If he'd known they were shrinks, he might have been more careful right away. Careful about what, he couldn't say, but he didn't want his attraction to Scott to give him away.

Someday, Ryan thought, *I won't have to feel afraid of this anymore, but when?*

They all shook hands again and the climbers waved good-bye to the boys.

Ryan stood by the passenger side, not getting in yet. "Hey, let me drive."

Scott eyed him as Ryan rounded the Jeep to the driver's side. "I don't know."

"Just while we're in here."

"Well, okay," he reluctantly replied. He handed Ryan the keys once they swapped places. He wondered why he didn't protest the request. Perhaps it was that he couldn't say no to someone as good-looking as Ryan? He looked in the back for a moment, making sure Shakaiyo was okay. Still wary though, he buckled his seatbelt with ceremony, and held onto the dashboard.

"What are you doing?" Ryan asked as he watched his deliberate actions.

"I'm just trying to be safe."

He started it up, made sure it was in low, and gunned it immediately. Gravel flew back behind them as the vehicle bucked forward.

Scott gave him a stern look. "Be careful!"

"I'm just testing the horsepower." He turned it around and went toward the main road. Scott pointed the direction and they headed back north toward the west entrance.

About a mile further, Ryan spied the shallow ruts of a trail he saw the day before. It led down a gentle slope to an unusually grassy area populated by what looked like a sprawling orchard of mature Joshua Trees, little underbrush, and few upward-protruding boulders. He slowed, and before Scott could say anything, turned down the trail.

There was just a hint of alarm in Scott's voice. "Hey, where're you going?"

"This is an off-road vehicle and we haven't off-roaded yet."

In a way, the impromptu side trip was called for. After all, they hadn't done any off-roading at all. But quickly enough Ryan was a little too much of a daredevil for Scott. He left the rutted trail and dodged a cluster of short creosote bushes, weaving around the Joshuas. The remains of the ice sloshed noisily back and forth inside the cooler as Ryan took a sharp right turn. Scott was sure the driver's side wheels left the ground.

"Hey, not so fast!" he yelled, now feeling a little trepidation.

Ryan felt a surge of adrenaline. He was frustrated about being with Scott and yet being unable to really be himself. A considerable amount of tension had built up inside between what he had experienced last night and from this morning with what Lisa had said. Now, that familiar out-of-control feeling he so often felt was replaced with exhilaration.

"I can handle it."

As Scott held protest, and now that panic was beginning to etch itself onto his face, Ryan felt he wanted to irritate him even further.

A Joshua Tree branch brushed the side of the Jeep as they ran too close. Scott leaned inward to avoid it as it flew past, remembering the jab he got last night. "I mean it. Cut it out!"

"Don't worry. I know what I'm doing."

"Like hell, you do!"

Up to this point, Shakaiyo was simply enjoying the ride, despite the abrupt shifts to the left and right, and the bumping around she was experiencing. But now, at Scott's exclamation, she stuck her head between them and whined loudly several times. They hit a narrow low spot and at the same time the right front tire hit a small rock. They were still in two-wheel drive and the added torque on that tire slung it up into the wheel well with a loud thud. It startled Scott as they bounced up and back onto a level stretch. Ryan gunned it even more now and swerved to avoid a Cholla cactus. It seemed to Scott that Ryan was now completely out of control since he hadn't slowed down even a little. He could only remember two other times he'd felt panicky. This was his third. "Stop right fucking now!"

Ryan hit the brakes while the steering wheel was slightly turned. It caused the vehicle to turn almost ninety degrees as it came to a stop. Sand flew all over them from the short skid.

Scott scrambled to unbuckle his seatbelt. Jumping out, he nearly screamed. "Out! Now, asshole!" Ryan hesitated, enjoying how much he had riled Scott. Scott picked up a sizeable rock lying at his feet and with a wild-eyed look threatened him with it. "*Now!*"

Ryan stumbled out. "Ha, ha, had you going." *Scott's a pussy,* he thought. *All of my friends would have just laughed at all that. He took it way too seriously.*

"Fuck you, dickweed!"

"You don't have to be such a *faggot* about it!" Ryan spat back. He blurted it before he realized what he had said and immediately regretted it. He had said it with an intensity he was sure Scott felt.

He felt it. Scott threw the rock as hard as he could past his head. Ryan ducked, but saw he wasn't the actual target of his aim. He popped back up quickly, his hands in front of him. "Hey, I'm sorry. I didn't mean that. I…" He stopped as he heard the sound. The left rear tire started hissing steadily. Scott, still furious, went around to look.

"*Fuck!* Now you did it, shithead." Scott kicked the tire. His boot tread scraped the ground before it hit the tire and sand went up into the air.

"Chill. It's just a flat tire. I can…"

Scott cut him off. "What kind of excuse did you make when you wrecked *your* fucking car?!"

The shouting match continued. "The Jeep is *not wrecked!*"

Ryan was sincerely sorry for what he did. And Scott blasted him for just having a little fun. Now it brought his totaled car back to mind. No, worse. He had called Scott a faggot in the heat of the moment. To his only friend in Yucca Valley.

Scott wouldn't talk to him now as he tossed camping gear from the back to get the jack and tire iron. Ironically, Ryan felt a lump in his throat. Calling Scott a faggot when he didn't really mean it brought up a torrent of emotion he wasn't prepared for. That's exactly what Crawford did to him on more than one occasion: he called him his 'little fag boy'.

Scott stood with his hands on his hips as he watched Ryan methodically search under the chassis for the proper spot for the jack. He wrestled with the tight lugs, using his foot on the tire iron to loosen them. It took a while, but finally he had the spare on. He didn't bother asking Scott to help him. He knew what kind of answer he'd get. It seemed Scott wasn't the kind to change a tire. Still feeling regretful, he hoisted the heavy flat onto the brace on the back of the Jeep. In a way, doing it all without Scott's help was a punishment he felt he deserved for acting stupid.

Scott still wouldn't speak, yet began to mellow out as he put their belongings back in. Ryan poured water on his hands, then wiped them with a rag to get as much of the tire black off as he could.

"Listen, Scott. I'm sorry. It was only a flat. I-I promise I won't do stupid stuff like that anymore."

"Yeah, well, you're not driving anymore."

"I'm sorry I called you a fag. *I didn't mean it.*"

"Just get in. Luckily, everything was here, stupid, or we'd 've been stranded. I didn't check to see if there were any tools in this thing before we left." He started the Jeep back up, testing its traction as he headed back toward the trail.

Realizing Scott had a few things to learn about vehicle maintenance Ryan tried to assuage his fear. "Really, if you stick with me you'll have no problem when we go up north." He said it more as a question than as a statement. At this point, his fear was that Scott would say 'see ya'. There'd be just he and his uncle, alone, in his house on that lonely street; just the employees, all older than he, at AeroSun; and Scott would still be pissed at him. He couldn't deal with that future at all.

Scott waited until they reached the rutted trail before he answered. "Maybe," he finally said.

Thank God, he didn't just say no, Ryan thought. He sat back, watching the ground pass by as Scott drove them back to the paved road.

Scott was watching his anger as much as experiencing it. *Ryan's such a butthead at times*, he thought. *But I couldn't just up and leave him in the middle of the Monument. He's so strange. One minute he calls me his friend, the next he deliberately riles me up.* "Why do you have to be so crazy?"

Ryan didn't really know how to answer. He liked to antagonize people, but Scott was different, so why he antagonized him didn't make sense. To make things worse, he was feeling sorely isolated just now. "I promised," was all he could find to say. *What a strange mix of feelings*, Ryan thought. His natural inclination had always been to irritate people and exploit situations when he knew others felt helpless. After all, his grandmother hadn't sent him away for nothing. Now he actually felt regretful about it, and that was something he wasn't used to. Right there he resolved not to do anything like that to Scott again.

Had Ryan actually apologized, Scott wondered? "I'm gonna make you stick to that promise when we go up to Crescent City."

Ryan wanted to leap for joy. Scott hadn't turned against him. And right when he promised himself about not bothering him, he had said that. His joy was evident in his voice. "Then, we're…still friends?"

Scott glanced at him, then looked straight ahead at the road. "For now."

Ryan decided he meant longer than that, mentally crossing his fingers that he wouldn't actually provoke him anymore. He thought about their odd friendship. So far, this was the shortest but the best one he'd ever known. Not a moment of pretense from him. Not a hint of fakery. Just straightforward interaction and Scott's unique brand of character humor. As they flew down the highway toward town he hoped he could keep his antagonism to himself. In spite of doing stupid things around him, he was becoming more attached, as well as attracted to him. He just had to figure out a way to stop himself from being like that around him. He let out a long sigh, then turned to pet Shakaiyo. "Pull into the first gas station and I'll pay for the repair," he said as the wind whistled past.

CHAPTER 9

More than a week had passed since their rappelling excursion and neither had seen the other. Despite the time apart, it was distracting how captivated Scott felt about Ryan, despite the argument that had ensued. After thinking about it more, Scott was sure that he had overreacted anyway. Perhaps it was just a sense of possessiveness over his new vehicle that made him react that way. The attraction he felt toward Ryan far outweighed all the other things he didn't like about him. It made him have to concentrate even harder at tasks on hand whenever he thought about him. As the days had passed he imagined Ryan more good-looking than he knew he really was. But what was the most compelling aspect of their short friendship was how Scott figured Ryan must be gay. Unfortunately, his earlier plan to simply tell Ryan he was, and to see if Ryan would come out to him seemed to be on permanent hold.

In the last week, he had two significant conversations with his parents. One was about the trip to Crescent City. He was just testing the waters really. The other was still a sore spot with him and he had regretted talking about it again.

"But Ralph, do you realize how far it is to Crescent City?" Elaine had asked.

"He can read a map," Ralph had countered. They had been talking as if he wasn't even present. "As long as he goes the speed limit and stays awake they'll be fine. And he can take a week off."

Scott had thought he heard wrong. He had been prepared for the protest from his mom about the distance, but he hadn't been prepared for his dad's agreement without even a warning of some sort. He didn't even try to guess why he was so easy.

Ryan's comment, back in the VFW auditorium, about him seriously pursuing music had opened up an old argument as well. Now that it was Ryan who had suggested it, the idea somehow seemed more worthwhile. Funny how no one in the band ever discussed it with him. Maybe it was because he was still in high school and the entire rest of the band wasn't. The age difference must have been some sort of factor, he surmised. Maybe it was because he considered being Centauri's soundman nothing but fun, not something serious.

His mother's voice was still distinct in his mind. "Honey, it only *sounds* like a good idea. After high school things change. It's important to make sure you have a secure future. You'll understand once you're off to college," she had said. She had sounded even more concerned this time and almost convincing. "You know business will help you more in the long run than music."

That was where his dad really protested. His forehead had even gotten red. He hadn't seen his father's forehead get red from frustration in a long time. "Out of the question," he had said. "We've already discussed the fall semester at High Desert College after you graduate. You've even filled out all the registration forms. If you have time you can take music appreciation courses, but *major* in music?" Scott had never mailed the forms. They still were at the bottom of a pile of papers on the desk in his room. He had even thought about just pushing them until they fell behind the desk. He hadn't done that just yet.

Ralph really expected him to follow his lead. Scott's older brother, Steve, had been a business major. But much to everyone's surprise he had announced years previous that he was not only not going to help run Faraday's, but he was moving entirely out of the country and started an import/export business. Ralph had gotten it into his head that Scott was the next candidate for succession. It was implicit in the way his dad interacted with him from there on in. Until recently, Scott just ignored the more serious aspects of the tacit agreement. Now he was beginning to feel smothered. He had no idea that music would be the outlet for him that it had now become. Somehow, being the baby of the family made him more dependent than he expected, despite being a virtual only child since junior high. The role he was being set up for was difficult to break free from.

"Yeah, Dad, I know…." Scott had rebutted, but the discussion ended up being more of a showdown than anything else. It did no good when he pointed out how involved he was with Centauri and how much fun he was having. His mother had been quiet for a while, thinking before she asked. "Honey, we've been through this."

He'd already given them enough reasons but tried the most recent one as well. "Well, even Ryan, who's not a musician, asked me why I wasn't majoring in music."

His dad had spoken even more firmly. "Son, how can a seventeen year old boy possibly know what's best for you?" That really hurt.

He wondered why they were so adamant about business school. Neither of them had gone to a full four-year college. His father had gone to a community college. And his mother had only a year of college behind her. So how could they possibly know what it was like for him?

Instead of pursuing it further, he just dropped it. His conversation with Colleen later that week hadn't helped any. She was under the impression that his parents knew just what they were talking about.

"Look at me," she had said. "I've got a bachelor's degree and I still haven't made it."

"But you weren't a music major," Scott had responded.

"No, but I should have majored in something worthwhile like economics or finance. I'd have a real job and not just be hanging around with a bunch of flunkies like you guys." He knew she was just razzing him but her answer had stung as well.

That night, the frustration he felt was confusing. Everyone was saying one thing and his body said another. Didn't it make sense to want to follow one's natural strengths? Hadn't that been one of the most important lessons he'd learned so far in his short life? And over the last year music seemed to be the singular thing closest to his heart. Maybe Mom and Dad did know best, he had thought. How, he didn't know, but they *were* paying his tuition.

∗   ∗   ∗

"It's so nice to have a real holiday for the 4th this year," Beth said to Scott as they stood at the host station. "You can go as a real family this year."

"Yeah, it *is* unusual for us all to go together, isn't it?" Since the Fourth was a holiday, and plenty of people were in town for the fireworks at the Marine Base some twenty miles away at Twentynine Palms. Faraday's was usually open late on the Fourth. It was always a bonus day for them economically. That meant Scott was either working late or he'd end up seeing the fireworks with friends. Starting this year, the fireworks display was on the third. That meant hardly anyone made reservations for that evening. For once, it wasn't economically viable to stay open late for that holiday. The excuse was there and the entire family was going to the Base to watch the display.

"Mr. St. Charles and his nephew are still coming with us?" Beth asked.

"They're supposed to show up at our house later," Scott replied.

"Great. We'll all have a good time."

Elaine came by just as Beth was about to leave. "Meet you at our apartment." Beth and her husband lived off base in a duplex apartment building.

"Don't worry. We'll be there well before dark."

Late in the afternoon, Howard drove Ryan to the Faraday's house in his bright red sports car. Scott was changing when there was a knock on his bedroom door. "Hey, Scott," Ryan said through the closed door.

Upon hearing Ryan's voice Scott felt his pulse quicken. T-shirt in hand he let him in. Any lingering reservation about Ryan's stunt with his Jeep faded into insignificance upon seeing his face. Somehow, the sexual antic he performed on the camping trip seemed a million miles away.

"Hey, how's it going? We're just about to leave," he said. His eyes lingered on Scott's unclad upper body.

Scott quickly pulled his shirt on and looked at his intercom for a second before they left the room. Yes, the LED still glowed brightly. *Hmm,* he thought, *Ryan elected not to use it though that's the preferred method in the house.*

Scott reminded Shakaiyo that dogs weren't allowed on the base. She wagged her tail, looking like she agreed with him, as he left her in the backyard.

Ralph drove them all in the station wagon. As they passed the VFW, Scott pointed out the flags he'd raised earlier. There were quite a few of them, Ryan noted.

They stopped briefly at Beth's apartment to get her and her husband. They drove in their own car, which was packed with chairs, a cooler, and munchies. They arrived at the big stadium at one corner of the base with plenty of time to spare, and found parking. They grabbed lawn chairs from the cars while the two boys took the big cooler. Beth's husband helped spread out the blankets and soon they had snacks and sodas passed around.

Scott sat next to Ryan. Ryan was eager to know if he was going to get his ride. "Well, did you ask your parents?"

"Yeah."

"What'd they say?"

"No problem. What'd Howie say?"

"I think he'd rather I stayed here. But he said okay."

"You know, you'd think that if you were eighteen by that time, you wouldn't have to ask anyone anything."

"I think I have to be on some sort of good behavior or something before he trusts me."

No doubt, Scott thought. "What did he say about the week off?"

"Since I'm his assistant it really makes no difference. And I can deal with a week of no pay if we're partyin' instead."

"So, this is for real?" Up to this point, Scott figured a trip all the way to northern California was more imaginary than real.

"We're happenin', dude."

Scott noticed that Ryan wasn't his usual thoughtless self tonight. He seemed completely at ease, and likable. *Is he deliberately holding his attitude in check and trying to keep his promise about not being an asshole after all? Tonight he seems extra cute and irresistible. How could that be,* he wondered. He stretched his legs out. That's when the envelope crinkled in his pocket.

"Oh, I almost forgot." He extracted the envelope, then stuffed the inside of his pocket back in. "This is from my aunt in Parker, uh, a town on the Arizona border." In it was a letter-size advertisement. He showed it to Ryan. "There's a speedboat race on Lake Havasu every year. It's on the second weekend in July. And I always go. See if you can come, too."

"Awesome. I've never seen a live speedboat race."

"You'll love it. My aunt and uncle run this bed and breakfast on the Arizona side of the river. They've got a ton of space. They also own a marina on the lake. And we can watch the whole thing out *on* the lake in their boat. It's bitchin'. We can stay over. They usually have at least one room available. I already called her today to let her know I was coming. I could let 'em know I'm bringing someone, too. They wouldn't mind." Scott knew he was rambling, but he wanted to sound excited enough to convince him to go.

"What happened to band practice?"

"Just so happens no one wants to practice that weekend. So, tell Howie you're comin' with me. We can leave late Friday night. I don't get off 'til after nine-thirty. But I could head straight out to your place from the restaurant. It's only about an hour and a half away."

"Road trip. Bitchin'. I'll tell him right now."

Ryan told Howard the plan. He listened, then looked at Scott. Ryan was back with him straight away.

"We're there."

Scott pulled another soda from the cooler and cracked it open. "Celebration time," he said as he slurped loudly.

Ryan held up his soda and they touched them together. He whispered so the others wouldn't hear. "Not as good as Jim Beam, but it'll do." Scott grinned, then took another sip.

The day completely faded and only the faintest wisps of red crossed the sky in the west. The mountains obscured them as twilight faded in a cloudless sky. A half-hour later, the fireworks began.

CHAPTER 10

The pleasing scent of cologne wafted into the master bedroom as Howard hummed to himself at the mirror in his bathroom. He had a date tonight. It was seven-thirty and he was just about to take off to meet Krysta at Faraday's. And it was formal since he was wearing a tie. Ryan was leaning against the bathroom doorframe and observed as Howard put the final changes to his hair. They had been talking the last few minutes, but now there was a short silence.

"So, Ryan?"

"Yeah," he answered slowly.

"Has Scott introduced you to any girls around here?"

"Why?" he answered defensively.

"Well, you haven't shown any interest in dating since you got here."

"You're not exactly Don Juan, yourself."

Howard frowned and pointed at Ryan with his comb. "Hey, careful." He added, "I just don't want you to feel left out."

"There'll be so many babes in Parker I won't know which ones to choose."

Howard narrowed his eyes. "Remember to choose wisely." He put the comb down on the edge of the sink.

"Not to worry. I always use protection."

Howard grinned and slid the medicine cabinet mirror shut. Despite the fact it was just the two of them in the house, Ryan felt he had to keep a certain emotional distance with his uncle. He was sure he wasn't going to end up using any of the five condoms he had in his toilet kit bag anytime soon. Nonetheless, he didn't want his uncle to think he didn't have plans.

After Howard left he put a frozen dinner in the microwave. While eating in the big leather recliner he spent the next hour and a half watching music videos at a high volume. He ended up eating two dinners.

The later it became the more excited he got about their road trip. Since he was going with Scott it was somehow even more exciting. It was as if Scott had cast some sort of spell over him. He couldn't get over how much he really liked him. The past week couldn't go fast enough. It had been a long time since he'd experienced this level of exhilaration and anticipation.

*   *   *

It was only a ten-minute drive to Faraday's, but Howard didn't want to feel rushed when he got there, so took his time even more so than normal. Krysta had insisted that she would meet him at the restaurant. He had protested, but she had to watch her sister's baby that evening and wouldn't be able to leave until she got back. He gave in, knowing that this was a one-time thing.

"Hi, Mr. St. Charles," Scott greeted as he came in. "We've got the best table in the house waiting for you," he pointed.

"And I have a nephew at my house waiting for *you.*"

He looked at his watch. "I'm gettin' there."

Howard also looked at his watch as well. "When Krysta gets here let her know where I am."

"Where is she?"

Howard explained her delay.

"Not to worry. I'll personally escort her to the table."

Howard chuckled. "Don't trip her on the way."

Scott wasn't sure what he meant, but saw the smile on his face. He led Howard to the table, handed the menu to him, and he immediately surveyed it.

Elaine had seen Howard, but up until now was too busy to come by. She brought him a wine list and took a moment to talk.

"It's nice to hear that you and Krysta hit it off so well," she said with a big smile. She looked around. "Is she here?"

He briefly waved his hand. "She'll be right along. Family stuff."

"Oh."

"It's going to be nice to finally eat a meal with her. We don't see each other all that often at work since her department's in a different building than mine." He noticed the concerned look on Elaine's face. "Something wrong?"

"It's probably nothing. It's my son."

He watched Scott seat a family across the room. "He looks okay to me. Is he sick?"

She followed Scott with her eyes as he greeted the next guests.

"No, nothing like that. I'm…worried about Ryan's influence on him."

Howard was all too aware of Ryan's bad traits. "Oh, boy. What did he do now?"

She touched his shoulder. "I never pry, Howard. I'm just wondering what kind of boy Ryan is. I think he's putting some strange thoughts in my son's head."

Expecting the worst when Ryan first arrived, Howard was somewhat apprehensive. But he quickly realized that what Ryan needed was direction. He'd known him since he was born, and knew he had been rebellious ever since his parents had died. Since he was rapidly approaching eighteen, any sort of positive influence he felt he could have over him was sure to be useless sooner rather than later. Luckily, Ryan still had a bit of 'follower' in him and could be led, somewhat. After an initial acclamation period Ryan's behavior grew from unruly to at least contained. Yet, Howard was justifiably surprised at Elaine's pronouncement at this point. "That's news."

"Oh?"

"Ryan talks more than he realizes. He thinks Scott has it made. Scott lives at home. He has a wonderful set of parents…who, by the way, are still married.

"Scott's athletic, seems well-connected socially….I can't imagine what kind of *negative* influence my nephew could have on him."

Elaine was taken aback, yet nonetheless welcomed the compliments.

Howard continued and looked a little more thoughtful now. "You know, since he's been running around with Scott he's mellowed quite nicely. He's doing his own dishes, helping around the house more than I expected…doing his own wash. I hope *your* son is like that at home."

Elaine visualized Scott's bedroom. It was usually picked up. Not liking to meddle in his personal life, she let him do what he wanted back there in Steve's old room.

"Well, yes. He has good habits. It's just that lately he seems to be getting a little rambunctious. I'm sorry I thought Ryan was the influence. It must be that band he's involved in."

"Ryan tells me Scott really seems to like it with, what do they call it…?"

"Centauri."

"Centauri. Yeah, in fact he says he's surprised Scott's not majoring in music after high school."

She gestured with a finger. "That's another…" She didn't get to finish. Howard's attention was clearly directed across the room. Scott was leading Krysta to the table. Elaine excused herself although she was annoyed she couldn't complete her thought. Nonetheless, she put on her greeting smile as Scott pulled the chair out for Howard's date.

*   *   *

Just before twilight faded, Ryan opened the blinds on the big picture window in the living room that faced the street. He wanted to be ready as soon as he saw headlights. So far, not a car had come down the street since Howard had left.

It was only nine-fifteen and Scott wasn't going to be there for at least another half hour. For the third time he went through his bag by the door making sure he had everything. He turned off all the lights except the one in the front hall. Now the only lights on in the living room were from the TV and the stereo components in the entertainment center. *Thank God Howie has a satellite dish*, he thought as another music video from one of his favorite bands, *Low Orbit*, came on.

A vehicle slowed to turn, then quickly pulled into the drive. Ryan took a sharp breath then dashed to draw the curtains closed. With a quick flip of the main stereo power switch, the living room was silent. *Damn*, he thought. That was his second favorite music video. He remembered to lower the volume of the receiver this time. Howard had warned him several times already about turning off the stereo with the volume so high.

Scott was on the front porch with a hand poised to ring the bell when Ryan yanked the door open.

Startled, Scott quickly pulled his hand back. "Whoa."

"Saw ya pull up. Ready to boogie?"

"We're gone, dude."

Ryan grabbed his bag and locked the door behind him. He dropped it next to Scott's in the back and jumped in. Soon they passed through Twentynine Palms and headed into the dark of the open desert.

Scott tried to keep it at a steady sixty-five mph. He had a full tank of gas and figured he'd get good mileage at that speed. He wasn't sure what to expect from him this weekend. So far Ryan seemed to be watching himself, almost as if he was thinking carefully about what he would say before he said it. In fact, if Scott could hear over the wind he would swear Ryan was, well, purring.

"You really do need a top for this thing," Ryan said.

"You keep talking about that. Why?"

"What if it rains?"

Scott surveyed the clear, cloudless night. Stars shown brightly, twinkling in the dry desert heat. "Rain? Here?"

"Well, up north."

"Oh."

"Just reminding you."

The dashboard lights shone on Scott's lower body. His skin tone had been completely even for months due to having been outdoors so often from track. His firm thighs and round calves, with his thick, ankle-high socks and running shoes, egged Ryan to stare. Over the last week, he'd been thinking about his fascination with Scott. How he moved, how he looked, with and without his shirt on. Those legs and the way they stuck out of his shorts. His buttocks were perfectly proportioned to the size of his thighs. Again, Ryan let his imagination take control and a growing erection found his attention. He squirmed in the seat and poked his hand into his right pocket to adjust himself.

Scott couldn't help but notice Ryan digging in his pocket. It was too dark, though, so when he glanced over he couldn't see exactly what he was doing. Ryan caught him looking and quickly pulled out a pack of gum that was conveniently in the way of the endeavor.

"Want a piece?"

"Yeah, the biggest one you have." He wasn't going to let any comments get past him. Playing the game to the hilt was the order of the weekend, he decided. He was going to come out to him even if it was the last thing he did on Sunday night. Before that time he was going to hint as much as he could. If he were the first to come out, and if Ryan really were gay after all, maybe he'd come out, too.

"They're all the same size, dumbass."

"Yeah. I want a piece." Scott wanted to answer that he knew they all weren't the same size as he took the proffered stick. In fact, he remembered that Ryan's was thicker than his.

Scott's thoughts drifted as they listened to music. His brother's old car would never have been trusted to go clear across the open desert like this. What a relief that his Jeep was far newer and would assure him safe passage to Parker and eventually to Crescent City.

Only two vehicles passed them before they reached the junction to Highway 177. Between Twentynine Palms and the junction were miles and miles of salt flats from the Sheep Hole dry lakebed. Ryan absent-mindedly studied the light reflecting off chunks of halite along the sides of the road as they flew along. Mixed with dirt and sand, they reflected light from their headlights and from the moon that hovered over the far mountains to the southeast. *How ironic*, he thought, *to be going further into the desert to watch a speedboat race. But, it sure will be nice to get back near water again.*

Scott slowed down as they reached the yellow flashing lights of the junction. The only business there was Keith's 24 Hour Cafe and Truck Stop. They saw only two semis outside and both cabs were unoccupied.

It took only a few moments to pass through the crossroads. More miles of open desert surrounded them. Around a curve to the north, just after they passed over the Colorado Aqueduct for the second time, Ryan spotted four red eyes staring at them from the side of the road up ahead.

"What do you suppose those are?"

"Probably rabid coyotes."

Ryan wasn't sure if he was kidding or not. He knew to be extra careful when he listened to Scott. But he still couldn't quite tell when he was in character and making something up or merely being himself. He unconsciously edged a little closer to the left in his seat as they passed by.

Further on, Scott saw the fourth pair of headlights he'd seen so far on their trek in his rearview mirror. The others had either only followed for a short while and fell way behind him, or had long ago passed them. As the vehicle approached, he also saw the distinctive glow of fog lights lower to the ground. It was going fast and was soon going to overtake them. It turned out to be a large pick-up truck. It flashed its lights to pass and Scott slowed a little. Ryan watched as it started by.

In the bed of the truck sat two young bikini clad women in their mid-twenties and two guys about the same age wearing swim trunks. They sat in as much of a circle as they could muster on their squat lawn chairs. Three other people were in the spacious cab; its back window was slid open.

The pickup was pulling a long sleek black speedboat with the number '57' written in huge white numerals on the side. Various speed boating brand names were written along the side. Ryan surmised they might be contenders for tomorrow's competition.

He held onto the roll bar and rose up to see what was the center of attention in the bed of the truck. It was a cooler. He noticed beer bottles in everyone's hands.

"They're partyin'. Check 'em out," he said as he pointed.

Scott glanced over at the silly grins on their faces. Discovered now, they held up their beers in a mock toast.

Ryan yelled across Scott, "PAR-DY!"

He heard them whoop and they all took a swig. One of the girls wearing a bright yellow bikini top pointed to her upheld beer with a questioning look on her face. Ryan threw up his hands, indicating they had none. She quickly stuck her face in the window and spoke to the driver who looked back briefly and nodded. Scott wondered why the driver hadn't passed him yet: they were still in the oncoming lane. In fact the pick-up was slowing just enough to match Scott's speed now. He didn't see the girl gesture to Ryan and started to speed up.

"Hey, wait." Ryan said. "I think we're getting some party goods!"

She leaned over and lifted the lid of the cooler, pulled out four beers, and slid them into a wrinkled grocery bag. Ryan stuck his fingers in his mouth and let out a loud whistle.

Scott held a palm to his ear. "Hey, not in my ear!"

She stepped over to the side of the bed. Ryan climbed into the back, stepping over their belongings. Scott glanced over just as he had one leg in back in time to get an eyeful of crotch. It was only a split second but worth it, he thought.

He reached across the chasm, hanging onto the roll bar as she handed the bag over to him. She shouted something, but it was drowned out by the wind. He yelled a thanks and the pick-up immediately sped up. He clutched the bag as if gold were inside, carefully making his way back to his seat.

"They're all mine," he said with a wide smile. Scott frowned and looked at the bag. "Just kidding, my boy," he added as he opened the bag and took two out. He cracked one open and sat it on Scott's bare thigh. Scott smiled widely and held up the beer in a toast to the fast receding pickup. A cold beer in the hot desert night was going to hit the spot nicely. Ryan was still incredulous at their bounty. "Who would 'a thought?"

"Too cool, I say."

"Well, we have to root for '57' tomorrow."

"If we see them. Unless you're in one of the official's boats, or in a balloon it's almost impossible to see all the boats. Mostly, you hear a bunch of noise. It's the good kinda noise. Makes your dick hard."

"That's the kind of noise I like."

Scott took a couple of swallows and sat his beer between his legs. "See, I can already imagine the sound now," he said as he looked at the bottle.

Ryan took a swig and glanced at Scott's crotch. Scott wondered how many more ways he could play with his mind. One way or another he was going to say it. If he could just muster up enough courage to just do it he'd be a lot happier. So far, every time he thought of doing it the direct way, his heart pounded too much and he just couldn't.

The next sign they saw said 'Parker 15 Miles' when Ryan put the second set of empties in the bag. A little after midnight, in the little town of Earp, they saw the last sign: Parker 2 miles.

"I've never been to Arizona," Ryan said offhandedly.

"It's the real southwest. Cowboys…"

"…And cowgirls."

Scott frowned and looked at him. "Rodeos, and loud speedboats hauling giant rooster tails on the lake."

"You can forget the rodeos."

"Yeah, I don't really like rodeos either."

As they approached the bridge, the air temperature dropped slightly. The smell of water was thick in the air here and it brought a sigh to Ryan as he was reminded of back home.

After passing through the inspection station on the Arizona side, Scott turned north, now parallel with the river to his left. He took a short blacktopped road a few miles further and came up to a tall Victorian style house. Ryan could just see the black stretch of the river beyond it. Huge willows and eucalyptus trees grew in two straight rows, one to the left of the driveway and the other on the far side of the property line. Both rows extended all the way to the river. An engraved sign that read "*Atcher House Bed and Breakfast*" was attached to posts driven into the ground at the head of the drive. Across the water, lights from people's backyards were all up and down the length of the visible stretch of the river.

The Atcher's house was two stories tall and quite deep. It seemed to have plenty of rooms, Ryan surmised, from the amount of windows he could see. They pulled up in back where he spied three separate smaller buildings. Two of them were cottages, which faced each other across a gravel drive just up from a boat launch and pier. A third looked like a large shed. A wide carport was behind the house. Four cars were parked in the gravel lot.

Scott pulled up next to the carport and shut off the engine. A streetlight on the driveway illuminated a large area of the drive. The smell of water from their proximity to the river was thick in the air. The main house was dark upstairs, but there was light coming from the window of a side entrance.

"I guess we got here too late for 'em," Ryan said listening to the silence.

"They're probably all out partyin'. Not to worry, I got a key."

With Ryan in tow, Scott inserted it into the lock of the side entrance door. They walked into a spacious kitchen. He flipped on a light switch and two overhead lights illuminated the space. The big island in the center had a deep double bowl sink, a funky modern-looking faucet, and plenty of counter space. The top of the counter was finished with undulating Mexican tile that contrasted with the plain gray floor tile in wild colors. A sealed envelope at the end of the counter said 'Scott' in greatly embellished letters. He tore one of the ends open and out slid a key with a note.

It read, "*Make yourself at home, Scott. We'll be up early tomorrow for the first heat. Take the big cottage tonight. Hope you and your friend sleep well.—Aunt Cin.*"

Scott wondered why they gave them the cottage instead of a smaller room, but didn't think twice about it. "Awesome, we get one of the cottages." He turned around in time to see Ryan yawn, which made him yawn too.

The bigger of the two cottages had a peaked roof with wood shingles. It was painted yellow, except for the white window sashes and shutters. Ryan opened the screen door; its spring rang as he did so. Scott unlocked the door and they went in. A single light from a lamp between two double beds illuminated the space. A small window air conditioner was on low and the room temperature was a pleasant change from the outside air.

A small round table with two chairs was against a partition separating the small kitchenette from the sleeping area. The kitchenette contained a row of miniature appliances and the entire bathroom was tiled, even the ceiling.

Scott dropped his bag on one bed and Ryan dropped his on the other. He saw the note on the table next to the lamp and read it aloud, '*Cookies in the fridge. Enjoy.*' The refrigerator was empty except for the covered plate of cookies. Ryan pulled the chilled plate out. "Hey, check it out."

Scott bit into one. "She knows how much I love her homemade coconut chocolate chip cookies"

Ryan set the plate on the counter in the kitchenette. "Coconut. My favorite." They both devoured several before another yawn overcame him.

"I'm fallin' asleep. I was having a hard time staying awake the last twenty miles."

"Wimp."

"I'm crashin'."

"Wimp," Scott said again.

"You can stay awake all night if you want." He took another cookie. Part of it stuck out of his mouth as he crunched it and started pulling clothes out of his bag.

Scott went to the bathroom as Ryan undressed. When he came back out Ryan was already down to his underwear, his clothes piled on the table.

Scott was glad to see a bed as well. He had been up early, worked all day, then drove nonstop. It was time to find dreamland. He pulled the covers down and slid in.

Ryan hit the bathroom, too. His eyes quickly adjusted to the dark after he came back. He propped his pillow up against the headboard and listened to the quiet sound of the air conditioner. In the soft light from the streetlight in the parking lot, he could see Scott's face. He looked so cute. His arm, outside the covers, the blanket up to his pecs, and the look of Scott's bicep, flexed by the position of his arm, made him long to tell him how he felt about him. *God, if only Scott would let me sleep with him. No,* he thought again, as he looked away. *That wouldn't work at all. Scott wouldn't understand.* Ryan slid the pillow down and lay back. The sound of the air conditioner was so soothing he didn't remember falling asleep.

Chapter 11

"Hey, it's morning," Ryan heard.

"Liar."

He opened his eyes as he heard Scott start the shower. His pulse was quickened by the distant sound of a turbo motor prop coming from the direction of the river.

Later, Scott came out of the bathroom in shorts, his hair still wet. Ryan hadn't gotten out of bed yet. "Hurry up. There'll be a big breakfast in the kitchen."

Ryan pulled himself out from under the sheet and was in and out of the shower in five minutes. When they were both done, they went in the house. Two more cars had pulled up overnight and one from last night that had a boat trailer attached was already gone.

Cinnamon was in the kitchen and greeted them right away. Ryan noticed that she had a vague resemblance to Scott's mother. Her hair was dark red like Scott's, she had an almost even brown tone to her skin, and some scattered freckles here and there. She was a few inches shorter than Scott and had a great figure for a woman Ryan guessed was in her late forties. Her shorts looked expensive, her light cotton pullover shirt was loose fitting, and she wore tennis shoes with short pink socks.

"Give me a kiss, you handsome young man!" She grasped Scott's shoulder, and then pulled him to her to hug him. They swung back and forth a couple of times as they hugged. Her high energy level made Ryan wonder if she was full of caffeine or if she was naturally that way.

Ryan raised his hand and waved self-consciously. "Hi. I'm Ryan."

She pulled away, took his hand, and greeted him warmly. "Nice to meet you. Any friend of Scott's is a friend of ours. Did you sleep okay?"

Ryan could already tell he would like her. He sniffed the air. "Yeah, but I could do with some of that coffee."

She led them in, as they were still standing at the door. "Right over here." On the far counter, a half-full pot of coffee sat in the brewer. Several upside-down coffee cups, none matching, sat on a wicker and bamboo tray.

Scott poured for them as Greg, Scott's uncle, came through the Dutch door from the dining room. He looked younger than her, Ryan noted. He was tall, and well tanned. His wide smile was noticeable right away. His short dark hair was complete with a balding spot on the crown, though not a hint of gray graced his head. He sported shorts, a thick pullover polo shirt, and old beat up tennis shoes. Despite his dress, he had the air of a successful executive.

Scott introduced Greg to Ryan who asked him to call him by his first name. "Sure, Greg. You should talk to *my* uncle. He wants me to use 'Uncle' when I address him."

Greg chuckled. "Can you guys stay all weekend?"

Scott added cream to his coffee and stirred. "We don't leave 'til Sunday night."

"Great, I look forward to it. As I'm sure you both will."

A young girl came in and put some dishes on the counter next to the sink. Behind her, a little shorter and younger, was her sister. They giggled excitedly and hugged Scott.

Scott introduced Ryan to them. "This is my cousin Michelle. She's ten. This is her sister Becky. She's seven."

She slapped his arm as she twisted back and forth a couple of times. "And a half."

Scott corrected himself. "And a half," he said with great exaggeration.

They said hello to Ryan and giggled to each other again. Scott could tell they thought he was cute. He knew their giggle quite well.

Snatches of conversations by the guests in the dining room drifted into the kitchen as they talked. Cin went back and forth between the boys and the other guests as she took donuts, milk, fruit, cereal, and other breakfast foods to them. There was much talk among the couples and the various kids staying there about the upcoming day on the lake.

Breakfast lasted another half-hour while Greg stood in the kitchen and made small talk with Ryan about his job at AeroSun. Scott listened, not really all that interested. He wanted to be off to the lake.

Cin came back into the kitchen for the last time and announced it was time to go. "You boys can either go with us or take your car."

Scott stood up. "Mine's the Jeep."

Greg picked up a gym bag of clothes from the floor next to the refrigerator. "You got it? How's it drive?"

"Perfect. In fact, I'm taking it up to the redwoods later this summer."

"Vacation?" Cin asked.

"Kinda." He looked over at Ryan. "His birthday's a week after mine and he's from up there. So we're going up for his birthday party."

Scott showed them the Jeep and gave more detail about going up to Crescent City later that summer.

"That's quite the haul," Greg indicated.

"But it's smooth sailing," Ryan replied.

Scott wondered for a moment about how accurate that statement was. But the more Ryan said it the more reassuring it sounded.

Greg patted the roll bar. "We need to get the girls ready. You can go on ahead if you want since you know the way. Oh, and Jeanine will probably be at the café, so you might see her there." Scott recalled the girl who had a crush on him last year.

"How would you know that?"

"We hired her on for the summer and I happen to know that she has the afternoon off," he explained with a grin. Scott hadn't seen her for a year despite having visited three times since last summer.

The boys went on ahead, passing dozens of cars parked along the main roads. Crowds of people of all ages were going from store to store in the small, quaint downtown area. The waterfront boardwalk along the river was also lined with shops, some accessible by pulling a boat right up to the many docks strategically placed along the walk. More people were all around that area as well. They by-passed the downtown area and went several miles further north past the dam. A narrow, winding, canyon road, devoid of any greenery except for palmettos that grew in the ditches, led them to the entrance of the marina. From there a huge parking lot came into view.

The lot was already nearly full and half-clad people were everywhere. Ryan could see this was an extremely popular event

"Something like fifteen hundred people come here for the weekend." Scott saw Ryan's eyes grow wide.

He parked near one end of the parking lot, not caring if they had a long walk to the marina. At the far end of it was the large, blue aluminum-sided marina shop. Ryan reached underneath his seat for last night's empty beer bottles as they came to a stop. He took the bag. "This reeks."

There was row after row of *Port-A-Johns* along one edge of the parking lot. A couple of trash bins with slanted open doors stood nearby. As they passed one of the bins, he pitched the empties with a basketball-style jump shot. He was glad he had mirrored sunglasses as they continued along the sidewalk. He knew none of the guys they passed could tell he was checking them out.

The marina's air-conditioned shop sold the standard fare of hotdogs and hamburgers, and was complete with a gas station out back on two piers. Along several long, floating T-shaped moors were docked large pleasure boats, houseboats, and various fishing boats.

Weaving in and out of the crowd, they finally reached an open cafe that faced the water. Ryan placed his sunglasses on his head. He noticed the stark contrast between the brown desert and the deep blue-green of the lake. "This place is too cool."

Scott was busy looking for Jeanine. He saw someone who could have passed for her sister, and wondered about it as they approached.

"Scott!"

He turned to face the voice. "Jeanine?" Her face was radiant, without the pudgy cheeks he remembered. Her hair was sun-bleached to a fine light sand color. Her teeth were brilliant white now. He couldn't see them that well before due to braces. *And those boobs!* he thought She really changed in the last year. "Wow. Jeanine, you've, well, you're differ-ent."

"Uh, I'll take that as a compliment?"

"Yeah, of course." He pointed. "This is my friend Ryan."

"Hi," he said, noting Scott was surprised at seeing her.

"Hi." She saw a customer waving a five-dollar bill. "Oh, just a minute." She ran off to help her.

Ryan jabbed Scott in the arm. "You didn't say you knew hot babes here!"

Scott was confused. "I don't, well, I mean…"

She returned rather quickly. "Dr. Pepper or something?"

"No thanks, we're waiting for my aunt and uncle."

"I'm getting out of here in about fifteen minutes. I guess I'll see you guys out on the lake."

"Yeah, we're supposed to meet up with you later."

"My mom and dad are waiting for me on the boat. Hey, here come the Atchers." She pointed as Scott's aunt and uncle came through the crowd along the boardwalk. As they gathered, and Jeanine left again to help another customer, Scott spoke with Cinnamon.

"I don't remember Jeanine looking so, well, fine," Scott told her as she stood near him.

She grinned and winked at him. "We'll see her and her boyfriend later."

Ryan heard it all, especially the part about the boyfriend. He looked at Scott. "Too bad she's going out with someone, huh?"

Cin was occupied with Michelle now, but nonetheless overheard the comment. Until now, she didn't know how to surmise Scott's relationship with him. Now she realized they were just friends. "And, the only way we can see them is if we get onto the lake ourselves," she said as she looked back at the boys.

Ryan was able to recognize their houseboat right away as they approached it. On the stern, it said 'Atcher House II' in the same stylized letters as on the sign in the driveway.

Becky and Michelle ran up ahead and jumped onboard. Soon they were all aboard, untied from the dock, and were off.

An armada of different boats hugged the shore and made their way up the narrow, watery canyon to the wider parts of the lake. They entered the lane of traffic and the boys sat on the upper deck in lounge chairs.

Ryan pulled up his sunglasses to look around at the people on the boats surrounding them. "This is the life," he said.

Scott leaned back some more. "That's why I visit as often as I can."

Ryan pulled off his t-shirt and smeared a line of green zinc oxide onto his nose. The contrasting florescent green to his tanned torso urged Scott to keep his eyes off, lest they wander too much. Ryan proceeded to put sunscreen on his legs and arms, then worked on his chest. Scott adjusted his chair, trying not to stare, as Ryan worked the lotion into his skin.

Greg was at the helm, just in view of the deck opening below them. Cin looked up the opening at them, then climbed the stairs to join them. She sat on one of the padded seats at starboard and directed her question to Ryan. "Nice, huh?"

"I'll say. I could stay all summer."

"We'd have to put you to work if you stayed that long."

He poured more lotion onto his palm and started on his neck. "If this is the work, I'll take it."

She grinned at him. "Here, let me get your back."

He shot a glance toward Scott who was busy spreading oxide onto his lips and nose.

She squeezed some of the lotion out and wiped her hands together. Working slowly, she completely covered his back. It had been such a long time since he'd been touched by anyone and suddenly he missed Crawford. *How can I possibly miss him*, he wondered. Nonetheless, he relished her gentle touch. When she was done, his nipples were hard. He missed the feeling. Every time Crawford had caressed him, even a little, his nipples got hard, too.

Scott was still occupied with his own endeavor. He turned the zinc oxide jar top over to its shiny side to see if he could make out the line on his nose and the two he placed under his eyes, then placed his sunglasses back on.

"Your turn, clown," Cin said, observing his nose.

"Sure."

She spread lotion onto his neck and worked it down his back too. Ryan looked on in fascination. It was such a simple thing and yet it was a turn-on to watch her, though it wasn't about watching her. It was about watching him. He felt a little jealous that it was her doing the touching him, and not him. He wanted her to move out of the way so he could take over. He felt a stir in his swim trunks signaling that it was time to stop fantasizing.

In the distance, a noisy speedboat engine grabbed everyone's attention. Greg called up from below about finding a good place to stop further on and pointed out the marker buoys.

Cin pointed up ahead to the boys. "There'll be a cluster of boats up there. It generally turns into a party, so get your crazy-hats on."

Soon they slowed, then coasted to an area near a cone-shaped spire
sticking out of the water some distance from shore. Trampled paths
were cut into its squat sandstone structure from past antics. Some kids
were already perched on it, but most of the people were still in their
boats. Several clusters of boats of all configurations were tied off nearby
with their anchors cast.

Cin called down to Greg. "The Baumanns are up ahead to port." He
shaded his eyes as she pointed the direction. He navigated slowly to the
tall white double-decker houseboat. He coasted perfectly until they
were alongside. Scott wondered how they had gotten ahead of them,
then spied Jeanine in the back on a chaise. The Baumann's were
Jeanine's parents. He figured the guy beside her was her boyfriend.

She stood and waved from the rail. "Hey, you guys."

Greg tossed a rope to Dr. Baumann and in no time, their boats were
one floating platform. They unlatched the rail gates and everyone was
able to go back and forth between the two boats.

Jeanine introduced the boys to her boyfriend Ken, and the other
older couples on board. Ryan learned that Dr. Baumann was one of
three dentists in town and the other couples were in medicine in some
fashion or another. He looked around, feeling uncomfortable now. He
realized that he and Scott were the only people either without a date or
not married. He wondered if Scott was concerned about it as well. *What
the fuck*, he thought, *at least I'm having a good time.*

After all introductions were made, everyone settled back to watch
what they could of the speedboats as they screamed past. There were
several officials' boats with their bullhorns all along the route, one of
which was near them. The race had full TV coverage on a local channel
via an overhead blimp, and the Baumann's miniature television provided information they couldn't glean from their vantage. From lake
level, Ryan couldn't tell if it was a race or just random boats speeding
past. Whatever was actually happening, the event seemed like good rea-

son to party and socialize despite his initial awkward feeling around all the people he didn't know.

Cin finally got to speak to Scott alone while on the lower deck of the Baumann's boat.

"Scott, Ryan seems a little lost without you. Maybe you should go back up and be with him."

Scott looked at him leaning on the upper railing. Ryan had the binoculars up to his face scanning the water up ahead. Scott turned back to speak to her. "Sometimes I think he's *completely* lost."

"How's that?"

"I wanna hang out with him 'cause he's cute…but he's such a butt sometimes…I don't know why I bother."

"Sounds to me that you do like him or you wouldn't be so concerned. Maybe there's a connection you haven't seen yet." She changed the subject. "Does he have a girlfriend?"

"No."

"Well, maybe he needs to find one."

"Maybe he needs a boyfriend."

"Scott."

"I have my suspicions."

"I think you're projecting."

"Maybe. Maybe I should just ask him and get it over with."

"Ask him what?"

"You know, if he's…"

"Now why would you do that?" She was sure now that Scott was indeed projecting.

"I have my reasons," he repeated.

"Don't do anything that doesn't feel right."

"I know. *'First Rule of the Heart,'* like you keep reminding me."

"Well, don't forget it. Plus, I wouldn't just up and ask a friend something like that unless I had a really good reason. You don't want to insult him."

"I don't think it would be an insult."

"Well, anyway, isn't it wonderful how there's so many textures to a friendship? Sometimes we don't know why we like people. Sometimes we don't need to know. A friendship is like a chrysalis sometimes."

"A what?"

"You know. What caterpillars turn into before they're butterflies."

"Oh. Yeah. What are you saying?"

"Maybe you're in the chrysalis stage. Some friendships have to develop first. Sometimes they take a while, but when they emerge they're different and full of energy."

"I feel like I'm in a washing machine, on an extended spin cycle," he said with exaggeration.

She laughed cheerfully. "Well, who knows? Maybe someone's going to raise the lid soon." She smiled and massaged his shoulders briefly.

Hours later the competition was finally over for the day. They never saw 'Number 57' from last night, though they had scoured the water with and without the binoculars quite a few times.

Ryan thought the party was ending, but he was mistaken. Most of the louder boats passed and were gone from the racing lane. That was the signal for the spectators' boats to spread out and tie off in other locations. The Baumann's untied from the Atcher's boat and they maneuvered closer to the pointed rock. Once close enough, they dropped anchors and retied back together. Now the people on the rocky pinnacle were jumping, diving and being pushed into the water and climbing back up to do it again. Scott invited everyone to join him for a swim, a climb, then a jump from the spire. He dove headlong into the dark water.

Ryan, Jeanine, and Ken joined in moments later. The adults watched while Becky and Michelle, wearing their bright orange life jackets, ate frozen pops onboard.

They spent almost an hour horsing around with other kids and younger adults on the somewhat cone-shaped rock. The boys attempted to dislodge each other from it by pulling, pushing, and using their weight against each other. Each in turn would follow through and they'd go tumbling in.

On more than one occasion Ryan was sure his penis was going to spring to life if he didn't dive in. Scott wanted several times to pull Ryan toward him and take him in his arms. Instead, when the urge to do so came up he pushed harder to make him tumble in.

Late in the afternoon Cin announced that they had made sandwiches to go along with the other picnic food they had brought. They swam as fast as they could to the boats. Breathless and exhausted from their hours of exertion, they ate voraciously.

Jeanine invited the boys to a party later that evening at one of her friend's houses. She told them to be there no earlier than 10 p.m. Cin said she knew where the street was and would give them directions later. The Atchers, Baumanns, and the other adults made plans to meet later that night at a local watering hole.

As they headed back, Cin watched Ryan's eyes as she leaned against the railing astern. She'd noticed the almost constant attention he had been giving Scott most of the day. How he stared at Scott and drank in what he saw. In her mind, she replayed the intensity of their horseplay on the rock earlier—the constant grabbing, pulling, pushing, and general roughhousing they did. Not familiar with anyone who was gay except Scott, and some of the kids she had counseled many years back, she nonetheless figured Scott must have figured it out: Ryan was gay after all. *Funny*, she thought. *I wonder why I didn't notice that before.* The more she observed, the more she was sure. He sure seems moved by the male figure, especially Scott's. *Enough of this*, she thought. *If Scott's friend is gay, that's fine.*

She readjusted her sunhat. "Oh, Scott, I forgot to tell you this morning. The big cottage is rented for tonight. I'll need you guys to move your things to the small one."

"No problemo. We'll do it as soon as we get back."

The way back was choppy as they passed through the wakes of dozens of other boats. The constant rocking must have done the trick since the little girls were asleep below when they finally returned to the marina. The long day in the sun was ending as clouds came in and darkened the water. *It looks like it might actually rain*, Ryan thought. *That would be a relief. I haven't seen rain in over two months. I feel like I'm going through withdrawal.*

After everyone had disembarked, they finally made it back to the house a short time afterward.

Cin gave Scott a key to the small cottage. The maids had already changed the sheets and their bags were inside the front door when they returned to the larger one. From the outside the smaller one looked similar to the other one, only was half its length. Inside there was a single queen-sized bed, a tiny kitchenette, and a tiny dining table. The bathroom was half as big as the other one, with just a shower stall instead of a full bathtub and shower combination.

"There's only one bed," Ryan said.

Scott laid his bag on it. "Wow, you can count."

"Fuck you."

"Maybe," he said, not paying much attention to him as he unzipped his bag.

Ryan bit his lip as he deposited his bag on the other side of the bed. Crawford's bed was this size. It was comfortable, that was for sure. He sat on it and it bounced only slightly. And his bed felt this firm, too.

Scott pulled clothes out of his bag. "Did you get the cookies from the fridge?"

"I ate 'em all."

"*All* of 'em?"

"Just kidding." He pulled the plate out of the bag and took off the plastic wrap. "I saved 'em for us." He offered the plate to Ryan after popping one into his mouth.

None of his friends in Crescent City would have bothered to save the cookies. Scott did. He was almost positive now he never really liked his old friends. Maybe Muh was right about those guys after all. In fact, it was beginning to become obvious that none of his friends back home even came close to being, well, nice, like Scott.

Ryan's hair was a mess. He wetted then re-combed it in the bathroom as Cin knocked, and stepped inside.

"Hi. Just making sure the air conditioner was working." She went to the window and turned it on medium. She looked out the top of the window to the far hills past the river. "The Weather Channel said it might just rain tonight. I hope there's not much wind on the lake tomorrow or it'll be choppy for the heats. Just in case it actually does rain, I would pull your Jeep under the carport. I'll have Greg move the van before you boys get back tonight. Oh, and dinner's almost ready."

Ryan looked at him. "See, it does rain here."

Scott furrowed his brow. "Yeah, sometimes it does," he said, thinking about how much a top would cost for the vehicle.

They hurried and shortly afterward entered the house through the kitchen.

Cin made the crispiest fried chicken Ryan had ever eaten. There was also squash, which he usually found repulsive, and spinach linguine with an Alfredo sauce.

"I don't think I've ever had squash that I liked. But this is an exception," Ryan commented.

"We grew it out back. That's the only way to have squash, if you ask me. Then there's cinnamon," Cin said.

"Yep, you're a good cook." Ryan took another bite.

She grinned. "Actually, I meant the spice."

He chuckled, finished off his helping before scooping more onto his plate.

The girls made faces at each other and whispered comments about how cute Ryan was. He overheard them and tried to tickle Becky, who was closest, a couple of times. He felt so at home. The environment culled memories of a long time ago. Memories full of bad times to be sure, but right now the good ones were on the surface.

CHAPTER 12

Cin gave them directions to the Jeanine's friend's house and shortly before 10 p.m., they took off. It was completely cloudy now and the wind had picked up, but it wasn't yet raining, and it hadn't gotten much cooler. The wind buffeted them as they slowly rode among the rest of the partygoers through the small downtown area.

They slowed as they came to a freshly blacktopped residential street. They found a parking space near the very end. The street seemed brand new; there were only six houses on their side. Two across the street were in various stages of construction. One had pallets of bricks in front and the other looked only recently framed on its cement slab.

It was obvious where the party was. Music blared from the backyard as they approached. The driveway to the house was jammed with several four-wheel drive trucks. Two were on huge tires, with roll bars, fog lights, and other accouterments. A dozen other cars were parked close by on both sides of the street. They could feel the bass beat of the music now.

"Jeez, heavy metal," Ryan said. Right away didn't want to stay too long.

"Hmm, whatever." Scott didn't mind heavy metal music all that much but wasn't something he would have chosen for a party. "At least they'll have beer. Maybe we can slip some of the right kind of music into the CD changer."

Walking along the side of the house they reached the backyard to see several Tiki lamps lit along the perimeter of a wide octagonal shaped bricked back porch. It was packed with people. Most of the backyard was filled with a good-sized swimming pool that was surrounded by a wide concrete walkway. The speakers were near the pool, and as they made their way into the house through the back door, the music was almost as loud inside from more speakers.

From the kitchen, Jeanine saw them. "Hey guys. Glad you could come. There's plenty of beer and other stuff outside." She was dressed in a skimpy bikini bottom with a short t-shirt over her top that said 'River Rat' on the front. An airbrushed speedboat was in the background with a humanized rat holding a huge frothy beer in an oversized mug.

"Hey, where'd you get the shirt?" Ryan asked.

She held out the bottom of it so he could see the entire design. Her cleavage disappeared for a moment as he looked at it. "We sell 'em at the shop. Most are already gone since there are so many people here. If you want one I'll keep one back for you."

"Large. In blue or green."

"I know we have some in those colors." In a flash, she was off to the back porch with a two-liter bottle of cola. Scott hung around with Ryan most of the time. Jeanine was quite the social butterfly, barely stopping long enough to talk to them, but nonetheless introduced a couple of guys and girls to them. Both of them felt out of place though since the party seemed to be quite cliquish as the evening progressed.

The music never stopped and the selected type seemed only to have loud screeching guitars, which no one else seemed to mind except Ryan. After another hour, it started to give him a headache. He pressed on his temples for the second time, trying to stave off the pain, when they heard yelling by the pool. Scott looked through the crowd to see what was going on, and poked Ryan in the side to get his attention. Two guys were launching verbal salvos at each other. They were both big, very drunk, and ready to fight.

Scott looked at Ryan, remembering the incident back home. "That guy in the car at the drive-in back in Yucca Valley could have been that guy."

"But he wasn't. And he wasn't drunk. And he backed off."

"I don't think either of them are going to."

It was inevitable. The characters were well lubed from the nearly empty keg. A few people watched as the two guys swung at each other while one of the girls attempted to keep them apart. But, unfortunately, she was just about as looped as they were and failed. Scott was sure one of them would end up in the pool. Someone must have called the police because only minutes later a cop car arrived and parked out front. He saw the blue and red flashing lights reflecting off the back fence and sparse shrubbery.

"Ditch the beer," Scott said as he dumped his over the rail.

Ryan clutched his cup a little tighter. "What for!"

"The cops are here and we're not legal."

"We're close enough."

"Yeah, tell *them* that. Plus I don't need my uncle to have to bail us out."

It took only a second for Ryan to mull it over. The cops already had his license in California. If he were busted for underage drinking out of state, he'd be screwed. No, another spot on his record should be reserved for something more worth it. He reluctantly agreed. "Let's just go. My head hurts anyway."

Scott thought about the previous headache Ryan had given himself, back on the campout. "Wimp."

"Fuck you."

He wasn't going to let anything get by now and looked him directly in the eye. "That's the second time you've said that tonight. You'll have to wait till we get back."

Was that an invitation, Ryan thought. *How am I ever going to figure him out?*

Scott saw him hesitate. "Come on, let's go," he ordered. Just as he said that, one of the two big guys ended up in the pool with a huge splash. It was the perfect cover as contained chaos started to break out.

They sneaked around one side of the house and crouched down by some of the shrubs. The cop car's front tires were on the rocky yard with its lights still swirling around. That was clearly not the right direction to go. He led Ryan along the fence to the neighbor's backyard, where they stopped. Scott checked out the situation, then decided to take advantage of the darkness, sticking to the remaining backyards, as he led them up the street in the direction of the Jeep. No one had seen them and they finally got in and started up the vehicle. The cops were still in the backyard as they drove past the front of the house.

"I can't imagine how Jeanine's gonna get out of that one," Scott said. "I bet we'd 've be busted for sure," he added.

"That would suck."

Scott grinned. "But it would feel really good, wouldn't it?"

Ryan didn't reply. That was another comment Scott had managed to get away with.

Now, closer to downtown, cars were everywhere, even though it was well after midnight. He had to be extra careful to avoid the revelers. In another fifteen minutes, they were through town and back to the quiet street along the river to the bed and breakfast. He parked under the carport. As they headed across the gravel to the little cottage, they saw two men and two women come out of the larger cottage. The driver jiggled his keys as he spoke to the others. They all got in a car parked at the door and drove away. Except for the crickets nearer the river, all now was quiet.

Once inside, Ryan swallowed a couple of aspirin, and shed his shirt and shorts, leaving him in only his underwear. As Scott pulled his shorts off, his underwear came down a little in the back, revealing the delineation of his tan and the pale skin below his waist. Ryan watched as he pulled up on the waistband. They pulled the covers down simultaneously and Ryan turned out the light as they slid in.

He faced outboard trying to stay as far as possible from Scott. Scott did the same, prying into the shadows of his clothes hanging on the chair next to the bed. In just a few minutes he fell asleep. Shortly after, so did Ryan.

Thunder rolled somewhere in the distance. It woke Scott up. He realized the storm must have made it their way after all. An instant later, he realized another thing: Ryan's arm was touching his. His regular breathing was steady and rhythmic, telling him Ryan was still asleep. Scott had already started getting hard. All the scenarios he'd imagined about he and Ryan together all these weeks would come true if he took a dare now. His imagination started going full blast.

Slowly he turned to his side. Ryan was on his back and didn't move at all. A flash of lightening outside briefly illuminated his face. His lips were just barely parted and his eyes were still closed. Scott desperately wanted to kiss him.

As he adjusted his position a little more, Ryan, still asleep, turned and faced away from him. After a moment's hesitation, Scott steadily shifted his body and finally was able to slowly slide his left arm under Ryan's pillow. His heart was racing now, and it was difficult to keep his breath steady. He continued to inch closer and molded his body to Ryan's, pressing his penis against his rear. He slowly rested his other hand on Ryan's side. Ryan's body was warm and his skin was so soft Scott felt he might melt with emotion. His erection pulsated with his rapid heartbeats as he slowly pressed in more tightly. He ran his hand down to Ryan's waistband and rested it there. Now he could smell Ryan's hair. It smelled vaguely like the lake, but another scent was stronger, though not overpowering. He was sure it was Ryan himself, his skin, a slight armpit smell, the smell of pure boy. Scott took in a slow deep breath to inhale as much of the scent as he could. He didn't think it was possible for his penis to get any harder, but he thought it had now.

Another flash of lightening and the thunder was a little closer. It pealed louder and rattled one of the windowpanes. This time it woke Ryan up. The first thing he realized was that an arm was under his neck beneath his pillow. He felt Scott's fingers as they flexed slightly on his hip. Scott was pressing him from behind. Adrenaline shot through Ryan's veins, causing a sharp breath to involuntarily lurch his body.

Scott felt the sudden breath but kept his hand on Ryan's hip. It was a wonderful fantasy but hadn't Ryan ignored every hint he'd given him over the last several weeks? Scott was sure that the problem was that hinting just wasn't the answer. The direct approach was the only way and he knew it. He decided finally to simply tell him the next morning and be done with it.

Ryan opened his eyes. Just a crack at first, then all the way, trying to determine if Scott was awake, or whether he was doing this in his sleep. He was rapidly getting hard now and he needed to adjust the confined angle of his penis in his tight underwear. But he didn't want to make any purposeful moves until he could determine if Scott were awake or not. In the next instant the deliberate movements of Scott's hand and head told him the truth. He was very awake.

The craving he felt inside was overwhelming. He had been trying to deny everything as much as he could: what Scott had been hinting about himself to Ryan, how he felt about Scott, everything. *I am so stupid*! The feelings were mutual and he knew it even through his constant denial. He hoped he wasn't too late as he quickly rolled over to look Scott right in the eye in the dim light.

The sudden turn startled Scott. The look on his face was of complete surprise. Ryan laid his hand on Scott's chest and pressed his palm against it.

Scott found that he had lost his voice and could only whisper. "Fuck, I'm sorry…"

Ryan sounded breathless as he whispered. "God, Scott, I've wanted to do this for weeks."

Scott managed to get his voice back. "Y-you what?"

Ryan didn't answer him. Instead he pulled him in close and planted his lips against his. Scott thought he would ignite on fire from the sudden surge of adrenaline that engulfed his body. While Ryan kissed, he slowly turned Scott onto his back so that he could lay directly on top of him. Scott could feel Ryan's rock hard penis pressing against his own.

He let Ryan take the lead for a long moment. Finally, needing to catch his breath, he pushed Ryan up a bit. "Oh, my God!" he said aloud, not believing it. Finally, he had been kissed by a boy!

Ryan rose up on his knees to Scott's side. The sheet that had been over them floated to the side. He took Scott's waistband in his hands and slowly pulled them off. Scott lifted up his hips to assist him, then moved Ryan onto his back and pulled his underwear off as well, not believing he was copying Ryan's actions so smoothly. In seconds, they were entwined in each other's arms again, mouths locked, while Ryan gave Scott a deep French kiss. Scott was sure his heart would explode from excitement as Ryan's warm chest touched his. They pressed their groins together, their hips undulating as their tongues explored each other's mouths in long passionate kisses. In a few moments, their breath had a sweet, musky odor as their saliva combined.

Scott almost felt like crying. He mind almost screamed it. *Why did I wait so long?* He then sat up, his pulsating penis arching out in front of him. He looked down to see Ryan's penis bobbing up and down, too. Somehow, despite having never done this before he knew exactly what to do. "I gotta suck your dick," he said. He knew he sounded pitifully desperate.

"What are you waiting for?"

Ryan pulled his pillow up and leaned it against the wall. He pushed himself back and rested his head back on it while he spread his legs apart. Scott got on all fours in front of him and lowered his head to Ryan's crotch. He cupped Ryan's tightening balls in one hand. Scott was impressed with himself. He had always thought he would be shy when it actually came down to this. Now, as Ryan's penis filled his mouth he could only see an action plan in his head. It seemed his whole life had been designed for this one moment.

He tried his best, but fumbled at first, as he went up and down on it with his mouth. It took a few moments to figure out how to do it, all while keeping his teeth out of the way. Ryan alternately rested his hands on Scott's head and ran his fingers through his hair as Scott's head went up and down. The more he bobbed the more Ryan moaned. In only a few moments, Ryan whispered to him. "Uh, stop. Stop!"

Scott didn't want to stop and Ryan had to forcibly pull him off. Scott leaned back on his knees. A wide grin had spread over his face. Ryan's chest heaved up and down as he caught his breath. As lightening flashed again, Scott saw the look of ecstasy on his face. He scooted a knee as close to Ryan's crotch as he could. Ryan took Scott's penis in one hand and started a slow pumping action. With his other hand he reached up, ran his palm up and down Scott's chest, and then stopped at a nipple. He took it with his thumb and index finger and pinched lightly. He did that for a moment, then went to the other one, then back again. Scott had to stop him. His nipples had always been sensitive, but never like right now.

Scott steadied himself by putting one of his hands on Ryan's shoulder and another on his knee. Ryan turned his face to the hand on his shoulder and rubbed his cheek on it. He kissed and licked the back of it, reveling in the feel of Scott's downy hairs against his cheek. Scott pushed on Ryan's knee. "Move up a bit," he whispered.

Ryan adjusted the pillow and his body so he was more in a sitting position. Scott grasped both their penises at the same time. Ryan marveled at how Scott seemed to know what would turn him on. Scott spat into his hand several times and applied the saliva to their touching penises. A considerable amount of pre-come started to well up out of Ryan's. Passing his palm over the head several times, Scott was able to use some of the natural lube he so generously provided. Ryan moved his hips up and down to accommodate him as he continued to pump. Scott could tell he was almost there—his eyes stayed closed and his breathing was becoming ragged. Ryan's whole body tensed then and in another second his penis erupted. He emitted guttural sounds as it shot up and landed on his chest and abdomen. A second later Scott thrust his hips forward a bit as it landed on Ryan's chest. The volume of it from them both quickly ran down his left side to the sheet. It took several moments before Scott could open his eyes. The only sound inside the little room now was the air conditioner and the almost frenetic breathing of the two teenage boys.

Scott had semen all over his hand and fingers now. He dropped down on his back to Ryan's side with his hand up over his chest. He turned his head to observe the wet mess all over Ryan's torso as lightening continued to flash outside the cottage.

Ryan looked down at himself and started to chuckle. The thunder from the previous flashes of lightening was now almost overhead but it didn't drown out his laughter. He continued laughing as he put a couple of fingers in one of the translucent blobs. He reached over and rubbed wet circles around Scott's nipples. Scott's penis stayed hard. It continued to bob up and down in front of him. Ryan's only lost partial hardness as he lay there and kept laughing. It was contagious. Now Scott was laughing, too. Only he couldn't figure out why. He tried to catch his breath.

"Why...are...we...laughing?"

Ryan pointed to the bathroom. "I don't know. Get me a towel."

Scott scooted off the bed and went into the bathroom. Now that Scott was no longer in view, they both stopped laughing. Scott ran his hand under the water to wash it off then heard the rain hit the window by the shower. He retrieved a hand towel, wet a corner of it, and then came back to the bed. He was still at full mast.

Ryan started to take the towel from him but Scott brushed his hand aside. "I'll do it." He gently wiped Ryan's chest and stomach clean. Next was Ryan's penis, then his. He tossed the towel off the bed and listened to the rain now audible on the roof. Ryan kicked the sheet off the foot of the bed and it spilled onto the light blanket already in a pile on the floor. Scott turned onto his stomach and scooted over so he could lay his chin on Ryan's chest. He rested the fingers of his left hand in Ryan's right armpit. He felt Ryan breathing, looked at Ryan's nipples only inches from his eyes, and moved his index finger ever so slightly to feel the hairs in Ryan's armpit. He lay like that for only a moment then rose up just enough to kiss him repeatedly. Ryan didn't resist either. It had been a long time since anyone had kissed him like this, and Scott seemed starved as well.

He was. *Forever is a long time,* Scott thought, *even if it's only about seventeen years. If this is what it's like to kiss a guy, to lay on him, to rub hard-ons together, I can't believe I ever waited.* But that was the past now. At this very moment, he was kissing Ryan St. Charles.

Scott finally moved aside. Ryan pulled the pillow up against the wall again and leaned back, his penis hanging down over his somewhat loose scrotum. The sight of Ryan there in the semi-dark continued to keep Scott rigid.

Ryan reached over and flipped Scott's erection with his forefinger. "Man, you stay hard for a long time."

"It takes a while for it to go down sometimes."

Ryan felt a sudden flash of fear as Scott answered. The thing he had been hiding all summer was right in his face. Scott, who he couldn't imagine was gay, had just unloaded all over him. And now, his secret was out.

Scott was too full of energy to keep still. He sat up on his heels in front of Ryan. He didn't want the moment to ever be over and drank in the sensations: them naked on the bed, Ryan's hairy leg touching his calf, the sounds of the rain and the air conditioner, their breathing; the smell of their skin and the taste in his mouth, it was all so heady. He ran a hand up and down one of Ryan's furry legs. Ryan watched Scott's hand and didn't stop him as he flexed his thigh muscles. Scott's action made him grow more tumescent, but not fully hard. Scott, though, stayed hard.

"How do you *do* that?" Ryan asked admiring it.

"Good genes, and what's in 'em," he replied, trying to make a pun.

The rain was coming down in torrents now. The downspout was rumbling with the runoff from the roof. Scott went to the window to turn off the AC. Finally, he started to go flaccid. His round buttocks, framed by his tan, shone in the semi-darkness. More lightening flashed and filled the room with a brilliant brief light. Warm air spilled into the room as he opened the door. The sound of the rain splattering on the concrete porch slab filled the quiet room. The light from the telephone pole illuminated a corner of the room, reflected off the white walls, and covered them with an even dim glow. He dove back into the bed and propped a pillow up next to Ryan. Ryan crossed his outstretched legs. His genitals were perched in the middle as if a prize for Scott to admire, which Scott did. They listened to the soothing sounds of the rain and the now distant rumble of thunder.

Scott was filled with a satisfaction he'd never known. "I've never done that before," he confessed.

Ryan pulled up on his scrotum, and then re-crossed his legs. "You mean with a guy?"

"With anyone."

"You're a virgin?"

"I don't think so now."

Ryan squinted at him. "You're lying. You knew what you were doing."

Scott took his somewhat tumescent penis in his hand and pumped it a bit, and rolled his thumb over the slit. A drop of semen clung to it, which he licked off. "Must be all the practice."

Ryan felt so close to Scott. This was nothing like being with Crawford. It was completely different. Scott seemed so innocent, so unlike Crawford. He looked down at a ridge in his pillow and ran his finger over it, pushing it down. He started to speak slowly, as if trying not to say the words, yet coaxing them out anyway. "I have...done it, that is...lots of times."

Scott's mind whirled. He *had* done it before. He had liked it, that was for sure, or he wouldn't still be sitting there naked with him. "With guys?"

"Just one. His name was Crawford."

"From high school?"

"No, but I knew him my entire senior year."

Experience with another guy. Lots of it. But it was obvious Ryan wasn't going to elaborate. It nonetheless aroused Scott's curiosity, making him intensely jealous all of the sudden. That was an emotion he hadn't felt before and was struck by how crazy it made him feel.

Scott he rose up on one elbow. "So, when we beat off on the campout, you didn't get it?"

"Get it? About what?"

"That I'm gay."

"I just thought you were horny. I was, too."

"And the next morning? That wasn't an obvious enough clue?"

"No. I just thought you were fucking with me." He fell silent, not sure what to say next. Scott had indeed been hinting. Ryan had thought so, but had been denying it.

The rain continued to splash on the sidewalk outside the door, making slapping sounds on the cement. Scott finally lost most of his tumescence as they spent long minutes just watching and listening to the rain splash outside the door. He reached over and fumbled for his watch. It was only two o'clock. They had barely been asleep for an hour before they were woken up. He felt he should be sleepy after the long day and all the exertion, but he felt wide-awake instead. "Hey, lets go out to one of the piers."

"It's raining."

Scott tensed a corner of his mouth. "You noticed."

Ryan thought for a moment. "We have to put some clothes on. I'm not going out there like this," he said looking down at himself.

"Sure."

Scott turned on the shower and adjusted the water until it was warm. He took their cold damp shorts that were hanging over the shower door and wet them. They stood in the semi-dark bathroom, wrung them out, and struggled into them. Scott pulled out some sandals from his bag, as did Ryan. They looked out the door for a second before heading to the pier.

The rain was still coming down steadily and the whole area was getting a rare soaking. Scott was glad they were there to participate in it, yet wondering what was going to be washed out. He was well aware of the damage that could be caused by a rainstorm, especially in a thirsty summer desert.

Both piers were covered to about halfway out with a metal corrugated roof held up by tall metal poles. The sound of the rain on the metal was quite loud once they were under it. The boards weren't slick, although there were puddles in places where they were warped. At the end of the pier, Scott took off his sandals and sat with his legs dangling over the side. Ryan sat next to him. His legs were a little longer and could just skim the dark water with his big toes. The choppy water slid past as the rain splashed on them and all around them.

Scott leaned back on his hands, letting the raindrops hit his chest and face. He opened his mouth in an attempt to catch some of them.

"It's almost like back home," Ryan said. "Only I wouldn't go out in the rain there. Too cold."

Scott reached over and put his arm around Ryan's waist. Ryan brushed his wet hair off his forehead but didn't take Scott's arm away. *Good*, Scott thought, *he likes it*. With his other hand, he pushed a lock of hair from Ryan's ear. Still Ryan didn't stop him, but neither did he look at him.

Scott's penis started to spring to life again as he continued to touch him. As the lightening continued to illuminate the area periodically, he observed that Ryan was also getting hard again, though it seemed he was trying not to let Scott know. *Why is he pretending not to notice,* he wondered.

Back at the house, the thunder had woken Becky. When she came into her parent's bedroom complaining she was scared, Greg reassured her and Cin took her back to bed. When she came back, she pulled aside the curtain and looked out over the river. Lightening both near and far flashed from cloud to cloud. Although scary to her child, the rare desert storm always had a soothing effect on her although she, too, was aware of the danger of flash flooding, and wondered if the marina was okay.

There was movement on one of the piers. She knitted her brow, trying to discern who could possibly be out in the rain in the middle of the night. It was far enough away that she couldn't make out any detail yet when a brighter flash illuminated the area, she recognized two shirtless boys and realized that it was her nephew and his friend. The smile that crossed her face made her feel warm and young again. How wonderful that they can enjoy it. *Ah, to be out there myself,* she mused, *to feel the rain tickling my face.* She sighed and watched for a moment more. She went back to bed and gently kissed Greg's cheek before falling asleep again.

Scott swung his legs back and forth as he tweaked one of Ryan's nipples for a second time. He tensed his bicep as Scott squeezed it. Scott pulled Ryan's arm up and ran his tongue up and down over it, tasting the rain that ran down it. If it were possible he would have tried to eat it right there.

The heavy rain abruptly tapered off but still came down steadily. Scott reached around to get his sandals then whispered in Ryan's ear. "Show me what you can really do with that dick," he said seductively.

He studied Scott's face. He couldn't believe he heard it. Scott wanted him to fuck him? Crawford never let him fuck him and he knew this was his chance. His hardening penis strained in his wet shorts. "Let's go in."

Scott took his hand and lifted Ryan up. Ryan let go as he gained his footing, then slipped his feet into his sandals.

They shook themselves of as much water as they could under the door awning before going back inside. Quickly they went into the bathroom and dried off. Scott squeezed their shorts and hung them over the shower door.

Scott watched as Ryan rummaged in his toiletry bag. "What are you doing?"

"I'm looking for a condom. I'm not fucking you unless I have one."

"You *have* some?" Scott had never bought one.

"Be prepared. Didn't you say that a while back?" He pulled out two condom packages, then took a tube of aloe gel from the bag.

Before they were on the bed, Scott was rock hard again in anticipation. He lay on his back with his knees bent slightly. His hair was sticking up every which way now that he had toweled it off. His hands were clasped behind his head.

Ryan placed the condoms and the aloe on the nightstand. Scott lowered his knees and spread his legs open. Ryan straddled one of them. He ran his hand up and down Scott's thighs and lingered as he fondled his penis. At first, Scott's balls were loose but at Ryan's manipulation, they quickly grew tight. Scott felt the familiar feeling of excitement in the pit of his stomach. At last, he'd know what it was like to have a penis inside him!

Ryan scooted back and took Scott's penis in his mouth. In only a few moments of tonguing, he had Scott right at the edge. Scott pulled him off. Ryan had done it so expertly he figured that Crawford guy must have been a good teacher.

Scott's penis bobbed up and down with each heartbeat as he lay there. Ryan pumped his own a few times, then leaned over and started sucking on Scott again, this time much more slowly. He changed his mind only a few moments later. Reaching over the end of the bed, he had to lean over Scott's middle. He took one of the condoms from the stand, lingering only long enough to rub Scott's stomach with his erection. Scott was sure he would never lose the smile on his face. Ryan took the condom and rolled it down his shaft while Scott watched. He lifted Scott's legs up, resting his Achilles' heels up on his shoulders as Scott adjusted his body. "When I go in, push out. That's makes it easier."

"Okay."

Ryan spit into his hand, then squeezed out some of the aloe gel into the spit. He smeared the gel and saliva on the condom, on Scott's ass, then the remainder on Scott's rigid penis. Then, with his hands at Scott's sides, he leaned forward and touched his anus with the tip of the condom. Slowly he pushed, raising Scott's legs higher by lifting his shoulders up as Scott tried to relax. Ryan penetrated just a little, then backed out. Scott reached around and guided Ryan in as he pushed again, this time deeper. This went on for quite a few minutes as Ryan pushed a little more each time, until Scott felt himself sufficiently loosened up. He was sure it was going to hurt like hell, which it did at first. Now, though, it was an indescribable mixture of pleasure, a little pain, and a feeling of odd fullness. Another thrust, then another, and Scott felt Ryan slowly slide all the way in with one long slow motion.

"Oh God, it's unbelievable," Scott whispered.

Ryan slowly pulled out, then pushed just as slowly back in.

"Yeah, just like that. Real slow," Scott said, his eyes now closed.

Ryan listened, following along with exactly what Scott wanted. His arms quaked as he rested most of his weight on his hands while he slowly pushed in and out. Scott's legs, still draped over Ryan's shoulders, added to the burden. The anticipation was almost unbearable. He was glad he was going so slowly or he would have already come several minutes ago.

After the long minutes of going quite slowly, Scott loosened up considerably. Ryan started thrusting harder and faster. Scott had no idea it would feel this good. He took his hand and slowly massaged his penis to Ryan's timing.

Scott's face looked pained, but Ryan knew it was sheer enjoyment. After all, he spent a good year letting Crawford fuck him at just about any time of the day or night. He knew just how excellent it was. Scott beat off even faster as Ryan thrust more quickly. He knew it wouldn't be long before he came again.

Just watching Scott's face was enough to get him off. Ryan let out a series of moans as his entire body tensed. His hips were moving in only short strokes now. Scott felt Ryan's body tense. He grasped his penis tightly now, pumped good and hard this time, then felt himself getting close. "Pull out! Uhhh, pull out," Scott commanded. Ryan pulled out slowly, reluctantly. Scott continued to stroke himself, his ankles still high on Ryan's trapeziums. It was just in time, as his moans filled the room.

Ryan took Scott's legs by the ankles and gently let them down on the bed. He let out a long breath of relief. He'd done all the work and it was quite the workout. Scott lay motionless, his hand still on his rigid penis as he caught his breath. It was heaven. Sheer heaven. After all this time he'd finally been fucked. It was better than he ever imagined.

Ryan slowly pulled off the filled up condom and tossed it onto the rug next to the bed. He took the hand towel and raised Scott's legs up to wipe the aloe off him. Before he could wipe Scott's chest off, Scott pulled him down and started another round of kissing. Ryan was reluctant at first to lay in it and tried to resist, but almost immediately gave in. A broad smile crossed his face while Scott covered his cheeks with kisses. They lay there for a long time until Scott felt himself about to fall asleep. He pulled Ryan up and wiped off the sweat that had generated from them with the already wet towel. Ryan pulled the sheet and blanket up onto the bed.

"I never did that before," Ryan said.

"Did what before?"

"Fuck a guy."

"Right," Scott said disbelieving.

It was true. It was his first time with a guy. "Crawford wouldn't let me."

That feeling of jealousy passed through him again and he tried to make it go away. It was intruding on his feeling of ecstasy. He was only partially successful. He looked at his watch. It was close to three-thirty and he was finally feeling really sleepy.

Scott had a satisfied smile on his face. "Well, for the record, I'm now *officially* not a virgin."

Ryan faced away as Scott snuggled up against him, pressing his still hard penis against Ryan's buttocks. This time, though, a layer of cotton fabric didn't separate him from Ryan: they were both completely naked. He wiggled his hips as if inviting Scott to enter. Despite being spent, he was still fully hard. He slipped a hand under Ryan's pillow, and rested the other on his side, just like before. Caressing Ryan's lats a few times, Scott slid his hand slowly down and finally reached his crotch. Ryan was still hard, too. *Look who doesn't get soft*, he thought. It was the last thing he remembered before sleep took him away.

CHAPTER 13

Scott rustled the sheet in his sleep while Ryan lay very still and very awake. A bird chirping incessantly outside in one of the willow trees had woken him what seemed like an hour before, but the clock indicated that it had been only ten minutes ago. Now it was beginning to annoy him. He moved toward the edge of the bed and quietly got up to turn on the air conditioner. It hummed loudly for a moment then quieted somewhat as the compressor engaged. He looked back at the bed. Scott hadn't so much as stirred.

It was dawn, and in the gray light, he found his underwear at the foot of the bed under the bedspread and slipped them on. He then put on some shorts and sandals. He briefly looked back at the bed again, then quietly opened the door and went outside. The bird making all the racket was behind the cottage. He tossed a small rock in its direction. It hit the tree trunk with a sharp cracking sound. The bird flew off to the next yard to resume its chirping on top of a swing set.

The storm had completely passed them now and the sky was almost clear except for an occasional fast-moving dark cloud. Far away, at the horizon, low clouds from the front were just beginning to be lit up by the early sun. He could still see a few stars in the west ahead of him as he went out to the end of the pier by himself. It was the same one as they were on last night.

It was almost as if it had never rained. The few puddles he saw were back under the awning by the door of the cottage and several small ones on the boards of the pier. It was hard to imagine that just a few hours ago he and Scott were sitting there with torrents of rain pelting down on them. The early morning light breeze gave him goose bumps across his arms and chest as he sat and pondered last night's events.

It had been weeks since he last had sex. He could barely imagine Scott would be one to break his fast. *And it seems like he enjoyed it even more than I did*, he thought. As the scenes of last night replayed in his head he noticed a tiny crust of dried semen in his navel. He scratched at it and it blew away, landing in the swift-moving water.

A tug-of-war seemed to go on in his mind. Racked by images of Crawford, who he now despised, and images of Scott who he was attached to like no one before, he couldn't decide how to handle what happened. The more he attempted to escape the feelings, the harder they resisted. If this was what it was like to be gay, he hated it. Still, he couldn't bring himself to say it was completely true. Neither Scott nor himself seemed to fit the pictures in his head. Images that Dolf and the rest of his so-called friends back home had reinforced. Images that Crawford had dogged him about as well.

The spring on the screen door from the big cottage stretched and rang as it opened. An older woman, perhaps one from last night, wearing a white windbreaker and a red scarf tied securely over her head, walked briskly toward the pier. He pretended he hadn't seen her, but as soon as he heard her footsteps on the pier he turned around.

"Hi," she said. "I see someone else likes the early morning, too. Are you in the race?"

"No," he croaked. It was hard to talk this early. "I'm a spectator. I'm here with the Atcher's nephew."

"Nice place they have, huh?"

"Yeah."

She sensed his melancholy and studied his face for a second. He was very much aware she was staring. "Just wanted to say hello. I'm off for my morning walk. I hope you feel better," she said cheerfully.

Better, huh, he thought. *Is it that noticeable?* His reverie now broken by her presence, he couldn't think anymore. He waited for her to be out of visual range, then headed back to the comfort of the cottage.

As he stood by the bed, he slipped off his sandals. Still in his shorts and underwear, he quietly slipped under the sheet. Scott was on his stomach. When he pulled the sheet up, he saw Scott's legs and the downy reddish-blonde hairs that ran up the back of his thighs. They disappeared into the crack of his hard round butt. Part of him wanted to caress Scott, to again experience the exquisite sensuous feel of his post-virginal body. Another part of him held protest. If he didn't watch himself now he'd go too far. That's how it began with Crawford. It was innocent at first. It was supposed to be a quick blowjob and nothing more. What was supposed to be a one-time thing became two, then a month long, then over a yearlong entanglement. He just didn't want that to happen again. Nonetheless, he reached out and touched Scott's back, tentatively at first, then put his entire palm down against his warm flesh. He was so beautiful. He let his hand slowly move down to his sensuously curved butt, slid it up and down a couple of times, then rested it there. He closed his eyes. An odd mixture of relief and anxiety was alternating inside his head. Soon, though, he fell asleep.

Scott whispered in his ear. "Wake up."

"What time is it?" Ryan sounded groggy.

Scott glanced up at the alarm clock next to the bed. "Almost seven-thirty."

Ryan turned around and opened one eye to look at him. Scott's cheeks were puffy and both eyes had bags under them.

"You look half-dead."

Scott yawned. "You kept me up half the night."

"I didn't start it." Ryan sounded gruff. He was trying to see if he was going to tell him to drop dead. No, the look on his face wasn't anything of the sort.

Scott studied Ryan's face, not sure how to respond. "You're right, I did." He touched Ryan's exposed shoulder. "And I'll start it again if you want me to."

Scott wanted him for sure. He let Scott continue to touch him; slowly feeling himself let go, even if it was just a little. If he went too quickly though, he wouldn't be able to sort out all that was going on. But as Scott continued his caresses, he felt it was a little too fast too soon.

Ryan pulled the sheet up. "It's too early." He turned over onto his back and tucked a hand under the pillow.

Scott edged over to him and lifted the sheet up. "Hey, when did you put clothes on?"

They heard the screen door slam shut from the other cottage across the drive.

"It's only shorts."

Scott pulled the waistband away and saw that he had underwear on, too. "I should get up anyway," he said. Without hesitation, he pushed the sheet away, sporting a noticeable erection. Ryan watched him as he went into the bathroom. In a moment the shower started.

Ryan pulled off his shorts and underwear and went into the bathroom. He could just make out Scott's shape through the steamed up translucent shower door. He pulled it open and quickly stepped in.

Scott was lathering up his hair but now stood motionless. "I've never showered with a guy like this before."

"You were on the track team. You've showered with dozens of guys."

"I never had *sex* with any of 'em."

Ryan looked at the water and soap bubbles sliding down his face. He reached out and wiped them from his forehead. He reached around Scott's waist and drew him close. His heart raced as he hugged and kissed Scott while the warm water covered them both. God, it felt so good to kiss him. When he released his embrace, his voice resonated in the confined space. "We need to talk."

Scott could hardly catch his breath. "How about after I'm done."

"How about on the way home."

"That late?" Scott wasn't sure what Ryan really wanted. His body was saying come and get it, but his voice was saying wait.

Scott let Ryan go despite being completely hard now. The sensation of being with him in the shower seemed more than he ever could have thought. He'd often imagined, more like fantasized, what it would be like to be in this situation but never figured it would produce such a wide range of emotions and thoughts all at the same time. It was overwhelming. Ryan didn't touch him again, nor speak, as they quickly showered together, leaving Scott to deal with not knowing what was on Ryan's mind. It wasn't until they were completely dried off that Scott lost his erection.

As they dressed, Ryan could tell it would never be the same. His life until now was a thorough set of lies, a trail of illusions he had carefully fashioned before and behind himself. He had hoped that being with Crawford, wanting him, needing him, was a fluke, but was slowly becoming cognizant that it wasn't so. Yet, he would be damned before he admitted he was queer. He winced at the thought.

They packed their bags and dressed. On their way to the big house, Scott draped their still damp swim shorts over the headrests of the Jeep so they could dry out a little more.

When they came in the kitchen entrance Cin was just coming back into the kitchen as well.

"Good morning," she greeted. She briefly hugged them both. Cin felt something odd as she hugged Ryan. He was too quiet. Must be too early for him, she figured. The thunderstorm must have kept them up longer than she thought. She knew what might help. "Coffee?"

He hesitated just long enough for Scott to interject. "I never say no to coffee," he said as he started for the counter. Ryan followed, still quiet, and poured his black, as usual. He went to the TV room and sat with a couple watching the morning news.

Scott leaned against the counter in the kitchen and sipped from his cup, then put more cream in it. Cin noticed the bags under his eyes.

"Storm kept you boys up, huh?"

"*It* woke me up. But *he* kept me up," he said with a wide grin. It was just the right tone of voice, the right inflection. The look he gave her made her instantly realize what he meant.

She tilted her head ever so slightly. "Uh, what?"

He still had a wide grin on his face as he leaned over to whisper in her ear. "We did the wild thing," he said proudly.

Cin pulled back. Yesterday, she was sure they were just friends. Maybe Ryan initiated something? She studied his face. "This sounds sudden."

Scott kept his voice down. "I suspected, and it's true. I took a chance and he took my lead." He touched her shoulder. "He loved it. And you don't know how glad I am to 've *finally* done it."

The news almost made her jaw drop open. "You're embarrassing me." She started the water in the sink and washed her hands. *So, Scott had been the initiator instead*, she thought. *And it was his first time. In addition, here he is telling me about it.*

She shut off the water. "I wasn't going to say anything, but I noticed yesterday the way he looks at you. And he follows you around like a puppy." But something about the way Ryan was reacting now seemed to put a different spin on the situation. For example, he was nowhere to be seen.

Scott wiggled a shoelace back and forth while he inspected the floor tile under his foot. She'd been observing them, he realized. Good ole Aunt Cin, always on top of everything. Too bad he wasn't aware of it. It might have saved him a step or two.

She took a dishtowel and dried her hands. "I'd go slow with him."

He wrinkled his brow. "Whadda ya mean?"

"I learned a few things about this, although it wasn't my specialty. You remember the community youth center I used to work at back when we lived in Banning?" She referred to the volunteer work she had done many years back.

"No. Oh, yeah…"

"Well, I think his reality is about to be permanently altered." She folded the towel and placed it back on the counter. She picked up a wooden spoon, took the lid off a crock-pot, and stirred what looked like chowder. Its aroma drifted to Scott and he took a deep whiff. "But if he's just anxious he'll get over it," she added.

"Get over what?"

She whispered again. "Do I have to hit you over the head? You're could be bringing him out of the closet." It seemed obvious enough to her. He was quiet, seemed withdrawn compared to yesterday, and now wasn't even within earshot. If he had been as happy as Scott about it, wouldn't they both be carrying on like nothing was wrong?

Scott thought about the person Ryan talked about, that Crawford character. He wasn't sure how that could be true if Ryan had been having sex with someone already. He started to talk in a normal tone of voice, then went back to whispering. "I wouldn't say that."

She continued to whisper. "Well, he's probably not out there really watching the news. When something close to you—your sexuality—is threatened, it takes time to sort out your thoughts and feelings."

What the heck was she talking about? He needed to tell her what Ryan had told him last night, that he'd done it with a guy before. "Wait a minute…"

Ryan reappeared before he could continue. "Mmmm, something smells really good."

Scott could tell that even though he sounded cheerful, he wasn't.

Ryan carefully avoided looking at Scott and directed his attention to Cin.

She turned her attention to him as she put on her best smile. "And I'm sure you're hungry. It's cream of broccoli, with bacon, potatoes, and other tasty things. Really hits the spot."

She felt awkward, knowing the silence between the boys was because she was present. "Here are some bowls. There are muffins and fruit on the table in the dining room. Help yourself while I get the family ready," she said. She disappeared up the back stairs as Scott picked up a bowl.

"Well?" Scott asked.

Ryan felt uncomfortable looking at him. "Well what?"

"Did you like last night or what?" he whispered.

Ryan quickly looked away as he took a bowl as well. "We're not talking about that right now."

Scott scowled. He didn't understand what was going on at all. First his aunt warned him and now Ryan was still acting like nothing was going on. Here he was still feeling more alive than he'd ever felt in his whole life and Ryan wanted him to just shut up. It was as if the connection just disappeared. Maybe *Aunt Cin's right*, he thought. *Maybe I am going too fast. We're going to be with their friends all day so I guess I have no choice but to keep my mouth shut.*

This time they went up to the marina in the car with the Atchers. Scott let Becky sit on his lap so they could tickle each other. Michelle tried to get Ryan to tickle her, but he felt a growing awkward embarrassment as she kept touching him. She let him know she noticed by putting a finger at each corner of Ryan's mouth. She giggled as she raised them and made faces at him. "Smile. You smiled yesterday."

Ryan decided he better cheer up or everyone was going to notice. It was time to forget about what happened last night and just have a good time. He wasn't going to pass up a day of fun because of his confused feelings.

The Baumanns were already on their boat when they arrived. Once out on the lake they tied off together as they did the day before. The boys went to the top of the Baumann's boat and found Jeanine and her boyfriend. Scott was quite surprised to see them both.

Once they settled down Jeanine leaned over to Scott. "Where did you guys go last night?"

"We're underage, just like you are, so we boogied. I didn't feel like getting busted over a lousy beer." He didn't say that they both couldn't stand their choice of music and didn't mind leaving anyway. "What happened to you guys?"

"Nothing." She was surprised he even asked.

"Nothing?" He was the one surprised now.

Ken chuckled. "The cops checked IDs, but they really couldn't do anything. The keg was already empty when they got there."

"What about those two drunk guys?" Ryan asked.

"The cops put Tom in the squad car until he cooled off. Eddie was pretty pissed that he ended up in the pool. The cops told them to go home. We ended up inside anyway when it started raining. We partied 'til, like, three."

"Nobody got busted?"

"Are you kidding?"

"Well, shit," he responded. "You mean we coulda stayed?" He asked just to say it since he knew they wouldn't have stayed much longer anyway.

"The jail isn't big enough to hold all the people who're partyin' on the race weekend," Ken explained. "They just patrol around and make sure people aren't killing each other." That was an exaggeration to be sure, but Scott didn't know that.

Ryan felt he had to explain himself anyway. "I don't have a license and haven't gotten a state ID yet, so it would have sucked if they had nailed me."

Scott thought about it while Ryan spoke. If they had stayed, last night might never have happened. He was glad they had left after all. He sighed as a wide smile grew on his face. No one noticed.

Today's heat was much shorter than yesterday. By the time it was over it was still early afternoon. Ryan couldn't stifle his yawns as the day progressed. Luckily, the Atchers and Baumanns decided to head back to the marina early. It was still a good time, although more subdued than the day before.

Back at the marina, Jeanine asked Ryan if he still wanted the t-shirt. He said yes and she pulled a couple from a box for him. He chose a green one with a silkscreen speedboat on it, silhouetted by a huge setting sun. Underneath a choppy wake was written *River Rat.* In small print in the lower right, it said *Lake Havasu.* "This is great!" he exclaimed. He pulled off his shirt and wore the new one. It smelled new, which contrasted oddly with the coconut sunscreen fragrance already on him.

Finally, back at *Atcher House,* Michelle and Becky jumped out of the car first after they stopped under the carport. Cin looked at both boys as they both continuously yawned. "I don't want you to fall asleep driving back."

"I could use a nap," Scott said.

"Me, too," Ryan added, then yawned again.

Greg tried to sound funny. "I won't tell the guests you're napping in the same bed."

Scott's eyes darted to his aunt, then back to Greg. He knew it was a joke and cut off Ryan's impending alarm. "Like, I like sleeping with this snoring dude next to me."

Ryan's ears rang but knew Greg couldn't have known about last night. Despite himself, he found that he couldn't wait to fall into bed with Scott.

Cin and Greg herded the girls inside while Scott dragged his tired body into the room. He shut the door then fell backward onto the bed.

Ryan rubbed his eyes then pulled off his tennis shoes. He turned on the air conditioner and stood with his back to the breeze, as it grew cooler.

Scott opened his eyes to see what he was doing. "Are you coming?"

"Yeah."

Scott held up his arms, inviting him. "Well, what are you waiting for?"

Scott was like a magnet he couldn't resist. He approached the edge of the bed and rested his knees against the edge. Scott stroked the short dark hairs on Ryan's thigh. Ryan yawned and stretched, then pulled off his shirt. He didn't know whether he should run away or fall on top of him.

"Peep, peep, peep," Scott said with a smile.

Ryan made a face. "Peep, peep, peep?"

"It's what little ducks sound like."

Scott pulled him down on top of him. Ryan resisted. He pulled him close so he could gaze into his eyes. It was hard, at first, to keep him from looking away. *"Fear is the mind killer,"* Scott recited from one of his favorite books. "And you say: *'Fear is the little death'.*"

Ryan didn't know what he was talking about. "Why do I say that?"

"Because that's what the rest of the saying is."

"Fear is the little death," he answered in a monotone. "And sleep is taking me away." With that he yawned again and rolled onto his back.

Scott lay on his back, too, feeling Ryan's body heat. It was just like back in the Monument. Somehow, it was electric. And it wasn't just anyone's body heat. It was Ryan's. If he'd known that something as simple as lying next to him could make him feel this way, he'd have gone for him the first day they met instead of playing all those stupid hinting games. He gazed at Ryan's long, dark eyelashes, his deep-set eyes and the strands of hair layered across his head. The little crescent moons in his fingernails jumped right out at him as Scott examined the hand that lay across Ryan's stomach. The very same stomach that last night was draped in a bath of warm sticky liquid from them both. The ebb and flow of Ryan's breath became the ebb and flow of his breath. Before he knew it, there was a knock at the door.

Scott had his wrist to his face even before his eyes opened. His watch showed that more than an hour and a half had passed. He was surprised. He went to the door and opened it. Cinnamon was standing with the screen door open. Ryan sat up and looked for his shirt.

She stood at the threshold, not sure if she was intruding. "I figured you guys had passed out, but it's getting toward six o'clock and I wanted to make sure you were awake."

Ryan found his shirt and pulled it over his head. He stopped, looking disoriented. "Ugh, I feel zombieish."

"With some food in your stomachs, and some more cookies for the trip, you'll be ready to rejoin the living. Dinner's almost ready."

One of Scott's eyebrows arched up. Ryan's face lit right up as well. She knew that would perk them up.

Just before dinner, Michelle presented a crayon drawing of the boat race. When Scott asked about the two stick figures standing next to each other, almost touching, on top of the houseboat, she innocently proclaimed it was the boys.

Ryan felt his face grow flush and looked at Cin. As close as he felt to the Atchers in just the last two days, he didn't know what they'd think about her drawing. Michelle must see something, he figured. Cin noticed Ryan's ever so slight reaction and told Michelle to put the drawing away. "They can take it with them, dear. Go wash up for dinner now."

It was still well before sunset when they were ready to leave. Everyone followed the boys to the Jeep. There were the usual smiles and hugs and this time two coffee cans full of coconut- chocolate chip cookies. Scott laid the cans on the floor in the back.

"Bye honey, call us when you get back," Cin said.

"Not to worry," Scott answered.

Michelle gave Ryan the drawing, which he rolled up. He lightly bopped her on the head with it then placed it in the back seat. That made her giggle and she put a finger to her mouth as she stood back. They waved good-bye for the last time and were off.

It wasn't until they were past Vidal Junction that Ryan felt like talking.

"Scott I'm…not sure about this."

"I am."

Ryan looked at him. "I mean I'm not like that."

Scott noticed Ryan had said it conclusively. He hesitated before answering. "Seems to me you are."

"I'm not a fag."

Scott looked at him, not believing he'd said that. "Don't *ever* say fag. Only assholes say that."

Ryan looked down at his hands not sure what to say next. Scott's heart was racing.

"It's just…too fast."

"Get a grip."

"Get a grip, he says. There's nothing to hang on to."

Scott thought for a moment. He had the perfect rebuttal, but figured he'd save the obvious for some other time. His aunt said he might be coming out anyway. "Okay. Let's make up some rules," he offered.

"Rules? Huh. I've already broken all the rules."

"Well, don't break these." The wind rushed over the windshield as Scott kept his speed steady. It was hard to contain the excitement he was feeling. "Deal?"

"What kind of rules are you talking about?"

"Us. What we're doing."

"We're not doing anything. What we did was a mistake."

Right! Scott thought. *Last night was all I needed to seal it. And this morning when Ryan hugged me in the shower, what was that? He loved it. He's just resisting the inevitable.* "Rule one. You don't ever use the word fag."

"Well, that's the word."

"It is *not*! The word's gay. Only say gay."

"Okay, okay…*gay*," he said with emphasis.

"Rule two. You have to stop being an asshole."

"What the fuck does that mean?"

"Like that! No more saying stupid stuff, like fag. No more acting stupid either. Especially around my female friends. I like girls, you know, just not that way. Rule three…"

"There's more?"

It was a stretch to be sure, but Scott just had to make it a rule anyway. "This one's the last one….Starting today, you and I are going out with each other."

"We're both guys, Scott."

"These are our rules."

"What do you mean 'our rules'?"

"Our rules. We can say we're going out if we want to."

Ryan thought about it for a moment. He was being hauled into a relationship. As much as he liked Scott, he felt a familiar feeling of being trapped.

Scott intently watched Ryan's reactions now. The very fact that he kept answering gave him away. *His mouth holds protest, but I know the truth. He just needs a little nudging to give me the right answers.* "My guess is that you don't want to date girls anyway."

Ryan laid his elbow on the door armrest then rested his cheek onto his fist. His voice was weak. "I don't."

That proved it. Scott grinned, but tried to keep from being noticeable. "So say it: 'we're going steady.'"

A sudden odd thought struck Ryan. He looked at Scott. "Do they know about you?"

"Of course."

"For how long?"

"I don't know. A little less than a year?"

"What? So, they think I'm a fag, too?"

"What the fuck did we just agree about?"

"I'm sorry! See, I can't help it."

"The word is *gay.*"

Ryan ignored him. "Do they know about last night?"

"Aunt Cin guessed it."

Ryan looked out toward the side of the road, "*Fuck!*"

"What's wrong with that? She's probably the coolest aunt in the world."

"Your aunt knows we had *sex!*" he stated, incredulous. "What about your uncle? Does he know, too?"

"I don't think so, but I'm sure she's gonna tell him. What difference does it make? He doesn't care that I'm gay."

Ryan didn't ask any more questions. He had just spent all weekend with them and they all knew about Scott. The joke seemed to be on him, and it wasn't at all funny.

He watched Scott's hand as he shifted gears to slow at a yellow light at a crossroads. He was so cute driving in his beat up tennis shoes, his hair flying around in the wind, and the broad smile on his face. He felt a warm feeling, like a weight was lifting off, then lowering again, then lifting again as he thought about them together.

Scott let it sink in awhile before he asked again. "So, we're going steady?"

Ryan didn't answer.

Scott's heart was still racing. "It's okay if you say yes."

"Yes. Now will you quit asking me?"

The moment was frozen in time. It was all Scott wanted to hear. The most amazing feeling of warmth spread throughout his body as he thought about it. He was actually going out with a guy. And for looks, he couldn't have made a better choice. He thought the smile on his face would be permanently etched there. *Steady. As in a boyfriend. Finally!*

Nothing was said for almost a minute. Finally Ryan spoke up. "You really had that girlfriend?"

"Really."

"Well. What happened?"

"I talked to Aunt Cin."

"She told you to stop seeing her?"

"Fuck, no. I just stopped pretending."

It should have been easy to say no to Crawford, and to make Little Trout get lost. Somehow, though, it was impossible at the time. They both had been continuously backing him into a corner. *Maybe that's what I'm doing*, Ryan thought. *Pretending. Pretending I like having sex with guys. Pretending I want Scott now. Worse than I've ever wanted anyone? Is it pretending? Why is it so fucking difficult to tell?* "When we go up to my place, don't tell my friends you're like…my date or anything."

"Boyfriend," Scott corrected him.

"Jeez."

"Well, that's the right word."

"You don't have to say it like that. It sounds so…final."

Scott was suddenly alarmed. "You're not changing your mind are you?"

Change his mind? He wanted to change his life. They fell silent for a moment before Ryan asked the next question. "Do you like me?"

"Duh! What have we been talking about? And what do you think happened last night?"

"Well," he began.

Scott interrupted. "Well, yes."

"But *why* do you like me?"

He didn't mind coming up with reasons. "For starters, you throw a mean Frisbee. You don't know how hard it is to find someone who can throw a Frisbee as good as you. Second, you're the cutest guy I've ever known…"

"No way."

"Yes way." He wrapped his fingers around Ryan's bicep and squeezed. "Then, there's how you play along with me when I do my characters. Nobody'll hardly do that with me."

Ryan felt the weight lifting off again. No one had ever said these things about him. "You're funny. I like it when you do that—sometimes."

"And the way you kiss. God! Then there's this…oh…kinda feeling I get from you. Like you need hugs all the time. I like that. Can I hug you?"

"You're driving."

"Later then?"

"Maybe," he answered, trying to be coy. He was eating up the compliments and the weight was completely off him for the moment.

"And also you're like me. You're alone." He meant to say different. Unique. Not like the rest.

The weight came back. Scott noticed right away. "What's wrong?"

"It's no fun being an orphan, believe me."

"What?"

"You're parents aren't dead, stupid."

"Hey! Stop being an asshole."

Ryan sulked for a moment, not knowing why he felt angry every time he thought about them.

"What happened to them anyway?"

Ryan bit his lip as he tried to figure a way to encapsulate what happened. He rushed to tell it all before he became overwhelmed by emotion. "When I was ten my mom went into the hospital for surgery. She had this weird thing called a tubal pregnancy. It was a week before Christmas when she started getting these abdominal pains. She should have gone in earlier, but by the time she did, it was too late. She had been bleeding internally for so long they couldn't help her. She died three days before Christmas. I went to her fucking funeral the day after Christmas."

"Whoa!" Scott said under his breath. He didn't dare ask any more about her, as Ryan was visibly upset. A minute later, he had regained his composure and Scott ventured his other question.

"What about your dad?"

"He started drinking even more than normal. He died eight months later. I...I found him in the kitchen one night. There was a broken glass on the floor and blood was everywhere. He had passed out and cut himself. I was glad he was gone, though. He was getting too bizarre and started scaring the shit out of me and my brother all the time. We went to live with my grandmother after that. I hated him."

Scott could tell Ryan was fighting an intense sadness now. "Hey, I'm sorry. I just wanted to know why you never mentioned them. Is Howard cool?"

"Huh! Howie's the only sane one in the family."

Scott stopped asking questions and mulled over the weekend. The tape ended and he changed it, turning the music up a little more. Over the next half-hour, Ryan had time to think about what Scott was doing to him. *Scott's right,* he thought. *I am alone. More like lonely. He pays attention to me and I like that. Maybe it'll be okay to see if what he wants from me will work. At least for now.*

He inspected some huge rock formations that came up on the left and right as they continued down the highway. Scott saw them too. It gave him an idea. A character shift would be needed for effect. First he'd need to turn off the road. There wasn't a vehicle in sight—the last one passed them a half hour before. He slowed as he pulled across the lanes and onto the opposite shoulder, searching the rocky ground for a makeshift trail.

"Hey, where're you going?"

"You're going hitchhiking."

"You're not letting me out!"

"Hey, just play along." Scott maneuvered over to a less rocky area and they bounced along until they were around the other side of the tall rocks. The road was nowhere in sight from this vantage. In front of them was the shimmering yellowish-brown horizon. Not a single man-made structure was in view. He shut off the engine in the shade and got out. Kicking the ground, he thrust his hands in his pockets acting like he was waiting for something. Ryan got out and tried to follow along, not sure what Scott had in mind just yet. "So you want a ride, huh?"

Ryan studied his silly accent and decided to play along. Already it was a turn-on. "Yeah. But I ain't payin' ya."

"How far ya goin'?"

Ryan flipped one of Scott's t-shirt sleeves with a finger and gave him a coy look. "As far as you can go."

"I'm liable to go all the way with a hunk like you."

"You gotta catch me first." Ryan turned and dashed up a stacked cluster of rocks, slipped, then re-caught his footing. He got just out of reach as Scott pursued. His evasive maneuver was no good. He was immediately at an impasse with nowhere to go. Scott stood on the narrow rock ledge, almost stepping on his feet.

"Make out with me."

"Out here?"

Scott leaned in and pinned Ryan against the irregular rock face. Despite Ryan's initial protest Scott reached out and pulled his shirt up. He ran his hands along Ryan's lats, then downward to hold onto his slim waist. "Do you see anyone around?"

Ryan couldn't resist, closing his eyes in response. Taking Scott in his arms, he held him close. He totally gave in. "God, you're too wild." He devoured Scott's mouth, sucking in his tongue, giving him his. In another moment Scott had Ryan's shirt completely off. Ryan pushed him back and jumped down. Scott followed and took Ryan's hand where he led him back to the Jeep.

By this time, Ryan's erection was evident beneath the thin material of his shorts. Scott decided both of them needed to be freed up. He leaned Ryan against the wheel well, his groin against him. He watched as Scott took the single button of Ryan's shorts in his hand, undid it, and unzipped his fly. His penis strained against his underwear. Already there was a small wet spot on the white fabric. Scott also undid his shorts and stepped out of them. Ryan pulled his underwear down, and accidentally ripped them trying to get them around his tennis shoes.

They stood there in each other's arms, naked except for their tennis shoes, slowly rubbing their groins together. Warm gentle breezes caressed their naked bodies as the blood rushed in their heads. Ryan felt fire in his stomach and he found it difficult to catch his breath as adrenaline raced through his veins. Scott knew tricks he hadn't ever thought of before.

Without taking his eyes off him, Scott reached into his bag in the backseat and took out his bottle of coconut-scented sunscreen.

Ryan's eyes grew wide. "Oh, yeah. Go for it."

Scott squirted some of it out on his palm and smeared it all over Ryan's penis. It seconds he was in Scott's control. As he worked on it, Ryan's neck and upper chest got redder and redder as he sucked in labored breath. Another few slow pumps and Ryan stopped him, taking some of it in his hand. He took Scott's penis, working it as slowly and deliberately as he could, while they kissed. This wasn't like last night at all. In the middle of nowhere it was ten times more exciting.

Scott seemed to be fighting him, but it wasn't that at all. He leaned back and watched as the first spurt launched half a foot up, then a second and third draped over Ryan's hand in quick succession. He waited until Scott's breath was a little more even before he stopped stroking. Without hesitation, he applied what had oozed down his knuckles onto his own penis and let Scott pump him up and down now. His animal-like vocalizations were a perfect compliment to the wild, open desert. A powerful orgasm paralyzed him as it obliterated his senses. It took a few moments before he was breathing normally again and he could open his eyes.

"Ugh, I think I'm damaged," he announced as he looked down at his red slicked up penis still fully at attention.

Scott pulled out a small towel from his pack and gave it to him so he could wipe up. "Why'd you suggest this?"

"*You're* the sex maniac."

Scott examined his still hard dick, flipping it out a little with his thumb and letting it smack against his belly. "It's quite the phenomenon, isn't it?"

"More like a freak of nature."

"One *you* seem to have pretty much fun with."

They each wiped their penises off, then dressed slowly, as if not wanting it to be over. In all his life, Scott wouldn't have ever believed he'd be leading the way in matters of sex. And Ryan didn't resist, protest, or otherwise stop his advances. He guessed it meant Ryan was his. How else could he explain it? He was a funny one that was for sure. His mouth said no, while his actions said 'Hell yeah!'

Scott drove until it was nearly sunset. Ryan had leaned the seat back and had fallen asleep before they reached Howard's place. He pulled to a stop in the driveway. "Hey, we're back."

Ryan removed the cap from over his eyes. Howard's car and someone else's was in the driveway. "That's Krysta's car," he said. The living room lights were on and he gave Scott a worried look. He figured that if he had to talk to Krysta and Howie both he'd need Scott with him to keep the edge off. "Come on in," he invited.

"Are you sure?"

"Yeah, just come in." Ryan took his bag and they went in the back entrance through the kitchen.

They heard Howard talking in the living room. Krysta was sitting across his lap in the big recliner. When she heard the sliding glass door close, she jumped, looking embarrassed.

"Hey, guys," Howard said. He had to hold onto her to keep her from getting up. Her hair wasn't at all in place and Howard had a silly grin on his face.

She brushed back her hair and looked at Ryan. "How was the lake?"

Ryan put on his familiar serious demeanor, which Scott noticed right away. Before Ryan could answer, he spoke up.

"It was great! You should have been there."

Howard looked at Krysta. "We had a nice quiet weekend while you were gone."

Ryan looked over at the stereo that was playing soft quiet music. "I'm surprised you're not in a coma with that adult music going."

Howard looked at Krysta for a moment then back at him. "You'll like it, too, when you're our age."

"I don't plan on living that long." Scott turned his head and looked at him quizzically.

Krysta sized them up. They looked tired, and the scent of coconut was strong in the air. She sniffed a couple of times. "Smells like you were out in the sun all weekend."

Ryan immediately felt embarrassed, yet he knew she couldn't tell that they had used the sunscreen as lube only an hour and a half ago. He immediately diverted her attention. "His aunt and uncle have the coolest houseboat. We were on the lake most of the time."

They sat on the couch while he talked about the trip in more detail, carefully leaving out any scenario where he and Scott were alone together for any length of time. He deliberately sat on the far end making sure the middle cushion was well between them. The fact that Krysta seemed perfectly at ease now while still sitting on Howard's lap weighed on him. Scott, on the other hand, wished he could do the same with Ryan so he could touch his foot, run a finger along the back of his hand and hold his arm around his waist, just like Krysta was doing with Howard. Scooting any closer to Ryan was out of the question. *It just didn't seem fair!*

When Krysta yawned, Scott figured he should go. Ryan quickly stood and picked up his bag. "Let me show you that shirt I was telling you about," he told Scott.

What was he talking about? He realized Ryan wanted him to go to the bedroom with him. "Oh, yeah…"

Howard let Krysta up and she went to the kitchen. Scott followed Ryan down the hall, watching his butt in his tight shorts. His room was cold since the door had been closed and the vent in the ceiling was going full blast. They heard ice cubes clinking in glasses back in the kitchen.

"Let's see that 'shirt.'"

"Huh. I just wanted to get outta there. She was looking at me too much."

"Did it have anything to do with you talking with her?"

"She, like, looked at my crotch a couple of times, too."

"Who wouldn't? Besides, she probably likes the way it looks when you sit down. It's quite noticeable."

Ryan fidgeted with his bag then unzipped it. Scott saw he was nervous and took a step closer. "*Fear is the mind killer,*" he recited, not knowing what else to say. Ryan glanced up at him but didn't complete the saying.

Scott whispered. "Give me a kiss before I go."

"No. Not in the house," he whispered back in alarm.

"Why not?" Scott asked aloud.

"Shhh!"

"What are you shushing me for?"

"Look, I have to get up early tomorrow and go to work."

"So?" Scott protested, but whispered back anyway. "Why can't you kiss me?"

Ryan started pulling clothes out of his bag, then stopped in mid-pull. His tone was almost pleading. "C'mon. Go slow with me."

Scott felt terribly rejected. He wasn't prepared for him to act like this after their near perfect weekend. He scrutinized the situation. "Maybe I *should* go. Call me?"

"Yeah."

Scott knew he wouldn't see him for several days. He and Howard usually got home late at the beginning in the week, but usually just after five o'clock on Thursday and Friday.

"Promise?"

"Come on, you gotta go," Ryan said impatiently.

Scott stood for a moment and wanted to do his peeping sound to cheer him up. No, to cheer himself up. Where had the excitement gone? What happened to Ryan now? How was Howard going to know what was going on between them unless one of them said something?

Ryan opened the bedroom door and motioned Scott to go past him. He went out without a word. Krysta and Howard had the TV on now. As they passed them in the hall neither of them looked back at the boys.

Ryan crossed his arms and shuffled his feet back and forth a few times on the porch as Scott went to the Jeep. Scott motioned him to follow. Ryan reluctantly pulled the front door shut and went down to the driveway.

Scott got in and started the engine. "So you're gonna call me?"

"I said I would."

"Oh, here." He reached back and felt for one of the cans of cookies in the back. "Don't eat 'em all at one time." Ryan rolled the can in his hand but it was so packed with cookies it barely rattled.

Scott took the steering wheel, touching the tips of his thumbnails together as he gripped it. He wanted to look at Ryan again but didn't as he backed away and left.

Despite Ryan's reluctance to fully take pleasure in their newfound relationship, Scott was overjoyed. It was a dream come true. The thing about Ryan pretending he wasn't gay was, in a way, a turn-on. His penis stirred with the thought. Boy, was it sore, despite using lube. *But, what a great reason to have a sore dick*, he thought.

When he reached the highway, his mind was a jumble of different thoughts. He remembered the first day he saw Ryan. How it seemed he was a dink from the word go. *He's still a dink*, he thought. *And he seems so sensitive about this. Hmm*, he wondered, *how would I know if I was going too fast? Maybe I should talk to Aunt Cin about it*, he decided. It seemed like a thousand emotions were surging through him. *Who cares if Ryan's not excited? I am!* Before he could stop himself he let out a loud 'Yahoo!' at the top of his lungs.

Scott greeted Shakaiyo at the gate and his face was quickly covered with kisses. Ralph and Elaine were in the den when he came in. They talked about his exciting weekend for a while. Elaine noticed he was unusually animated about it.

"Dad, we should all go next year. It's such a blast," he said as he scratched Shakaiyo's neck.

"Yeah, maybe Christmas isn't the only time we should see them," he replied.

"I'm glad Ryan had a good time, too," his mother said.

"Yeah." Scott knew he had a far away look in his eyes, but didn't care. "He really liked it. We're pretty good friends now." Scott pulled out the can of cookies from his bag and opened it.

"I thought you were friends before," she said off-handedly.

He hadn't told her that he had been hanging around him only to please Howard and her. Nor had he said anything about what he really thought about him at first. Nor about his attraction to him. And he sure couldn't tell them he was no longer a virgin because of him. Regardless of the fact that his mom knew he was gay he couldn't tell her he was going steady with him either. That would be too weird. He opted for the easy route for now. "After a plate of Aunt Cin's cookies he became my friend for life." He popped one into his mouth and offered the can to them.

"Put them in the cookie jar. I'm sure we'll have one later," Elaine said.

Scott offered one to Shakaiyo who snatched it out of his hand. She looked longingly for another, and he couldn't resist. He emptied the remainder into the ceramic container in the kitchen. Checking his watch he saw it was almost ten o'clock, and he still needed to call his aunt.

"I'm heading for bed. See ya tomorrow," he told them. Shakaiyo dashed into the backyard as he slid open the patio door.

She ran ahead of him and stood against the door, her tail thumping heavily on it. It was hot in the little room, something that could be fixed in a few moments with the window AC on full blast and the ceiling fan on high. In another moment, he was down to his underwear in the dark, and on his bed. He picked up the phone and dialed the Atcher's house.

"Hey, Aunt Cin? Too late?"

"No, Scott. How was the drive back?"

"Uneventful." He skipped any mention of their little side adventure. "What a great time, as usual. I love you, you know."

"And I love you."

There was a short silence, as if she was waiting for him to say something.

"Do you have a few minutes?"

"Sure. Let me go to the other phone."

He could hear static come and go as she went through the house with the cordless. The line was much clearer after she switched phones. "There. Now, tell me about it."

"I think you know already."

"I just know you're excited about him."

"Yeah. That's it. But he has me totally confused."

"Rejoice, confusion is the beginning of wisdom."

"I am rejoicing. He's not. Not at all. I don't know what to do with him."

"Did you talk with him?"

"Sorta."

"Are you going too fast?" she cautioned.

That was going to be *his* question. "Well, I told him we were going steady."

"What do you mean 'you told him'?"

"Well, I guess I did it that way so he wouldn't say no."

"And what did he say?"

"He said guys can't go steady with guys."

"Maybe that's what's so for him."

"But I told him it was okay, that we can make up our own rules."

"Did he agree with that?"

"Yeah."

"What else did you talk about?"

"I told him not to act like an ass." He almost said 'asshole'. but thought better.

"He was a perfect gentleman here."

"Well, sometimes he acts like a dink."

"Oh, and you don't sometimes?"

"Not like him."

"He's going to handle coming out differently than you did, Scott."

"And his parents are dead. I didn't mention that."

"Dead? How?"

"His mom died from some sort of pregnancy problem when he was, like, ten. His dad died later that year. He cut himself really badly and Ryan was the one who found him. I don't think he got over any of it."

Cin thought for a moment. "Those are big issues. Are you sure you want to get involved with him?"

"Hell, yeah. He's way cute!"

"That's not the only thing that counts. He's probably confused about a lot of things. Unless he's handled his parents' deaths he'll have all sorts of unresolved issues when it comes to relationships."

"Yeah, that's what I mean. He acts weird sometimes. Like he's trying to impress himself, or me, or someone."

She could see he wasn't going to hear everything she needed to tell him. "You've got a lot on your hands. But I think it'll be good for you in the long run."

"Think I should teach him how to meditate?" He was referring to what his aunt had taught him last summer.

"He doesn't seem the type."

"Yeah, you're right. He's always thinking. You know, he wants to be an engineer."

"Greg told me. He was impressed with him."

"Did he think he was good-looking, too?"

Cin laughed. "He didn't say. But just the same *I* think he is."

"Thanks. You know, I don't get it. How could he be dealing with his parents? That was, like, a long time ago."

"Sometimes people never get over traumatic issues like that. Think about what you'd feel like if you were ten and your mom died and you found your dad dead. You'd be a mess."

"I guess. But he said he hated his dad."

"Well, that's what he *said.*"

He thought for a moment. "Hmm, maybe you're right. Maybe I should get him to talk about it."

"Good luck. Sometimes it takes years for therapists to get people to handle stuff like that, much less talk about it. But if you're in a relationship with him maybe it'll help."

"I hope so." They talked for only a few more minutes. After he hung up the phone, he snapped his fingers at Shakaiyo. She came up to the bed and laid her chin on the top of the blanket and blinked each time he petted her head. She padded around to the foot of the bed and jumped up to lay there.

Scott slid off his underwear and lay back, playing with his dick. He flipped it several times against his belly once it was fully hard.

"A boyfriend," he said to her with a big smile. "*I* have a boyfriend."

CHAPTER 14

The first part of the week went by quickly. By Thursday afternoon, though, Scott was starting to feel a heart wrenching sadness creep up on him. Ryan hadn't called, nor had he or Howard stopped by the restaurant during Scott's shifts. Granted, the timing for an actual rendezvous or phone conversation wasn't very good. Ryan worked eight to five while Scott was going to the restaurant at one o'clock and not leaving until a little after nine-thirty at night. That left little time for them to connect. The only phones in Howard's house were in the kitchen and the master bedroom. It wasn't exactly private for any kind of conversation Ryan might want to hold with him. The silence was the worst part.

Every time Ryan's face came to mind, he felt his heart pound. Dozens of times over the last several days he had had to stifle an erection at work when his dick seemed to take on a life of its own. He thought *that* problem had ended in eighth grade.

What Cin said about Ryan being a difficult endeavor weighed on him, too. He knew he wasn't prepared for what might be ahead. As the week wore on, he reasoned it out. His conclusion was to call off the boyfriend thing. But his body said that would be stupid. Besides, his body always won whenever there was any kind of decision to be made. His track coach wasn't dumb. He taught the team to listen to their bodies. And Cin followed that up with listening to your heart. What sense both of them made. It was funny how the brain wasn't even on the list.

Unfortunately, it seemed clear that Ryan was listening to his brain most of the time, not his body. His brain seemed to be haunting him. Silence seemed to be Ryan's defense now. Tonight Scott resolved to end the shield of silence. If he wouldn't call, Scott would have to make the move himself. If Ryan were his boyfriend, he would call him. Since he was getting off at seven o'clock tonight, the timing was better this evening. Just after eight, he ventured the call. "Mr. St. Charles? Is Ryan there?"

"No. He just took off some place on that scooter he fixed. Must have been about ten minutes ago."

"Oh," he sighed. The let down weighed heavily on him. "Don't know where he went, huh?"

"No. But I'll tell him you called when he comes back."

"Sure."

"No problem. Talk to you soon."

"Bye."

Crestfallen, Scott punched the off button and let the phone fall onto his bed. Shakaiyo whined and put her paws up on the windowsill, growled and wanted to be let out. He opened the door, wondering if that tortoise had gotten into the backyard again. That's when he heard the sound of a two-stroke engine at the gate.

His heart pounded at the sight of Ryan as he flipped the kickstand down. Shakaiyo recognized who it was and wagged her tail. Scott didn't hesitate as he nearly ran for the gate to let him in. "Hey, I just called your house."

Ryan got off the scooter and pulled back on the body to put it into position. "I got this thing fixed and had to try it out."

Scott stepped forward. "You fixed it all by yourself?"

"Sure. It was easy. It's only a 125cc engine. It only needed some minor work anyway."

"You really are a gearhead."

"I had to use duct tape on the seat since it was pretty torn up. It looks crappy, but otherwise the engine's in great shape."

Scott instantly got an idea for a birthday present. "What do you call this thing anyway?"

"It's a P-series Vespa 125. It's about eleven years old."

Scott made a mental note of the make and model. "That's kinda old isn't it."

"Yeah, but it was repairable. See, we'll have no problem going up to my house."

"Yeah, on a moped."

"It's not a moped. And no, I'm not gonna drag you behind me on a skateboard."

"It was just a joke. Come on in." He walked backward for a few steps, smiled, and stared at Ryan's face.

"You're embarrassing me," Ryan said as he came through the gate.

"Sorry."

When they got inside Ryan took Scott in his arms and hugged him until Scott felt a little lightheaded. Scott took his face and planted a kiss on his mouth. Ryan gave him a deep French kiss. Scott figured he had a lot to learn since Ryan knew how to do that perfectly. He had stumbled his way through French kissing his girlfriend, but never really enjoyed it until he met Ryan.

"I was thinking you weren't gonna see me anymore."

"That's why I came over."

Scott lost his smile, not liking the tone with which Ryan had said it. Ryan saw the look on his face. "I didn't mean it like that."

"Whew. Good." Scott turned on his stereo and turned off all the lights. The blinds were opened slightly and low sunlight from the west spilled into the room. They sat on the bed with their backs against the wall while Shakaiyo stuck her face in Ryan's crotch at first, climbed up on the bed to lick his nose, and finally wanted constant scratching

behind her ears. The air was thick with expectation. Ryan had something to say and Scott could just about feel it.

"I don't like all those rules. I had enough of 'em when I was living
with Muh."

"Muh?"

"You know, my grandma."

"Oh, yeah."

Scott knew he had made up the rules only to protect himself. The
third one was specifically because he didn't want Ryan to decide to try
to date someone else. Had Ryan changed his mind? "Y-you don't want
to go out with me, do you."

"Why do you have to call it…a rule?"

"All right. We won't call that one a rule. Do you want to like, do it,
with someone else?"

"There *is* no one else. I didn't want to start this with you either. I- I
was afraid of what you'd do."

"Do? You mean like suck your dick or something?"

"No. Like call me a fag or a queer boy."

"What!? Fag is out."

"And queer boy."

Scott nodded. *Of course*, he thought. "And that, too. Why would you
think I'd say shit like that?"

Ryan thought for a moment, searching for the right words. "I wondered all week what you really thought about me. I wondered what your
aunt and uncle were thinking about me, too. I was scared that Howie
would figure it out and I'd be on the street. I don't want to be kicked
out, Scott. I would just die. I don't make enough money to get my own
place yet."

Scott saw his dilemma. No parents. Kicked out of his home. Living
with a single uncle. It was rough, he guessed.

"You think Howie would kick you out if he found out we were seeing
each other?"

"I don't know."

"Did you ask him?"

"Yeah, right."

"Well, nobody knows except my aunt and uncle. And her." He pointed to Shakaiyo. "She thinks you're cute, you know." Ryan ate it up.

Shakaiyo thumped her tail and wiggled her head back and forth, shaking her dog tags.

He scratched her side, looking for her tickle spot, until she was kicking at the air. Scott was glad she liked him, too.

"You don't know shit about me. You haven't been hurt like I have."

Ryan tried to hide it, but Scott saw anxiety in his face. Scott wasn't sure what Ryan was talking about so made a guess. "Was it that Crawford guy?"

Ryan's chin trembled as he clamped his mouth shut. He finally spoke though. "Yeah."

"You wanna explain it?"

"There's nothing to explain." He lied. There was a lot to explain. He just didn't want to go into it just now.

"Then you'll be my 'advanced boyfriend.'"

"Your what?"

"You're way ahead of me. You already have a lot of experience and a whole relationship behind you. It's kinda exciting knowing that."

"I wouldn't exactly call it a relationship."

"Whatever. At least you and I met. Lucky Howie and my folks are friends, huh?"

"What about us? Who's gonna be the girl?"

Scott raised his shirt up. "Notice, I'm not a girl."

Ryan looked at his chest and pursed his lips. "You know what I mean. I don't wanna be the girl." He almost said *again*, but stopped short.

"Who says there has to be a girl?"

"I always think about that." In a way, despite loving how Crawford used his penis, he always thought of himself as the girl. It wasn't true by any stretch of the word, but he felt that way anyway.

"Well, *stop* thinking about that. Sheesh. Just because I let you stick your dick in me? There's two guys here. I'm a guy. You're a guy. Hey, I thought you didn't want any rules?"

"That's not a rule."

"Yes it is. It's *your* stupid rule. Look, let's just make this up as we go, huh? Neither of us is a girl. Neither of us wants a girl. We make it up ourselves as we go. That's what makes it fun."

"It doesn't seem all that fun yet."

Scott shifted on the bed to face him. He felt irritated now and spoke slowly, emphasizing every word. "That's because you're not trying."

He's right, Ryan thought. *Not knowing what to do is fun. Not having any rules is fun. If there are none to break, there can be no consequences.* It was scary and a relief at the same time. As the logic of the idea went around in his head, he started to lighten up a little. Scott saw it on his face.

He took Ryan's hand and pulled him off the bed. Taking the two pillows off with him he tossed them to the middle of the floor. He lay down and stuck one under his chest and neck, motioning for Ryan to do the same. Facing him on the floor, he put a finger to his lips. The last tune on the tape had ended. It was another Centauri original. The next tune started slowly and echoed as if in a huge chamber. It was Scott's flute.

Ryan saw the flute case on the floor at the foot of his stack of stereo equipment and noted all the dents and dings in it. He was sure Scott wouldn't reject him. In fact, he was positive Scott was trying his hardest to keep him. Maybe last weekend wasn't a fluke, or an illusion, nor was it a reason to run away. Scott genuinely liked him. Unlike Crawford, Scott didn't only like him for how cute he was, although it was fine that Scott found him cute along with everything else.

Ryan's pillow was stuffed under his chin enough to obscure his mouth and nose. Just his eyes and fuzzy ears showed as Scott opened his eyes. He touched Ryan's shoulder, then slipped his hand up his sleeve to squeeze his deltoid. Ryan stroked the hair on Scott's forearm, giving him goose bumps.

In no time Scott felt himself grow hard and wondered if Ryan felt the same. He shifted his weight slightly to the side and Scott decided it was so. "Why didn't you just tell me when we were on the campout?"

"Tell you?"

"That you like guys. I gave you every chance. I figured you could tell about me from all the stuff I said."

Ryan looked away. "I just…couldn't." The way he said it was so odd sounding. Like he was terrified, or sad, or something.

Scott really couldn't say what it was, but his tone was almost frightening. He shifted the topic slightly. "I know you had that wet dream."

Ryan lifted his head a little. "What? How did you know?"

"I woke up when you left the tent. I saw you standing in the moonlight against the Jeep. I saw you wipe yourself up." Scott snickered. "I saw you drag your underwear across your face—that was especially…interesting. I saw your dick get hard. I saw everything. That's when I figured it out. "

Ryan buried his face in the pillow again. His voice was muffled. "I just know you didn't see all that."

Scott squeezed his deltoid again. "I did."

Ryan raised his head again. "I had no idea you were awake."

"You should 've seen me after you came back into the tent."

"Why?"

"I came so fast it wasn't *even* funny."

"You beat off again. In the tent? How did I miss that?"

"No, when I went to take a leak."

Ryan put a finger to Scott's mouth, indicating that he wanted Scott to be quiet. He pivoted so they were parallel to each other. Shakaiyo got up and circled them, trying to figure out what he was doing. But it was clear to Scott what he was doing. He tugged on Scott's shirt. In another moment, it was off, so were his shoes. They embraced in a long sensuous kiss. Scott came up for air for a moment. "God, you kiss *so* good."

"As good as you play the skin flute, I mean, the flute?" Ryan asked with a grin.

He studied Ryan's face, shifting his gaze from eye to eye. "Yeah," he said as seriously as he could. "Both." He felt blood pounding in his head and the familiar burning sensation in his solar plexus as he groped Ryan through his shorts.

"You want me to put it in you?" Ryan whispered.

"I just wanna kiss…and feel you up. Can you wait 'til the weekend?"

"Why wait so long?"

"Hey, when do I get to do you?"

Ryan tensed up and just barely pulled away, but Scott noticed it. "Maybe later."

"Well, hopefully not too much later. I've been wanting to since we left Parker."

Ryan licked his thumbs, then lightly caressed Scott's nipples until they were tight little bumps. It was as if little electrical charges were connected directly to his penis as Ryan did so. Scott couldn't stand it anymore and wriggled out of his shorts and underwear. He pulled Ryan's shirt off and flung it aside. Now he was naked on the floor with Ryan's shorts unzipped. The stereo equipment lights and the dim evening glow from outside were all that illuminated their bodies now that the sun had set behind the mountains. Ryan put up a playful struggle as Scott tugged on Ryan's shorts, but he soon had them off.

Ryan led him to the bed where Scott sat at the edge. He spread Scott's legs apart. He sat on his knees in front of him and expertly wetted Scott's penis with plenty of saliva. Slowly he took it in his mouth and pressed his face right down to his pubic hair while playing with his balls with one hand. He adeptly sucked for a few minutes until Scott's back arched and he tried to push Ryan away. Ryan held fast as he felt the spasms start. Scott held his breath. He gushed into Ryan's mouth. It spilled out a little as he continued bobbing his head. Scott's moans filled the room as Ryan slowed down. Finally, he gave up as the last drop oozed out.

Scott couldn't believe it had happened so fast as he fell backward on the bed. Once he caught his breath, he was able to open his eyes. A narrow trail of translucent fluid ran down Ryan's chin. He hadn't swallowed though. He opened the drawer of Scott's nightstand, took the rag, and spat it out.

"How did you know that was in there?" Scott asked as he raised up on his elbows.

"One of the corners was sticking out. I figured out what it was right away." That wasn't true. He declined to say he had seen it before.

Scott's dick was still hard and he was virtually glowing. He dropped his head back down on the bed. "Don't ever forget how to do that."

He spread his legs wider to let Ryan come closer. Ryan sat on his knees in front of him. His erection arched out in front of Scott, pulsing with anticipation. Scott could tell it wouldn't take much to make him come either. Ryan fondled Scott's still hard penis and balls while he jerked with the other hand. In a few moments, his hard stomach tightened several times in quick succession. Gritting his teeth, a long thin white streamer launched onto Scott's shoulder. He kept jerking and bucking back and forth, as several short sticky strands crossed Scott's chest. Finally, the last drops fell to his abdomen and pubic hair. Leaning forward onto his fists now, he looked down at Scott's face. Ryan's dark hair framed his face in a curious way from his angle. Before Ryan knew it, Scott pulled him down in an embrace. At first Ryan resisted, since he'd end up laying in it, but Scott pulled even harder and he collapsed on top of him, making sucking sounds on their bellies as they moved. The tape ended and the deck shut off, making the room quiet. Only their breathing disturbed their reverie. Shakaiyo was still in a ball in one corner of the room and didn't bother them. Ryan peeled himself off and examined the front of his body. Scott retrieved the rag and wiped Ryan clean. He went to the bathroom to wet a washcloth and returned to wipe the residue from Ryan's torso. He wiped himself clean. When he was done, he sat on the edge of the bed squeezing the last drop out as Ryan stepped into his underwear. He slid in between Scott's legs and took his head to his chest. It was the first time Scott ever actually listened to another boy's heart. Ryan's warm chest against the side of his face and the sound of his heart beating just inches away made him feel like shouting and crying at the same time. Scott reached up and gently caressed Ryan's back as he listened. He felt he was in another world at how sensuous Ryan's skin felt, how beautiful Ryan was standing there against him. Ryan's willingness to join him in getting naked at a moment's notice like that amazed him. He was happy he had such an experienced partner as well. His initial jealousy was almost completely faded away now, he noticed, as he thought about it. At Ryan's insistence, he reluctantly got dressed and followed him to the scooter. Ryan sat on it, pushed forward on the body, and flipped up the kickstand.

Scott followed as he rolled it to the bottom of the driveway into the street. "Damn, I didn't kiss you good-bye."

The scooter's tinny sound filled the quiet cul-de-sac as he started it. Ryan rested foot on the baseboard. "We can kiss all weekend"

Scott scuffed the asphalt with his bare foot, then touched Ryan's tennis shoe for a second. "See ya, cutie."

Ryan mouthed the same in return, and was off. The wind blew his hair back as he took off down the road. Scott stood at the end of the driveway and watched until he saw only a pinpoint of red as he braked at the intersection.

He thrust his hands in his pockets. He hadn't put his underwear on and could feel his genitals against the fabric while he walked back up the drive to his room. Once back inside he picked up the pillows from the floor and tossed them onto the bed. He quickly shed his shorts, lay on his stomach on the bed, and hugged one of the pillows tightly. He released his grip on it a moment later and rested his chin on a balled up fist on top of it. *The sex is great, that's for sure, but there's something missing. There's something he's not telling me. Something I know he wants to say. I just can't quite put my finger on it yet.*

*   *   *

Friday morning, just before Scott went into the house for breakfast, he got a call from Bryce Owens, the drummer from the band. His next call was to Ryan.

"Ryan?"

Ryan lowered his voice. "Scott. Why'd you call me at work?"

"I just got a call from Bryce. He and Mitch are going to a movie tonight. It starts at eight. Wanna come too?"

"I guess so."

"Whadda ya mean 'you guess so'?"

"I mean yes. See you tonight."

"See you tonight, cutie."

There was a pause at Ryan's end and Scott heard him whisper something. "What?"

Ryan whispered a little louder. "I can't wait to see you."

Fifteen minutes later Ryan called back. "Scott?"

"Ryan. Why are you calling me at home?"

"Fun-ny. Don't eat dinner tonight."

"Why?"

"'Cause I'm cooking for us."

"You can cook?"

"Fuck, yeah. It's only spaghetti, but it's good. I make it like my grandma's."

"Howie's gonna eat this, too?"

"Howie won't *be* here. He's going out tonight. I just found out."

The wheels were already turning in Scott's head. "Just like we will be."

It was almost six-thirty before Scott got off work. He quickly showered, changed, and dressed in his tightest shorts and a thick white cotton t-shirt that said *Ski Gorgonio* in bold black letters along the hem. He dabbed on some cologne and headed into the house.

Elaine sniffed as he passed by. "Scott, where are *you* going?"

"To the movies with the band."

"Home late?"

"About eleven or so."

"We'll probably still be up."

"Okay. Later."

He snapped his fingers as he remembered to go back to his room to retrieve his Frisbee. It sat on the passenger seat as he hurriedly drove up the highway to Howard's place. When he arrived, he saw that Howard's car was already gone.

He went up the several steps on the back deck and peered in through the sliding glass door where he spied Ryan in the kitchen. He waved for Scott to come in.

Ryan was clad in a bright yellow mesh shirt, which looked similar to a football practice jersey. It came down only to the top of his navel. The bottom of it stood away from his stomach making an S-shape wave in the hem. His sky blue corduroy shorts had the distinctive logo of *California Surf* sewn onto the left thigh. He also wore leather sandals. In his hand was a just opened box of linguine. "Just in time. It's almost ready."

The aroma of spaghetti sauce filled Scott's nose as he slid the door shut behind him. He wanted to take the box out of Ryan's hand so he could kiss him right there. Better yet, he wanted to throw him on the floor, take that damned inviting shirt off, and suck his nipples until he screamed for mercy. Instead, he simply leaned against the counter next to the stove where a large pot of water boiled. Ryan briefly grinned at Scott and dropped in the stiff noodles.

"You know that muscle right there?" Scott lifted Ryan's shirt a little and pointed to the abdominal muscle that was prominent on top of Ryan's lower ribs.

Ryan knitted his brow and looked down at it. "What about it?"

"Well..." Scott stepped forward and licked it. The wetness glistened as he stepped back. "I can't help it. I love that part of a guy's body almost as much as I love dicks."

Ryan rubbed where he'd licked.

Scott watched the water roiling in the pot for a second. "I see Howie left."

"He was in a hurry, too, since he was here for only, like, twenty minutes before he left again," he said while stirring the noodles. "He said he might not be home tonight."

All by themselves in the empty house, Scott thought. It was excellent.

Ryan put the lid on the noodles. "But don't get any ideas, stud."

Scott gestured first at Ryan then at himself. "*You* call *me* stud and say not to get any ideas?"

He took a step toward Scott and pressed his body against his. He slowly ran the tip of his tongue across Scott's lips, then kissed him until he felt Scott getting hard. Scott felt up his pecs and pulled up on the shirt, trying to get it off.

"Don't. We don't have time. I thought you said the movie starts at eight."

Scott felt somewhat taken aback. He glanced at his watch. "Yeah, uh, eight."

"This will be ready in another five minutes. Here." He opened a cabinet. "Put these on the table."

Scott took the two plates and laid them on the dining room table. "I love it when you command me." Ryan cracked a smile, opened a drawer, and pointed to silverware. Scott laid out two place settings.

Scott was impressed that Ryan knew his way around the kitchen. Even the other pots and pans he'd used earlier were already washed and stacked in the dish drain.

They served themselves and ate hurriedly. Scott picked up the last little piece of his garlic bread as Ryan belched and laid his fork down. "You know, when I was with you in Parker I couldn't believe I was eating with you guys."

"Huh? Did you think we were gonna let you starve or something?"

"No. I mean it seemed like I was in a family again. Your nieces were so cute and funny. Your uncle was joking around and your aunt seemed like a real mother."

Scott hesitated for a second. "Well, she *is* a real mother."

"I know. I guess it felt like I was part of your family or something.... I made dinner for you 'cause I liked that feeling."

Scott scooped the last bit of sauce with the bread. "I wish I could tell everyone about you and make you part of my family. For real."

Scott inspected his t-shirt, making sure no sauce had splashed onto it. Ryan changed into a thick pullover shirt with a psychedelic print on it, then donned a well broken-in pair of deck shoes. They quickly put the remaining dishes in the dishwasher and zoomed to the theater in Scott's vehicle.

Once they parked in the usual spot at the shopping center Scott took the Frisbee and tossed it to Ryan. He reacted immediately and tossed it back. Soon they were tossing it back and forth expertly. Ryan stuck his tongue out at Scott every time he caught it between his legs. This went on for a few tosses before Scott tantalized him by turning his back to him, bending over, and catching it between his legs. He wiggled his butt as he caught it and stuck his tongue out at him. Bryce and Mitch pulled up just as he did it.

Bryce stopped the vehicle and rolled his window down next to Scott just as he stood up. In the back were their dates watching them, too.

His face was full of mirth as he stuck his head out the window. "Wiggling your butt in the parking lot again. Haven't we talked about that?"

They rolled past and went to the spot next to Scott's Jeep. While they were on the way Ryan approached Scott. "Why did you do that?" There was a touch of anger in his voice.

"He was just razzing me. Mellow out...or I'll call up rule number two."

"You didn't tell me they'd have dates."

"They didn't tell me either."

"I don't feel so good about this now." He sounded nervous.

"They don't know anything about us." Ryan seemed so worried about what they would say, or what they'd think, he just had to take a jab. "And if they guess, don't deny it."

Ryan gave him a shut-up look and threw the Frisbee at him. It bounced off his side and landed on the asphalt. Scott stashed the Frisbee in the Jeep.

"Dudes," Mitch said, "it's slash and burn night at the Bijou. I can't wait to see who *Billy The Stalker* gets tonight."

Scott looked up at the marquee then back at the guys' dates. He already knew the girls. The guys had been dating them off and on now for about five months. Ryan didn't know them, of course, and didn't feel like striking up a conversation with them. He was afraid they would misconstrue anything he said as an admission that he was now Scott's boyfriend. He ended up sitting at the end of the row next to Scott away from the rest of the entourage.

Three times during the course of the movie, Scott reached down, acting as if he was doing something with his shoe. What he did was stroke Ryan's ankle twice, and once reached his fingers into Ryan's shoe and stroked the outside of his foot. Each time he did it Ryan pulled his leg away. Scott wanted to put his arm around him, to do what Mitch and Bryce were doing with their dates. Ryan would kill him if he tried.

After the movie Bryce made it clear that they were going parking. He kissed Susan, then gave her a look that Scott was only too familiar with. "I guess you guys don't want to come with us. Besides, there's not room in the car for two more."

"That's okay, Bryce. Us homos are gonna go make out at my house."

Ryan eyes grew wide and he socked him in the arm. "*He's* the homo," he said in defiance.

"Shit!" Scott yelped as he rubbed the spot and took a pace away from him.

Ryan didn't care what the others thought of his outburst. He wanted to get Scott for saying something like that aloud. "Serves you right for calling me a homo."

Scott laughed nervously. "He gets like that when he hasn't had his nap."

Bryce unlocked his car. "Have your mother video all the juicy parts. We'll critique it at practice."

"Gross," Susan said. "I don't believe you said that."

Bryce shrugged his shoulders. "I'm kidding, okay?"

"Like *I* was, of course," Scott directed it to her, trying to get himself off the hook with Ryan.

The two couples left the parking lot as the boys stood by the Jeep.

Ryan was still angry. "Don't say shit like that."

"Look. Those guys are my friends. They know I say all kinds of crazy shit. They don't know what we're going to do. By the way what *are* we going to do?"

"*We're* not doing anything."

Scott looked at him, waiting him out. "Oh, come on."

Finally, Ryan had shuffled back and forth enough. "I don't know."

"Let's watch music videos at your place. Plus, we can see if Howie's coming home."

Ryan took a deep breath and sighed noticeably. "Okay, whatever," he said as he climbed in. He still wouldn't look at him. They took off through the crowded lot and arrived back at the house about ten minutes later.

Scott sat in Howard's big recliner as Ryan went in the kitchen. Ryan had finally mellowed out, which Scott was grateful for. He returned moments later with bourbon and cola. Scott took a whiff after Ryan handed him one. "Bitchin'."

"Howie still hasn't said anything about the bourbon I took on our camping trip. I guess he hasn't noticed." He left again and returned with the coffee can of cookies. He rattled it in front of Scott.

Scott was quite surprised. "I thought you'd 've eaten 'em all by now."

Ryan removed the lid. "I saved some so I could eat 'em with you."

They munched on the cookies, drank their bourbon and cola, and watched music videos. The countdown had them rocking nonstop for most of an hour. Just after eleven, Scott yawned and stretched out on his back on the floor. Band practice was starting early tomorrow and he decided he should be starting back soon. Ryan lay next to him and rested an arm on Scott's chest. He rubbed the soft material of Scott's shirt then rested his chin on his hands. "Spend the night?"

Scott closed his mouth in mid yawn. "What about Howie?"

"He's usually home by this time. If he even bothered to tell me he'd not be coming home, I can guess he won't be here at all."

"I didn't bring anything to sleep in."

"Are you wearing anything under your underwear?"

"Of course not."

"Then you brought something."

Scott wanted to see just how sincere Ryan was. "And I don't have a toothbrush."

"I have another one."

"You wouldn't let me even kiss you in your bedroom last week."

"That was last week. And Krysta was here. And it was all so new and everything."

"So I can kiss you?"

"Kiss me."

They sat up and kissed while the music continued to blare from the speakers. Scott noticed the peculiar taste of cookies and bourbon and cola and decided he liked it because he was kissing Ryan on top of it all. It didn't take long before both their erections were demanding attention.

Ryan flipped the stereo off and led him to his room. The only light on was the nightlight on the far side of the room as he closed his door.

"Why the nightlight?"

"It was here when I moved in."

"Wimp."

"Fuck you."

"You seem to like that phrase. So…go for it."

Ryan pulled off his shirt and dropped it to the floor. Scott sat down on the bed. He kicked off his shoes, then let Ryan pull his shorts off. His erection pressed against the sheer white cotton of his underwear. Ryan kicked off his shoes. Scott unzip Ryan's shorts. Scott pulled on Ryan's underwear, first from one side, then the other. He slid them down to his knees and Ryan stepped out of them. He pushed Scott back and fell on top of him as he gyrated against his warm body.

Unexpectedly, Scott got a strange idea. "Let's not do it tonight."

"What!?"

"Let's not do it. Let's sleep together and not do it."

"Are you insane? You just got me naked!"

"Just so we can say we didn't."

"But Howie isn't home. We could do it in the living room if we wanted."

"I know. But we'll have a million times to do it. Besides, we've already done it this week. And I'm sleepy."

Ryan was incredulous. "I can do it, like, three times in an afternoon and you're bitchin' about two days ago?"

Scott had his hand on Ryan's neck and could feel his carotid artery pulsing. "No, it's not that. I just want to see what it's like to sleep with you and not do it."

He couldn't believe it, but reluctantly agreed to the ridiculous idea. It made him lose his erection in record time.

Scott noticed right away, of course. "I didn't say go away. I just said let's not do it tonight."

Scott's idea sounded stupid, yet it was compelling at the same time. *I guess it wouldn't hurt to just sleep this one time*, he thought.

They kissed each other's face, neck, armpits, and chest until their breath took on the scent of each other's body. Ryan grew hard again and stayed hard. As usual, he leaked like a sieve. As much as Ryan wanted to do it, he complied with Scott's wish and eventually let up. Scott didn't know what time it was when he drifted off.

The clock said 1:33 a.m. Ryan's body was pressed against his back. His hand was slowly massaging Scott's erect penis and occasionally cupping his tight scrotum. He had a sense he hadn't lost his erection all night. He turned, stretching his arms above his head. "You awake?"

"Duh."

Scott reached around and found what he was looking for. He ran a thumb around the top of Ryan's glans and felt his tight balls, firm beneath his hardness. "I guess," he whispered. He turned around and pressed his mouth against his. The little bit of stubble on Ryan's chin rubbed against his face as they kissed. Despite its sparseness, the masculine feel of it made him want to renege on his plan of action, or lack thereof, for the night.

Ryan stuck his head under the covers and sucked on Scott's penis a little, making it good and wet from his saliva. He came up for air. "Are you sure you don't want me to fuck you?"

"I don't know what the hell I was thinking. Do me."

Ryan immediately flung off the sheet and left the bedroom.

Scott rose up on his elbows and called out. "Where the hell are you going?"

Ryan answered from the hallway. "My condoms are in the bathroom."

"Oh." Scott scratched his head and lay there waiting.

Ryan returned in less than five seconds. He was already peeling off the top of a condom package. He had his tube of aloe gel in his mouth as he did so. He stopped at the edge of the bed and quickly rolled the condom down onto his hard shaft, dropped the aloe tube onto the floor next to the bed, then flung himself on top of Scott. They wrestled, and Ryan attempted to hump his abdomen with his condom-covered penis. He forcibly turned Scott over onto his stomach, helped him stuff a pillow under his pelvis, reached down to retrieve the tube, and quickly smeared the gel over the condom. He applied a glob onto his finger and proceeded to smear it all over Scott's anus. He paused only long enough to get first one digit in, then a second. He pumped with his fingers a few times while Scott raised his hips up to meet his motion.

"God, go for it now. Don't just use your fingers."

"You don't have to ask *me* twice." His breath was already labored. He had never waited this long in his life and was just about to explode.

Ryan placed the head against Scott's anus. With a slow, but continuous motion, he pressed harder and harder. He felt himself slowly penetrate and in only a few more seconds was completely in.

Scott grimaced. "Oh my God."

"Did I go too fast?"

"No. It feels so good, I can't believe it."

Ryan took that as his cue to start pumping. And pump he did. Unfortunately, it took less than a minute before he came. He moaned and kept pumping long after he had filled the condom, not happy that it had happened so fast. He had been well primed from several hours of feeling Scott up. He didn't know it at first, but Scott had come all over the pillow. The pressure applied to his prostate combined with the sensual feeling of being humped on the soft downy mound made him lose it. Scott's muffled moaning gave Ryan the clue.

"Did you just come?"

Scott was still breathing heavily and humping the pillow. "Yeah," he moaned.

Ryan slowly pulled out and turned Scott over. Scott had left quite a sticky mess. The pillow had a wide smear on it, and it was all over Scott's abdomen and his pubes.

"Damn it, you came all over my pillow."

"Oh, and that's the first time that's ever happened, huh?"

"Fuck. It's gonna stain."

"What did you expect?"

"How am I gonna explain this to Howie?"

"Don't tell him. Wash the pillowcase. I don't know!"

Ryan tensed his abdomen as Scott pushed him. Ryan got up and went to the bathroom. Scott heard the toilet flush then the water running in the sink. He returned a few moments later with a wet washcloth. He carefully wiped up Scott's abdomen, then attempted to clean up the pillow. He dropped the washcloth to the floor and finally sank, exhausted, into the bed. "That was a stupid idea."

"What?"

"We're all alone in the house and you say *don't*? That better not come out of your mouth again."

"Yeah, it was pretty stupid."

Scott had a wide grin on his face. In a way, they'd been having sex all night due to Ryan's constant groping. In a few more minutes, they both fell asleep, side-by-side, on their backs.

Early gray dawn light was coming through the partially opened blinds. Ryan rose to his knees, pulled the blinds back to look out, and rested his arms on the narrow sill. From his vantage, he could see the upper part of the driveway. He surveyed what he could of it for Howard's car. He cocked his head to listen. Although he couldn't see if the car was in the drive or not, judging from the fact that it was four in the morning now and they hadn't been woken up by any noise from inside the house, he was sure Howard wasn't there yet.

Despite being quiet, Ryan's movements woke Scott. He could see Ryan's half-hard penis and his round buttocks, tensed and firm as he balanced himself at the sill. Their whiteness contrasted quite nicely with the darker skin on his back and legs. He ran a finger up and down the crack of Ryan's butt. He cleared his throat. "What are you looking at?"

"I guess he's still over there." Ryan lowered himself to get out from behind the blinds and turned to face him. Covered up to his neck by the sheet, Scott's erection was quite noticeable.

Ryan looked down at his own now fully erect penis as it pulsated with anticipation. Scott knew what to do and pushed off the sheet. Ryan got on top, holding his torso over Scott by putting his weight on his palms. Scott watched as Ryan rubbed it up and down along side Scott's. It took a lot longer than the previous time, and it was sort of surprising that dry humping did it. But it was, after all, friction. Finally, as Ryan's muscles tensed and his breathing took on a ragged sound, a tiny white pool appeared on Scott's abdomen. He collapsed on top of Scott in a heap.

Scott let Ryan catch his breath before he stirred. He turned the pillow up on end against the headboard and leaned into it. Ryan sat on his knees in front of him. Scott placed his legs over Ryan's thighs and motioned for Ryan to scoot a little closer to him. Slowly Scott pumped as Ryan smeared the now runny liquid around on Scott's abdomen with his fingers. Scott figured he'd finish himself off but Ryan didn't want that to happen at all. He pulled Scott's hand away and wrapped his fingers around Scott's penis. He started slowly at first, stopped for a moment, then started again.

"Go a little faster now," Scott said as he watched Ryan's fist.

Ryan complied and adjusted his body so he could get a good rhythm going. He figured that since Scott usually came quickly that he wouldn't last long at all.

Scott's mind was reeling. The sensation was unbelievable as Ryan's warm grasp continued in a constant rhythm. Scott's heavy breathing turned into short moans, which became louder ones that filled the bedroom. He tensed his abdomen as a single long thin streak arched across his chest while the remainder oozed down Ryan's fingers. Ryan only slowed down a little. Scott finally had to grab Ryan's arm and make him stop.

Ryan grinned, and fished over the edge of the bed. He grabbed what he thought was the washcloth. It wasn't. It was his underwear. He wiped Scott up with it. Scott took the balled up underwear from him when he was done, getting his lips and nose wet as he inhaled.

"What are you doing?" Ryan asked.

"How could I resist? Can I keep them?"

"*No.*"

"I want 'em."

"That's too queer."

Scott threw the underwear at his face. "Don't say 'queer'."

Ryan caught it and dropped it to the floor. "Sorry, but no."

"I was just kidding anyway."

Scott sat up and looked through the slats of the blinds now, looking for Howard's car, too. He didn't know why either of them bothered to look since Howard clearly wasn't coming in this early. He flopped back in the bed. He still felt a little miffed that Ryan had used the 'queer' word, but in another moment, a big smile drew across his face. Ryan lay at his side and pulled the sheet up to their navels. They lay side by side, as Ryan clasped Scott's hand in his. Scott held it tightly for a moment before he released his grip.

"Hmm," was all Scott could muster. The house was completely quiet as they both slowly drifted into a satisfied sleep once again.

Ryan stirred and stretched his arms out. He bumped against the side of Scott's face. That woke Scott up. It was a little past six. Ryan pulled the sheet aside and went to the bathroom. Scott followed a moment later, sure that the coast was still clear. He shut the door and locked it. "Can I shower with you?"

Ryan protested. "Howie," was all he said.

"We'll make it quick. Besides, if he shows up he wouldn't have any idea we were in the shower *together*."

Scott let Ryan soap up his chest and dick, which made him fully hard again. But he was spent and didn't go for another try. How many times he imagined doing this in the shower with some of the guys on the track team, he couldn't remember. To think it was finally happening! This time, though, in his boyfriend's house. He examined his face in the mirror after he dried off. He needed to shave again and all his things were back in his bedroom. "I need to get home."

"I can't believe I let you spend the night."

Scott turned around to look at him. "What does that mean?"

"I mean, I can't believe I didn't freak out about lettin' you stay over."

Actually, Scott was more surprised than he. "Less freakin', more kissin'." He strapped on his watch and went into the bedroom to put on his clothes. Ryan was in tow directly behind him. Scott almost decided to keep the underwear after all, but had no place to stash it. "Hey, wanna come to practice?"

"I don't know." He thought about their all-night sex and how it seemed that despite the shower, that he was virtually advertising that he had had sex with Scott.

"We're gonna do more original stuff."

Ryan thought about it again. He'd essentially be home alone today if he weren't with him. "Okay. But you'll have to come back and get me. I'm gonna sleep some more. Your hot body kept me awake."

Scott reached down to adjust himself. "Don't I know."

He drove home, yawning most of the way. In effect, he barely slept at all either. And it was beginning to be weird that he liked Ryan this much. First, he was attracted to him. Then he thought Ryan was an asshole. Then he got this strange idea that Ryan must be gay. Then he found out the truth. The most amazing part of it all was that now he was going out with the guy. His dick was doing all the thinking now. It was difficult to resist. As he drove, he wondered what he would do when Ryan started school. The thought that he would soon be over a hundred miles away while he remained in Yucca Valley without him made him reel with a sudden feeling of loss. *Not so fast,* he thought, *he's not even close to being gone yet.*

Shortly after seven, he arrived home. Even though it was overcast, it was quickly becoming the usual hot day. He drew fresh water for Shakaiyo and roughhoused with her for a few minutes before shaving his sparse beard, then changing clothes. Food was on his mind now and he went inside to get some cereal. He had just reached for a bowl from the cabinet when Elaine came in the kitchen.

She looked at him, took a cup from the cabinet, and poured some of the already made coffee for herself. No hello. No good morning.

"Scott. Where were you last night?"

Although he had a tremendous amount of autonomy, he knew she still checked on him. "Sorry Mom. I was out late."

"You mean you didn't come home. You could've called." Her tone was disturbing.

Scott could tell she wasn't happy with him. "I forgot." He placed the bowl on the counter and pulled open the drawer to retrieve a spoon. She rarely got this way but when she did, it was unnerving.

"Well, where were you?"

"With Ryan."

He wanted to elaborate. He was still excited about last night and could have told her a lot more: how they had eaten his Aunt Cin's cookies and drank Howard's bourbon. That they kissed and hugged, and

Ryan had felt him up for hours while he tried to sleep. That Ryan and he had done it twice even. And they showered together again. All that was impossible. She was his mother.

She showed her familiar face of concern. "I talked to Howard about him last week."

It was too early in the morning for him to think about the situation from her perspective and he took the defensive. He didn't want to be in a bad mood going to band practice but couldn't avoid what he was feeling.

"About what?"

His tone was evident to her. That wasn't the Scott she was used to, and it only strengthened what she was about to say. "He seems to be affecting your judgment."

"What the…" He wanted to say "hell" next, but didn't. "What did he say?"

"He disagreed with me, of course."

"I'm not surprised."

"I think Howard's too close to the situation to know how his nephew is affecting you."

What does she know, he thought. *He's affecting me just fine. She doesn't know the situation.*

"Now I know why." Her intonation told him everything. She knew. How, he couldn't begin to guess.

Scott pulled the milk out of the refrigerator and sat it on the counter. He let go of the door and it closed with a muffled thump. He leaned back against the counter, his arms crossed. Ironic that he was doing the same thing just last night in Howard's kitchen although the situation was completely different. "I think we need to talk," he said as his heart started to race.

"I should say so."

"I found someone else, Mom."

"Ryan?"

He nodded.

"Was Howard there? Did he let you spend the night?"

He started to raise his voice. "No. He was with his girlfriend. And he spent the night with *her*."

"*He's* an adult. He can make that choice."

He was even louder this time. "Be serious!"

"I *am* serious."

This time he shouted. "I'm nearly an *adult* myself!" He flung his arms up as he said it and knocked a magnet and piece of paper from the refrigerator door.

Elaine was already exasperated. "Son, you're only *sixteen*."

"What difference does that make?"

Kids his age were having sex all the time. He knew that. Some of them were his friends. Why was she arguing with him about it? Just because he was having sex with a boy, and not a girl? Why didn't she understand what he was up against? This was an opportunity he never figured he'd be partaking in, especially at his age.

She quickly realized the conversation was going to go nowhere. She reached out and took him in a hug. He wouldn't hug her back as he fought to control the confusing feelings that were coming up. On the one hand, he didn't want to disappoint her, but he sure wasn't going to just up and shut Ryan out of his life over motherly concerns. He was in what he considered a real relationship for the first time in his life and now he had to figure out how to defend it with her.

She chose her words a little more carefully. "I'm sorry, son. I'm worried about you."

"You always worry about something. There's nothing to worry about," he said as he pulled her away.

"What about AIDS?"

He was perfectly aware of AIDS. Only once had she spoken about it to him. That was when he came out to her. "He's only been with one other person."

"That's enough to infect someone."

Maybe, maybe not. He wasn't sure. He realized he was eventually going to have to get Ryan to talk about that guy Crawford. "We've been safe. Look, Mom, I'll tell Dad myself. Don't go blabbing this to his uncle either. He doesn't know about him, or us." She stood there, not saying anything. "Mom, I want you to be *happy* for me. I like him and he likes me. He even cooked dinner for us last night." Granted, it was only spaghetti. Anyone could make spaghetti. The fact was that Ryan had indeed bothered to cook.

She picked up her coffee cup and looked at him. "He can cook?"

He guessed that since she seemed a little calmer now that their usual rapport was returning. "I was surprised, too."

"How was it?"

"It was good." He looked at his watch. "Speaking of food, I need to eat and get to band practice. Mom, please, we can talk about this later?"

What else could she say? "Go to practice."

He poured some cereal into the bowl, drowned it in milk, and ate quickly.

She poured some sugar into her coffee, then picked the magnet and piece of paper up off the floor. Outside she was keeping calm. But inward she was a wreck all of a sudden. She had known this would happen one day, that her son would say this exact thing to her. One day she'd have to hear about a gay relationship he was in. The scenario played once, maybe twice before in her mind. She remembered thinking it would be awful to have to finally admit it once and for all. She expected him to be much older, not a teenager, and certainly not while he was still living at home. In a way it was fine he'd found someone he liked. Now, though, she had a whole new set of concerns. But she couldn't just pass up her bad impression of Ryan, despite Howard's denial. Even though the news was so quick and disturbing, she could tell that Scott was happy and a small part of her felt happy, too. *I just hope to God he's careful*, she thought.

Chapter 15

Howard's car was in the driveway when Scott came back to pick him up. Ryan was waiting outside, looking nervous.

"Why are you out here?" Scott asked.

Ryan got in. "I didn't want to talk to Howie anymore."

"Why, did he say something about last night?"

"What would he say? He didn't know you were here."

"I don't know. Did you get rid of the two glasses?"

"Shit. I didn't think about that. They're still in the kitchen sink. I don't think he'll smell anything. He looked pretty sleepy."

Scott grinned and put his foot on the clutch. "Sounds like everyone got some last night." As he looked back over his shoulder, he made the announcement. "My mom knows about us," he said as he pulled out of the drive.

"What! Why did you tell her?"

"I didn't *tell* her. I didn't come home last night, remember?"

Ryan was panicked. "And she figured it out from that?"

"Dude, she knows I'm gay."

"Fuck! You didn't tell me that!"

"Hell, *you've* only known for a week." Scott started to notice that he was doing a fair amount of arguing with him when they interacted. *It's not supposed to be like this*, he thought.

"Is she pissed?" Ryan asked.

"No. More worried than anything. But she worries about every-thing."

"What did she say?"

"She's surprised you're gay."

Ryan mulled over the thought that Scott's mother now knew about the two of them. He didn't want everyone thinking he might be gay, much less anyone knowing what was going on between he and Scott. How awful that sounded to him most of the time. To identify himself the way Scott so easily did unnerved him. "Well, *I'm* worried now."

"Not you, too." *Maybe* that's *his problem*, Scott thought, *he worries a lot. He panics at the drop of a hat.* Scott, on the other hand, just let a lot of things slide.

"What if she tells everyone?"

"Duh, *my* mom? Not. Besides, I told her not to say anything to my dad. Or Howie."

"Please, not Howie," he said somewhat to himself.

Scott thought a moment how Ryan continued to put up this grand façade to pretend he was straight. "Look. Things aren't gonna be any different. I tried. It didn't work. You are what you are."

"I doubt it."

Scott countered. "Bullshit. I thought if I hung out with the guys more often I'd get over it. It didn't happen. So, there's nothing to get over. And Aunt Cin told me to just enjoy the fact that I'm different."

He was sure Scott was right. In fact, he had tried the same thing. Hanging out with Dolf and the other guys back home only made him long to get in their pants. And how could he explain Crawford? He couldn't, no matter how much he tried. He felt so fucking different, like a misfit. Sure, his show was good. People thought he was one of the guys. To his friends back home he acted the part perfectly. Some of the time he even believed it himself. Despite the disturbing thoughts that swirled in his mind, he realized Scott was trying to calm him down. He looked at Scott's face and sighed.

Before he could stop himself he blurted out, "God, I want you to be my friend forever." He knew exactly how sappy it sounded and wanted to take it back. But it was too late. He had said it aloud.

Scott was grinning broadly. "As long as you do me whenever I ask."

*   *   *

Bryce, Mitch, and Sparks had arrived at practice just before them.

After they parked, Ryan jumped out, ran ahead of Scott, pivoted, and waited.

Scott figured out what he was doing, grabbed the Frisbee from the back seat, and tossed it to him. Ryan caught it with precision—its dead center landed right on his outstretched index finger, and spun until he bopped it up. He whirled around and caught it behind his back. Mitch, who had watched the entire interaction, stopped what he was doing, blinked, and looked at Sparks. "Not bad."

Mitch turned his attention to Ryan again. "Come on!" he said as he held his arms up, waiting for Ryan to toss it back.

Ryan stripped off his shirt, pulled it through a belt loop of his shorts, and followed them to the backyard outside the Royal Garage. Now that the other guys had gotten involved, Scott declined to horse around and instead decided to set up the recording equipment for the day's take. Heat waves shimmered in the distance as the sun burned off the thin overcast. As usual, it was a good dry heat. Although it was already in the upper eighties, none of them felt particularly uncomfortable yet.

Colleen came out of the back door of the house. She stood for a moment watching the guys tossing the Frisbee, then went to the garage and found Scott setting up.

"Hey, why aren't you out there with the guys?"

"Too sleepy." That was the second reason. The first one was that he didn't really like playing Frisbee with the guys. He relished playing only with those that were good. He knew it was an awful thing to think, but couldn't help it.

"So, how was the road trip?"

"Loved it. You should have gone."

"I wanted to. A weekend on the lake would have been just the thing, but I had to work."

"Did you see Jim again?"

"Yes."

"And?" Scott saw her coy smile.

"And he was great, as usual."

Good. She was talking, so he could as well. He raised an eyebrow. "Can you keep a secret?"

She whispered back, her face animated. "Depends. You have to tell me who I *can't* tell."

He pulled back and made a face at her. "No one!"

"No fair. I have to at least tell my mother."

"She would puke."

"Pay me?" she said laying her hand out.

"Look, do you want to hear it, or not?"

"Hey, where's that famous Faraday sense of humor?"

"I left it with my boyfriend."

She cocked her head, not sure if she heard him correctly. "With who?"

"Him." He pointed to Ryan as he came into view, jumping to catch the Frisbee.

"Him?" She asked, incredulous.

"I did point to him."

"Isn't it kinda sudden? How did you...how did you convert him?"

"I didn't *convert* him. It happened in Parker."

"How did you know?"

"What? That he's gay?"

"Well, yeah."

"I didn't exactly. It just sorta happened. I'm not even his first. 'Mr. Supposedly Straight' has been in a relationship already."

"You mean with a guy?"

"Yeah. That's what gay means."

"He's awfully young. And so are you."

"Yes, mother. We're consenting teenagers, you know," he answered as he uncoiled a cable.

"Well, he *is* cute. Do you like him? I mean is there more than a physical thing going on?"

"Yes, and maybe. Why are *you* asking? You and Jim don't have more than a physical thing going."

"It's more than physical," she said, now crossing her arms. "We just haven't defined what it is yet."

"Well, neither have I…I mean, we. Anyway, I had to tell you, 'cause you'll probably see him and me together a lot. I had to tell someone besides my mother."

"Your mother? Did she puke?"

"She spazzed. Actually, I didn't tell her. I spent the night at his house last night and she found out."

"You mean, you 'slept' together."

"Slept? As in sleeping?"

"No, the adult definition of 'slept.'"

"Of course." He grinned, then added, "Twice. I'm running on fumes today."

She cracked a smile. "I take it she wasn't supposed to find out?"

"Exactly. I didn't call about not coming home and she figured it out."

"Is she some sort of mind-reader?"

"She has this way of figuring some things out. Not many, but some."

"Well, I'm happy for you, even though you razz me about Jim all the time."

"Believe me, I need all the support I can get. It's not easy with that guy."

"Why so?"

"He's an orphan. And he still bitches about not having parents."

"Hello. You have parents."

"Well, he's pretending that he's not gay either."

"Pretending?"

"You know. He's lived around only straight people his whole life, so he thinks he's straight."

She furrowed her brow. "Well, so have you."

"But I know I'm gay and that's that. He thinks he can stop himself from being that way."

She laughed. "That's silly."

He stopped to ponder her choice of words. "Yeah. Silly. He's being silly."

She took a microphone and plugged it in the soundboard. Her voice boomed loudly as she spoke into it. "I can't imagine how…" she started. He glared at her, while quickly twisting the potentiometer to zero. At that instant, a loud bang against the vinyl siding of the garage startled them both. Scott quickly withdrew his hand from the board in reaction. The Frisbee wobbled on the sidewalk in front of the side door before it came to a rest at the threshold. They both turned to look at it.

Colleen retrieved it as the guys came toward her from the yard. They piled into the garage and stood in front of the two big fans to cool off. Ryan leaned forward with his hands on his knees and caught Scott's attention. Barry showed up and listened as Ryan spoke.

"Scott I forgot to tell you," he said as he huffed. "Howie's invited everyone over to our place, not this coming Friday, but the next one for the birthday party. I already told the guys. Make sure your parents show up. And you, too, Colleen. And Barry."

She bumped Scott with her elbow, and whispered to him. "This is what happens in relationships. You're the last one to know anything."

Band practice was long and involved since Scott taped every tune this time. Ryan sat on a stool next to the soundboard while he watched and listened with much interest. It was evident that Scott was in his element. He couldn't see Scott working as a host at any restaurant for a career and decided he belonged in a music studio for sure. It was as if he changed into a different person. Serious, concentrated and definitely into what he was doing.

After filling up two 90-minute tapes, Scott played back some of the cuts. They downed sodas and ate munchies while they listened and analyzed the performances. It was late afternoon when they ended for good. Contrary to their normal procedure, no plans were made for after practice.

As Scott drove Ryan back to Howard's place, he thought about what Colleen said about him being the last to know.

"How come you didn't tell me about the party plans this morning when I picked you up?"

"Howie had just told me like ten minutes before and I forgot."

"How could you forget about something like that?"

"I was gonna tell you, but then you blurted out that your mother knew about us. I was freaked and forgot."

"Oh." It was simple. Ryan was upset. It wasn't a big deal at all.

They pulled up in the drive and Scott saw that Howie's car was gone. "Does he ever stay home?" Scott asked.

"This thing with Krysta's still new. It's hard to say what he's up to nowadays."

"Then let's go in for a while."

Ryan looked around, then stared at him.

"Don't look at me like that," Scott said.

"Why not?"

Scott looked down at his crotch. "It gets me hard."

Ryan ventured a hand to Scott's lap. "You're not kidding."

They got out of the Jeep. Scott reached into his pants to adjust himself, then pulled his t-shirt down a little farther. They went up onto the back deck. Ryan turned around at the sliding glass door and looked at him.

Scott looked back with a distressed look. "Open it up. I'm standing here with a hard-on."

"Let's wait 'til the neighbors notice before we go in."

Scott shot a glance to the neighbor's house on the left, then the one on the other side of the house. He saw no one but decided a character shift was overdue.

Ryan loved it. For once, he had Scott going.

Scott then did what passed as his Bella Lugosi voice, hunching his shoulders, and raising his hands as if he were going to lunge at him. "I vant you to suck my deeck," he said in a rhythmic cadence.

"Fuck! A homo vampire is after me," Ryan said with a make believe look of concern.

He scrambled to slide open the door, and quickly launched himself inside. Scott burst in after him and grabbed him around the middle. His car keys flung loose from his hand, went sliding across the kitchen floor, and smacked into the baseboard. Ryan ran down to the end of the hall and Scott tackled him to the floor just as he reached the carpeted den.

One of Ryan's sandals went flying as he tried to extract himself from Scott's grip. But Scott held him tight. Ryan struggled and finally got out of the hold. Before Scott could try anything else, he started to pull off Scott's t-shirt. It was one of Scott's favorites and he didn't want it to rip. He lowered his head and raised his arms up so it would come off smoothly. Despite the exertion, the sexual energy kept him mostly hard. He noticed Ryan was also sporting an erection now, as well.

Scott pinned Ryan to the floor again, this time with a wrestling move he had learned from his brother, one that had been used on Scott plenty of times. Ryan drew his knees up to his chest as he tried to pry him off. But Scott turned him over and gave him a wedgie instead.

Ryan's hair was completely messed up now and his face was beet red as he tried to catch his breath. Scott was laughing hard now, while breathing heavily from the exertion. Ryan tried to stand again but Scott caught his shin with an outstretched hand and Ryan went to the floor again. His left shoulder just barely missed a corner of the coffee table. This time, Scott straddled him and pinned his arms together above his head with one hand. Immediately he started to tickle him with the other one.

"Don't...tickle....Stop!" Ryan spat out between fits of laughter. Scott reveled in the discovery that Ryan was ticklish. As quickly as he could, he spun around. His shins pinned each of Ryan's arms above his head in such a way that he was unable to get himself free. Scott knew it would be difficult. After all, his brother had done it to him lots of times.

Scott's crotch was directly above Ryan's face. Ryan thought briefly of several things he might do with the opportunity. Before he could react, Scott took the hem of Ryan's shirt and pulled it back to get access to his stomach. He lowered his head, plastered his lips on the taut skin just above his navel, and blew as hard as he could. That made Ryan go into another bout of laughter at the loud farting sound and the ticklish feeling.

Scott took a deep breath, ready to do it again. As he did so, he thought he heard something behind him. From the corner of his eye he saw Howard coming into the kitchen. Krysta was standing there with him. Each had a box of pizza in their hands. The boys were in direct view of them both. Scott was in an embarrassing position so he scooted off to Ryan's side. Both of them sat up on their knees, catching their breath.

"What were you guys doing in there?" Howard called out. He pulled his sunglasses off, put the pizza box on the kitchen table, and immediately headed down the hall toward them.

Ryan responded immediately, trying to sound innocent. "Playing."

"Boys your age, playing?" Krysta asked, upon reaching the den. Both boys were still breathing hard. Scott had a big smile on his face. But Ryan looked somewhat angry. She observed the sandal at one end of the room. Scott's shirt was draped half over the couch arm, half on the floor, and she wondered briefly if they had broken any of the furniture.

Scott was artful in his comeback, though sounding completely serious. "Ryan needs to play more than most boys his age." He hiccupped loudly then put a hand over his mouth.

Krysta looked at Scott, then Ryan. Her laughter startled the boys. Howard laughed, too, and then eyed her.

Ryan was mortified. He was still half-hard and was sure Scott was, too. And it must have been obvious what they were doing. Surely, Howard would figure it out in another second and freak.

But that wasn't the case at all.

Howard took Krysta's purse and set it on an end table. She looked at him quizzically until she figured out why he was so deliberate in doing so. "Oh, no you don't, Howard!" She turned and headed for the kitchen but he was too quick for her and barred her way.

"I'll scream!"

He shrugged his shoulders, grabbed, and started tickling her.

She screamed.

Scott had no idea what to think of the situation. He was shirtless, Ryan's shirt was still pulled up to his pecs, and he thought for sure both of them had noticed the intense sexual energy they had stirred up.

Krysta was down for the count in the hall now, laughing hysterically, as Howard tickled her. Scott thought his penis had shrunk to nothing now, that it was even hidden inside his body somewhere. Ryan tried to smooth his hair back into place as he stood up. Scott continued to kneel on the carpet.

"Get up," Ryan whispered as he found his errant sandal and started to put it on.

Scott stood with Ryan in the hall watching Howard as he tickled Krysta on the floor. She was dodging his hands by constantly moving her arms around her middle, then attempted to grab him to make him stop. His hearty laughter echoed above them along the high vaulted ceiling of the den.

Ryan wished Scott would put his shirt back on. When he didn't bother, he picked it up for him and threw it at him. Scott shot him a nasty look as he grabbed it. Ryan pointed at him and mouthed for him to put it on. "Okay," Scott said out loud, as he looked for the sleeves.

Howard had finally stopped tickling and was letting Krysta catch her breath now. "Okay, what?" he asked looking back at them.

"What's the big idea of sneaking up on us?" Ryan interjected.

"It's my house. I'll sneak up on anyone I feel like here."

Howard let Krysta up and she straightened her top and hair. She looked so embarrassed that she didn't ask any more questions. Howard chuckled a few more times before he kissed her cheek.

"Did you have a good laugh?" he asked his nephew.

Ryan couldn't believe it. He was waiting for the worst possible scenario and none seemed forthcoming. His serious mood gave way to a less cheerless tone. "Yes, thanks to him," he answered accusingly, pointing to Scott.

"You loved it," Scott asserted.

While the adults weren't looking, Ryan mouthed 'fuck you' to him. Scott scowled and stuck his tongue out in return, surprised to find himself doing so.

Back in the kitchen, Howard asked Krysta to forgive him for being so rough on her. She told him that that was the only time he was ever going to get away with something like that.

The aroma of cheese and sausage from the pizzas was now quite evident and it made Scott's mouth water. Howard then lifted the lid of one of the boxes and took a whiff. "You guys will, of course, stay for pizza?"

Scott's eyebrows went up. "Pizzeria Turano? You don't have to ask *me* twice." He searched for his keys, found them, and quickly retrieved them from the floor. No one noticed him doing so.

Howard pulled some videos out from a plastic bag. "We went to the video store, too. Either of these two interest you guys?"

Ryan read the labels. "Nah."

"I insist. You don't spend much time around here anymore."

Scott looked at his watch, then back at him. "I can stay. I have time."

Howard was still acting as if nothing happened. And nothing had happened. Except that Ryan wanted to take Scott in his arms and kiss him the whole time they were roughhousing. Okay, not the entire time. He wanted to kill him when the tickling started.

Howard popped the video in while they ate. Krysta sat with him and when all the pizza was eaten they sat side by side with their hands clasped in his wide recliner. The boys sat at either end of the sofa. It may as well have been miles apart since they couldn't touch each other.

The chosen video was a love story woven around a murder mystery. Ryan was bored about fifteen minutes into it. Finally, though, it was over and, full of pizza, he found himself quite sleepy now. Scott notified them that he was leaving.

"I'll show you to the door," Ryan said after he yawned.

You better do more than just walk me to the door, Scott thought. *I want you to hold my hand. I want you to give me a kiss. I want to spend the night with you again!* He slipped on his tennis shoes and headed for the front door.

Standing on the porch, Ryan shut the door with a decided slam. "Fuck!" he whispered.

"What?"

"I was so fucking embarrassed."

"Nothing happened."

"But it could have."

"You're beginning to remind me of my mother. She worries *all* the time."

"I'm not your mother."

"Well, *I'm* your boyfriend. So kiss me."

Ryan jammed his hands in his pockets and whispered back. "No way. What if they're looking out the peephole?"

"Put your finger over it," he said, sounding exasperated. He pecked Ryan on the cheek and took a step down the stairs. The front porch light wasn't on and the dim light from the lone streetlight half a block away silhouetted Scott's face.

Ryan wanted to hug him as hard as he could, but couldn't bring himself to do it in front of the house. "I'm gonna miss you," he said.

Scott looked at his dark figure. There was a distinct bizarre ring to how he had said it. "I'm just going home. Are *you* going somewhere?"

"No."

He wasn't convinced. Something was wrong with his tone. "Where 're you going?"

"Nowhere." He quickly changed the subject and came down the stairs. "I'm calling my cousin Adina tomorrow so we can plan the party up north. Soon I'll be eighteen. And later we'll be in Crescent City."

"And in *one* week I'll be seventeen," Scott said. He raised a hand and met Ryan's in mid-air. The slap of their palms echoed from the front porch.

Scott started for his vehicle. "See ya tomorrow?"

"Come on over."

*   *   *

Scott examined a large yellow poster board, which lay on the dining room table. Various colored pencils lay all around it, one of which was in Ryan's hand. Figures of dancing guys and girls were hand-drawn in detail. Musical instruments were drawn with precision. Colored balloons were drawn all over the edges of the poster. A bold, highly stylized '18' lay in the center. Caricatures of the band members were drawn all around the center in a circle. Not only the figures, but also the lettering was all done in elaborate detail.

"I made it for the back door for the birthday party. Every once and a while I gotta do something creative and this is a good excuse."

"Dude, this is great," he exclaimed. "Colleen and Barry said they'd have to approve the promo poster you talked about, but I'm sure when they see this they'll say yes."

"Cool. It took a couple of days to get it all exact. I'm just filling in some color now."

"I can't draw a thing," Scott commented. "So what'd your cousin say?"

"We're lucky."

"Why's that?"

"Her parents are gonna be out of town that entire week, so we can party at her house. It's huge, so plenty of people can come."

"Bitchin'."

"Hey, did you tell your parents about the party? It's as much for you as it is for me."

"They were asleep when I got home so I left a message on the blackboard."

"Well, they all have to come. Howard's invited some people from work. He's invited just about everyone he knows actually. Make sure the band can come, too."

"They better all show up."

"I sure hope people show up for the party."

"Why wouldn't they?"

Ryan rubbed a pencil smudge on the top of the table with his finger. "I didn't exactly leave Crescent City on the best of terms with everyone."

"Why would that make any difference? Your cousin's doing all the work. And who hates to party?"

"I didn't tell too many people I'd be leaving. No telling what they're gonna think."

"Do they know her?"

"Adina knows everybody."

"Then you're just worrying again. I'm sure if anyone asked, she told them everything. I'm gonna start calling you 'mother', if you don't stop worrying all the time."

"Fuck you."

"Just say when. I'm ready right now, actually." A wide grin spread over his face.

Ryan remained aloof the entire time Scott was there before he went back home. It had made Scott feel like something was wrong. Nothing was wrong though. Ryan was simply concerned what people would think of his abrupt departure. He had been on his back for almost a week after the car accident. While he recuperated, Howard and his grandmother had arranged for him to leave. He had left Crescent City the day after he went to traffic court. That was only two days after graduation. He knew very well the grief he put his grandmother though all those years, hanging out with his fucked up friends, talking back to her, fighting with his brother, and all the other adolescent craziness. His one juvenile detention as a sophomore scared him enough to decide to never go through that again. Nonetheless, he was sure it was a miracle he didn't end up in jail.

Ryan didn't have the right words for what he had been struggling with. He just knew a horrible fight seemed to be going on inside him most of the time. Whoever was vulnerable, that's who he had verbally attacked. If there was a rule to break, he had broken it, short of ending up with a rap sheet. Muh had told him several times she would send him away if he didn't straighten up. He knew she had only been kidding. Even the part about sending him to military school years back. Maybe that's what started it with her. He had known she wasn't serious, and figured since he could get away with just about anything with her that everyone else could be pushed over. Nonetheless, by the time Howard had appeared he had felt so awful about everything that the only person he had told he was leaving was his cousin Adina.

Adina's mother and father didn't like him at all. They had known him well enough to know that he wasn't the type of person they wanted their daughter around. In fact, he had been politely asked not to come around their house anymore, even though he lived only a short distance away. Adina, on the other hand, liked him just fine. They were the same age and had had several classes together in school. Her parents couldn't keep them apart during the day at all.

"I can't believe a cousin of mine is so cute," she had once told one of her friends who, in turn, had told him. Naturally, Ryan liked her once he found that out. He kept a measured amount of emotional distance from her anyway and never could bring himself to confide in her. He knew it wouldn't go over well in school if people found out that he was secretly attracted to guys.

*   *   *

It was all Scott could do to contain his growing excitement about Ryan being his boyfriend as the week passed. Every waking hour he thought about him at least once. Many times in the next couple of days he caught himself having to break from a reverie, imagining Ryan's face, them kissing, them showering together, the feel of Ryan's dick inside him or in his mouth.

Wednesday morning after he woke up, Scott called AeroSun.

"Ryan St. Charles, please," he asked the receptionist.

"I'm sorry. That extension is busy. Would you like to leave a voice mail or a message?"

"No. I'll call back."

Twice more that morning he still couldn't reach him directly and declined to leave a message. Finally, on his shift at the restaurant, Scott got through.

"Hey, what's up, Scott?"

"I just wanted to hear your voice and-and I wanna see you tonight."

"Looks like we're gonna be here late. We're working on a special project. It's good overtime, though."

"How about if I come by tonight?"

Ryan hesitated. "I'll call you."

After 6 p.m., Scott got a call from Ryan. "Looks like we'll be here 'til seven or seven-thirty. If I can get some privacy later, I'll call."

Scott left the restaurant at eight o'clock that night. Ryan hadn't called before he left and there were no messages at home when he got there. Despite Ryan's lack of phone privacy, he still waited for the call. It didn't come. He figured it was time to buy Ryan a phone for the bedroom but didn't recall if there was an outlet in there or not.

By ten o'clock he was fuming. If Ryan wasn't going to call, then he'd do it. The phone was busy yet again. Ten-thirty, and it was still busy. He played his flute in an attempt to diminish his frustration. He only succeeded in butchering one of his favorite tunes. Finally, he gave up and lay on the bed after starting a cassette.

The tape deck clicked to a stop. He must have dozed off, he figured, since he didn't remember anything past the second tune. Shakaiyo got up on the bed and licked his face, seeming to know he was concerned about something. The clock showed twelve-thirteen. Time to see him, he decided.

"You, stay here. Better yet, go back to sleep," he told her. Being as quiet as possible with the gate, he left the backyard. The cul-de-sac was always quiet, so if he started the Jeep in the driveway his mom or dad was bound to ask him about it in the morning. It was nice having the amount of autonomy he had, but they kept an eye on him when they were home. If they heard him leave this late at night, he'd be questioned for sure. He coasted down the slight incline of the drive, rolled to the far end of the circle, and started it.

He took off down the sleeping street and headed to Howard's house. He parked the car on the street well away from the house, walked up half a block, and went around to the side of the house. He found Ryan's south-facing window and tapped on the glass. He waited. Nothing happened. He tapped again and stood back, waiting in the shadows. Finally, he saw the mini-blinds move around, then raise up. Ryan's sleepy face appeared. Scott's heart raced as he saw him. Ryan's eyes grew wide and he gave Scott a big smile. Scott motioned him to come out. Ryan slid open the window and whispered.

"What the hell are you doing? It's, like, the middle of the night."

"So what. Come out."

He drew in a deep breath. "Just a minute." He withdrew to dress, then reappeared a few minutes later. Scott pulled the screen off the window, and with him offering a hand, Ryan climbed out. Ryan wore his ubiquitous painter's cap, a dark t-shirt, and khaki shorts.

"The phone was busy all night," Scott whispered.

Ryan whispered back. "Howie was talking with Krysta 'til late. I finally just crashed."

"Dude, I can't stand it!" he exclaimed in a hoarse whisper. They leaned against the side of the house, passionately hugging and kissing. They rubbed their bodies together until they could feel each other grow hard.

Ryan pointed across the yard. "I know a trail through that field."

He led Scott through the dark of the backyard. The night was cloudless and there was no moon. The wide band of the Milky Way stretched unobstructed across the entire sky. Starlight illuminated the night enough to not need a flashlight. *It has to be a dream*, Scott thought. *Here I am in the middle of the night with my first boyfriend, and the night was as gorgeous as it can be.*

They came to the edge of the property and jumped down the wide cement ditch that separated the backyard from the soybean fields. The other side inclined at the same forty-five degree angle, which was no problem to climb with a running start. On the other side, Ryan led Scott down a narrow dirt trail toward the middle of one of the huge circular fields. The dark green undulating leaves of the soybeans surrounding them contrasted sharply with the stark dirt and rocks just beyond.

Up ahead loomed the tall-wheeled sprinkler assembly used to irrigate the green circle. Ryan squeezed Scott's hand as he led the way. Scott wanted him to lead him to some place where they could stay in each other's arms all night, not just to the center of a field.

Soon they were well into the dark greenery. "I bought you a birthday present," Ryan said, no longer whispering.

"What is it?"

"You think I'm gonna tell you?"

"You better or I'll start tickling you again."

Ryan let go of his hand and started forward to elude capture. Scott stopped in his tracks. A warm breeze caressed them as Ryan stopped, too.

Scott held up his hands. "I promise. No more tickling."

"I don't believe you."

"Peep, peep, peep."

Ryan chuckled, shoving his hands as far as he could into the pockets of his shorts. "Okay," he said slowly.

Scott started forward haltingly, and Ryan stayed put. Scott touched Ryan's forearm and ran his hand up to his shoulder, pulling himself even closer. Ryan willingly let Scott take his tongue as he kissed him ever so softly. He pulled away and took Scott's hand as they continued toward one of the wheels of the long mobile sprinkler.

"I don't have it yet," Ryan continued about his present. "But one of the guys I work with is bringing it to the party."

"Well, this weekend I'm going to San Bernardino to buy your present. It was a bitch to find. I called three places before I found one in stock."

"Whatever it is I'm sure I'll like it."

"You'll like it. I guarantee it."

Ryan continued to lead the way. His fingers cupped Scott's and every once in a while he lightly caressed his fingertips. The sensation made Scott shiver. Ryan's features against the backdrop of stars looked awesome. Scott pulled off Ryan's cap and put it on his own head. It covered his forehead and almost touched his eyebrows.

Ryan observed how it looked. "You don't have enough hair."

"You have a big head."

"I have another head that would love to get big." He took Scott's hand and put it on his crotch.

"Feels like it's already big."

Finally, at the central wheel of the sprinkler Ryan leaned against one of the spokes and pulled Scott close again. He took the hat and laid it aside, then pulled Scott's shirt up and off and laid it across a pipefitting. Scott pulled off his shoes with his toes and wiggled his feet in the dark earth. Scott pulled up Ryan's shirt, then caressed his warm chest. He unzipped Ryan's shorts. He was wearing no underwear and his erect penis popped out, holding fast at a sixty-degree angle. Ryan pulled Scott's shorts down to his ankles, and motioned for him to step out of them. He put the cap back on Scott's head and stood up to let Scott pull down his shorts now. It was all so methodical and precise as they draped their clothes over a spoke of the wheel.

Scott stood in front of Ryan, completely naked except for the cap. Excitement filled his body in waves. Ryan wetted one of his fingers with plenty of saliva, reached around, and pressed it against Scott's anus, getting his finger inside him just a little. Scott humped Ryan's abdomen as Ryan rhythmically pushed tip of his middle finger in and out. Before he knew it, Scott's moans were reverberating against the metal as an orgasm shuddered his body. Ryan pushed his finger in as far he could from his awkward angle as Scott thrust his pelvis even harder against Ryan's groin. Finally, he felt Scott's body relax a little. Ryan reluctantly pulled his finger out.

It seemed like a long time before Scott was able to catch his breath. When he finally opened his eyes, he saw Ryan scoop up the white globs from his abdomen, spit into his palm, then apply it all to his own penis. Ryan spit into his palm then grasped himself. The sound of Ryan's wet jerking kept Scott hard.

"Go down on me," Ryan whispered as he let go of his penis.

Scott knelt on Ryan's shoes and took his slicked up penis in his mouth. Not being an expert, as was Ryan, he used his hand, too. It was an interesting sensation and taste what with his own semen, Ryan's spit, and the salty taste of it all. It was something he didn't expect to enjoy, but it was keeping him hard as a rock.

With his other hand, he massaged Ryan's balls, feeling them grow tighter and tighter as he bobbed his head up and down on Ryan's hard shaft. Ryan laid his hands on Scott's shoulders as he continued to go up and down.

It didn't take much before Scott felt tiny jerks in his mouth. There was a loud moan from Ryan. A gust of wind blew the cap from Scott's head. It rolled to his side just as Ryan's penis erupted. Scott attempted to swallow but it made him gag. He wasn't used to a mouthful so, as it issued forth, he let it slide between his lips to the dirt below him. Ryan's chest didn't stop heaving even as Scott pulled away. Finally, spent and sated, Scott smeared his fingers on his leg in an attempt to wipe them dry. Still hard from the spectacle, he stood and poked Ryan's now softening dick with his own.

"Ha, ha, I stay hard longer than you do," Scott taunted.

"If you didn't just about put me in a coma every time, I'd probably stay hard, too."

The wind quickly dried the remaining wetness from their skin as they brushed up against each other's bodies, hugged, stroked each others face, neck and, of course, each other's still-tumescent penises. Finally, Scott felt his legs getting wobbly since he hadn't had a chance to even sit down yet. Ryan started dressing while Scott stepped back into his underwear and shorts. Ryan retrieved the cap and leaned back on the spoke as he wiped off his feet and tied his shoes.

Scott watched as Ryan finished tying the last lace. Still shirtless, his lat muscles showed as he moved. "God," Scott said softly.

"God, what?"

"You. Where did you come from anyway?"

Ryan picked up his shirt and held it up by two corners, letting it flap in the light breeze. He cleared his throat and tried to sound serious. "Many moons ago my people came here seeking others who were like us. We traveled to Venus and saw only clouds. We tried the moon but found only footprints. We saw this little blue planet and sought out Scott Faraday. They sent me here to see if you could be trusted."

Scott wondered if his grin was noticeable. Ryan was playing his game and stealing his heart even more. In a whiny voice, he responded. "Mr. Alien, did I pass the test? Can you trust me with your sex...uh, your secret?"

"It'll take a few more orgasms, but so far you pass."

Scott used his normal voice now. "Thank God."

Ryan tucked his shirt through a belt loop. Scott tried to tuck his in the back of his shorts as they started back but Ryan kept hold of one of his hands, hindering his effort. Finally, he managed to stuff enough of it in.

Then it was as if Ryan's mood just shifted. "Do you think we'll have to hide all our lives?"

"From what?"

"Me, from Howie. You, from your dad. And everyone else."

"I don't plan on hiding much longer about this."

Alarm was in Ryan's voice. "You're not just gonna tell everyone."

"Dude, hiding's fucked up."

"Oh, yeah. You're just gonna tell everyone in your class. How long do you think you'll be alive after you do that, huh?"

Ryan was right of course. He still had an entire year left of high school, which hadn't even started yet. The thought of it weighed on him. "You're right. Only those who matter."

Ryan really didn't know what that meant. "How do you know who those people are?"

"I don't know. My aunt and uncle know. My mother knows. I told Colleen."

"Colleen? She knows, too? Is there anyone *else* you want to tell me about?"

"That's it, just them."

"And you think Colleen didn't tell anyone else in the band?"

"Uh, I don't think so. I'm sure if she told them I'd have heard about it by now."

Ryan thought for a moment. "And no one you've told is a guy our age, right?"

"So?"

"See? Get ready to not be in the band."

"I'm not telling anyone else. At least not yet. And I bet nobody'll care when *you* get to school. Hell, I'm sure *nobody* cares in L.A." He couldn't believe he just said that and it suddenly pained him to think about the implication. Eventually, he was going to have to acknowledge that Ryan was going away. Then he'd be alone again in Yucca Valley. It was the first time he ever thought about feeling alone and it made him feel awful.

"I don't think I'm even gonna make it to nineteen," Ryan said weakly.

He loosened his grip but Scott, still feeling awful, held on tighter as he stopped walking. "You keep saying shit like that. What the fuck does that mean?" He didn't mean it to come out like that, but he was still thinking about Ryan going away and it made him angry now.

"Nothing."

"Nothing, shit."

Even under cover of the darkness that enveloped them, it was still painful for Ryan to look Scott in the eye. But he felt this little window of opportunity and decided to let him know what he felt. "It's…like I have this shadow…in my heart. Sometimes I can't even breathe it hurts so much. I close my eyes and see all this darkness…It's like I'm swimming against a current to…just stay alive."

Scott was honestly startled to hear something like that.

"And every once in a while when I see you, or touch you," he reached out and touched Scott's face, "it's like you're a life vest and I can…feel my heart smiling."

"Believe me, I'm your life vest." He tried to lighten up both their moods. "And I'm your love slave, too."

"It's not funny. I'm serious." Ryan hand dropped to his side.

"I-I didn't mean it to be funny. It's just…well, you're so…like yourself when we're together."

"That's why it's scary."

Scott took him by the shoulders. He made him look in his eyes and tried to find words for him. "Fun. You mean fun. You say, 'This is the most fun I've had in my whole life.'"

"This is all new for *you*. For *me*, it's not."

Maybe Ryan had something there. How would Scott know? This was the first time he had ever been with anyone in any kind of intimate relationship. Scott let go and they stood there in silence for a brief moment. Finally, Ryan turned and started walking again.

They retraced their steps and the long cement ditch came up. It stretched left and right looking somewhat like an abandoned road in the dark. Before crossing it Ryan stopped and yawned. Scott pulled the cap off his head and put it on his own head backwards.

"Stay with me, buddy. I like you." He touched Ryan's hair. It was as if electricity was going through his body from simply touching it. *How is that possible*, he wondered.

Ryan smiled so big that the chill of his strange earlier statement faded into the background. He took Scott and kissed him as passionately as he could.

They came up the other side of the ditch and eventually made it back across the backyard. Scott boosted him up through the window and quietly helped him replace the screen.

"See ya this weekend, cutie," Ryan whispered before shutting the window.

Scott leaned against the still warm bricks of the side of the house and sighed. His heart pounded with anxiety and excitement. There it was again: the weird mixture of completely different emotions at the same time. It was odd how being in a relationship did that.

CHAPTER 16

Several days later, in the morning, Scott called his aunt. It took twice before he got her and not the answering machine.

"Aunt Cin?"

"Scott, honey. Did you get our gift?"

"Yeah. One hundred and fifty bucks! Thanks."

"It's a special seventeenth birthday gift. It's also an enticement to have you over again. Soon. And bring your new boyfriend. By the way, how is he?"

"You don't have to bribe me. I'd be there all the time if I could. And he's the other reason I called."

She heard the slight worry in his voice. "Did you have an argument?"

"No. Just the opposite. We went walking in this big soybean field in the middle of the night."

Cin sighed noticeably. "Sounds romantic."

"God, it was."

"What did he say?"

"It was more like what he didn't say. But he talked about going away and not making it to his nineteenth birthday and stuff like that."

She remembered their conversation after they had left Parker. Scott had said that Ryan might be dealing with some serious issues. "Good."

"Good? How can you say that?"

"Stuff's coming up."

"Stuff?"

"Junk. Baggage. Some of the useless stuff he's carrying around inside. Sounds like a purge, of sorts. He's asking for your support."

"How do you know that?"

"That's how we grow. We lift ourselves out of our emotional funk by letting go of stuff that's a hindrance. Talk like that is a cloaked way of asking for support."

"He scared the hell out of me!"

"That's good, too."

He'd never heard her talk like this before. "How can *that* be good?"

"You'll grow from all this, too."

"I don't understand, Aunt Cin. I can rappel down a sheer fifty-foot rock wall, go down it face first, and not be scared at all. But all he has to do is say weird stuff like that and it scares the hell out of me. It doesn't make any sense."

He could tell she was smiling. "Ah, youth," she said almost under her breath. "Hon, it doesn't have to. Just recognize that your support for him is very important. Trust me. You'll be fine."

"Does this happen with guys and girls, too? I mean when they're together?"

"Pretty much. You might just have an extra challenge because two male egos are involved."

"I feel like I need someone to steer me through all this."

"Just keep your eyes open and you'll steer yourself just fine."

He heard a car door shut outside and pulled the string on the blinds to raise them up. "Hey, gotta go. One of my friends just pulled up. We're going birthday present shopping."

"Remember, *go slow.*"

"All right. I love you. Give my nieces a smooch and say hello to Uncle Greg."

"I will."

Mitch knocked on his door and pushed it open at the same time. Scott slid the antenna down on the phone and tossed it on the bed.

"Sound Dude!" Mitch said as he came in.

"Mitch, dude," he said as he high-fived him.

"Ready to boogie?"

"Soon as I get my keys."

Mitch moved his car to the top of the drive in the shade of the carport. They both pulled off their shirts to take maximum advantage of the sun and tossed them into the backseat. Scott, nonetheless, spread sunscreen on his shoulders, neck, and nose. They jumped in the Jeep and headed for the highway to San Bernardino. "Where's this parts store again?"

"Up on Watson St."

"Watson. Watson. Not the best neighborhood, if I remember. And your vehicle isn't exactly secure."

"It was the only place that had the *Vespa* seat in stock."

Mitch was fiddling with the radio. "*Vespa*? Oh, the scooters. What kind of stereo are you getting?"

Scott looked at the radio faceplate. "I've narrowed it down to three models. I'll decide when we get to *Berdoo Sound*."

"I got my tools in the car and all afternoon to help you."

"Great. Thanks for coming with me."

"I'd do just about anything for our Sound Dude."

Scott had grown to respect Mitch a great deal this last year. When Scott first met Mitch, he was the quietest member of the band. All that had changed in the last year. As soon as Mitch strapped on his guitar, he was a different person; one of the best showmen he'd ever seen. Nonetheless, off stage he was still the same mellow person Scott had originally gotten to know and like. Yet, as much as Scott liked him, there was a barrier he put up to keep him just slightly away. He was all too aware that it was because he knew Mitch liked girls.

The ride down into the valley from the high desert was always a thrill since the road rapidly declined many hundreds of feet in just a couple of miles. It had always reminded Scott of a much larger scale *Hot Wheels* track. It seemed as if the road crew had built it at the crazy steep angle so cars could race down it on purpose. Soon they passed the huge signs along the shoulder of the road that said "Danger High Wind Speeds Possible in the Valley." Today no gale force winds buffeted them, although he'd seen some monster windstorms in the valley before.

Just northwest of Desert Hot Springs, they passed the three brown and white AeroSun buildings. The contemporary design of the building fit in well with the earth tones of the surrounding desert. Scott pointed. "That's where Ryan works."

Mitch knew the company's name since it was displayed prominently on one of the buildings that faced the highway, but that was about all. "What's he do there?"

"I guess he's mostly a go-fer. But his uncle's got him on some engineering projects, and stuff like that, so he'll have a head start when he gets to college."

They ate lunch at a sit-down restaurant when they reached San Bernardino, having to put their shirts on to enter.

"I don't understand why we can walk around without a shirt in broad daylight, but can't walk into a greasy joint like this without putting one on," Mitch said when they stepped into the lobby.

"I guess people are afraid your hot bod'll turn 'em on," Scott answered as he pulled his down his over his head. Mitch wasn't Scott's type at all, but the way Scott said it made him note the remark.

They ate quickly and soon afterward reached the parts store. Scott had asked the clerk to hold the *Vespa* seat so it was a simple matter of going in and paying for it.

"Eighty–nine dollars, forty nine cents. That's with the mounting hardware," the man behind the counter said.

Mitch watched him shell out the cash. "Hmm, medium expensive."

There was a gleam in Scott's eye. "Ryan's worth it."

He didn't want to haul the box around all day and figured if he put an old blanket over it in the back no one would mess with it. It seemed like it might work since the box looked unobtrusive as he draped the blanket over it. Their next stop was the music equipment store.

They spent some time trying out keyboards and guitars before Mitch bought new strings for Barry and himself. Scott bought a box of a dozen blank cassette tapes and some long patch cords. They checked out microphones in detail but only kept the literature.

The box was still there under the blanket when they came back. Scott hesitated as he scanned the store names from the parking lot. He saw a new clothing store at the end of the mall.

"Let's go in there," he pointed, "before we go to the stereo place."

They kept their bags with them and Scott showed Mitch two t-shirts.

"Think Ryan would like these?"

"I thought you already bought him a present."

"A replacement part isn't enough."

Scott spent another thirty dollars while Mitch leaned on the counter noting Scott's excitement. "Are you gonna have enough for the tape player?"

Scott counted out the cash. "Sure. I've got a whole lot more."

They walked down a little further before heading out of the mall and back to the Jeep. The stereo store was another mile further down the road.

Scott listened to his three choices in the sound booth before choosing the one with the pullout auto-reverse tape deck. A set of speakers was also easy to decide on because of Mitch's discriminating ear and their demo tapes. Scott finally ran out of money at that point.

"Don't worry," Mitch told him. "I'll still help you install it even if you don't have any more cash to pay me."

"Pay you? You should pay me. I hauled you around all day."

It was difficult to juggle all the packages now. He could see that it would definitely be better to have a top on the Jeep.

Later, with everything stowed in the backseat, they headed out of town back to the high desert.

Scott couldn't wait to get back and install everything. There was just enough room in the dash for the deck and the speakers were mountable in just the right place as well.

Mitch was usually quiet, but he was more so now that they were out of town and away from the crowded streets and shops. He was mentally going over the details of everything he saw and heard on their shopping trip. Scott noticed Mitch was deep in thought. "Hey, why are you so quiet?"

He looked at Scott's hands on the wheel, then to the rear view mirror. "I was thinking about when we were back in the cycle shop."

"Yeah?"

Mitch touched the mirror with his index finger. "I was gonna buy you one of those garter belt air fresheners to go on here." Scott adjusted the mirror a little. "But I thought it wasn't the right thing to give you after all."

He noticed Mitch was avoiding something. He glanced at his face. "Why not?"

"If this sounds fucked up just tell me."

"What?"

Mitch asked point blank. "Are you gay?"

Scott felt shocked but responded almost immediately. "What if I said yes? Would it matter?"

"It hasn't so far."

"I'm gonna kill her."

"Huh?"

"How much did she blab to you anyway?"

"What are you talking about?"

"You mean, Colleen didn't tell you?"

"No. But if I knew she knew something I would've just asked *her*."

"Well, it's true. I'm gay. Are you afraid I'm gonna give you AIDS or something?"

"*What?* You can't get AIDS from hanging out with someone. Why, do you have it?"

"Fuck no. Well, who told you? If Colleen didn't…"

"Sound Dude, mellow out. It's pretty obvious since I know you. You never talk about girls. You don't hang out with any, except Colleen, and that doesn't count. You never make jokes about girls. And you look at guys the way I look at girls. So, what would *you* think?"

"You noticed all that?"

"I watch people. And I thought it was kinda funny you bought all that stuff for Ryan. So that finally made me figure it out."

"Why is it funny?"

"Well, I mean, you asked me if he'd like those shirts. How would I know what he likes?"

"So Colleen didn't say anything to you?"

"No, she didn't. Bryce and Barry said no way either."

Scott's eyes widened. "The whole band's talking about me?"

"No, it was just us." He figured out what Scott was so concerned about. "And they said there was no way 'cause they didn't believe it, not 'cause you can't be in the band."

"When did you guys talk about me last?"

"I just made a comment one day. That's all. I swear."

Mitch wasn't condemning him at all. In fact, he was doing his best to keep the conversation from going in the wrong direction.

"So we're still friends?"

"Fuck yeah. Just don't try any of that homo stuff on me. I'm not that way," he said as he grinned.

"Have I ever before?"

"I don't know which one of your characters wants to eat me." He was smiling now, but Scott hadn't caught on yet.

"None do. Besides, you're not my type."

"That's good news."

He just had to say it. "Ryan *is* though."

"I figured as much."

"We're going out."

"Going out, as in dating?"

Scott grinned. "More than that even."

"More? As in *more*?"

Scott nodded and smiled. "More."

Mitch held up a hand to cut him off. "I don't need to know any of the details."

The wind whistled in their ears as they passed the last yellow caution light. Scott opened it up and was up to sixty five mph in a moment. "Mitch, you still like me?"

"I told you I'm not gay."

"Seriously."

"Like, am I gonna help you install the stereo?"

"Yeah."

"You're our Sound Dude aren't you? And you're my friend, huh, Scott?"

"God, I was sure if I told any of you guys I'd be out of the band. But as far as I'm concerned, I'm like anyone else. Except for one thing."

"You're funny," Mitch responded. He looked at the fast-moving shoulder, then back to Scott. There was an awkward silence again as he looked at him strangely.

"What?"

"Since you told me the truth I'm gonna tell you something I've never told anyone."

"You told me you were straight."

Mitch turned up a corner of his mouth and looked at Scott. Scott looked at him but didn't say anything else.

"Remember Julie from last year?"

"That girl you dated, like, four times?"

"Yeah. I got her pregnant."

"No!"

"It was an accident. The condom broke. I was going crazy thinking I was gonna have a fuckin' kid with some girl I only fucked twice."

"When did that happen?"

"Last November. It wasn't until the end of the year that I found out. I convinced her to not keep it after her doctor confirmed it. That next weekend I drove her to Palm Springs to get an abortion. It cost me some good cash, too…she wouldn't pay a dime. You're the first person I've ever told."

"I remember that weekend. 'On-time Mitch' didn't show up and didn't tell anyone where he was. I thought that was a lame excuse you gave afterward. But why tell *me*? Why now? That was a long time ago."

"You were honest enough to tell me you're gay. I thought I should be man enough to tell someone about my secret, too. Besides…I've been wantin' to tell somebody…*anybody*…for a while. And I trust you. You don't know how good it feels to tell somebody. It was just too fucked up."

Mitch was telling him something he never told another human being? "You mean, you never even told the other guys?"

"You're the only one in the band who knows."

"Awesome!" Scott sucked in a few deep breaths, realizing he'd been suffocating himself the past ten minutes. Despite the relative comfort with which he felt inside about being gay, telling one of his male friends was *the* barrier he hadn't been willing to breach so far. The grin on his face grew wider as he realized that his fears about what the guys would do to him were unfounded. Now he wondered how he would announce it to the rest of them. But what was even more dumbfounding was that Mitch hadn't even told anyone else about the abortion. Scott could have kissed him right there. "I swear I won't tell anyone," he said instead.

"I know."

"You won't tell the other guys about me, will you?"

"And have them think I was like, you know, messing around with you?"

Scott grinned. "Good. *I'm* gonna tell 'em. When I do, act surprised."

"You're gonna deliberately embarrass me in front of the band?"

"I'm not gonna take a mike and, like, yell it. I don't know. I guess I won't tell everybody at once."

"Well, let's see, Colleen already knows." Mitch looked at him. "So, she's been keeping secrets about you, huh?"

"And you've been keeping secrets. And I've been keeping secrets. And Barry, and Sparks…. Should I go on?"

"All right, all right. Point taken."

One of the plastic bags in the back rattled constantly as they flew through the hot desert air. There were lots of clouds today, the kind that are pure white on top and dark and foreboding-looking on the bottom. Their shadows scattered all across the landscape alternating them with sun and shade. Soon the long incline leading home came up.

When they got home, Mitch pulled his car out from under the carport and Scott pulled up under its shade. He let Shakaiyo out of the backyard and she went back and forth between them looking for attention. He went in his bedroom to retrieve his boombox so they could have some music going while doing the installation. Mitch got his tools out and soon had parts laying all over the seats and floorboards. Unfortunately, the breezes died, leaving them hotter than before.

"I'm dying of thirst. Let's get something to drink."

Mitch followed Scott into the kitchen. Just as they came in the phone rang. Scott was sure it was Ryan wondering if he were back yet. Scott pointed to the refrigerator and Mitch opened it. He pulled out a soda while Scott answered the phone. Scott figured if he took the phone into the living room Mitch wouldn't hear him say all sorts of gay things he was bound to say. He was surprised to find out it wasn't Ryan after all.

"Is this my kid brother?"

Scott thought it was a joke at first, then recognized his brother's voice. "Steve!"

"How ya doin', birthday boy?"

"Hey, this phone connection's too good. Where are you?"

"The airport."

"Where?"

"Ontario."

"What are you doing in Canada?"

"The Ontario in California. You've been here plenty of times."

"Whoa! When did you get in?"

"We just landed."

"What? You didn't write or call. Nobody said you were coming in."

"It was supposed to be a surprise for your birthday this weekend."

Scott was literally jumping up and down now. He put his hand over the receiver. "Mitch, you won't believe it. My brother, you know, the one who lives overseas…?"

"You only have one brother, dude."

"…he's here. My brother's here!"

Mitch jumped up and down and made a face, trying to let Scott see how stupid he looked. "Mellow, dude. You'll wake the neighbors."

Scott idolized his brother and now he was talking to him for the first time in months. He uncovered the mouthpiece of the phone. "You said 'we'. Does that mean Muktiara is with you?"

"You think I'd leave my wife behind?"

"Hell no! I just haven't seen her yet. Do you need a ride? I can come pick you guys up."

"Calm down. And, no. We rented a car. Where are Mom and Dad?"

"Where else?"

"Of course."

"Should I call them?"

"No. Just clear out your old bedroom. Or did they rent it out?"

Scott laughed. "No. There's, like, some laundry on the bed, but I can put it in the utility room."

"Since we're a day early, we're gonna stop at the restaurant and surprise the folks. Meet us there in say, two hours?"

Scott looked at his watch. "Okay."

"See ya little buddy." There was a click and Scott replaced the receiver.

Scott still couldn't believe it. "This is so cool," he told Mitch. "I haven't seen him in years. I've never even seen his wife, either, except in pictures."

"Is she Singaporean, or whatever?"

"Singaporean? She's Malaysian. She's not from the island."

Mitch hadn't exactly kept up with all of Scott's relatives. He was aware, though, that his parents were a bit on the conservative side. "How'd your folks handle that?"

"They didn't like it at first. But they got over it."

"I've noticed you have to really train parents."

"Sometimes you have to teach them the same lesson over and over again." He looked at his watch again and set the countdown timer. "Think we can be done in an hour and a half?"

Mitch looked at his watch, too. "How's an hour?"

Forty-five minutes later all the wiring had been run and both speakers were in place. "Put the fuse in," Mitch said, after twisting a cap on the last set of wires.

Sitting in the driver's seat, Scott inserted the fuse in the tape deck's power line. He held up one of their practice tapes with two fingers. "The holy cassette," he said in a monotone, trying to sound reverent.

"Jam."

Scott popped it in, adjusted the balance and fader, then played with the volume as Mitch moved tools from the passenger seat. Mitch sat down, too, reveling in Scott's glow as he listened to the new sound system. "Thanks for the assist," he told Mitch.

"Thanks for being the bitchin'est Sound Dude we've ever had."

Mitch put his toolbox in his backseat. He backed down the driveway as he pointed at Scott from his open drivers side window, then took off.

Checking his watch again, Scott realized that he still had plenty of time to get to the restaurant. He headed for the highway, cranked up the volume, and drove around for another half hour while enjoying his new tape deck and speakers. He couldn't wait to see the look on his mom and dad's face when they saw Steve and his wife.

He pulled up into the parking lot of the restaurant and parked around back. He stepped out, pulled the stereo out by its handle so it wouldn't be stolen, and went in through the back door.

Ralph was in his tiny office and was busy with a pile of receipts from boxes of produce delivered just a little earlier.

"Dad, a surprise is just about here."

"I hope it's not like this surprise shortage I've got here."

He pointed to a large red '-2' on the bottom of the receipt indicating that two boxes were missing. Scott recognized the carrier on the heading of the bill of lading. "I thought we were changing shippers."

"We did. This was supposed to be their last shipment."

"I bought the stereo." He showed it to his dad, when he asked to see it. He expressed mild interest, then went back to his reconciliation. Scott continued to the front of the restaurant and found his mother at the bar talking to the bartender.

"Scott, you're off today," she said.

"I know. I wanted to be here for the surprise."

"What are you grinning about? Do you think you're having a surprise birthday party or something?"

"No. It's better than that."

Beth was up front attending to the guests arriving for late lunch. She went to a couple that just arrived. The man was a little over six feet tall with hair that vaguely resembled Ralph's in color. He was slender, with sharp features. His five o'clock shadow was noticeable because of his fair complexion. The Asian woman next to him was strikingly beautiful.

She had light brown skin and long black hair. Part of it was braided on one side with a single thin braid. Her eyelashes were very long and dark. Beth felt a little jealous when she assessed her beautiful, very expensive-looking dress. The couple spoke with her a moment, then seated themselves in a booth near the door.

She went to the bar looking concerned. "Elaine, that couple over there demanded to see you."

Scott's heart quickened as he put his stereo behind the bar and quickly followed. Elaine's face showed she was worried. Steve was faced away from her in the booth as she approached. Muktiara smiled as she saw her coming, then touched Steve's hand. She nodded, then looked away as Elaine came up to them.

Scott followed behind her as Elaine approached the booth. "Is there someth....Steve!"

"Mom! Scott!" He scooted out of the booth and hugged them both at the same time. Beth, had only worked there for about a year and had never met Steve, but knew the Faraday's had an older son by that name. The joyous reunion made her sigh.

"You weren't supposed to be in 'til tomorrow. Why didn't you let us know?" Elaine asked, chastising him.

"I took a chance and it paid off. I got Scott on the phone at the house and he helped set you up."

"We were supposed to surprise *him*." She wiped a tear from her eye as Steve introduced his wife. "Mom. Scott. This is Muktiara."

Elaine had spoken to her daughter-in-law on the phone and had seen her in photos, but this was her first time to actually meet Muktiara. She took Muktiara's hand, then gave her a long hug. "Finally my son brings home his bride. Please call me Mom."

In perfect, yet British-accented English, she answered. "I'm so happy to meet you, too. Where's Dad?"

"Dad? Ralph! Scott, get your father."

The commotion had already spilled into the back and Ralph was on his way. It had been a while since Scott had seen his dad smile so broadly. His first-born son was home and he was supremely happy.

"Steve! Son! *And* my daughter!" He took them both and gave Muktiara a kiss on the cheek.

Steve turned to Ralph after glancing at his wife. "Well, Dad, what do you think?"

"Gorgeous. Better than the pictures."

"I know she's the most beautiful woman I've ever known."

Muktiara's eyes went to the floor. "Steve, you're embarrassing me."

"Tiara and I have a surprise of our own."

Elaine could tell just from Steve's tone what he was about to say. Beth rested her elbows on top of the host station with her chin on her fists and smiled as she listened intently. This was better than a soap opera.

"Tiara's two months pregnant."

Elaine took Tiara from Ralph's arm and hugged her again. Ralph took his son and hugged him. Scott wondered why they were so excited. It was just a baby, nothing to be worked up about. Then it hit him. He was going to be an uncle. The thought of it was curiously odd.

Elaine wiped more tears. "We already planned on being home tomorrow. Now we can spend the whole day with you both."

"That's great." He looked at his watch. "It's early morning according to this and I need some sleep."

Scott led the way back to the house in his Jeep. Tiara took to Shakaiyo right away and vice versa. Once inside, with their luggage in his old bedroom, he insisted they tell him about the flight and what it was like living in Singapore. When Tiara started yawning Scott knew he had to let her go to bed.

He went to his bedroom and turned on some music. His adrenaline had just about run out. It was such a great surprise. What a summer. Indeed, what a summer.

CHAPTER 17

Morning sunlight streamed in the window as Steve lay awake. His watch indicated it was just past midnight, but the clock on the night table showed that it was a little after eight o'clock. He went into the bathroom while Scott ate at the counter in the kitchen. Scott hoped he'd see him before their parents woke up.

Seven months ago, Scott had written Steve his long-deliberated coming out letter and now was eager to talk to him about it. Because a letter from Singapore would be read by the whole family, he had asked him not to write back about it, due to him not having told his dad yet. He had told Steve everything in one long monologue, but the letter wasn't a proper coming out by any means. He had told his brother how he couldn't tell his dad just yet. How their mom kept worrying and how much it bugged him, the frustration he felt in living in Yucca Valley, and being the only gay person he knew in school. One day, he was sure he'd be able to talk to him about it in person. That was long before he met Ryan. Now, having a boyfriend was a brand new chapter in his life, one he also wanted to share with his brother as well.

Steve eventually padded barefoot into the kitchen in a robe. His freshly showered scent caught Scott's nose as he sat next to him. "Morning. Coffee's made."

"Morning." His brother was quite cheerful sounding.

"How'd you sleep?"

"I'm vibrating like I'm still on the plane."

"Tiara's still asleep?"

"She'll be up in a few."

"So, I'm gonna be an uncle, huh?"

"And I'm gonna be a daddy. Where's that dog of yours?" Scott whistled and they heard Shakaiyo's nails clacking in the hallway as she approached the kitchen. She stopped at the counter and sat, looking up at them both. "Too bad I couldn't have been here to see her as a pup," Steve said as he petted her head.

"She was cute then, and still is. How long are you guys gonna be here?"

"'Till next Saturday."

"Perfect. I'm having a double birthday party at a friend's house next Friday night. And the next day we're leaving for Crescent City way up on the coast."

"Say what?"

"I have this friend who's from upstate who lives here now. His birthday is the weekend after mine, so we're having a party over at his house this weekend for my birthday, then having another one up there."

"How are you getting there?"

"I'm driving us."

"I guess you won't be seeing us off at the airport."

"Oh. I guess not." He felt he'd just betrayed his brother, but banished the thought. After all, Steve showed up unannounced.

Scott could tell Steve was avoiding something. It was in his eyes, the way he sat there, and the way he looked away. He looked at Steve's hairy chest through the V-shaped opening of his robe. The dark hairs spread across from pec to pec in a wide band, wider than Ryan's did. So far, only light peach fuzz graced his own chest, and only down to his sternum.

"Just say it," Scott said. "I can tell you wanna talk."

"All that's true? In your letter?"

"Of course. All of it."

Steve took a kiwi fruit from the refrigerator. "I read it, like, five times, you know. I couldn't believe it at first, but I know you don't just up and say 'I think I'll be queer.'"

"Please don't use that word. The word is gay."

He sliced the fruit down the middle and gingerly placed the halves in a bowl. "Sorry. Gay, it is. Did you tell Dad yet?"

"No."

"Why not?"

"Mom said I shouldn't. And I guess I'm scared, too."

"You? Scared? Of what?"

"He had some choice words to say about you after you left the country."

"I heard 'em later. And he got over it."

"I don't think he'll get over this. It's not like I'm gonna change or anything."

Steve retrieved a spoon from the drawer, then sat next to Scott in the bar stool at the counter. He furrowed his brow. "Who said you had to change?"

Scott stopped thinking ahead. So far, he had been waiting for the worst possible scenario again. But it wasn't coming. In fact, it was ridiculous to think his own brother would have disowned him or he wouldn't have come home for his birthday. First Mitch, now Steve. That made two in a row. Apparently, it really didn't matter what people thought. It was just bad programming that made him think it wouldn't go over well.

"No one, I guess. But I love Dad and I don't want him to blow up at me or something."

"Good God. Since when did you care what people thought about what you did, much less what you were? You've always been unconventional. Just like me. This is just another one of those unconventional things."

"It's not so unconventional. And it's Dad we're talking about here, not just anyone."

"Okay, it's a little out of the *ordinary*," he said, then put a scoop of fruit in his mouth. He chewed thoughtfully. "You know, neither of us seem to be following the neat little 'normal' path our folks have tried to set for us."

"They're the only ones who think anything's supposed to be 'normal'. So, I'm still your brother?"

Steve squeezed his shoulder. "Jeez, I hope you didn't think I wrote you off or something. You've been my brother forever and will always be my brother."

It was difficult for Scott to speak because of the emotion he was feeling. "Well, it was kinda hard to tell since I asked you not to write back."

"Promise me something."

Scott was so filled with relief he felt he would burst. "Anything!"

"Tell Dad."

"*What?*"

"Tell him. Just don't do it in a letter. Take him aside. Ask him to go somewhere with you or something. He might panic at first, but he's not going to disown you."

Scott just looked at him, not sure how to answer that one.

"Promise," he said sternly.

"Okay. Promise."

Scott took his spoon and dug into his cereal, trying to avoid Steve's eyes.

"When?" Steve said still staring at him.

"Not 'til I come back from Crescent City. It's too close to us going. And I-I don't wanna just up and take off like that. It'll just give him time to freak out."

"You promised."

Scott made a face. "I swear."

Steve didn't want to back him into a corner. He only wanted Scott to make the commitment.

"What?" Steve said as Scott continued to look at him. He could tell Scott wanted to say something else.

"Can I tell you something?"

"Something good, I hope."

"Of course. I have a boyfriend."

"You do?"

"Yeah."

"Oh. When did this happen?"

"It's only been a couple of weeks but we've known each other all summer. You'll meet him pretty soon. When we have our party."

"Our party?"

"Our birthday party. It's the other guy. His name's Ryan."

Steve sipped his coffee. "So, you really like this guy? That way?"

Scott couldn't help but grin. "Especially that way."

Steve studied Scott's face, then lowered his voice. "I did it once."

Scott's eyes grew wide. "You what?"

"In junior high. With a guy I spent the night with. I don't think you ever met him."

"You?"

"We were only playing around. We didn't, you know, go all the way. It didn't do anything for me."

"Too bad."

That got a short laugh from Steve. "Did you ever like girls?"

Scott was indignant. "Yeah. Just not the way you do."

Steve smiled and patted Scott's back a couple of times. "Too bad."

Elaine seemed to have sneaked up on them. Steve coughed dryly which caught Scott's attention.

Her sudden appearance startled Scott. "Mom!"

"I didn't want to interrupt."

Steve was as bold as ever. "Interrupt what? Us talking about girls?"

Elaine pursed her lips, yet tried to act as if she hadn't heard the question. The boys exchanged a 'who does she think she's fooling' glance.

She started for the refrigerator, ignoring his comment. "I can't wait to be a grandmother. Your father is excited, too."

She sat with them and made small talk while the boys finished their breakfast. Tiara and Ralph eventually came into the kitchen and everyone migrated to the dining room. The coffee aroma and friendly chatter filled the air. A single shiver shook Scott. He was with the whole family, plus one. His dad seemed lit up like a Christmas tree. It reminded him of when he and Steve were younger, before they moved from Banning years back. That was when Steve was his age now. He loved it then, since Steve was usually there for him despite their age difference.

Even though their parents took the day off, there was only so much sitting around and talking that they could do. Steve had made plans to show his wife around town and later to visit L.A. She knew quite a few of the local place names as she had gone over a map of the area with him on the plane. Tiara seemed excited about spending time in "the big city." They were both used to a fast-paced urban lifestyle.

Scott declined to go with them since they planned to spend a couple of nights there. And it was as much for business as it was a vacation since his brother had arranged meetings with some of his suppliers.

Tiara winked at Scott when he caught her looking. He winked back. He could tell she liked him and the thought that he might meet her family one day, which meant traveling to Singapore, whetted his imagination.

During all the conversation, Scott realized he hadn't heard from Ryan. Eventually he broke away to make a quick phone call from his bedroom phone. Ryan answered on the first ring and sounded worried. Alarm was in his voice. "Scott! Come over here."

"Why? What's going on?"

"Just come by and pick me up."

"All right. I'll be there in a few minutes."

He returned to the kitchen and jiggled his keys to signify he was leaving.

Steve was emptying the coffeepot into the sink. "Where're you going?"

"Guess?" Scott said. He pulled one corner of his mouth back.

"Oh."

Tiara joined them in the kitchen and put her purse on the counter. She sat the rental car keys next to it. They were getting ready to do some sightseeing.

"We'll see you later, I hope," Steve said. "We'll be back way before dark. There's not much to show around here."

Scott thought about his remark, knowing that Steve never really appreciated Yucca Valley the way he did. He could show her all sorts of places and things. Granted, they wouldn't be museums, or skyscrapers, like in L.A., but he could show her all sorts of interesting things nonetheless.

Scott couldn't imagine what might have made Ryan sound so upset but withheld speculation until he saw him. As he turned down Howard's street, he saw Ryan standing on the curb half a block away from the house. *That's strange,* he thought. Ryan waved as he went into the street.

Scott slowed to a stop next to him. "What're you doing way down here?"

"I'll tell you when we leave." Scott turned the vehicle around after Ryan got in. He noticed the new stereo but didn't say anything.

"Go up to Baseline Drive," he instructed.

Scott headed north to the edge of town. The north side of the road was at the bottom of a long rocky range. Just past the shoulder of the road, the range gently sloped upward for several dozen yards before steeply inclining several hundred feet. Once there, he parked on the shoulder and they took a trail up the gentle slope of the range.

"Now, why are we out here?" Scott asked as he took the lead.

"Howie asked me some questions."

"Oh boy. About us?"

"About *me*. Krysta saw my sketchbook."

"You have a sketchbook? You never showed it to me."

"I never thought to."

"What's in it?"

"Pencil sketches. There's about six pages of drawings of you."

Hmm, Scott thought, *he's been drawing pictures of me and hasn't said a thing about it*. The thought was curiously endearing.

Ryan continued. "You didn't exactly have all your clothes on in some of them."

"And you *showed* them to her?"

"Fuck no. I accidentally left it on the dining room table. She must have looked through it when I was gone. Howie asked me the questions."

"So, what did she see?"

"Mostly sketches of your head and upper body. I was just experimenting. But on the last couple of pages I have some of the best ones of you. I put in the rest of your body, too. And you didn't exactly *not* have a hard-on in them."

"You drew me nude?"

"Well, yeah. All of them are."

"Oooh. So what did he say?"

"He wanted to know if there was anything I wanted to tell him."

"And you told him I'm your boyfriend, right?"

"Right. Just up and tell him I'm fucking queer!"

Scott was suddenly furious. "Don't say that!" He simultaneously raised a fist up. Ryan tried to dodge the impact, but Scott managed to punch him quite hard squarely on his deltoid before he could maneuver out of the way.

"Fuck that stupid rule! And I'm not telling him anything," Ryan whined.

Scott shouted at him. "You can't hide this forever!"

Ryan looked like he was on the verge of tears. Scott heard his voice crack as he spoke. "I can't tell Howie."

Scott's hands went up, palms out. "Sorry. Just chill." He didn't need Ryan to start freaking out over this and kept his mouth shut as well.

Ryan rubbed his upper arm for a moment, then jammed his hands in his pockets as they continued their slow trek up the almost invisible trail.

Scott turned around once they were some distance away and looked back at the Jeep. There was only a single car stopped at a stoplight several blocks away. It was headed away from them. "What did you tell him?"

"I told him they were just sketches, that that's what I do, I draw stuff. I asked him why he was interested. He didn't say anything after that. But, boy was I freaked. I thought he was going to ask me why I had drawn your dick with a hard-on."

"Unless he's a complete idiot I bet he figures something's going on." He instantly regretted saying that.

"Fuck, fuck, *fuck*!" Ryan exclaimed as he kicked several rocks. "This was not supposed to happen!"

Scott knew he couldn't keep Ryan from getting angry and just let him fume for a few moments. Finally, he stopped kicking things and settled down. Scott tried to divert his attention. "You like my new stereo?"

"Yeah. Sorry I didn't say anything about it. Who got it for you?"

"I did. With money everyone gave me for my birthday. Mitch helped me install it. And, I, uh, came out to him yesterday."

Ryan looked up from the trail. The question was in his eyes.

"He's the one who asked *me*."

"Right. He just asked you out of the blue if you're gay."

"He went with me to San Berdoo. He said he figured it out a while back and finally had to ask me. Besides, we're friends. So I told him the truth." His hands were also shoved in his pockets and he swung his elbow to touch Ryan's arm as he said it: "I also got some stuff for your birthday, too."

Ryan didn't care about that. "What'd he say?"

"That we're still friends."

"He didn't slug you?"

"Fuck no. I figured he'd make sure I was kicked out of the band, like, right there. But he said I'm still in. Hell, he even helped me install the stereo. And, sorry, I told him you were my boyfriend." Scott hesitated, expecting him to say something, but he didn't, so Scott continued. "I couldn't help telling him about you. I *like* it that you're my boyfriend."

"As long as he didn't say all sorts of stupid shit to you. I don't get it. Everything's okay when I talk to you. How do you do it?"

"Cuteness? Charm? Did I mention cuteness?" Scott asked with a grin.

Ryan deliberately bumped into him as they walked. "I think you did."

"I don't think I would worry about Howie just yet." But he wondered when the big question would come up and how Ryan would react to it.

They walked quietly for a few moments. Ryan thought about how he had responded to Scott telling Mitch. Again, it was like Scott was some sort of elixir making everything fine just by being near him. "Now that I'm with you, I'm not worried about anything. I don't even know what I was so worried about at first."

"Well, what would you say if you were Howie?"

"I thought about that. 'So, Ryan, are you drawing porn now?' or, 'So, Ryan, what's up with those hard-ons you're drawing?'"

Scott piped up. "I'd wonder what was going on, too. My supposedly straight nephew's drawing his friend with a hard dick. It'd make me wonder. Now if you'd drawn me with a limp dick I'd think it was just a regular sketch. But then *I'd* be pissed 'cause it's designed to be hard as often as possible, you see."

"Shut up, you're giving *me* a hard-on."

They were now so far up the hill they would have been just dots if seen from the road. His hands still in his pockets, Ryan stopped and turned around in front of him. He leaned forward and kissed Scott. Scott pulled his hands out of his pockets and grasped Ryan's arms. He kissed back, feeling himself swell in his underwear. He reached in and adjusted himself. "God, every time I do that my dick starts crawling around."

Ryan grinned, then licked his lips. "No kidding."

They started back down the trail.

"You feel better?"

"Yeah, I guess."

"Good. I had a huge surprise waiting for me yesterday."

"What?"

"My brother and his wife flew in from overseas."

"Are they gonna be here long?"

"They leave the same day we do."

"They're coming to the party, I hope."

"They better. I want them to meet you."

"Don't tell them, too."

"Steve already knows about me, too. I-I told him about you and me this morning."

Ryan halted in mid-stride. "Why do you keep telling everyone?"

Scott kept going. Ryan followed, even though he didn't want to. Scott explained the letter and how he didn't want a response his dad might read.

"See. You haven't told your dad yet. So why should I just up and tell Howie?"

Scott was defensive now. "My dad's different."

Ryan instantly found some leverage. "I bet he's not. He'd probably throw you out."

Scott thought about it a moment. No, his dad wouldn't throw him out. He was essentially already out of the house in his brother's old bedroom. He couldn't tell Ryan to come out to Howie and, in turn, not come out to his dad. "Steve doesn't think so," he finally said.

"But *you* do. I think you should tell your dad *now*. How do you like that?"

Scott couldn't dispute the complaint. But he had it planned for after they returned. "I'm telling him. *After* we get back. *Not* before," he shot back.

Ryan thought about it, but didn't harp on the subject.

They finally returned to the vehicle and Scott took Ryan home. He reluctantly agreed he wouldn't call Ryan until later in the week. Maybe Howie would forget about the sketches if he weren't around so much. Plus, they had plenty of time to be together while they were up north.

*   *   *

Tiara turned in early the night they came back from L.A. Their whirlwind tour had worn her out. Steve wanted to have a conversation with his mother so deliberately stayed up with her to talk despite still feeling tired as well. His dad would be next, after Scott told him. Unfortunately, he'd have to have that conversation over the phone or via letters. That certainly wasn't the best method, but it would have to do. His dad had already turned in as well, and Scott had told them he was visiting with some of his track buddies that night. Only the TV turned down low on the enclosed back porch broke the quiet in the house.

Steve muted the sound with the remote control. "Mom?"

"Yes, son."

"Scott told me the 'big secret'. I've known for a while now actually."

Elaine hesitated for a moment in the awkward silence. "I knew you were talking about it the other morning."

Steve shut off the TV now and put the remote down. She seemed not to know how to handle the conversation so he decided he'd better take the lead. "You know, he's gay, and that's all there is to it."

She looked away, not wanting Steve to see the concern in her eyes. "I don't want my baby to die from some horrible disease."

"He's not that stupid."

"You don't know. That boy he's seeing…"

"Mom," he interjected, sounding disappointed, "just because his friend's gay doesn't mean he's got a disease."

"I didn't mean it like that. I just didn't think he'd ever act on it."

"He's entitled to a sex life just like anybody."

"He's sixteen years old! You talk like it's…so matter-of-fact."

"You don't want to know how old I was then. And, it *is* matter-of-fact."

"I'm afraid if he gets into a gay relationship he'll want to leave us."

"Like move to L.A. or something? Do you blame him? How could anything be any more boring than Yucca Valley? And Scott needs his own life. You know that."

Elaine felt indignant at Steve's assessment. "There's the restaurant. And a very good living for our entire family because of it."

"But for Scott? He has more going for him than you give him credit for. The same thing happened to me."

She ignored his last remark. "It would kill Ralph if Scott left town."

Steve knew her only too well. "You mean it would kill *you*."

She looked him in the eye now. Steve had always been bold and brash. He always told it like it was. And it was true. She was the one who originally told Scott not to tell Ralph. When he told her, they were going through a rough time with unexpected repairs at the restaurant and a recent rise in property taxes. The financial strain it caused, that coincided with Scott's announcement, was a little too much for her to handle at the same time. She told him that when things evened out a bit he could say something to his father. That better time came, more quickly than expected actually, but Scott didn't come forward. And, as she thought about it more and more, she developed what she could only describe as a phobia. What would happen to the restaurant's reputation if word spread about their son? How about their friends? What would they say? When he didn't tell his father, she was relieved that she didn't have to confront it again. Now it was back.

"Mom. I know Dad hasn't been let in on this 'secret'. And Scott knows he can't keep it away from him forever. But it's not really about him is it?"

It would do no good to avoid it any longer, she thought. "You're right. I'm the one who told him to keep quiet. Maybe it's time he told your father. I asked him before the school year ended if he thought it was odd that Scott didn't have a girlfriend, just to see what he'd say. I thought he'd get the hint. He reminded me that he hardly dated through high school either." She let out a long sigh. "I'm tired of keeping it a secret from him, too. It's not fair to him or me."

"I think you're worried *you'll* be alone more than anything else."

She sighed. "I was afraid I'd never see you again when you went away."

"Mom, look. Leaving this town was the best thing I ever did. And it's not like I wasn't ever coming back. I'm still a US citizen so it's not like I *can't* return." She seemed like she was lost in thought now.

"Mom."

She didn't answer, and he knew she was working up her 'worried mom' routine. She took him, then hugged him until tears came to her eyes. "I love you, hon. I guess I've been afraid you'd leave us for good. I've been afraid Scott would hate us and leave, too."

"Just because he's gay? Where do you come up with these weird ideas?"

"Because he'd want to live a lifestyle that has nothing to do with a family anymore."

Steve pulled her away and she sat back down in the rocker. "Well, first, it's not a lifestyle, it's his life. And that's ridiculous anyway. Scott loves all of us. If you act like you're gonna lose him you just might. Don't give him any reasons to resent you."

She looked hard at him. "You've grown quite a bit for being only twenty-five."

"Travel broadens the mind…Do you know this kid he's seeing? Ryan, is it?"

"Yes. He's a year older than Scott and wants to major in engineering at UCLA if he gets accepted. He's new in town. That's about all I know about him. We know his uncle pretty well though. Ryan's staying with him until he goes off to college."

"Well…he must have at least half a brain if he wants to be an engineer." He chuckled. "My brother's…'boyfriend'. Sounds funny, but I'll get used to it," he said before he hugged her back. He yawned and finally turned in.

Elaine sat in the light of the single lamp on the porch. She pulled the family album from underneath the coffee table and opened it to a random page. The first photo she saw was one of Steve and Scott playing in the backyard when they lived in Banning. She even remembered taking the picture. Steve always loved his brother, and the photo showed it, although they were almost eight years apart in age. She closed the album and rested her arm on the cool surface of its cover. She knew Ralph wouldn't take it well at first, but she also knew he understood a lot more than he let on to people. All along it had been her who was afraid. All this time she was afraid her baby would want to leave before she was ready to say good-bye. Saying good-bye was always so difficult. She knew she would have to muster the courage soon.

*   *   *

Ryan pulled the coolant tester from the opened radiator and checked it. He poured in a little more coolant from a large container and checked it again. Satisfied with the result he replaced the radiator cap. He opened the windshield wiper fluid cap and started pouring in blue liquid until the receptacle was full. It took the remainder of his con-

tainer to fill it. He tossed the empty container into the paper bag that
was laying next to the front tire. An empty can of oil lay in it already,
along with an empty can of *SuperSlick 2000*. "Start it up," he said as he
lifted his head.

Scott started it up and got out, still looking at the dash. The oil pressure appeared to be normal and no other warning lights were lit. Ryan
listened closely to the engine for a few seconds, then inspected underneath. His butt stuck up in the air as he kneeled over. Scott looked
through the slats of the back deck. Howard's head was buried in his
newspaper. He licked his lips as Ryan stood and wiped his hands.

"Nice butt," he whispered as Ryan leaned over to look at the instrument panel.

Ryan ignored him. "No leaks," he stated. "You can shut it off."

Ryan picked up the paper bag and rolled down its top. "Howie does-
n't have a tire gauge here, so we'll have to check the air pressure later."

Scott helped him pick up the tools and followed him inside to wash
up. Ryan wet his arms up to his elbows in the kitchen sink, then squirted
dishwashing soap on them. "Party tomorrow night, and then we're
gone!" he said as he pulled several sheets of paper towel off the roll.

"Tomorrow I turn seventeen." Scott took his turn under the water.
"And I can't wait to get outta here. I've been ready for a month. By the
way, how did you get your grandma to let you go back?"

"She's a pushover on most stuff. And just for a visit? She couldn't say
no. It's not like I'm moving back in or anything."

"And Adina's ready for the party, too?"

"She made a big deal out of it. She's called twice already to let me
know how things were going." He unrolled more paper towels and gave
them to Scott. "Expect to party like a banshee," he said with a wide
smile.

Scott finished drying his hands then looked through the sliding glass
door. Howard wasn't in view so he gave Ryan a peck on the cheek.

Ryan's eyes grew wide then he drew away. He made a guttural sound with his throat and jerked his head toward the deck.

"Don't start," Scott warned as he pointed to him. He stuck his hand down his pants to adjust his penis. "See, you did it again," he whispered.

Ryan tossed the wad of paper across the kitchen for a perfect dunk into the trashcan. "You're gonna love my gift."

"Tell me or no more sex."

"Yeah, right. *You* holding back? You'll find out tomorrow. Just make sure you bring your vehicle with you."

"Why? Do we have to go get it?"

"No. It just wouldn't be right if it wasn't here." Scott didn't try to guess what that meant.

Ryan led him to the bedroom where two piles of clothes were neatly folded on the bed. A small gym bag, his toiletry kit, and a larger clothes bag were poised and open, ready to be filled.

"I'm finishing packing tonight."

"I'm already done. Got the bags all set in my bedroom. I can't wait to be alone with you. I'm bringing the tent in case we want to stop off someplace."

Ryan slowly closed the bedroom door, and shut it with a deliberate push. He moved Scott to the middle of the floor, and gently pushed him to his knees onto the carpet. He also went down to his knees and held Scott's head against his chest while hugging him tightly. He rested his head on Scott's shoulder and ran a hand through his hair, messing it all up. "God. This week's been so long. I can't stand it. I wanna do it with you right now," he said as he breathed deeply of Scott's hair.

"I thought you said none of this in the house."

"The door's shut."

Scott saw he was finally starting to lighten up. He didn't think it would be this soon though. "So Howie didn't say anything else about the sketches?"

"Nothing. It's been like he never talked to me about it."

"Lemme see 'em."

Ryan released his hold and retrieved the sketchpad from under the bed. They sat on the floor against it as he opened the cover.

Scott looked on as Ryan turned the pages. "Wow. They're good. But in this one," he pointed, "my dick's not big enough."

"Be fucking serious. I already drew it bigger than it really is."

Scott pushed him. He took the pad and flipped through the remaining pages before handing it back to him. Ryan closed it and slid it back under the bed.

Scott looked at the hot rod poster on the wall in front of him. The bottom right corner was slightly curled up where the tack was missing. "You're gonna make that promo poster for us aren't you?"

"Yeah. But my best drawing pens and stuff are up north. When we get there I'll buy some heavy poster board and a few more things and do it there."

Howard made a somewhat noisy entrance into the house by dropping his coffee cup on the kitchen floor. They heard it break on the tile. "Shit," they heard from the kitchen. Any idea Scott had of messing around with Ryan faded as they heard the crash. Ryan opened the bedroom door and they went to the kitchen.

Howard was picking up the pieces of a black ceramic mug. The pile of newspapers was on the counter and the top section was slowly feeling gravity's tug. "It slipped," he explained, just as the section fell to the floor as well.

Ryan retrieved the whiskbroom and there was no trace of the mug anywhere except in the trash. The boys headed for the front porch.

"See you tomorrow night," Scott said as he started up the Jeep.

"Par-dy!" Ryan responded with a wide smile.

*   *   *

Although they didn't eat at the restaurant that late afternoon, Steve and Tiara commandeered a table near the host station while Scott worked. They spent the next several hours laughing, joking, and talking about their recent adventure in L.A. and about living in Singapore. The fact that Tiara was from a completely different culture fascinated him to no end. Although, for the most part, it sounded like growing up there wasn't anything out of the ordinary, it was nonetheless interesting.

Finally, Scott's shift ended. Carmen was locking up tonight so Ralph could leave earlier than usual. Steve and Tiara took Scott home where he readied himself for the party at Howard's house.

They all arrived a little after 9 p.m. There was still some twilight left, and the backyard was already lit up from the spotlights from under the eaves. A set of small, but powerful speakers on the deck provided background music. Inside, crepe paper and *Happy Birthday* in cutout letters were strung across one wall of the kitchen. The dining room table was cleared and was covered with condiments and other foods. The birthday poster was neatly attached to the back sliding glass door.

Scott thought Ryan was dressed to kill. He wore the tightest surf shorts he had and a red polo shirt. Scott wore shorts, a t-shirt, and new tennis shoes. He was almost sorry he wore the shorts, afraid he'd embarrass himself in Ryan's presence.

Steve, Tiara, and the rest were introduced to Krysta and Howard's coworkers, and soon the band showed up in two groups. They didn't intend to perform tonight since they wanted to party as well. Later, toward ten o'clock, some of the employees from the restaurant showed up.

Ryan made sure they played at least one of the band's tapes and insisted that Colleen announce the tunes as they came up. Scott was glad the band took the edge off any possible stuffiness from all the older adults. Their silly antics made everyone laugh and have a good time. They even got everyone to join in a rousing and unique rendition of Happy Birthday to both boys. Ryan was a little aloof since he was being

Mr. Host. The atmosphere was festive and even Ralph loosened up, which made Scott happy.

Since neither of the boys had touched their presents, Howard finally told them they had to open them or else. Steve and Tiara gave Scott an ebony Buddha and a set of traditional Indonesian handmade puppets on strings, a fancy handmade hardwood jewelry box, and a bottle of expensive Chinese cologne.

Next it was Ryan's turn. He opened the gifts from his brother and grandmother that had arrived in the mail more than a week before, and set them aside. Next, Scott retrieved the wrapped scooter seat and the shirts from the Jeep. Ryan tore at the wrapping and peered into the first box. The surprised look on his face was classic.

"Uncle Howard. Look no further. Here's one." He held up the seat and showed it to him.

"Didn't he tell you I was looking for one of those?" Howard asked Scott.

"No. But I knew he would want it," Scott said as he blew on, then rubbed his knuckles on his chest. Ryan unwrapped the t-shirts and expressed his thanks for them, too. Howard was generous with money and more clothes, the only thing he knew Ryan really wanted.

Ryan deliberately didn't mention the present in the garage until now. Gifts from the band members were conspicuously absent. Ryan wanted to lead Scott by the hand to see his gift, but that was out of the question, of course. So he simply took the remote out of Howard's car and opened the door as they stood on the driveway.

In the middle of the floor, sitting on two wooden sawhorses, was a black vinyl top for Scott's Jeep.

"Totally!" Scott exclaimed loudly. "Where'd you get it?"

"Thanks to Walter over there." He pointed to one of the AeroSun employees. "He overheard me talking about getting one last week at work. He just happened to have the right kind in storage and sold it to me. And the guys in the band helped contribute some cash. They kept their mouths shut?"

"I had no idea," Scott said. He raised his hand and Ryan gave him a high five.

Since they couldn't let it just sit in the garage, the guys lifted it off the horses and brought it to the Jeep. Barry and Sparks helped attach the metal ribbing and the rest of the gang helped push and pull and attach everything. They all took turns pulling it back and forth, attaching the door windows, and sealing the Velcro seams together. In no time, it was properly put in place and completely secured. Scott stepped back to admire it. It didn't exactly look new—there was a dark stain along the top on the right side—but it still had a vinyl smell to it, so that helped. Ryan stood next to him as Scott stuck his head in the driver's side door to inspect it from inside.

Scott thought about their trip up north. "Perfect timing," he pointed out.

"Perfect is right. I didn't want to be rained on. Plus, we don't have to worry about our stuff getting stolen as easily if we have to stop somewhere."

Scott whispered from the corner of his mouth. "I want to kiss you, cutie."

"I want to kiss you, too," Ryan quickly whispered back.

Bryce came around from the back end, drumming his fingers along the outside of the top. "Dudes. Time to rejoin the party. You can admire this thing tomorrow."

As the party progressed, Ryan hadn't noticed that Elaine was periodically watching him. She was thinking about the aborted conversation that she had had that night with Howard at the restaurant. The new revelation of her son and Ryan being together had gone around in her mind quite a bit. She looked around herself. There were the crazy antics of the band members, the contemporary music, and the latest styles being worn by all the kids. It was suddenly clear she was growing out of touch with their generation. She had been so busy these last years help-ing her husband run a profitable business she had forgotten what it was like to be a carefree teenager. In that next moment Ryan went into the kitchen by himself. It was the perfect opportunity.

Up until that point, he had avoided almost all contact with her except for a perfunctory hello and even managed to stay at a distance from wherever she was. He was well aware she knew about he and Scott and felt uncomfortable with what he thought she might be thinking.

She deliberately sneaked up on him as he reached into the refrigera-tor. "Ryan?"

"Ms. Faraday," was his startled response.

"Can I speak to you, alone, for a moment?"

He could feel his body tensing already. What the hell was she going to say? Stay away from my son? Worse?

He looked at a clock, then back to her. "Can it wait?"

"No." Her tone said it all.

No use avoiding it, she was intent on talking to him. No one was at the end of the hall and she took him aside to the room at the end. She looked in, not knowing it was his bedroom she had entered and, as he came in, shut the door.

"I-I really don't know how to say this. I just wanted you to know that I know you boys like each other."

Ryan felt very uncomfortable. She was now sitting on his bed. "Look, M-Ms. Faraday, I…"

"Please let me finish."

Ryan took a step back, wanting to bolt for the door. He was only a foot from it and could dash out in an instant. *Good God*, he thought, *she's just Scott's mom*. She didn't seem angry. In fact, she seemed to be groping for the right words.

"My son and I have talked about this gay thing," she began. "And I know you and he are…seeing each other. I just wanted you to know that I love my son very much and don't want to see him hurt."

"I would *never* hurt him!" he blurted out. He clamped his mouth shut, sure his voice would crack from emotion if he said anything else.

"I'm sorry. I meant to say that I know I can't stop you boys from seeing each other."

He was taken completely aback.

She smoothed the bedspread with the palm of her hand. "I don't really understand it but I'm not in the grave yet. I know when things are the way they are. This is one of those things. At first, I thought you were a bad influence on him. Then I thought it must be that band he's in. But I know now that it's neither." She thought about the expensive gift Ryan and the rest of Scott's friends bought him and how they all felt proud for him. "I just wanted you to know that you have my blessing." She realized she was having this conversation so she could make real what she had concluded. It was a purge of sorts. Perhaps it was even a confession.

"What?" Ryan was incredulous. She was confiding in him. It wasn't like anything he had expected at all.

"When I found out that Scott liked you...more than just as a friend...I was angry and afraid at first. But I've thought about it. A lot. I know he just wants to be happy. Like you do."

"Did you talk to my uncle?"

She furrowed her brow. "No, why?"

"Please don't tell him. He..." Ryan didn't get to finish his sentence, as there was a knock at the door. Both of them looked when it immediately swung open.

Scott froze in mid-stride as he came in, wide-eyed, his hand still on the doorknob. He saw his mother sitting on the bed and Ryan standing next to the door. He had seen them come in the house and when neither returned he figured she was up to something. What, he didn't know.

"Hey, what's the idea? This is a party," he stated, deliberately breaking the tension.

Elaine looked to her son, then to Ryan. She looked a little embarrassed, but as she stood, she went to Ryan, took his face in her hands, and kissed his cheek.

Scott's mouth was agape.

Ryan felt he was in shock. He tried to speak, but nothing came out.

Elaine put a finger on his lips. She smiled as she flailed her arms in the air. "Come on, let's get out there, and have some fun."

Scott let them both walk past him. He looked at the bedspread where his mom had sat then back to them as they walked down the hall back to the kitchen.

What the hell, he wondered.

CHAPTER 18

It was unusual for Scott to wake up before his alarm went off, but the excitement of his imminent departure had made his sleep restless. He pulled the sheet down from his face and stared at the flashing dots on the clock as they counted off the seconds. Although the party had carried on well past midnight, he hadn't felt very sleepy at all. Now the past few hours of restlessness were cursing him. It was a few minutes before six o'clock, but he waited for the alarm to sound anyway. He poised his finger on the button and let the blare of the alarm quicken his pulse before turning it off. Shakaiyo approached the bed and nudged his armpit. She nudged again just as the phone rang. He turned over and rested the receiver on his ear, barely holding it in place. "This is Scott."

"Are you up?"

He ventured his left hand to his penis. "In more ways than one."

"Well, hurry up. I'm eating now. See you in a few minutes?"

"Yeah, give me half an hour."

He was in and out of the shower in record time. He dressed and tossed his bags by the door, then dumped a few crickets into the terrarium for his tarantula.

The early morning dawn was quiet and still as Scott quickly loaded up the tent, some other camping equipment, then stashed his bags in the backseat. Shakaiyo tried to jump in, knowing he was going somewhere. "Sorry, girl. You can't go with us. Mom and Dad will take care of you."

He pulled open the sliding door and went into the kitchen. Steve and Tiara were already up. His parents appeared a few minutes later.

"Sorry you can't see us off," Steve said.

Scott poured himself some orange juice. "I am, too. But it was fun, huh, Tiara?"

"I had a great time. This family is everything Steve said it would be." She smiled then put her arm around Steve's waist and kissed his cheek. Scott briefly wondered if she knew about him yet. Had Steve told her? He'd have to find out later. Scott wished that he, too, would one day be able to show Ryan as much affection around others, rather than sneaking a quick peck and clandestine hugs.

He ate in a hurry, not feeling much hunger after the constant snacking last night. The family followed him out as he went to the Jeep.

"Call us if you have any problems," Ralph instructed.

Is it my imagination, or does mom look different this morning? Scott wondered. Last night's tête-à-tête between her and Ryan came to mind. When he looked at her, she winked at him. He didn't know what to think, but there sure seemed to be a lot of winking going on now between him and the women in his life. "I don't expect a breakdown, but Ryan can fix just about anything with an engine," he assured them.

Ralph slapped a hand on the windshield frame. "Have a good time, son."

Scott hugged him. "I love you, Dad." Ralph squeezed a little harder. Scott hugged everyone else in turn.

"Tiara, take good care of my niece or nephew, or whatever it'll be," he said as he started the Jeep.

"Our baby will get the best of care. You take care," she answered, patting her middle.

Once out on the highway Scott was glad he had the new top. The road noise wasn't as severe with it on and the wind was out of his hair.

Plus, his stereo sounded even better than before, although he knew that when he got back he'd have to reposition the back speakers up on the roll bar for better sound.

Ryan was on Howard's porch when Scott pulled to a stop. He stood with his arms crossed, looking impatient. Scott grinned as he sat in the driver's seat. He could see Ryan's hair curling in a few places out from under his painter's cap. His sleepy early morning face looked so cute as he put his things in the Jeep.

"I wannna lick your face," Scott said as Ryan put a bag in back.

"Later," he said abruptly.

Jeez, Scott thought. *Maybe it's too early for him. He'll mellow out once we're on the road,* he finally decided.

The front door opened and Howard came out. He picked up one of Ryan's bags and handed it to him. Ryan stashed it in the backseat, then sat in the passenger seat.

"Got the map?"

Ryan rose up enough to pull a folding map of California from his back pocket, and opened it up against the windshield. Howard stood at the passenger side and tapped him on the shoulder. He stuck out his hand and they shook.

"I know I can't keep you from driving. But remember, you don't have a license." He looked at Scott. "I'll bail you out as far as Fresno. After that I'm not coming."

"Not to worry, Uncle Howard. I don't think he'll let me drive anyway."

Scott just had to respond. "If any cops get him I'll just say he's a runaway and they'll bring him back here."

"Not here, *please*," Howard said, trying not to crack a smile, but not succeeding. Scott noticed that Ryan didn't see the humor in their little joke. *I hope he's not like this all day,* he thought.

"Excited?" Howard asked him. Ryan didn't exactly know how to answer. As excited as his body was about the trip, his brain was saying all sorts of things about how stupid he was in suggesting the trip in the first place. His hasty exit from Crescent City weighed on his mind. What would he say to everyone when he got there? Then there was Muh. The escalated grief he dealt her the last year of school was haunting him. She wasn't overjoyed about him coming back. In fact, their earlier phone conversation, which he had carefully edited for Scott, contained a clear message of caution. She had acquiesced to the visit, but had listed conditions. Hopefully, Scott wouldn't notice the tension and enjoy himself. Perhaps Scott could be a buffer between he and her, he figured. With all that in mind, he nonetheless answered Howard with a lie. "I can't wait to get back."

Ryan studied the map as they drove through the quiet early morning and headed down into the valley of the low desert. Soon they were on a straightaway and Ryan leaned back to relax.

"So what did you and my mom talk about last night? I've been dying to find out," Scott asked.

Ryan adjusted his hat in the visor mirror. "It was weird as hell. She said she liked me. And she wanted to make sure you were happy and all. It completely freaked me out."

"Was that all?"

"There was other stuff about how it was okay we were together."

"*My* mom said *that*?"

"Yeah."

"So, that's why she looked at me so funny this morning."

"Whadda ya mean?"

"She winked at me. My mom never winks at me. She never winks at *anyone*."

"Maybe she wants you."

"You're sick."

"No, Elaine is."

"Elaine?"

"Are you retarded? Your mother," he said curtly.

Scott wondered if Ryan had suddenly reverted to his original self. He thought about last night some more. Apparently, his mother had figured it all out and was beginning to mellow. If so, it might just mean a completely new way of relating to her.

"You are, of course, gonna let me drive," Ryan told him.

Scott thought about what to say for a moment. "Only if you do me."

Ryan's cap was pushed forward in his face. He pulled it up and opened one eye. With his other hand, he grabbed his crotch. "Mmm, Mmm." Ryan seemed back to normal all of a sudden. *Thank God*, Scott thought.

"But only if you're a good boy...Great party. Thanks," Scott told him.

"It was more for me than you."

"Fuck you."

"No, you said I get to fuck you."

"And when are you gonna let me fuck *you*?"

"When the time is right."

"And that will be when?"

He looked at his watch, then out the window. "When I say."

Now he was back to his original self again. The ping-pong game Ryan seemed to be playing, first being irritated, then mellowing out, then irritated again, was becoming old already.

"You've been pretty ballsy this morning."

"That's cause I have big balls."

"Hmm, maybe I should lick 'em."

"I don't think so."

Maybe a change of personality is what's needed, Scott thought. *If Ryan wants to play games, I'll give him a good one to play.* "How about you taking all your clothes off and jack off while I watch."

"What?"

"Yeah, like, I'll watch while you drop your pants, right now. Look, there aren't any cars here."

"Yeah, right." He couldn't believe Scott would even suggest it.

"Okay, you wanna drive? I'll do it. I'm pretty horny. I didn't have time to…you know…this morning." Scott knew he had him since he wasn't using an accent. Funny how he never thought about using his own voice to fake him out.

Recalling what Scott did back on the campout, Ryan figured he might just do it, given the chance. He sat up and looked Scott in the eye. "You're serious, aren't you?"

"Look, I know you want it. I know you can't wait for it. I'm just telling you that if you want to jerk off, go for it. I like to watch."

"This is too weird."

"You want me to tie you up first?"

Ryan's tone immediately shifted from mild surprised interest to outright anger. "Fuck you!"

Scott frowned. His scenario was completely innocuous, not worthy of the abrupt attitude change. "Hey! Stop being an asshole!"

"No one *ever* ties me up again!" Ryan shot back. He tried to stop himself before he finished saying it. But it was distinct enough to Scott.

"What do you mean 'again'?"

"I meant *ever*," Ryan lied.

Something was up. That much Scott could tell. "I was just playing with you. You're supposed to play, too."

"Not like *that*."

"You are *so* bizarre today. What the *fuck's* your problem?"

Ryan looked out the window in time to see the sign that said 'San Bernardino 6 miles' whiz past. "I didn't get enough sleep," he said sheepishly.

Scott squeezed his arm. "Look, we don't have to drive all the way through if you don't want to. I brought the tent and other gear we'd need to stop for a night. We're not in a hurry and I wanna get there alive."

"I'm gonna take a nap," Ryan announced. Scott welcomed that. At least he wouldn't have to listen to his tirades over nothing for a while.

Ryan didn't just nap—he slept soundly. Scott popped a tape into the deck and plugged in his headphones so he wouldn't disturb him. Soon enough they passed Cajon Summit. He skirted the edge of Edwards AFB and then pulled over for gas in Mojave.

Ryan only woke once while he was at the windows paying for the gas. After getting his bearings, he went around the corner to the bathroom of the small service station. When he came back, he immediately fell asleep again.

Soon after they passed the tiny town, the road rose steadily until they reached Tehachapi Pass. Then they plunged into the haze of the San Joaquin Valley. Scott couldn't help but look at Ryan's crotch every so often. It just invited him to grope. But he kept his hands to himself so Ryan wouldn't freak.

It had been a long time since Scott was in the Valley. Acres and acres of cotton flew past, then a sheep ranch. Fields of flowers were next, then groves of various fruit trees. The variety of products grew even as he passed the sign that said "Visalia next two exits." At this point Scott was sure he had now driven farther than he ever had before in a single stretch. The trip to Parker seemed quite short now in comparison. His stomach told him to stop, and shortly after noon, he took the second exit into town and found a restaurant just off the highway.

He poked Ryan's side. "Hey."

Ryan woke up with a start. "What?"

"We're eatin'. And you're driving the rest of the way today."

Ryan pulled up his cap and stretched. Scott noticed Ryan sporting a partial erection. "Did I excite you?"

"Your Jeep did."

"Maybe you need some help with it. I know an excellent way to make it go away."

Ryan made a fist and bounced it on his crotch. "You have to wait 'til tonight."

"Why do I always have to wait?"

While they were both out on the sidewalk, Ryan checked his hair in the reflection of the big windows as they went inside to eat. He hadn't shaved that morning and could feel the sparse stubble on his chin as he dragged his hand across it.

They sat at a semi-circular booth in view of the Jeep so Scott could keep an eye on it. A team of adult baseball players was making a loud racket across the dining room so it was difficult to carry on a conversation. Scott tried to razz Ryan by playing with his feet. Ryan kicked him.

"What's the deal, butthole?" Scott asked.

Ryan leaned forward and whispered. "Look, those guys over there could see you and say something."

Scott snapped back. "Remember when we first met and we were at Tower Road Drive-In? You were the one who stood up when that guy fucked with you."

"This is different."

"How different is it?"

"You know what I mean."

Scott had no idea what Ryan was talking about. He surveyed the group of men. None appeared to be the least bit interested in them. He took the plastic ketchup dispenser and scooted closer to Ryan in the semi-circular booth. Ryan instantly moved over as far to his end as he could. Scott frowned at him, then smoothed out one of the burger wrappers, and proceeded to make some sort of design on it with the ketchup. Ryan figured out what it was on the second stroke. Scott squirted an arrow through the heart, and set the bottle down. He then scooted back to where he was as if nothing happened. He looked toward the baseball team. No one was looking in their direction. "I'm waiting."

"For what?"

"For those guys to come over and slug me."

"Oh, come on." Ryan wadded up the paper and let it drop from his hand onto the serving tray. "We've been here too long. Let's go."

Scott looked at his watch. Unfortunately, they had arrived just after the team did and had to wait for them to be served. Now that they were done almost an hour had passed. Ryan got in the driver's side and strapped on the seatbelt. He did a couple of turns around the uncrowded parking lot to get a feel for the transmission.

"What are you doing? The road's that way," Scott said, pointing.

"I'm just gettin' a feel for this thing. I didn't get much of a chance that one time."

Scott realized Ryan knew what he was doing. He shouldn't forget Ryan was a gear head. With that in mind he felt more at ease. Ryan was driving without a license though and he wondered if he should let him. But, as usual, his body won, telling him he was tired. He figured he could get some rest as long as he knew Ryan was going to drive safely.

Scott's eyes lingered on the seatbelt buckle across Ryan's crotch. He was becoming used to having sex now, and after a week of none, he was sure it was going to be a hot time tonight. Masturbating the usual twice-a-day this last week somehow wasn't the same now.

Despite his profuse yawning Scott watched the road until they saw the sign that said Fresno 49 miles. "I'm gonna crash. Wake me when we reach Sacto."

Ryan held up the map as he drove, trying to see how far it was. "That's like…five hours away."

"So? You slept all morning. Here. Crank up the tunes." Scott handed him the headphones and sat back. Soon he was lulled by the constant hum of the wheels and fell asleep. The next thing he knew they pulled up to a gas station. "Where are we?"

"Modesto. It's about an hour and a half before we reach Sacto."

"Cool," he said sleepily. He slept again until a big bump woke him. "What the…"

"Sorry. Pothole."

Scott took the map and looked. "Where are we?"

"Just past Sacto, going toward a campground. I saw a sign a couple of miles back. It's in a place called Fairplay."

Scott scanned the map along the road they were traveling. "I don't see it on here."

"Maybe it's too small."

"Well, we need to stop soon so I can take a leak."

"I'll pull off over there." He pointed to the shoulder ahead.

"Yeah, pull over."

Ryan pulled over and Scott peed next to the front wheel. As he looked around, he saw a sign over a rise saying *Fairplay Campground.* On it was an arrow pointing the direction. "I see a sign for a campground over there," he said through the open door. He got back in and Ryan followed the sign's directions.

They went down a winding dirt road several hundred yards long and came to a dead end. A huge open campground area extended directly in front of them but no one was around. Ryan stopped the Jeep in front of a low hanging chain between two posts. The chain was fastened to the posts by large padlocks. A rusty sign hanging from even more rusty wire was attached to the chain.

Scott read the one word painted on it, 'Closed'. "Well, shit. Whadda we do now?"

Ryan got out and inspected the chain and the distance between two other poles on the other side of a ditch. "I got an idea."

Scott surveyed the area in front of them while Ryan traversed the ditch and made mental calculations. Several huge oaks were scattered around an open field. A fence cordoned off a pasture to the right. Two bay horses stared at them, their necks over the top of the barbed wire. In the back of the open campground area was a single building made of cinderblock with a slanted corrugated roof. The only other structure was more like a pavilion.

Ryan inspected the situation. "Hey, come here." He spread his arms out as Scott approached. "I think we can make it through these two poles. Pull the Jeep up here."

"What about the ditch?"

"What do you think four-wheel drive is for?"

Scott shoved his hands into his pockets and looked more closely. "Hmm, you're right." He got back in, shifted to four-wheel and pulled up to the shallow ditch.

"If you get stuck we can lighten the load and try it again."

Scott went for it. With a minor bump, he was through the ditch and beyond the poles.

Ryan jumped in. "We're happenin'! Go over to that building."

Scott stopped at the small building. It turned out to be two long, narrow communal showers with toilets at one end. One door was marked *Men*, the other *Women*. Ryan tried the plumbing but the water wasn't working. He went outside looking for a water valve and immediately found it. He turned it on and heard water coming through the pipe. He went back in, tried the spigot in the shower stall, and waited for the rusty water to flush out. Running it for a few minutes, he noticed that although it wasn't hot, it was bearable. Scott checked for toilet paper in the bathroom. Coming back into the shower where Ryan was he held up a half-used roll. "At least we can wipe our butts."

Scott looked at him standing in the dim light of the interior of the showers. The single bulb in the ceiling had a cobweb surrounding its ceramic escutcheon. Desiccated bugs in the web hung all around the bulb. He took Ryan in his arms and closed his eyes as they hugged tightly. "I wanna fuck you right here," Ryan said. He wasn't kidding. His breath was already a bit irregular and Scott could feel his heart pounding against his chest. And it was no use hiding his erection as it pressed against his groin. He pushed Scott against the tiled wall of the showers and pulled his shirt up. He went for Scott's nipples, sucking and licking each until they were both tight little bumps.

Scott's little friend, which had already gone to attention, pulsed even harder in his pants. He pulled himself away. "Stop or you'll make me come."

Ryan stopped and stepped back, then stuck a hand in his pants to adjust himself. "I almost forgot how hot you were. Let's pitch the tent and eat. We've got this whole campground to ourselves!" He withdrew his hand.

Scott took it, brought it to his nose, and took a whiff. "I love that smell."

Ryan grinned and took Scott's hand as he led him to the door. He poked his head out and looked around. "Nobody's here."

"Well, someone owns those horses over there. And they'll probably be around to feed them. They might catch us."

"I doubt it. Look, the pasture goes all the way across that hill. There's got to be a tack room, or something out of view, where they get fed. We can check it out later. Plus, there's no other entrance to this place except through that chain—which we got around."

Scott pulled the Jeep behind the building so no one could see it from the road. Ryan stood under the roof of the pavilion and inspected their surroundings. A thick layer of wood chips was scattered along the ground under its wooden roof, which was held up by large stone support columns. Nearby were two iron barbeque pits on short posts, and a picnic table between them.

"This'll be a great place to set up the tent. And this barbecue pit is perfect." He tapped it with one of his feet.

"All we have is sandwiches and cold chicken. We don't need a fire. Unless," Scott moved toward Ryan, "You need my body to start one with you."

Ryan looked Scott up and down. "You're always hot."

Scott was glad Ryan had finally mellowed out. Apparently, he had really needed sleep after all, as he had said earlier. Spending the night with him was beginning to look like it would be a blast again.

They set the tent up and repositioned it several times before they decided on its final location. Black clouds started to gather from the west and Scott was glad they had found a sheltered area.

They dragged the picnic table under the pavilion roof, laid out all the food, and ate. The wind whipped up, blew their napkins around, knocked over Ryan's drink, and generally scattered their condiments across the tabletop. The horses continued to stare at them from the fence. Scott washed the last bite down with his soda. "Let's get the Frisbee."

Ryan nodded his agreement as he munched an Oreo cookie, then showed his black-speckled teeth.

"You're not planning on kissing me with those teeth are you?" Scott asked.

"I don't kiss with my teeth. I use my tongue and vacuum-like suction."

"I hope it works well on dicks."

"It works best on dicks."

Scott grinned. "I never thought you'd be talking like this."

"Neither did I."

They dumped their garbage into a nearby rusted fifty-five gallon drum that was chained to a post. Ryan packed the rest of the food in their little Styrofoam cooler, set it on the table, then put a rock on the lid so it wouldn't blow away.

Scott went into the bathroom to pee. Ryan went around the corner to the other bathroom marked 'Women'. He heard a scuffling noise through the ventilation duct that connected the bathrooms. "Hey," he called out, "what're you doing?"

He looked up at the screen covering the duct at the top of the brick wall that separated the two bathrooms and saw the light go out on the other side. Ryan appeared under the pavilion with an old rag in his hand. In it, he had a hot light bulb. He pointed upward. "There's a socket up there. If it's live, too, we'll have light tonight."

Scott eyed the empty socket. "Let's give it a try."

"Here, help me drag the table."

They moved the picnic table under the socket. Ryan stood on it but couldn't reach the socket. With every flat object they could find they made a pile. Scott stood against him as Ryan steadied himself. He just barely was able to reach the socket now and as he tightened it in, the bulb flickered, then shone steadily.

"Excellent. Light," Scott said as Ryan jumped to the ground.

"Hey, grab the Frisbee and come on," Ryan said as he started toward the pasture.

Although the wind was steady, no rain had fallen yet. The dramatic difference from the arid desert Scott was so used to was refreshing.

When they arrived at the fence, they offered the horses some of the tall grass that was out of their reach. They seemed to be happy with the offering.

Now that they'd made friends, the two horses followed along as the boys walked a rutted dirt road along the outside of the fence. Weeds grew between the parallel tire ruts. Scott took in the surroundings. The rolling hills were so peaceful and here they were, by themselves, to enjoy it together. Tall oak trees stretched into the distance in all directions. In some places, a lone tree gave way to a large tract of them. It was like being in some lost land that had been painted brilliant green and brown. The smell of water was in the air, but they saw no water larger than a creek that meandered nearby. Scott decided the smell was probably due to the impending rain. The setting sun broke through the line of low dark clouds, striking their undersides with the last rays of the day. Around a curve, white beehives at the edge of the pasture were visible. Far off in the distance, across the pasture was a small tack house. Still they saw not another person.

"Hold my hand," Scott said.

Ryan took a step away from him.

Scott quickly walked ahead of him, turned around, and stopped. "Do you see anyone else around here?"

The wind rippled Ryan's shirt, his sleeves slapped against his biceps as he looked around. "No."

Scott took his hand and they continued. A few steps later Ryan took Scott and hugged him as hard as he could. He rested his head on his shoulder and sighed. "You put up with me. Why?"

"Because you're cute. Why do you think?"

Ryan let go of him and they continued to walk at a leisurely pace for another twenty minutes. There wasn't a decent level place to toss the Frisbee and the wind was too strong, so they bagged the idea. At a rise was an overlook to a long, wide, undulating, grass-covered valley. They sat on a fallen tree trunk and watched the valley turn dark. In a few more moments, the sun set in front of them.

That was their cue. Scott took the lead, walked ahead of Ryan, and kicked a small rock. Ryan came up from behind him and kicked it ahead of him. Soon it was a challenge to see who could keep it in the rut and ahead of them without kicking it into the weeds on either side of them. The horses walked along the fence line as they played, eyeing them as they went. It didn't take long for them to make it back, and none too soon, as the first drops of rain loudly hit the corrugated roof of the circular pavilion. Scott stopped and dropped the Frisbee and his shirt onto the picnic table. Ryan tossed his shirt onto the pile and then pushed him. At first Scott didn't know what the push was for, but when Ryan pushed him the second time, this time with a grin, he caught on.

Scott headed for Ryan but missed as he feigned right, then went left. Now Scott was grinning from ear to ear as he crouched down to see if he could fake Ryan out. As quick as he was, he couldn't take him down, but ended up locking arms around his shoulders for a few seconds.

The rain that started as a series of loud drops against metal soon became a full-scale downpour. The two horses apparently didn't mind the rain and watched as the boys whooped and hollered at each other in the only dry spot around.

Ryan dived for Scott's legs but lost grip of one knee after catching it with only three fingers. Scott stumbled as he twisted and ended up out from under the rooftop as he whirled around, getting rain all over him. Quickly he dashed back, now wet with not only sweat but also the rain. Ryan took that second to pin Scott's arm behind his back. Scott acted like he was going to stomp Ryan's foot. As Ryan moved it to avoid him, Scott turned and was wrapped around him. He locked his fingers together as he squeezed around Ryan's chest. It was hard for him to catch his breath, and as he held on, he deliberately pressed his groin against Ryan's butt.

"Whoo! The dude has a hard-on!"

"You'll have to fight me for it."

Ryan gritted his teeth as he took a deep breath. With all his might, he strained his arms and broke Scott's grip.

"Ah, ha. Got you now."

"Not if I can help it."

They were laughing so hard now it was difficult to keep hold of each other. They were both covered with sweat, and pieces of wood shavings, by the time Ryan raised his hands in a time-out signal.

They shook on it and sat on top of the picnic table catching their breath while watching the ebbing rain in the dark. Its gentle sound was just the tranquilizer they needed. Scott sat transfixed until moths and other insects found their lone light bulb and whirled around above them. "I'm gonna take a shower. Wanna come?"

"What do you mean by that?"

"Both ways."

"Only if you shower with me."

"It *was* an invitation."

They took towels from their packs and ran to the shower through the drizzle. The bulb behind the cobweb was bright inside the confined space of the shower. The two spouts in the wall were both operational, and Scott started one. Rusty water came out at first, but almost immediately turned clear. The water was warmer than the rain and wasn't at all unpleasant after their exertion. Scott stripped off his underwear and beckoned with his finger to his still-clothed boyfriend. "Afraid of the water?"

"No, I just wanted to see your hot body all naked and wet."

"It's easier when you're next to me and naked as well. So come here."

When Ryan pulled off his pants, Scott watched him get increasingly more rigid. He was fully erect in seconds. Ryan swung his hips back and forth, shaking it from side to side. "Here I come."

He got under the water with Scott and they washed the sweat and grime off. Scott massaged Ryan's penis but only seconds later he had to stop him. "Don't make me come. I want you to do me in the tent."

"Finally!" Scott said. He turned off the water and grabbed his towel. After he was dried off, he tried to get himself to go limp but it wouldn't listen to him even after he put underwear on. Ryan put on shorts with no underwear but the anticipation was so great his erection didn't subside either.

They gathered their clothes and other things and looked outside. The rain had stopped completely. The only sound was a light breeze that made an occasional shower of water fall from the leaves of a nearby oak tree. Not a light was to be seen except for the one inside the shower and the one under the pavilion.

"The coast is clear," Scott said as he turned off the light and dashed to the tent.

They spread out the thin blankets and the sheets and Scott took off his underwear. The soft lighting from the bulb outside evenly illuminated the inside of the tent. Ryan lay on his back and raised his hips as he shed his shorts. His erection flopped back onto his belly. Scott wasted no time. He grasped it in his hands, moistened his lips, and opened his mouth to take it. Ryan moaned as Scott slowly went up and down on it.

Ryan leaked until Scott's mouth was awash in its sweet flavor. He pulled Scott over in a sixty-nine position and started to lick on his balls and fondle his rigid penis with one hand as he caressed Scott's hard butt with the other. "I gotta have that dick inside me."

Scott took his mouth away. "Beg for it."

"No way. Don't make me wait or I'll go nuts."

This time Scott went to his toilet bag and produced a condom.

"When did you get those?"

"I go to the store, too, you know."

Ryan groped around in his bag then flipped him his tube of aloe gel. The inside of the tent was getting quite warm now even though he had unzipped one of the mesh windows at the top. Scott could just imagine how much hotter it was about to get.

Ryan took the little packet and broke it open with his teeth. He slowly pressed it down onto Scott's penis, unrolling it down to the base. He opened the tube of aloe, squirted some on the condom, and let Scott smear it around. He put some on his finger, smeared it on his anus, then poked his finger in and out a few times, lubing himself up. The gleam in his eyes was Scott's invitation. "Go for it," Scott told him as Ryan withdrew his finger completely.

Scott lay on his back and bunched one of the thin blankets under his head. He spread his legs slightly, and motioned Ryan to straddle him. Ryan slid his ass back and forth across Scott's lubed up dick, then bumped the tip at his anus several times. With one hand, he grasped Scott's dick at the base and held it vertical. With little ceremony, he slowly pressed down onto it. Several seconds later Scott's entire length disappeared.

Ryan's eyes were closed and the look on his face was just what Scott needed to see. Now Ryan started a slow up and down motion, his rigid penis bouncing above Scott's stomach.

"God, that feels great. Sure you haven't done this before?"

Scott wasn't sure what Ryan was talking about since he was doing all the work. All he was doing was lying there. "Not…that I…remember," Scott replied between gasps. He couldn't believe how intensely good it felt, too.

Ryan had started slowly at first, but was now riding up and down with a much quicker motion. Several times Scott made him slow down since any minute now he was sure he was going to come. The head of Ryan's penis was turning purple now and a vein on the underside was starting to bulge out. Scott drank in the scene, watching Ryan's thighs flex with his bouncing, his hand as it occasionally pumped his dick, the vein, and the look on Ryan's face.

Ryan's breathing was fast becoming laborious. Another second later he erupted all over Scott's stomach and chest. He had barely touched himself. His moans filled the small tent as he continued to bounce up and down, but more slowly now. He grasped and pumped his shaft rapidly while his orgasm wound down.

It was more than Scott could stand. He came, too, holding Ryan by the hips to stop him from bouncing. Everything disappeared from his consciousness except for his penis hidden inside Ryan. Finally, Scott let go of him and let him slowly slide up and down a few times. He was sure it was the most intense orgasm he had ever experienced. Once he was able to open his eyes, he felt the fast liquefying semen rolling down his sides.

Ryan just sat there with Scott's penis still inside him, as his own continued to pulse and drain. Finally, Scott pulled him up and off and his penis flopped out. The condom was opaque with white goo. Ryan reached for a tissue from his bag. He wiped his anus, cleaned off his penis and thigh, and then leaned back on his hands.

Scott sat up on his heels with a huge grin on his face, his hands on his thighs. Clear streams of semen slowly ran down his chest to his abdomen. His penis was still at high noon, the filled up condom completely obscuring most of the shaft.

Ryan inspected it by squeezing it a little with two fingers. He was amazed that Scott still hadn't gotten soft. "That was fast."

"Look who's talking. You came first."

"You always come fast."

It was true. Now that Scott thought about it, it seemed to be a bit of a problem. He never lasted long. He had never had a partner before and didn't know how to pace himself.

Ryan rose up on one elbow and with the other hand reached out and tugged on the condom. "You can take that off now."

Scott brushed Ryan's hand aside. "No. And I'm never gonna wash my dick."

"I'm not a movie star."

Scott tried to correct him. "Porn star."

"Not that either."

"You had me fooled." But he carefully removed it, and then pumped his penis, using his semen as lube. It pulsed even more now.

"How do you do that?" Ryan asked him rhetorically, as he observed Scott's steady erection.

"Lots of leafy green veggies," Scott answered as he wiped himself clean.

Ryan laid on his back now, knees up and his feet flat on the sheet. Scott lay on his side next to him and caressed Ryan's stomach as he alternately tensed and relaxed the muscles. "So do you feel cool now that you've fucked me?"

"Well, it was better than I imagined."

Ryan curled his fingers around Scott's bicep and pulled him on top of him. They hugged, kissed, and rubbed their bodies together for long minutes until Ryan was hard again. Scott had stayed hard, much to Ryan's surprise, then delight.

"Can I have more timeshare with you?" Scott whispered.

"I'm not a condo," Ryan said, trying to sound serious.

"Peep, peep, peep," Scott said as he sat on his knees straddling Ryan's middle.

"Alright, alright. Just don't 'peep' at me anymore."

Scott scooted back down and proceeded to run his tongue up and down his penis. Ryan's body squirmed and tensed as Scott licked slowly but continuously.

Ryan could only emit an "Uhhh! Uhhh!" as Scott started relentlessly sucking him. Ryan leaked more and more, but before Scott brought him to the point of no return, he stopped.

Ryan opened his eyes. "What the hell did you stop for?"

"I wanna fuck you again."

"Let me think about it."

"Well think fast."

He didn't actually think about it at all. Instead, he turned over onto all fours and spread his legs apart. Scott maneuvered himself so that he was behind Ryan and spat into the palm of his hand. He worked the spit all over and soon his entire shaft was glistening with saliva. He dropped another gob of spit on the head. Ryan's hairy anus was well lubed and felt loose enough as he poked against it several times. Finally, he kept a steady pressure and slowly worked himself in. He didn't intend to actually fuck him without a condom he just wanted to feel what it was like to be inside him without anything in the way. It felt almost the same as before but he definitely liked the feel of skin against skin better than with a condom on.

"You're not gonna come inside me," Ryan commanded.

"I just wanted to feel what it was like."

"Well, before you *do* come you better pull out."

"You don't trust me?"

"If you shoot inside me I'll punch you."

"Humph," he breathed. "Throw me that condom."

Ryan looked back to see Scott pointing to his bag. Ryan reached in and found another condom package right on top. He pulled it out and bit off the top of the package before handing it over his shoulder. Scott took it, slowly pulled out, and unrolled the condom down over his hard shaft. With more aloe, he smeared the condom all over. In a few seconds, he was guiding himself back in.

It was heaven again. The feeling of Ryan's tightening anus against his penis was a sensation he couldn't adequately describe to himself. His mind was on autopilot as he shut his eyes and slowly moved his hips back and forth, lingering on the thrust to feel the warmth of Ryan's insides surrounding him. He held onto Ryan's hips, and then ran his palms across his smooth flesh as he slowly thrust in and out. He seemed to have a little more control over himself this time. Each time he felt himself getting too close, he slowed long enough to make sure he wouldn't come right away.

All the while, Ryan had his head lowered and a hand reached down between his legs while resting the rest of his weight on his knees and other arm. On every thrust, he was able to caress Scott's balls, then his own as Scott backed off. Finally, after several long minutes, Scott found a rhythm that started building the tension higher and higher. Ryan could tell from the new motion, and the fact that Scott's balls were getting tighter and tighter, that it was only a matter of seconds now.

"Oh fuck," Scott whispered with a grimace on his face. He breathed rapidly a few times, then stopped moving as he let out a guttural sound. His halted motion lasted only a few seconds as he continued in short furtive thrusts. From the sound of things, Ryan thought Scott was choking on his own spit, but it wasn't anything of the sort. Finally, Scott caught his breath and fell over Ryan's back.

"Pull out. It hurts."

Scott was still feeling spasms. "I'm not done coming."

Ryan pulled his pelvis forward but Scott met his motion and followed him. Finally, Ryan was lying flat on the tent floor, being crushed by Scott's full weight. "Damn it, get up, you're smashing my dick."

"Sorry." Scott slowly pulled out. He deliberately took his time. Finally, though, he was completely out and leaned back on his knees. Ryan turned over to observe him. Sweat had matted Scott's hair down around his forehead and down by his ears. A single trickle of it was starting to run down by his left temple. His face had a stupid smirk on it and he looked drunk. Again, his dick was still at attention. This time, though, only the tip of the condom had anything in it. Ryan looked at it.

"I'm not taking it off," Scott announced.

"I didn't say anything."

Scott leaned over and began to suck on Ryan's rock hard dick. It took only a few minutes, and he, too, had the prize he was looking for. There wasn't too much this time, and he was able to swallow every bit of it. As he did so, he wondered if he would eventually get used to the slimy texture. He could handle all the pre-come Ryan could muster since it tasted sweet to him. A gob of the salty-tasting semen was another story altogether.

Ryan rose up on his elbows while Scott leaned back on his knees again. He had finally started losing some rigidity, although it was still at greater than a forty-five degree angle.

Ryan thrust his chin out. "It'll leak all over you."

"You mean, like all over my balls or something?"

"Or stain the tent floor."

Scott looked down abruptly. He didn't want stains in his tent and didn't want any of it on the sheets either.

He reluctantly pulled it off and wiped himself clean. Now completely spent and very satisfied, he laid on top of Ryan. He was finally going completely limp. Eventually, he slid over and got comfortable in a position to Ryan's side. The last thing he remembered was hearing breathing in his left ear.

The noise outside sounded like it was coming from the picnic table. It woke Scott up with a jerk and he put a finger to his lips as Ryan opened his eyes.

Scott didn't know what to do since, from their vantage, he couldn't see the table through the unzipped window. Both of them were naked, and it sounded like someone was rummaging through their stuff. As quickly and quietly as they could, they slipped on their shorts. Scott grabbed one of the flashlights and poised himself at the flap of the tent.

The noise outside continued. Now something crashed to the ground. It sounded like the cooler. Ryan took his flashlight and held it up at the ready. In one quick motion, Scott unzipped the tent flap and let out a piercing whistle as Ryan let out a loud war cry. They scrambled out on all fours, stood, and turned in time to see two frightened raccoons racing away into the dark, chattering loudly as they scurried off. The Styrofoam cooler was in several pieces. A previously unopened bag of chips had been emptied all over the bench, tabletop, and ground. The rest of their food was everywhere.

Scott let down his shoulders. "Shit!"

Ryan caught his breath. "I forgot about the 'coons all up through here."

They picked up the remains of the packages and dumped them in the rusted drum.

"We'll have to go into town for breakfast, I guess," Ryan said.

"Just as well. I could do with some hot food in the morning."

As Ryan dropped the last wad of packaging into the drum, Scott pointed at him. "Hey, was that you I fucked earlier, twice?"

"You're mistaking me for some other hot stud."

"No. I'm sure it was you." He pulled the front of Ryan's shorts away, clicked on the flashlight, and looked in. "Yeah. That was your dick. But it was hard before."

"They can always tell from looking at my dick."

He yawned and gave Scott a hug. Scott's skin against Ryan's bare chest felt wonderful. They went back into the tent and Scott zipped the flap back up. Scott pulled off his shorts again and motioned for Ryan to strip off his, too. Scott nestled his body to conform with Ryan's as they settled down.

It's all too wonderful, he thought as sleep started to claim him again. Ryan was more than he bargained for. He was cute, practical, and good with a Frisbee. And now he was leading him on a journey into a redwood rainforest he'd never seen before, even as a Boy Scout on all their campouts. It was all too good to be true.

Then he remembered. That Crawford guy. He would have to get it out of him tomorrow. He felt himself get jealous again and let the feeling fill up his mind. In a way, it was interesting to feel that way since he wasn't used to it. But he hoped that by tomorrow he wouldn't have to feel that way ever again.

The chattering of birds flitting around the picnic table woke Scott up at first light. He yawned and woke Ryan by searching for his erection. He found it.

Ryan sounded groggy. "You're gonna make me pee in the tent."

"Unless I make you have an orgasm first."

"My tank's empty."

"Why don't I believe you?" Scott slipped on his shorts and exited the dew-covered tent to the bathroom. He had to pee as well.

A few birds sat on the roof of the Jeep and on the cinderblock building, diving to claim the remaining pieces of chips that the boys hadn't picked up last night. Ryan came in to the bathroom a few moments later. He shaved and washed just his hair under the shower spout. Scott did the same, shaving just his chin, the only place he needed to today.

Still no one else had shown up. Neither cars nor people were anywhere in view. And the horses had disappeared somewhere, not visible anywhere in the pasture.

They took all of their stuff out of the tent, then packed it up. They repacked the rest of the gear in less than a half-hour and both sat in the Jeep, inspecting the roadmap. Ryan pointed out the way he figured would be quickest. "This route will get us through the Trinity Forest by afternoon. In the mountains it'll be a little slower. But let's find a place to eat first."

Ryan guided Scott through the narrowly spaced poles back onto the unpaved road. Soon they were by-passing Sacramento on their way north again. Ryan offered some gas money and they stopped to fill up in a tiny unincorporated town. Next door was a cafe and they opted to fill their stomachs there.

CHAPTER 19

In the restaurant, Ryan seemed a little out of sorts again and Scott noticed his agitation as they waited for their food to arrive. "You know I've been wanting to ask you about a couple of things."

"I figured."

"You know what I want to ask?"

"Yeah."

"You better tell me or you get no more dick."

Ryan looked dejected as they ate and kept looking at his watch, which made Scott nervous. What was worse, though, was Ryan's stony silence. *He had better tell me truthfully about Crawford*, Scott thought. After they ate, Scott asked for a soda to go and they paid the bill. He pulled into a convenience store a little further ahead to buy sodas in cans, ice, and a little Styrofoam cooler. Soon enough they were back on the highway once again.

Scott drove this leg of the way, but after fifteen minutes, he couldn't contain himself any longer. He turned down the tape volume. "Okay. Let's have it. Why the big secret about this Crawford guy?"

Ryan let out a long sigh and bounced his head back against the headrest. He lifted his cap and readjusted it back on his head. "God, where do I start?"

"How about the beginning?"

Ryan fidgeted with the map for a moment. "I met Crawford at a rest area."

"A rest area? You mean like on a highway?"

"Yes," he said sheepishly.

"When?"

"Exactly five weeks before my junior year ended."

"You were what? Sixteen?

"I told him I was seventeen."

"Did he kidnap you?"

"No....I...let him pick me up."

"You gotta be kidding. Why?"

"There's this truck stop nearby, where I used to eat before I worked the morning shift on weekends. You know, at *Haradon's Lumber* that I told you about?"

"Yeah."

"One morning I was eating breakfast there and I overheard these two truckers talking about the rest area up near the border on the PCH. They thought they weren't being overheard but the booths in back carry sound along the ceiling if you sit in the right spot. One was telling the other how some guy sucked him off in the bathroom. That caught my attention, so I kept listening. He said the best time to go there was in the evening and whenever he got horny he'd go in and get a quick blowjob. I, like, couldn't believe it. I really thought the guy was shittin' his buddy. But I figured it wouldn't hurt to find out if it were true since I knew where he was talking about. I wasn't gonna do anything except check it out."

"You were sixteen?" Scott asked.

"Yes....Now listen..."

"I'm jealous!"

"You won't be when I'm done."

Scott interrupted again. "How old was he?"

"Twenty-eight."

"Twenty-eight? That's old."

"Twenty-eight's not *old*."

"Well, what did he look like?"

"He's six feet tall, big arms, hairy chest, thick dark hair on his head but with a high forehead, and real hairy legs and butt. He's got a pretty thick dick, hazel eyes and wide lips."

"But twenty-eight? Jeez."

"Are you gonna let me finish?"

"Okay, okay. I just can't imagine, that's all."

"I parked the car in the parking lot one night about a week after I heard those guys, downed a couple of beers, and checked out the bathroom. I didn't see anything fishy going on at all and I left. A week later—it was on a Saturday—I boogied over there again. I don't know why. I guess…I wanted it to be true. That's when I saw a couple of cars parked across from the bathroom and guys coming and going."

"Did you just…go in?"

"No. I backed my car in near some others and just sat there and watched. Soon enough this pickup truck came up and parked next to me. The guy driving was Crawford."

"Did he kidnap you then?"

"He didn't kidnap me. Why do you keep saying that?"

"You said he picked you up."

"Well, he didn't kidnap me." Ryan looked exasperated for a moment, then continued. "I knew he was checking me out, but I pretended not to notice. The next thing I know he gets out of the truck. But instead of going over to the bathroom he came to my passenger side window with this big smile on his face." He let out an unconscious sigh, and then went on. "I had the window rolled down so it was easy for him to talk to me. He was friendly, so I let him talk. He asked me if I had a cigarette and I told him I didn't smoke, but I offered him a beer. He leaned on his truck and talked to me through the window while we drank. Then he asked me if he could check out my car."

"And that's when he seduced you?"

"*No*…. I got out, opened the hood, and told him what I was planning on doing with it when I got the money. You know new parts and all. Then he wanted to see the dash, so I let him sit in the passenger seat. I showed him my tapes and he wanted me to play one. We must have talked for, like, another half an hour. He kept telling me how nice my car was and how he liked to fix up cars and that he knew where he could get Chevelle parts really cheap. He even said he could help me and all. I thought that was really cool. Then he got even smoother."

"Whadda ya mean?"

"He said he had a nephew who was my age and they saw a lot of each other a few years back before he moved away. He said I looked a lot like him. I was feeling loosened up by then, mostly 'cause of the beers, and I thought about what his nephew might be like. But it was the perfect line. He asked me if I wanted to go back to his house where we could talk some more. He wanted to show me some of his hot rod magazines and other stuff and I said yeah. By that time, all I could think of was what it would be like to do it with him. I knew the whole time what he wanted even though he never let on. I pretended to myself that I didn't really know what was happening. I hadn't ever been with anyone before and didn't know what to expect or do.

"He lives off the PCH, a few miles south of the rest stop, so it was easy to follow him. And his house is really cool. It's, like, up on this slope off the highway, and it's all rough-hewn wood inside. His backyard is a couple of acres on the side of the mountain. It's a two-bedroom place, but he lives by himself. He has a real bearskin rug in front of his fireplace, and a rough stone floor in the kitchen and by the front door. He has a couple of pistols, some rifles, and hot rod magazines and all.

"So we sat on his couch and talked about cars and stuff. He showed me his guns and told me about the sawmill where he worked. I told him I worked at the lumberyard and how I was surprised I never saw him before. He said he rarely went to the lumberyards.

"All that time I was expecting him to do something with me and he didn't make a move. But then he finally stopped talking and scooted over more. I didn't stop him. I just let him take my hand. I remember it cause my hands were cold. He said he wanted to warm them up and he unbuttoned his shirt and put one on his chest. God, Scott, my dick just got hard in a second even though I was shakin'. He said I would quit shakin' once I had my clothes off. The next thing I knew we both had our shirts off and we went down to the bearskin rug. I was just about to lose my wad right there though. I wanted him so bad I ached.

"He sat on his knees on the floor across from me and hugged me. He kept telling me I was the hottest guy he'd ever seen. I felt I had, like, this control over him 'cause he was almost worshipping me. But it was really the other way around. He had control of me right then.

"When he laid back I could see his big dick through his pants. I was about to break my zipper, too. And I figured if he wasn't going to unzip me I would do it. So, I did.

"I pulled my shirt off and he pulled my pants down but wouldn't take off my underwear. It was like he just wanted to look at me like that. I finally had to make him take off his pants since he just kept feeling me up."

Ryan was quiet for a moment, trying to gather his thoughts. This was the first time he'd ever told anyone the story and it was beginning to smart. "So he started kissing me all over. I just got into it and kissed him back. He's strong, built, and smelled like a guy. I wanted to kiss him all night. I remember I had to tell him to stop cause I was about to get off just from *that*.

"It was funny, too. I was leaking so much he thought I'd come. I told him I hadn't and he finally pulled off my underwear. God, his body against mine was the best feeling....

"I let him feel me up for a while more. Finally, I couldn't stand it anymore and while I was humping his belly I came all over him. He rubbed it all over his chest like it was cologne or something.

"He let me jerk him off then. That was the first time I ever jerked a guy off. He came in just a minute. We fell asleep right there in front of the fireplace with the lights on and his arms around me, and my pants around my ankles. I thought I was in heaven."

Scott was so riveted by the story he didn't notice they'd driven twenty miles. The turn at Yuba City was just ahead.

"You know this is, like, really turning me on." He pointed to his crotch and the noticeable erection that tented his pants.

Ryan glanced down at Scott's lap. "Just wait, it won't."

Scott made the turn and prompted Ryan to continue.

"We woke up in the middle of the night and I got dressed and left. Before I did I asked him if he wanted to see me again. He said he couldn't believe I would bother."

"Well, why did you?"

"He was hot. And I knew he wanted me more than I wanted him. Plus, I loved it that he wanted to pay attention to me like that. I stopped by again a few days later. And again. And again.

"It usually started out the same way. As soon as I'd come into the house, he'd start to hug and kiss on me all over. I loved it. He was the only person in the world who was even remotely interested in me then. He taught me how to French kiss.

"A couple of weeks later he asked me about my friends and if I had a girlfriend. I told him there was this Choctaw girl in school I had my eye on. So, he said I needed to be 'depussyfied'. I knew it meant he wanted to fuck me. Just the thought of his dick in my ass made me hard. I was hooked the first second it went in. It was as if something had been missing all my life until then. I let him do me twice that night, and just about every time I saw him after that, too. Then he started doing weird stuff."

"Like what?"

"Like one Saturday he came by the lumberyard looking for me. I hadn't seen him the weekend before since I had to work both those days. He talked to my buddy Dolf, who I used to work with, and

Crawford told him he was my uncle. Dolf was, like, one of the guys I used to hang out with all the time—him and these two other guys. I was working that day, but was way in back and didn't see him. So Dolf came and got me. He thought it was strange I never talked about this uncle who lived so close by so I had to make up some stupid story about him.

"I went to his truck with him and asked what he was doing saying he was my uncle and shit. He said he thought I wasn't going to see him anymore and had like, run out on him, or something."

"What did you say?"

"I told him not to say shit like that anymore and that I would come by and see him that night. So I did. At first, all we did was talk. I was still pissed off at him, but he had this way of making me not pissed off anymore. Of course, it led to us having sex. It was great, as usual, and I couldn't figure out why 'cause I thought I should still be mad.

"I thought it was stupid for me to keep seeing him just for sex, but all I could think about was his arms around me and that fat dick of his and the way he sucks dick. The whole time I was thinking it was weird that all this started because I hung out at the rest area."

"This *is* getting weird."

"I *told* you. And it's all true. Every bit of it."

"Did Dolf believe your story?"

"I had to start lying to everyone. It sucked 'cause I wasn't used to making up stuff like that and wasn't sure I would be able to keep it all straight. I was at Crawford's house a whole lot then and not with the other guys like I used to be. Zirk, one of my other buddies, wanted to know where I was going all the time so I made up a story that I had this babe in Oregon that I was fucking. They didn't have a clue that it was completely the opposite, like a *guy* was fucking *me*."

"They kept razzing me and kept wanting to meet this babe. And I had to keep lying about it. One weekend night I went to see Crawford. When we were talking, I told him about having to lie to my friends. Not like it was funny, but like how stupid it was. He kept laughing at me while I

was telling him what I had to make up. I called him an asshole. That's
when he slapped me."

"He *slapped* you?"

"Yeah. And I didn't just leave then like I should have."

"What did you do?"

"I fucking cried. God damn it!"

"Whoa," Scott said. Now he wondered if he should ask any more
questions.

"Yeah. I fucking cried. Not like all out bawling, more like tears in my
eyes. I was scared. He was laughing at me like it was some kind of joke
or something. But I was serious. I didn't know how I was gonna keep up
with all the lies. He said he was sorry, that he didn't mean to slap me.
Then he started kissing me and taking all my clothes off. All my dick
needed was a little attention and in a second he had me hard. Then he
made me give him a blow job in his den."

"He *what*?"

"Yeah. I thought if I didn't that he would pull another stunt like the
one when he came to my work. So, I made him come. Then I sat on his
dick on his couch until he came again."

Scott didn't know if he should ask, but just had to. "Did *you* come?"

"Do I ever *not* come?"

"I get the picture. Did you use condoms?"

"Always. I made him."

Scott was relieved. "Good thing."

Ryan continued. "I didn't want any more scenes at work so I kept seeing him. But the more I did the more he didn't seem to care about much
else except how much I jerked off when I wasn't with him."

"Well, was it a lot?"

Ryan glared at him.

Scott made a face. "Sorry."

"I finally got up enough nerve to tell him I didn't want to see him
anymore. That's when it started getting really fucked up."

"It got worse?"

"He said if I didn't keep seeing him he'd come and make this big scene about how this babe I was supposedly seeing was really a fag and I was going there as often as I could to have him fuck me. He said he'd tell everyone I had AIDS and I wanted to fuck all my friends. Can you believe it?"

"What? And you *believed* him?"

"I didn't want him to tell people I was a fag!"

Scott bit his lip and looked at him. "You don't really think he would have said all those things, do you?"

"I didn't know what to think."

"So what did you do?"

"I was stuck. If I told him to get lost, he'd just make a scene I'd never be able to live down. So I kept seeing him."

"*No!*"

"What would you have done?" Ryan's eyes were red and he looked like he was going to cry. Scott waited as Ryan wiped away a tear from a corner of one of his eyes.

"Then he told me he was going to tell my brother and grandma. I knew he couldn't 'cause I never told him where I lived. The phone's in Muh's name. And her last name is different from mine. I even told him we didn't have a phone. I don't know how he believed that, but he never asked me about it again. And I always hid my driver's license in the car before I ever came in to his house so he never knew my address."

"I can't believe you were that smart."

"That was the *only* smart thing I did that whole time. But I felt like I was in a vise. The next day I decided to kill myself."

Scott swerved slightly at the sudden revelation. "You *what*? You...you tried to *kill* yourself?"

"Don't make me feel any worse than I already do. Please."

Scott suddenly realized he was dealing with something he'd never even conceived of before. Up until now, it was great fun to be with Ryan, what with his experience, his cute body, all despite his garish behavior. Suddenly, with this, it was different. "I'm sorry…I just never knew anyone who wanted to like…you know…"

"Tried. I only tried."

"How?"

"My granddad willed me this vintage Packard. It's covered and up on blocks in the garage. I'll show it to you when we get there. I closed the garage doors and started it up. I figured it would be an easy way to die."

Scott's mind was reeling. It sounded so strange to hear his boyfriend talking like this. Almost afraid to ask, he spoke anyway. "Did you leave a note?"

"No. That's the other reason I didn't do it."

"*Other* reason?"

"Yeah. I didn't leave a note, and I couldn't stand the thought of dying in a car that only had an AM radio in it." He managed a tight smile while Scott furrowed his brow at the thought.

"I was pissed at myself afterward and started giving all sorts of grief to Muh. After about three weeks, she threatened to kick me out if I didn't stop it. I was starting to get all gloomy feeling while this was going on and her threat made me feel even worse. I kept seeing Crawford 'cause when he'd hug me I felt better.

"And every time he'd start taking my clothes off I'd get this instant hard-on 'cause I knew he'd do me. So in a way it was sorta okay, 'cause I would forget about feeling depressed while we were having sex.

"A couple of weeks after that I started feeling a little better and I told him I was thinking about buying new stuff for my Chevelle. It was just talk then. But he said he'd give me some money to do it. I couldn't believe it. He just outright gave me nine hundred and fifty dollars for new tires, a new carb, wheels and some other chrome junk. I couldn't believe how happy that made me."

"And that's how you had the 'coolest Chevelle in Crescent City'?"

"And everybody thought I was *The* Dude. Including Little Trout—that was my girlfriend."

"Little Trout? Girlfriend?"

"It's her Choctaw name. She's like half-Indian and goes by it."

"You had a *girlfriend*?"

"It just sorta happened."

"Just *sorta* happened?"

"She kept hanging around me at school, mostly because of my car, I'm sure. Then when I started fixin' it up, she got way interested. So, I asked her out. I really wasn't all that interested in her, you know, like sexually. I didn't wanna call her up a lot, and figured if I sorta ignored her that she would eventually go away. But the exact opposite happened. Like when I'd ask her out on a date I would hardly talk to her during the week and mostly avoided her at school, but that somehow made her like me even more. So, we ended up together a lot more often than I thought. We got more attention than we knew what to do with 'cause she was pretty popular in school. And it was a great cover since I was still seeing Crawford once or twice a week.

"Then I thought that if I kept going out with her, like I should've done in the *first* place, I could eventually figure out how to get Crawford completely out of the picture. I figured that if I had this local girlfriend, and if he pulled another weird stunt, no one would believe him."

"Well, did it work?"

"Not even close."

"*Jeez.* Why not?"

"I managed to make everyone believe I was getting it on with her. And my buddies thought I was bad 'cause I had this girl in town and still had some on the side in Oregon and she didn't know anything about it. Then we had this big dance one Saturday night. I didn't normally bother to go to dances, but she wanted to go. Dolf, and his girlfriend, and Jack and Zirk, and their girls and I, all went. We went parking afterward and she was, like, all over me."

"I can't imagine why."

Ryan ignored him. "But I felt like stone. All I could do was think about being in the back seat with Dolf instead of her. That's when I started thinking I must be a fag after all."

"Gay, God damn it. Don't say *fag*. And being with Crawford wasn't enough information for you?"

"No....I figured it was just...I don't know! He always wanted to hug me and feel me up, and I loved the way he kissed. Plus, he was horny all the time, and so was I. All the attention he constantly gave me was the only thing that made me feel good about myself. But toward the end of the school year I started feeling crazy 'cause I was going out with Little Trout and keeping Crawford a secret from her, and everyone else. I was constantly bitching at Muh 'cause I felt so out of control. And my little brother started staying away from me 'cause I was always on edge. I didn't dare tell Crawford all this was going on 'cause I didn't want him to laugh at me again. That's when I met Frank Gaviota."

"You went *back* to the rest area?"

"Fuck no. He was a customer at work. He's one of the coolest guys I ever met."

Scott thought for a moment "Oh, yeah, I remember you saying something about him before."

"Yeah. He's the guy who lives north of us in Prieto Canyon. He and his wife have this house on some of the most expensive real estate on the river there just off the highway."

"He's married?"

"Very married. And don't think we were doing stuff."

"How does he fit into all this?"

"Well, he came in one day looking for the 'perfect plywood'. I asked him what it was for, you know, so I could get him the right grade and all. He said he was building kayaks and needed a load delivered. That's before he got his van and started getting it himself.

"We got to talking and I realized he was really different. Just from the way he talked, he seemed like he had his shit totally together. And I figured he must be rolling in dough to be living in the canyon—the houses are way expensive. He said he'd tip me if I delivered the wood. I wasn't about to pass up the easy cash. That's when I saw their place and met his wife.

"And everything about them was cool. He used to live in New York City and told me he had this dream of chucking everything to live in the woods so he could work with his hands. He was new to the county and didn't know a whole lot of people yet and he was really friendly."

"How old was *that* guy?"

"Mid-thirties…I think he said he was thirty-six. So, he did it. They sold their condo in Manhattan, their house in some place called Westchester, and moved to the canyon. He had a new workshop built and I delivered his first load of plywood."

"How can anyone make money building kayaks?"

"The way he makes them they're expensive, but worth it. And he sells 'em for about eight hundred dollars apiece. They're, like, top quality. Some are wood, some are wood and fiberglass."

"Okay, so go on."

"So, after he helped me unload the plywood I asked him to show me what he was up to. That's when he told me about himself. His wife invited me to stay for dinner with them and I did. They didn't know me from anyone and already were inviting me to eat dinner with them."

Scott suddenly realized Ryan must have never had any real allies before this Frank guy came along. For the most part, he seemed to have surrounded himself with people who were hostile toward him, judgmental of him, or about to be his enemies.

"I told him about the classes I was in—the ones I didn't skip—and about some designs of different things I'd done in shop and drafting classes. I had told him I was kicking around the idea of being an engineer. He said he liked me and wondered if I might want to help him design kayaks. I'd been ocean kayaking before but never thought about designing one. He lived closer to me than Crawford did and it was easier to see him. So, I started visiting him and helped draw out designs for him, and he'd try them out. Finally, he settled on two basic designs we got from some books."

"So you actually helped this guy?"

"Not really. More like he helped me. If it wasn't for Frank I'd probably be dead now."

"Huh?"

"When I wrecked my car."

"If he was your friend why didn't you tell him what was going on?"

"I'm getting there...I'd been helping him for weeks at that point. It was almost a year after I started seeing Crawford. Somehow, I managed to juggle everything even though I had an almost failing grade in one of my classes. Then Crawford said I needed a good luck fuck since finals were coming up. This time, though, he was really weird.

"It started in the den where our clothes usually ended up. He said he wanted to try something new and got out two handcuffs and some rope. I told him I didn't get into that kind of stuff, but he promised it was just for fun and it would make my dick stay hard for a long time. Who was I to turn that down?"

Ryan was having a noticeably difficult time continuing now and his eyes were red again as he tried to swallow the lump in his throat. "I was so stupid. He cuffed both my hands with two different cuffs and put the loose cuff parts over these rails that were spaced out really wide on his headboard. He even strapped my ankles with some rope around the feet of the bed. So here I was, laying on my back, totally naked, spread eagle, and my dick ready to go. Then he got out this little riding crop and started slapping it on my dick and thighs. I told him to stop because it hurt, but he didn't. He kept slapping it harder and then started on my stomach and chest. He was hard as a rock—like it was some sort of hard-on pill or something. Finally I screamed for him to stop and let me go."

Scott's mouth was wide open now. "Fuck! Did he?"

"Yeah, but he stuffed a sock in my mouth to make me shut up and said he had to go some place!"

Scott's heart was racing. "*He what?*"

"He left me tied up to his fucking bed and left—in my car."

"What did you do?"

"I was able to spit out the sock, but it was a good five minutes before I realized he really left. So, I tried to get my hands out of the cuffs, but I couldn't 'cause they were so tight. I was so tied down it was hard to move at all. God, I was so scared 'cause I had no idea what he was planning or where he had gone or anything. It wasn't for fun at all. It was just awful. I never suspected he'd do something like that."

Ryan stopped there and again wiped a tear from each eye. Scott's heart was racing and aching at the same time. It was the weirdest thing he'd ever heard.

Ryan began again. "I was stretched so tight I thought my arms would pull out of the sockets. I kept kicking and kicking and finally managed to get enough slack to slip the rope off my feet. I pulled every muscle in my neck and arms, cut my wrists from pulling with the cuffs, and bruised up my ankles pretty badly. At least my feet were free so I was able to scoot back and pull the cuffs up off the rails." He rubbed his wrists unconsciously as he related the incident.

"I ran out of the bedroom and the first thing I noticed was that the asshole'd hidden my clothes and shoes. I couldn't find them anywhere. I looked outside for them, but it was raining and I didn't see them from the door. That's when I realized he'd taken my car. I looked everywhere for a key to the cuffs but he had it the whole time. I even thought about loading one of the guns to shoot him when he came back but his ammo was always locked up in a steel case."

"You were completely naked?"

"After I did all the searching I put on some of his shorts. But I didn't have anything else, no shoes—his were too big for me—no wallet, no money, no keys, nothing!"

"Why didn't you just call the cops?"

"Are you *crazy*? I couldn't tell 'em what happened. Jeez, they'd probably take me to jail and kill me or just killed me right in the patrol car. And I still had those fucking handcuffs on. I didn't have my ID, and I had all these red spots all over me from the whip."

"When did he come back?"

"A half hour later. He had my stuff with him in a paper bag. He wanted to know if I liked his little joke. He wouldn't give me the key to the cuffs until I promised to give him a blow job."

Scott slapped his forehead with the heel of his hand. "*What?*"

A single tear rolled down Ryan's left cheek. All this time he had kept it a secret. Until now had never told anyone and the embarrassment was the worst of it for him just now.

Scott slowed down, pulled over to the side of the road, and stopped the vehicle. Putting an arm around Ryan's neck, he pulled him toward him and wiped the tear off his cheek with his index finger. The sign up ahead said 'Weaverville 2 miles' and he decided it was time to stop for a rest and maybe, if Ryan felt like it, eat some lunch.

CHAPTER 20

The tiny restaurant was empty except for the waitress and a cook. Despite the piped-in music, it was too quiet to ask any more questions until they left.

"I can't believe you never told anyone about this," Scott said after they got back out onto the highway.

The bitterness sounded in Ryan's words. "I hate his guts. All he did was trash my senior year."

Scott couldn't remember the number of high fives he'd given his friends at the end of the school year. It was a happy memory, completely the opposite of Ryan's.

They drove for a while and Ryan, now completely composed, told him more. "I didn't know it at the time, but it was the last time I saw him. And there was still Little Trout. We had a couple of weeks to go before graduation and I still didn't know if I would pass my Composition final. Muh was constantly pissed at me whenever I was at home—which was rare those days anyway. I was pissed 'cause Little Trout was pissed at me. And she thought it was time we started fucking 'cause I had kept holding her off. Remember, my buddies thought we were already doing it.

"She started saying I must be queer or something 'cause I rarely got a hard-on when I was with her. I really tried, mostly because I wanted to prove to myself that I could do it. It didn't work.

"I took her to senior Prom and we double-dated with Dolf and his girlfriend. We got a motel room and while he was fucking Ginnie, I was still trying to get hard. Finally, I managed to get hard enough to fuck her and the only way I could stay hard was thinking about Dolf and me doin' it."

"I hope you used a condom then, too."

"Are you kidding? I didn't want to get her pregnant. But it was the only time I ever didn't come. She didn't know though."

"I don't get how you could fake that."

"We didn't have any lights on. I managed to toss it before she saw anything."

Scott thought about Mitch and the secret abortion he told him about. "And?"

"The next day I decided I just had to tell Frank about this mess. I hoped he'd be able to help me sort all this stuff out. I didn't want to fuck her again and I didn't want Crawford to spaz out on me. I wanted to just drop the whole thing. She was only a cover for Crawford, I was just about over him anyway, but was still over my head with her.

"The whole time I was driving up to see Frank I was scared shitless. I didn't know what was worse though, still seeing Crawford or having to give in to Little Trout.

"They asked me to stay for dinner and we talked around the subject, but I felt embarrassed to talk to both of them and couldn't say anything. We went outside on their deck after dinner, and even though Carol went back in, I just couldn't tell him. So I left.

"I was so pissed at myself for not saying anything that I drove as fast as I could. It's always slick on that road when it rains. And it's pretty easy to wipe out on those hairpin curves down from their place if you're not careful. So, I wasn't careful."

Scott's mouth dropped open. "You *tried* to wipe out? I thought it was an accident!"

"It was the only solution I could think of! I could keep from fucking Little Trout and get back at Crawford at the same time. He's the one who paid for my car stuff, remember? The last thing I remembered was my head hitting the steering wheel."

Scott suddenly realized what Ryan had said. He started slowly, then finished loudly. "You tried to kill yourself. *Again*?"

Ryan was quiet for a moment before he answered. "And it didn't work that time either."

Oh my God, Scott thought. *What have I gotten myself into?* "How in the hell did you *really* get to Yucca Valley?"

"I don't know why, but earlier I told Muh I was going to see Frank and would be home by nine. She called him 'cause it was late and I hadn't come home yet. He told her he'd check the road since it had been raining pretty hard. He saw the skid marks, the torn up trees, and me in the car over the side of the road. I'd lost a lot of blood. He called the ambulance. I had to explain to Muh how I wrecked the car 'cause the police report said I was speeding. I told her Frank pissed me off. I knew that eventually she was gonna kick me out. So she did and Howie came up and later I was flying down to Yucca Valley."

Scott realized Ryan had lied to his grandmother about Frank. "Frank didn't piss you off, you just didn't tell him!"

"I know, but I was hurtin' and didn't have any other story I could tell her." He looked down at his lap. "I was in so deep I didn't know who to tell what."

Scott shook his head. "So, Howie just dropped everything to let you live with him?"

"Muh said she'd been talking to him on and off those last couple of months. He said he would take me in as long as I agreed to enroll into college. So, I agreed. I got my stitches out and was out of the sling on the same day. I went to court, packed some of my things, and was outta there. Muh said she didn't want me there any longer than I had to be."

"What happened to Little Trout?"

"I don't know."

Scott looked at him. "You don't *know*?"

"I didn't tell her I was leaving."

"Wait a minute, wait a *minute*. *Why* are we going up here? Crawford's a dick. Your grandma kicked you out. You didn't even tell Little Trout you were taking off. And, you haven't spoken to her in months now. She's sure to be at the party once she knows you're gonna be there." Scott was fuming now. "Something's *wrong* with this picture. And I think you're the *stupidfuck* in the center of it."

"I know, I *know*. But it's like I have someone to protect me for the first time."

"*Protect* you? From *what*?"

"You're so fucking sure of yourself. You know just what to say and do. All I just have are stupid feelings, fucked up thoughts, and do brainless things. I told Muh that I had a friend with me and I wasn't gonna start anything with her. She has that crusty exterior only when I'm around her."

"And you recognize that?"

"I'm *stupid*, not blind."

As the winding mountainous road led them downward toward the coast, the tall trees whizzed past, as the trek seemed to take on a new and somewhat darker tone to Scott.

Ryan let out a long sigh. Scott pulled to a stop along the shoulder so they could stretch. "Can I drive for a while?" Scott reluctantly swapped places with him and they were off again.

"So do you hate me now?" Ryan asked as he reached cruising speed.

"The closest thing is I feel is numb. I still don't get it. Why did you keep seeing Crawford if he was so weird?"

"I only told you the bad parts. He wasn't fucked up most of the time. Sometimes we would just watch TV or rent videos and watch them, too. Other times he'd help me fix up my car. Sometimes we would go up in the woods behind his house and shoot targets and stuff. I even studied for the ACT at his place and did some homework there since it was quiet. Whenever we'd have sex, I was learning something new just about every time. I'm sure I was having more than all my friends put together. He always wanted to hug and kiss me and I loved the way he smelled. And he can cook like nobody's business. I left his house most of the time with a feeling that I loved him."

That feeling of jealousy came back. "Did you?"

Ryan thought about it for a moment. "Maybe. I don't know now."

They drove in silence for a good five miles before Scott's feeling of jealousy completely subsided. Finally, he ventured something to break the too-intense silence. "Hey."

"What?"

"Feel any better?"

"No. I feel stupid."

Scott looked at him. *So do I*, he thought.

They reached the turn to Highway 101 a little after three-thirty. They had gone through beautiful scenic wooded and mountainous stretches which Scott had barely noticed since he was so absorbed in Ryan's story. Now the climate was distinctly different. They caught glimpses of the ocean as they headed northwest only a little over an hour from their destination.

Here along the coast the constant wetness, fed by cool Pacific winds, nurtured the temperate rain forest climate. The road wound back and forth through the vast forest of tall firs and deciduous trees. Patches of fog draped across stretches of the highway as they drove, forcing them to slow to a more moderate speed at times. Mostly though, the patches of fog obscured short stretches of the beach that were visible through the trees. Although it was summer and the sun was still high, the air was cool where it was foggy and it smelled of water and moss. Scott wondered what it must be like to live in a climate that was so wet and lush all the time. The closer they got, the more animated Ryan became. Finally, they saw a sign that read: Crescent City 15 miles.

Ryan accelerated. "I know this area like the back of my hand."

"You mean like your dick."

"Well, yeah…that's more accurate." He pointed over to his left as he slowed. "This is a scenic overlook." He pulled over and parked next to a fence that stretched in a curve on top of the high cliff. He breathed in the air with great ceremony. "Ah, the smell of home."

Scott noticed that Ryan was completely at ease now. He still was feeling a slight mixture of revulsion from Ryan's story and a little jealousy from Ryan's statement about perhaps loving Crawford, but now he was glad that Ryan was no longer feeling so despondent. So, with a quick glance around to make sure no cars were coming, he reached over and planted a kiss on Ryan's cheek. Ryan turned to him and softly pressed his lips against Scott's. He stepped closer and gave Scott a long satisfying French kiss. Scott's heart pounded in his chest. Every bad thought Scott had had about him for the last hour or so disappeared.

A car came up the highway. Ryan quickly pulled away. Scott looked down at the water below. He stood in awe of the expanse of the ocean from so high up on the cliff. He'd seen the ocean plenty of times, cliffs even, from Dana Point to Santa Barbara. Up here though, it was different. Huge surges of water crashed against sea stacks, some with tall evergreens growing on them in isolated clusters, way below. Wisps of fog stretched in low wide bands all along the rocky shore. Light blue sky and dark blue water stretched out in front of them while to their backs a seemingly unending stretch of green forest closed them in to the shore.

Scott looked left and right looking for sand below. "There's no beach here."

"The Dunes and the good beaches are north of the city. It's usually too cold to lay out though. But we've got whales, sea otters, and live running salmon. Stuff you guys don't have at all down south."

Scott breathed in the fresh ocean air and scanned the horizon again. It was indeed beautiful. Far off to his right, toward the north along the shore, he could just barely make out buildings against the water. He made out a distant lighthouse as the fog abruptly rolled away from it.

"That's the town," Ryan said with excitement.

They pulled back onto the highway and it finally sloped down to the shore. The town was built into the gentle rise of the hills and along the straight line of the narrow shore. Behind the town were hillsides densely covered with tall fir trees. No fog limited their visibility in this area.

Ryan pointed out the route to the jetty, the downtown business area, and the road that led to his cousin Adina's house. They only passed a couple of pickup trucks as they rode through town. Other than that the town seemed deserted.

"Is it usually dead like this?"

"Dude, it's Sunday. There's mostly fishing, logging, some tourists and other little businesses here, and on the weekends usually only the malls are crowded."

"Where's your house?"

"We have to go northeast another four miles. It's just off Del Norte Pass Road." He turned off the highway after they passed through town and headed up a well-paved two-lane road that wound through a tree-lined canyon. The forest surrounded them so densely that the only light came from directly above them where no trees obstructed the sky. Scott had his face up to the windshield so he could look up at it.

"Wait till we get to my place. You won't believe how tall the trees are there."

They passed a sign that said *Jedediah Smith Redwoods State Park*. Scott tried to look down the road, but the foliage was so dense he couldn't see past the first curve. Just a little further on Ryan slowed where two mailboxes stood side by side. A fenced-in area cordoned off a wood-shingled single-story building just off the road.

"That's the ranger station. Hmm, they fixed the hole in the fence."

"I take it you made the hole?"

"Me and Chris did it to razz the ranger. He couldn't say we did it. But I know he knows." He turned down a dirt road just past the station.

"Here we are," he announced.

Two long rows of tall old oaks stood on the shoulders of the drive and shaded the boys from the late afternoon sunlight. The narrow lane turned to the right and the woods seemed to just open up. A wide meadow, devoid of almost any trees except for obviously planted deciduous ones, greeted their eyes. The meadow defined the extent of the trapezoid-shaped property. The drive ran right up to a tall, two-story frame house. Many other structures were all along the property. Off to the left and further back was a whitewashed building that looked like a tall garage, with a triple-peaked roof. There was also an old building that looked like it hadn't been painted in decades. Its gray weathered boards beneath greatly peeling paint looked quite rustic. Various other single room buildings, all with chimneys poking up from the middle of the roof were off to the left. All looked old and abandoned.

Behind the house, down a short gentle slope, was an animal pen with several small sheds next to it. The pen was fenced around five closely spaced crabapple trees. Their roots were all exposed from three black and white goats pacing in the confined area. Hearing their arrival, the goats perked up their heads at the perimeter of the fence with curious looks on their faces. A small smokehouse stood at the edge of a mowed stretch of grass. Its cockeyed metal chimney was blackened from years of smoke. Scott wondered what it smelled like inside.

They parked next to a faded blue step-side pickup truck and a dull green station wagon. "Muh and Chris are both here. That's his truck," Ryan said as he came to a stop and handed Scott the keys.

They jumped out and stretched. The smell of organic matter was everywhere. Rotting wood, the heavy scent of the evergreen forest that enveloped them, a waft of goat manure, and faint wood smoke. Scott stopped long enough to listen to the new sounds. Wind. It was everywhere, except in his ears. It gently swayed the trees as insects buzzed by.

Birds called out from hidden places and everywhere crickets chirruped even though it was still afternoon. They had landed in the middle of a forest and were being serenaded by a soothing concert of sounds.

"Hey. You in Ozoneland. Let's go." Ryan trotted briskly up the front steps. The door opened before he could get to the knob.

Muh was dressed in a simple pink and white flowered print dress. Her face was etched with deep lines but her skin looked fresh and radiant. Her salt and pepper hair was long and drawn straight back in a tight ponytail. Her gray eyes were bright and alert and spoke of someone who was happy and well. Her smile was as radiant as the rest of her face.

Behind her was Chris. Scott could tell he was Ryan's brother the moment he saw him. He had Ryan's dark hair and looked vaguely like him, but his hair was longer, not styled like Ryan's. He was also shorter and thinner than Ryan.

"My boy is here!" She said in a strong and steady voice. Scott wondered what Ryan meant about her being a bitch. She seemed nice enough. In fact, she was greeting him with open arms. Ryan hugged her long and hard, then pulled away. Scott had thought Ryan didn't like her. Clearly, that wasn't the case.

"Muh, this is my friend Scott."

She kissed the side of his face and stated emphatically, "Come in, come in."

"I'm Chris," Chris said as he stepped in. Scott offered his hand. Chris shook it weakly.

Now Scott could see him a little better. His eyes were droopy and he seemed to have a far away look in them. He looked like he should not only comb his hair, but wash it, too. Ryan said hello to his brother before they proceeded down the hall to a huge den. Ryan didn't seem to be all that friendly to Chris and Scott wondered what that might have been all about.

Scott noticed how dark and masculine everything in the house looked. He had expected a much more feminine look to things. The floor was covered with wall-to-wall carpeting. It was so thick it was springy. Every sound seemed muffled by it. The furniture in the huge room was all dark wood and leather. Thick heavy draperies covered the windows. The dark mantel over the fireplace was a rough-hewn railroad tie set into large stones that made up the chimney. The room was big, but still dark because of the wood. The smell of home cooking filled his nose. Despite that, musty smells greeted him as well.

"Wow. This place is cool."

Muh spoke up. "Well, it's your house, too, as long as you're staying." She looked at Ryan. "Which is how long?"

"'Til next Sunday," he answered, not looking at her.

It was a simple response, which spoke volumes. Scott could see it. While she was trying to be warm, Ryan didn't really try to connect with her.

They were just in time for dinner. As Muh set the table, Scott called home to let his parents know they had arrived. Before he could get a tour of the house, they were ushered to the huge oak table in a separate dining room to eat dinner. The main course was a stew that smelled so good Scott thought he should ask for the recipe. It could possibly make an interesting addition to the restaurant's lunch specials.

At dinner Scott told Muh about the restaurant, the band, and what it was like back at home in Yucca Valley. He emphasized the difference between the desert and his initial impression of the coastal climate.

"Is it true about what they're gonna do to your property?"

"Unfortunately, yes." Muh explained how the government bought up several surrounding tracts to create the state park. With the redwoods butting right up against their property and their area already cleared, the government bought their homestead, too. They were on a lease until the last of the Covington's died. That meant her. She wasn't too happy explaining it. "They'll probably end up razing the house and put a concession stand on the foundation," she said.

"Why would they raise the house?" Chris asked, not knowing what she meant.

"The other raze, stupid," Ryan answered.

Muh cut him off in a stern voice, one Scott didn't know she had. "Ryan, try to be nice."

Ryan wouldn't look at her. Scott's eyes darted to him, then to Muh. She gave Ryan a continued 'I don't believe your behavior' look, then resumed eating. Scott broke the brief silence.

"Well, you'll have to show me that root cellar and the rest of the house after dinner."

"After dessert, you mean," Chris said.

Scott eyes widened. "Mmm, dessert."

Muh was ready to respond. "Dutch apple cobbler."

Ryan nodded. "And the apples are from the orchard-tree."

"Orchard-tree?" Scott asked.

"The big apple tree out back that's grafted with five different varieties," he answered proudly.

"Five?"

"Five."

"On one tree?"

"Orchard-tree," Chris replied.

"Oh," was all Scott could respond. After the dinner dishes were cleared, and despite being full, Scott had a second helping of the cobbler. It was dark outside when they were done.

He was led on the house tour next. They went to the second floor up a creaky oak staircase. The three rooms upstairs were fully furnished, although no one occupied them. Muh said it was silly to sell anything since the boys would get it all later and they could decide what to do with it. Muh led them back downstairs to a thick wooden door that creaked loudly when she opened it. A steep stone passage led into darkness. It looked dank and scary. Chris had his back to the wall and reached over his head. Without looking, he flipped on the switch and the cellar flooded with light. They scuffled down to the bare cement floor and briefly looked around. Trunks of belongings were along one wall. A passage built into another wall led up a short flight of stone stairs but was closed off by slanted doors. Rows and rows of wooden shelves held harvests of fruits and vegetables in clear glass jars. They could eat like fiends if they couldn't get to the grocery store, Scott thought. The quick look at the cellar was over and they went back up. Muh led them to the rear of the house. There was an abrupt transition as they went down a single stair. She explained that the house had been added on to several times in the last eighty-five years and that the back end of the house was the second to last addition.

Ryan and Chris's bedrooms, a big full bathroom, and several huge storage closets were in the back area. Muh didn't give him a tour of them, but rather just indicated that this was the back of the house. She explained that many years ago eight people were living in the house at one time. In addition, she told him, they had once rented out the small, now-dilapidated cottages to families many decades back. Scott thought it was neat that their bedrooms were essentially detached from the rest of the house, much like his bedroom at home.

"So, where would you like to sleep tonight?" Muh asked Scott.

Ryan headed him off. "Uh, he can sleep in my bedroom. We've got sleeping bags. I can make room on the floor for him."

"Ryan, we have plenty of bedrooms."

"Ms. Covington…" Scott began.

"Muh. Call me Muh, like the boys do."

"Muh. It's okay. Really. I can sleep on the floor back here. I really don't mind."

She hesitated for a moment, as if she'd been put out. "If you insist. But you'll change your mind, I'm sure. Now why don't you boys get your stuff out of the car and settle down? I'll be here all day tomorrow and can make breakfast for you whenever you get up." She turned and went back to the main part of the house.

Ryan nodded his head. "Let's get the stuff." He walked down the short hall and out a door on the side of the house. "We go this way most of the time. That way we don't have to go through the whole house to get to our bedrooms."

They exited into the cool early evening air. A single streetlight lit up the drive in front from a single telephone pole that also fed utility wires to the eaves of the house.

"This place is great. You even have your own entrance. I can't believe you got kicked out of here," Scott said.

"If you had to live with my grandma for as long as I did you'd hate it here, too."

"She's totally okay. How could you say that?"

"You haven't heard her jabber away yet."

Scott pulled the Jeep closer to the side entrance and they hauled their things inside.

Ryan's room was larger than his entire guesthouse back home. The tall double window on one wall would have given a great view of the expanse of the back yard had it not been too dark to see outside now. And not a light shone through it since the dark, forest-covered side of a mountain covered up the sky from that vantage point.

Thick curtains hung from halfway up the windows to the floor. On the pattern were ducks in flight and ducks in the water along with hunters aiming from various angles. There was a thick rug on the floor that almost touched three of the walls. A queen-sized bed was against an exposed brick wall. The bricks looked ancient and the bed was higher than his back home. Scott sat and it squeaked a little as he bounced.

"This thing's noisy," he said as he bounced again. "How are we gonna keep from being heard?"

"What makes you think I'm doing anything with you here anyway?"

"We're not going by Howie's house rules again, are we?"

"You can't touch me while we're here. That's the only rule." But he was unable to hide his grin. Scott tried to tickle him which Ryan fended off. Scott took him by the middle and pulled him back on the bed. It squeaked again a few times, then quieted as they stopped bouncing. He knelt over him as Ryan lay on his back, his feet still touching the floor. The soft curve of his penis was visible through the fabric of his jeans as he lay there.

Scott put a hand against his crotch and rubbed. "You mean I can't touch you like this?"

He heard a footstep, a scuffling at the door, and almost immediately it opened. Chris walked in just as Scott pulled his hand away and quickly whirled around. Ryan sat up like nothing happened.

"Hey, you guys wanna get high?" He had a loaded up bong in one hand and a lighter in the other.

Scott looked at him, then at Ryan.

Ryan saw the expression on Scott's face. "Not in my room. Let's go in yours."

"I don't get high," Scott told him.

"You don't have to."

They walked down the hall and into Chris's room. The first thing Scott noticed were two three-foot tall marijuana plants, with thick healthy-looking stalks, growing from white pickle tubs. They lay on a wide windowsill. Scott's mouth dropped open. He recognized the plants right away and approached them. "Holy shit. How did you get these in here?"

Chris shrugged his shoulders. "I grew 'em in here."

"Your grandma doesn't care?"

"She said as long as I don't sell it that she doesn't mind."

Scott looked at them both. "You gotta be kidding."

Ryan had already taken a hit from the bong and was holding his breath. Chris looked at him. Ryan shook his head no. He let out the smoke and took a deep breath of fresh air. "Honest. She doesn't give a shit."

"And you were telling me about rules?" Scott asked as he inspected one of the jagged leaves. He realized he shouldn't have said anything about rules in front of Chris. Chris looked at Ryan again and was about to ask him something.

Ryan spoke instead. "It had nothing to do with pot. She's never smoked it, but doesn't see why it's such a big deal. Besides, Chris is the dope fiend. I don't get high that much."

Chris punched him. "I get high only when you're around or when my girlfriend's here."

Ryan coughed several times. "Girlfriend? When did you get a girl-friend?"

"About a week after you were...uh, after Uncle Howard came up."

"Who is she?" Ryan passed the bong and Chris took a hit.

"Teresa Soto," he squeaked out.

"Slutty Teresa, huh?"

"She's better than Little Trout," he said indignantly, as he let out the smoke and took a breath of air. He reluctantly handed the bong back to Ryan.

So, Chris knows Little Trout, Scott thought. He immediately wanted to ask him about her. Instead he simply observed both of them interact-ing as they sat next to each other on the edge of Chris's bed. They looked like different versions of each other.

"So you fucked the slut, huh?" Ryan asked as he exhaled.

"She's not a *slut*." Chris went to his dresser and opened up a small wooden box. He took out a wrapped condom and tossed it at him. It smacked against Ryan's chest and landed on his lap. "I use those, too."

"Well, fuck me. My brother's no longer a virgin."

Chris looked embarrassed for a moment as he looked at Scott. "Not anymore," he responded. Ryan took another hit and they talked for a few minutes before they left his room. Chris turned up the volume on his stereo and shut the door behind them. The walls were so thick that by the time they were down the hall past the bathroom they could no longer hear it.

Ryan shut his door. "I'm buzzed. It's been a long time. Too long."

"I didn't know you got high."

"I only smoke the stuff he grows. And it's pretty good, too."

Ryan's hair reeked but Scott kissed him anyway. The smell was also on his breath as Ryan kissed back in an intense but disconnected way.

A skeleton key lay at the edge of a shelf and Ryan inserted it into the lock of his bedroom door. It clicked almost noiselessly as he turned it and left the key in. He flipped off the overhead light, then pulled the string in the closet to turn the light on. He closed the door until only a crack of light shined across the bed. He took Scott's hand and pulled off his shoes with his feet as he motioned for Scott to do the same. Scott did so, pulled his shirt off and unbuttoned Ryan's, too. He took Ryan in his arms and held his bare chest against his while licking his fuzzy earlobes.

Still pressed together, Ryan edged him toward the bed. They fell onto the thick soft covers side by side and kissed. The bed squeaked as they settled onto it. Scott had never been with anyone who was high before, at least not in a sexual way. He was intrigued at how intensely passionate Ryan seemed now. The smile on his face was a funny contrast to the dreamy look in his eyes.

Scott shed his pants and underwear while Ryan lay on his back and watched as they dropped out of sight to the dark floor. Scott straddled Ryan's left leg and unbuttoned his jeans while he grew harder by the second. Scott got off his leg, pulled the jeans down to his feet, and Ryan kicked them off. Finally, he had Ryan down to his underwear and it, too, landed onto the loose pile of clothes as he flung them aside.

The wonderful warmth of Ryan's body against his was different tonight. Although there was a definite sexual overtone to his actions, Scott felt different. He wanted to revel in the sensuous feel of Ryan's body against his as long as he could. Ryan kept his hand away from

Scott's penis most of the time, only lingering there briefly to make sure he was still good and firm.

They rose up on their knees and balanced themselves against each other as they hugged and rubbed their groins together. Ryan, as usual, leaked all over them. Scott went down periodically to lick the goo from Ryan's penis onto the tip of his tongue, and kissed him, passing the sweet pre-come taste between them.

Ryan pulled himself underneath the top blanket and Scott with him. He put one leg over Ryan's and they rolled around until the heat was roasting. The sweat they generated brought out their musky smell, which overpowered the lingering smell of pot smoke.

Oddly enough, fatigue slowly overwhelmed them both. As much as he wanted it to last all night, Scott eventually found himself falling asleep with his erection still throbbing away.

He woke up sometime in the middle of the night. He had to pee and pulled himself away from Ryan. When the door wouldn't open, he remembered Ryan had locked it. He turned the key, but couldn't get the door unlocked. There must have been a secret to it, Scott decided as he turned the key back and pulled it out. It slipped from his fingers, rang once as it bounced off the wood floor, and landed on the carpet.

Ryan stirred. "Hey," Scott whispered as he retrieved it. "How do you unlock this door?"

"Like you would any door," Ryan answered as he got up.

Scott looked at Ryan's naked body in the harsh light from the closet. He continued to whisper. "You know the difference between light and hard?"

"No," Ryan croaked.

"You can sleep with a light on."

"How did *you* get to sleep?"

Scott rested one of his palms on Ryan's chest, ran it over his nipples, then down to his stomach. His dick sprang to attention. "I better stop. I won't be able to pee."

Ryan took the key from him and unlocked the door. He then turned back around and flopped into the bed again face first. The springs squeaked twice as he did so. Scott hesitated at the door as he saw Ryan's round butt and the muscles of his back on top of the sheet. The dark crevice of the hair that ran between his ass cheeks invited him to stay, but his bladder said 'go now'.

When he came back, Ryan hadn't moved. He locked the door and put the key on a little shelf next to the doorframe. He then went to the bed. Putting a knee on it he slowly lowered his body against Ryan's. He lay on Ryan's back, grinding his penis between his butt cheeks.

Ryan gyrated his hips to meet Scott's motion. "I had a dream."

Scott ran his hands up and down Ryan's arms and then slid them under Ryan's pillow. "Yeah?"

"I dreamed you got up and tried to unlock the door."

"It wasn't a dream."

Ryan tried to move and Scott rose just enough to let him turn over. The shaft of light from the closet door still angled across the bed and illuminated his body. Ryan's erection came into view as he turned over. Scott lowered himself again. They hugged, kissed, and continued as if they hadn't stopped earlier. This time though the intent was decidedly different. Ryan pulled Scott up onto his knees in front of him. With one knee against his balls, and the other knee to the left of his hip, he took Scott's penis and pumped it slowly while fondling his balls with the other. Scott alternately leaned forward on his hands, then back on his knees as Ryan continued his pumping. It didn't take long before it was all over Ryan's forearm and chest. He didn't worry about the loud sound of his breathing as he sucked in air and moaned softly. As usual, his erection stayed at full mast while he worked on Ryan's. Ryan pulled Scott's hand away by the wrist. He pushed Scott's palm onto each drop. Scott figured out what he was doing and smeared as much as he could onto his hand. He spit into his palm and grasped Ryan's penis to slick it up. In only a few more seconds, Ryan's stomach tensed. As Scott pumped faster, Ryan grimaced and he moaned softly as his senses went on overload. Thin ropes of translucent semen landed all over his chest. The sound of his irregular breathing filled the quiet of the room. Finally, spent, he was able to breath normally again.

Scott wiped his palm off with a tissue. Ryan pulled Scott down on top of him again and they wiggled in the wetness as they hugged and kissed. Scott loved that Ryan didn't like to wipe it up despite the taut feeling it gave his skin after it dried. They slept until morning light illuminated the top of the tree-covered hill behind the house.

Scott moved the covers aside and looked at Ryan sleeping next to him on his stomach. The hairs of his thighs and hard butt were so sensual in the early morning light. He wanted to put his head down there and lick the back of his thighs but Ryan woke up and turned over. Ryan saw Scott looking at him. "Are you still my boyfriend?"

"What would make me change my mind?"

"You don't care that I made you do it in the middle of the night?"

"Let me think about it for a while." Scott counted off 'one thousand one' aloud, then added flatly. "No."

Ryan closed his eyes and tried to stifle the smile that crossed his face.

Scott leaned over to kiss him but realized his morning breath would probably kill him. "I'm gonna take a shower. Wanna take one with me?"

"No, Chris might see us."

"Why would he care?"

"Come on. He's my brother." He picked up Scott's pillow and bopped him in the side with it.

Scott put on fresh underwear and headed for the bathroom just in time to see Chris come out. He, too, had on only underwear. Chris grunted a sleepy acknowledgment and went back to his bedroom. Scott lingered at the door of the bathroom to see as much of him as he could. Chris and Ryan had the same shaped butt. *Except for Chris's slightly dopey look, he might pass as marginally cute,* he thought as he stepped into the shower.

Ryan had fallen back asleep when he returned. Scott opted for jeans, a t-shirt and a polo shirt, dressing quietly. He left the room and retraced his way through the hall into the den. Muh was up and the smell of coffee filled the front of the house.

"Scott, how did you sleep? Where's Ryan? Was it too cold for you?" Her rapid-fire questions were too quick for only seven o'clock.

"Whoa. I slept well. He's still asleep. And no," he said in succession, thinking the order of her questions was funny.

"I hope you didn't mind sleeping on the floor. You really can have one of the bedrooms upstairs."

Scott thought about that for a second. He'd better make it look good by spreading out the blankets before she went back there to see they had slept together. "Really. It was okay. I was quite comfortable and toasty warm," he said, recalling last night's experiences.

"That's good. Those boys tell me it gets a little cold back there sometimes. I'm afraid that part of the house doesn't heat as well as the front."

"It was fine."

"Coffee?"

"Sure."

"Here. Let me pour you some. Cream? Sugar?"

Her doting was a little extreme, he thought. Maybe this is what Ryan was talking about. She literally poured the cream for him and would barely let him stir it.

He took the mug and sipped it while he looked out the window over the sink.

"Has Ryan told you about why he's down with his uncle?"

Scott didn't know what to answer. Should he say he knew, or what? "He said he's going to UCLA sometime next year, if he's accepted."

"That boy. I never understood him."

He didn't want to get in-between Ryan and his grandmother, but it looked like she was already going to tell him the story.

"He's coming right along, Muh," he said, hoping she would know what to say.

She studied his face. He was aware he meant something he hadn't said. "I hope so. He needs nice friends. His friends here were so…well…unruly. You seem different than them. You must have a nice girlfriend, too."

"No, I don't."

"Well, that's too bad. A good-looking boy like you should have a nice girlfriend."

Scott was beginning to see what she was doing. She talked and pried, trying to get him to talk to her about everything. All and all, though, she seemed benign.

Luckily, Ryan appeared and her questions stopped. He looked like he was still half-asleep and his hair was a mess.

"Ryan, did you brush your teeth?"

He was wearing nothing but sky blue corduroy shorts with nothing underneath, Scott observed, as Ryan leaned against one of the kitchen counters. His hair was all which way and he looked half dead, yet as soon as he scratched his shoulder, flexing his bicep to do so, Scott decided he could be covered in mud and still look cute.

"No. Coffee will kill the germs," Ryan told her.

Despite her exasperated look she poured him some coffee, too. He drank it black as usual.

"Hey, you have to show me around here before we boogie into town," Scott said to him.

Ryan looked out the window. "There's nothing out here except woods."

"I live in a desert, remember?"

"Oh, yeah. We'll do the tour of the property and the park, then head to the shore."

Muh washed a couple of glasses, then turned to the boys. "I'll go make up your beds, then make you some breakfast."

Alarm went through Scott as he realized she hadn't asked, but rather told them she was going to do it. She wiped her hands and was gone seconds later. Ryan looked unconcerned as she left.

Scott bolted across the kitchen, and then stopped when Ryan didn't move. "Fuck," he whispered frantically. "She's gonna know we slept together!"

"I took care of that."

"How?"

"I unfolded all those blankets and tossed a pillow on the floor."

Scott's eyes grew wide with surprise. "Good thinking."

"You forget. I know that woman."

"Why does she bother?"

He shrugged his shoulders. "That's just the way she is." He sipped his coffee some more. Scott drank his while he looked out the window again at the quiet hillside. They heard Muh return a few minutes later.

"I hope it wasn't too cool back there for you, Scott," she repeated.

"No, Muh, last night I was plenty hot." He looked at Ryan briefly and cracked a smile. Ryan only gave him a quick glance.

She cooked more food than they could possibly have eaten at one sitting. Ryan had commented in Parker about Scott's aunt's home cooking. Scott was wondering what he had meant. There was clearly a lot of home cooking going on in this house. His own mother rarely cooked, since they so often ate at the restaurant or brought food back to the house. Here Muh was making a full-course breakfast. Maybe it wasn't about the food after all, but rather the intact family atmosphere that he was in at the time.

"So, will you boys be gone most of the day?" Muh asked as Chris came into the kitchen.

"Yeah. We might be back for lunch though," Ryan answered.

Chris acted as if no one else was there as he quietly picked a waffle up from the pile and covered it in syrup.

"Chris, is Teresa coming over today?"

"Humph," he said as he chewed.

"In English."

"I said maybe."

Scott wondered if their interactions were always this disconnected. But, Muh *was* being a busybody.

"Come on, Scott. I'm gonna get dressed so we can boogie," Ryan said as he pushed his plate away.

Besides making the bed, and picking up the blankets, all their clothes had been picked up too. Now they lay neatly folded on the foot of the bed or hung up over the back of the chair. Scott wondered what it would take to have a maid like her.

"I guess your granddad lived pretty decently with her taking care of everything."

"I don't remember him all that well since he died when I was like five or something. She probably killed him, though, from all the waiting on him."

Ryan stepped out of his shorts and draped a towel around his waist. Scott watched as he left for the bathroom. He spied a photo album wedged between some schoolbooks in a bookcase. Leafing through the pages, he saw pictures of Chris and Ryan when they were much younger. Some of the older photos showed who he guessed were their mom and dad. The zoo pictures showed the four of them when Chris was in a stroller. Those pictures must be old, Scott guessed. The very last page had some new 5x7s of Ryan. He was dressed in what passed as a hockey uniform and was in a parking lot on in-line skates. Scott was instantly taken by the smile on his face. It was so radiant and sexy and even the loose fitting shirt couldn't hide the fact that he had a body that made him hard just looking at it.

Ryan quietly entered the room and saw him looking through the album. "This one where you're wearing that hockey outfit is *so* cute," Scott said pointing.

Ryan's hair was still wet and the towel still wrapped around his waist couldn't hide the slight bulge in front as he stepped over to look. Scott flipped the page, then turned it back.

"That was taken last year. You can have it if you want."

"Serious?"

"Yeah."

"You look really happy then."

"Like, I'm not now?"

Scott didn't really know how to explain it. "Well, it's just that when I met you, you didn't seem as happy as in this picture." He peeled back the plastic, carefully pulled up the photo, and placed it on his bag.

Ryan took off the towel and dried his armpits and hair again. Scott watched his every move. He dressed and they went outside.

The morning was a bit humid, but still cool even though it was the end of July. Ryan explained it would warm up quite quickly in the glade as soon as the sun crested the mountains and cleared the tall trees.

Scott followed as Ryan took him down to the edge of the property by the goat pen. Chickens strutted around the enclosure and followed around behind the goats. It wasn't very interesting to him. What was more interesting was the extremely tall apple tree that stood in the middle of the back yard. It was heavy with different hued apples. It seemed amazing that one tree had so many branches as well as varieties all over it. Ryan saw the interested look on his face and led him to it.

"So this is the orchard-tree?"

"That's it. Muh'll can 'em and we'll get, maybe, ten bushels this year for sure."

"That's a lot of apples," he said, then laughed when he realized what he had said.

"Muh gives most of them away. Hey, wanna see my car?" Ryan asked.

"I thought you said it was totaled."

"No. The Packard. In the barn."

They trampled through the dew-covered grass as grasshoppers bounded out of the way. Insects were everywhere. As much as Scott liked the desert, it was refreshing to be here.

He remembered how freaked he felt when Ryan told him about his suicide attempt. It was in the same building they were now approaching. The thought of it was spooky as hell. Movies were nothing like when it was right in your face, he realized. Ryan walked backwards for a couple of steps. "This is the way to the park anyway," he added, then turned back around and continued walking.

Rows of small windows on two wide sliding doors were obscured by a thick accumulation of dust. It was impossible to see through them. Ryan knew where the key was to an old brass lock that held the doors secure, and in a moment, had the hasp flipped back and one of the doors rolled back. Inside the dark expanse he hit a switch and light hit the back corners, and right above them.

Old metal farming implements lay in piles and hung from the walls. Buckets of paint, painting tools, lumber and other unidentifiable items lay in various piles, some covered with cobwebs. Several bales of hay were randomly scattered within. One bale's twine had failed and cakes of straw were tumbled about like a row of fallen dominoes.

The item under a big brown dusty tarp had the obvious shape of a car. It was all the way to the back, propped up on cinderblocks. Only the bottom portion of the white-walled tires was exposed.

Ryan lifted up the tarp to expose a silvery, almost iridescent finish. "A real 1929 Packard Super 8. Only sixteen thousand miles on it. Can you believe the paint still looks new? Check out the signature grille!" He pulled the tarp completely off and cast it aside. Dust rose all around them.

Scott ran his hand across the driver's door admiring its beauty, but not being into cars like Ryan, didn't fully appreciate its age. "And this is yours?"

Ryan raised the hood. "Absolutely. It runs, but it's not in the best condition. The engine really needs to be cleaned since it's been sitting
around for so long. I'd fix it up, but I don't have my license back yet, I
don't live here anymore, and I don't have the money for the insurance.
This is the best vehicle though. And worth a mint." Hardly knowing
about engines Scott didn't understand what was being pointed out, but
he could tell Ryan was quite proud of it. "I need to replace some of the
engine components, but won't be able to afford genuine parts until after
I get out of college."

He opened the driver's side door and invited Scott to sit. The smell of
musty old leather filled the interior. Despite the dashboard's apparent
old design, it looked fairly sophisticated. Scott wondered what it would
be like to drive it. After they inspected the gauges and dials, they got out
and put the tarp back on.

He motioned with his head. "My door's over here."

"Door?"

It was leaning against the back wall and he pulled it forward so Scott
could get a good look at it. "It was gonna be my bedroom door, but I
ended up in Yucca Valley instead." It was an ordinary pine door, painted
white, except that it had dozens and dozens of designs drawn on it in
various stages of completion. The intricately colored geometric shapes,
caricatures, and slogans in highly stylized letters, ran into one another
in a mosaic of tiny graffiti-like designs. No scene was more than six or
seven inches square.

Scott tilted his head back and forth to get a better view of some of
them. "Whoa. I bet you were high when you thought up some of this
stuff."

"How would you know?"

"Come on. How could anyone think up a lion's head designed
around the shape of this fist, unless they were high? And this upside
down staircase drawn in the belly of a laughing rhino? I know you were
high."

Ryan tilted his head and looked at it again. "Busted," he said with a smile. He leaned the door back against the wall and they walked back to the entrance of the barn. He slid the door closed, replaced the lock, and they headed out toward the park.

At the end of the property, they climbed over a weathered wooden fence that zigzagged its way in front of them. Morning sunlight came through the open area and shone on a narrow, single-lane paved road. It also revealed their wet pants legs and tennis shoes from the dew of the tall grass.

"This is the park. We have to walk along here a bit, then we get to all the picnic tables and stuff."

Scott marveled at the huge trees that lined the road through the thick foliage. Ryan walked up to a huge redwood stump. It had steps chopped into its base. On each step grew a tangle of ferns in various stages of unfurl.

"They logged this area a long time ago, but someone was smart and didn't let 'em take everything," Ryan explained.

They rounded a sharp curve in the road and the asphalt came to an end. The view changed dramatically. Now they were standing at the edge of a giant open grove of redwoods, their dark red bark was streaked with moisture. And it was quiet here. No birds, no insects. Everywhere he looked Scott saw trees that had trunks a minimum of ten feet in diameter. A thick carpet of redwood needles covered the ground and at least one picnic table sat next to each huge trunk.

Scott surveyed the sky above him. "Wow! I've never seen anything like this."

"And camouflaged by the rainforest." Ryan was right. Unless one knew to come back this way, the redwoods would be hidden by the profusion of growth between them and the road.

Ryan led him through the picnic area. No one was around this early. Above them, the towering limbs completely obscured the sky. It was as if they were in a gigantic natural room. The trees were pillars and their high limbs supported a green canopy draped overhead. The thick smell of wood and pure pine-scented air was everywhere.

Here the only sound was the occasional drop of water from somewhere high overhead as it pelted the mat of organic matter below. Scott stopped to touch the craggy bark of one of the nearest trees. *This one's roots look like flying buttresses sticking out along its circumference,* he thought. He faced outward and leaned back, nestled inside the indentation made by one of the U-shaped curves just to get a perspective of its dimensions.

Ryan stood, arms akimbo. "What are you doing?"

"I don't know…Waiting for it to swallow me, I guess.

"This isn't *Poltergeist*. Come on. The river's down this way."

Scott stepped away and looked up at the canopy above them. "Wow," he said under his breath, before he turned to follow.

CHAPTER 21

They took a diagonal course through the soft spongy matter that was underfoot. Eventually they got closer to the river and here and there an anomalous rock stuck up through the undergrowth. The rocks in Yucca Valley grew multicolored lichens, but the ones here were only green, Scott noted. And instead of covering just the rocks, they covered the wet bark of the redwoods along with the moss. Ryan was making a beeline toward the dense undergrowth closer to the river, and was now well ahead of Scott. Scott had slowed to gawk at everything, but finally caught up. They finally reached a well-worn path that paralleled the wide expanse of the Smith River. Its swift running surface reflected the sky that opened up before them. A torrent of water from a spring gushed out from the undergrowth below them. It cut across the tilted gray shale of the bank and emptied into the wide river. Briefly surveying the steep wet decline before them, they slid down flatfooted. Pieces of small broken shale shards trailed behind them and spilled down to smooth rounded gray ones at the water's edge. The rocks along the bank clacked loudly as they trod across them. Stopping now, Scott surveyed the embankment. He spoke the obvious. "It's too steep to go back up."

Ryan pointed downstream. "There's a path around the curve and it'll lead us back. It's not as steep." He motioned Scott to follow and they walked along the alternately wet and dry rocks to the water.

A lone fisherman in waders, his fishing pole flicking back and forth at the opposite bank, looked tiny compared to the wide river. The air was warmer here, and a light but steady breeze drifted from upriver at the water's edge. As he knelt to touch the water, Scott saw a light fog rise silently from the forest as it gathered and headed downstream. "This is cold," he said as he wiped his hand on his pant leg.

"Wait till you see the beach this spills out into. It's even colder there."

Scott grinned. "And I bet it's salty, too."

The bank narrowed and turned with the curve of the river, then tapered up to a trailhead. They used a sapling that dipped down to pull themselves up onto the solid bank. After doubling back to the park, they found the asphalt road again.

"Let's head to town. I'll show you the beach."

He led them across the picnic area again and back toward the narrow lane near their property line. The huge redwoods towered above them once again. They seemed so ridiculously tall Scott couldn't help it as he burst out with laughter.

"What are you laughing at?"

Scott continued laughing as he leaned against one and stretched his arms around what he could of its diameter.

Ryan stood watching, his hands in his windbreaker pockets. "What the fuck are you doing?"

"Listening."

Ryan figured it was another of Scott's entertaining character shifts. He took a few steps closer. "And are we having an amusing conversation?"

"These trees talk."

Ryan continued to mock him. "And are they saying all sorts of interesting things?"

"I'm serious. I can't believe you never heard 'em before."

"Yeah. And they eat seventeen-year-old boys."

Scott grinned and let go of the tree. "I'm only letting *you* eat me."

When they reached the fence, they saw Muh at a small table by the smokehouse. "Look, Muh's smoking something," Ryan told him. They climbed over and started in her direction.

"What, pot?"

"Hell, no. Something in the smokehouse."

The sun had finally topped the far mountain. It was fully in their eyes as they approached. Scott watched Ryan's cute round butt, wanting to put his hands in his back pockets and snuggle with him right there.

Next to the smokehouse, a mass of blackberry vines grew in a tangle over wire mesh held up by rusted metal poles. An old, gray wood-handled shovel sat next to the door. Next to it a pile of wood, kindling, and redwood bark were haphazardly piled in bins under one of the eaves. Ryan plucked some ripe berries off the vine and offered some to Scott as they watched Muh.

She filleted thick orange slabs of salmon and put them through hooks. She worked silently on the old dilapidated table as they watched and munched the berries. A good kick on one of the table legs and Scott was sure it would fall right over.

"I'm making these for your trip back," she said.

"Good ole Muh," Ryan responded.

The smile that Muh gave him was so endearing that Scott wondered why there was antagonism between them.

Once all the fillets had been hooked she shook spices from three different bottles onto them then rubbed them in. Ryan helped collect the hooked pieces of meat and they carefully hung them up on horizontal wires that stretched across the top of the shed. Scott watched as they placed row after row of strips across them. She dug into a pocket on the front of her apron and gave Ryan a lighter. He flicked it a couple of times before it lit, then placed a few pieces of bark in a metal case that was full of holes inside the dark confines of the little smokehouse. He lit it and shut the lid before closing and latching the creaky old door.

"Should be perfect in a couple of days. And with just the perfect smoke flavor, too."

As the smoke came up the chimney and blew downwind, past bounties filled his nose. "I've never had salmon right out of the smokehouse," Scott told them.

She wiped her hands on a rag. "This is the *real* thing. I caught 'em myself right out of the river," she told him, as she collected the spice bottles. Scott wondered if the fisherman back at the river was having any luck yet.

Ryan jerked his head toward Scott. "We're goin' into town, Muh."

"I'll be here all day if you come back for lunch," she told him.

Scott shuffled his feet as she spoke. As convenient as it was for her to cook for them, he was sure if he had to endure her doting all the time, he'd eventually go crazy.

Ryan started for the Jeep. "Come on."

Scott went inside to get the hockey photo. Once at the Jeep, he put it in the glove box. A shiver went up his back as he started the engine. "This is the best place," he said as he drove down the long drive to the main road.

"It's too far from town."

Scott looked at his odometer. "It's only a little more than three miles away."

"It might as well be a thousand."

"What does that mean?"

"It's just that the house is so far from anyone else. Our closest neighbor is a quarter mile away."

"I thought you didn't like the 'big city'."

"L.A. big city. I wouldn't have minded living in town."

They wound down the two-lane road that cut through dense fir-covered hills. As they reached the flatter terrain, the trees thinned out to reveal the expanse of the city once more. Ryan directed him as they drove to an almost empty parking lot near a slip. The parking stripes had been recently repainted and some of the spaces were still cordoned off.

A few small shops ran along one side of the lot. Two different-sized tugboats, their hulls rusted and full of holes, were on trailers near a pier. Another boat at the edge of the lot where it met the rocky beach looked like it had been washed up like so much flotsam. Its hull was as badly rusted as the tugs'.

Several of the shops' windows were made of what looked like authentic portholes, round and framed with well-shined brass. Scott saw something lying in the sparse weeds at one edge of the lot. "What's that?"

Ryan shaded his eyes. "A whale bone."

"That big?"

"You've never seen a whale bone?"

"Yeah, they're all over the place in Yucca Valley."

They walked across the lot so Scott could look at it. It was partially buried in the dirt and short grasses grew from within it. It looked like it had been there for a long time. He recognized the shape as a vertebrae. He tested its strength with a push of his foot, then sat on its gray porous surface holding his arms out to his sides. "This thing's wider than my whole body!"

"There used to be lots of whaling up here a long time ago. They'd haul 'em up here on huge cement slabs that sloped down into the water. These buildings," he turned to look at them himself while pointing, "and others that aren't here anymore, used to be warehouses and butcher shops." He shifted his attention out to the bay. "On clear days, and in the right season, you can see 'em spouting out there in the water." Scott stood up on the bone and shaded his eyes hoping to catch a glimpse of something. Nothing was in view except whitecaps.

They continued on to the sandy gray shore. It was a scattered mess of sand, rocks, huge weathered redwood stumps, logs, and miscellaneous driftwood.

"Looks like a bomb hit here," Scott commented.

"Some of this is from the storm we had a long time ago. But it's mostly from all the logging. They drop logs in the rivers and float 'em down. Some of them get away and wash out to sea, then end up on shore. Others just naturally fall and wash out by themselves. They all seem to wash up here 'cause of the bay."

"No wonder you don't have a decent beach."

"There's miles of dunes further up north with a lot less logs, but the water's way cold," Ryan answered. "And it's usually a little warmer this time of year. I'm surprised it's not foggy today. It can get really thick, roll in just a few minutes, and stay all day"

"I like 'em thick."

"Jeez Scott, is everything sexual to you?" Ryan shook his head while Scott grinned at him.

Ryan led him down to a wide, two-story-tall concrete jetty. The wind was constant in their ears here. Waves crashed so furiously against the jetty that the water was tossed up two and three times as high as the structure. The tremendous power of the surges and the awesome sound made Scott's jaw drop. Far out past the jetty were odd sea stacks with lone gnarled windswept trees perched precariously on top. Their branches permanently pointed in one direction from the constant wind.

They passed the jetty and continued along the beach. Aside from the huge pieces of driftwood, flotsam of all kinds was strewn along the sand. Seaweed, plastic containers, rocks, desiccated fish and fish bones were all over, and hardly any people were to be seen. Scott turned around so the wind hit his back. The wind had never been this bad back home, except for the occasional windstorm, which mainly hit way below them near where AeroSun was located. Beach or no beach, he figured if the wind were this constant he wouldn't enjoy it either.

Scott came across what at first he thought was a jellyfish stuck in a net. He pushed the net, which was tangled up in seaweed and sand, with his shoe. It wasn't a jellyfish. He had uncovered a weathered green glass object about eight inches in diameter. A stem-like projection protruded from the spherical glass. Attached to it was a still-intact donut-shaped cork. He stooped to pick it up. "What is this?"

"Cool, you found one. They keep the nets afloat. The ones that don't break wash up every once in a while."

It tore easily from the tangled piece of net and he shook the sand from it. It was a souvenir worth keeping. The chilly wind stayed constant although the day was rapidly becoming bright and sunny. Scott ran ahead a few steps and turned around in front of Ryan. "Kiss me."

"Be serious. This is a public beach!"

Scott looked around. The only people he saw were a few people taking pictures of the breakers crashing against the jetty and some others rummaging around a redwood stump near the shoreline some distance behind them. Before Ryan could step aside Scott grabbed him and kissed him on the lips. "Ha, ha. Gotcha," he said as Ryan pulled back.

Ryan looked back, then wiped his lips. "Don't do that!"

"Who cares? You don't live here anymore."

"People know me here."

Scott pointed to the jetty. "They look like tourists. And those people," He looked the other way for the people by the stump but they were nowhere to be seen. "have disappeared. So...we should spread a blanket out and do it here."

"You think you're funny, but you're not."

It's kinda fun to razz him, Scott thought. *In fact, it's becoming easy to figure out how he'll react.* Oddly enough, Ryan still wouldn't razz Scott back and he couldn't quite figure out why.

"C'mon. Let's see if Adina's home."

They backtracked up the wood-littered beach to the Jeep. Ryan gave him directions and they crossed town to a well-kept neighborhood on the outskirts of town. This far from shore, there were just normal passing breezes, nothing like the constant wind off the ocean. Brightly painted totem poles on either side of the street demarcated the entrance to *Crescent Manor*. Beautiful stately homes lined a long boulevard and radiated out in three streets to the left.

"Second left. It's the fifth house down. The one with the black shutters," Ryan said. Scott complied and slowed when he saw the house. "Stop at the curb and wait here." Scott stopped and Ryan jumped out. He peered into one of the garage door windows, then signaled Scott to pull up the driveway and park.

Scott had the feeling he had been watching a prowler as he got out. "Why are we sneaking around like this?"

"I told you her parents don't like me. She said they were supposed to be gone and I was making sure their car wasn't here."

They walked along a perfectly manicured sidewalk to the front porch. Scott surveyed the profusion of flowers and vines that were planted in, and spilled over from, wide cement urns. Wood chips covered the dirt in the front garden. A massive oak front door with translucent beveled glass on either side stood in the middle of the wide front porch. Ryan pressed the doorbell. Almost immediately they heard the door unlock and the door swung open.

Adina was Ryan's age and wore her short, light-blond hair swept back on one side and straight down on the other. She was wearing pink tights with a white stripe down one side, which showed every contour of her body. She dropped a pair of tennis shoes as she yelled, "Ryan!" She launched at him and gave him a big hug. Her exuberance was refreshing. Finally, she pulled herself off him. "When did you get in?"

"Last night. Hey, this is the friend I told you about." Her eyes gave her away as she checked out Scott. She was pleased with what she saw.

He offered his hand. "Scott Faraday."

She briefly shook it. "You guys have tans. I'm jealous."

She let them in and they walked down a beautifully tiled foyer to a spacious living room with a high vaulted ceiling. The interior looked like it was right out of *Architectural Digest*. Scott couldn't help but express a "Wow."

"I thought you were Kathy," Adina said. "She's driving us to aerobics before work. You should've warned me you were coming."

"Ha, ha," Ryan replied.

She gave him a face. "I'd, like, offer you something to drink, but she's gonna be here any minute and we gotta leave."

"That's okay. I just wanted to show Scott where we're partying this weekend."

"Well, this is it." She gave Scott a mini-tour of the two-story house and showed him the big backyard. The redwood Jacuzzi in the gazebo off the back deck especially intrigued Scott.

"Are we gonna be able to use this?"

Adina wrinkled her brow. "A party without the Jacuzzi? I couldn't imagine." She turned to Ryan, "Hey, I talked with some of our friends. Some are going to be gone this week. Dennis moved to Portland with his girlfriend, so they're not coming. But don't worry. I took care of *everything*. Everybody knows the party's here."

"Great," he answered absentmindedly. She had already told him everything on the phone before the trip.

"I invited bunches of other people you probably don't know." Then to Scott, "My folks don't know we're having this party, so I'm going all out."

Scott could see that she was quite the wild one. If he were straight, he might even think she was attractive in her skintight bodysuit. He went to the edge of the deck to check out the long yard and heard her whisper something to Ryan. When he turned back around, he caught Ryan grinning at her. The sliding glass door was still open and they heard the doorbell ring from inside the house.

"That's Kathy." Adina waved them in and they followed her to the front door.

Adina introduced them both to Kathy, who said she knew of Ryan because of Little Trout. Scott noticed Ryan was noticeably uncomfortable now that Little Trout's name had been mentioned. Adina unconsciously jiggled her house keys and ushered everyone out.

"Hey, wanna meet for a bite tonight?" Ryan asked.

Adina turned to her friend. "Kathy, you want to?"

"Sure, why not?"

"We don't get off until nine-thirty," Adina said as she shifted her bag on her shoulder.

"We'll meet you at the regular café after you both get off. See you then."

The boys jumped in the Jeep and followed the girls out of the neighborhood. The girls turned right and they took a left.

"What was *that* all about?" Scott asked.

"What was *what* all about?"

"You freaked when Kathy mentioned Little Trout."

"I didn't know she knew her."

"So what?"

"I told you. I haven't exactly talked to her since I left."

"Well, when you see her at the party, and you know she'll be there, what're you gonna say then?"

"I'll figure that one out later." Ryan scratched just above his shirt pocket.

"Need some help?" Scott asked as he watched.

"I said I'd figure it out."

"No. Does your nipple itch?"

"I can do it myself."

"Just checking. I take it Adina doesn't know you like dick?"

"Fuck no."

Scott wondered how long it would be before she found out. "Where should we go?"

"Back to the house."

About a half-mile away from *Crescent Manor*, they reached a long bridge. Way below was the wide cold Smith River.

Scott slowed and pulled to the side. "I'm gonna check it out."

Ryan seemed a bit apprehensive as Scott got out and went to the railing. The wind was in his hair and almost drowned out his voice. "Are you coming?"

"Yeah, I guess."

The bank on this side of the river sloped steeply to a shoal of the same smooth, gray rocks that he had seen earlier. The shoal under the bridge extended out only a short distance before disappearing under the dark water. The trees that grew along the bank anchored the rocks forming a gray sandbar. In the middle of the rocky shoal was a redwood log lying on its side, with stump intact, mired in the rock and sand.

As Ryan reached the railing and looked down, a great sadness seemed to have overcome him. Scott scooted a little closer to him and touched his elbow.

"Hey, what's wrong?"

"I…this is where I thought about jumping.

"*What?*"

"I thought about it about a month before I left Crawford." He lowered his head as he finished. "I figured my body would wash out to the ocean and no one would ever find me." The quiet way that Ryan said it scared Scott.

"You're *shittin'* me," Scott exclaimed again.

Ryan looked him in the face now. "You think I just made that up?"

Scott gripped the railing tightly and looked at him. "How many times did you try it anyway? And don't *lie*."

"Once here, once in the Packard, and once in my Chevelle."

"*Three times? Three fucking times?* Have you thought about it recently? I mean…"

Ryan wouldn't look at him but interrupted instead. "Yeah."

Scott slapped his forehead. "When?"

"The morning we left." He looked up at him. "Are you satisfied now?" The wind continued to blow through his hair, making it stand up in a ridge of black locks.

Scott was trying hard to digest it. Ryan had been acting particularly weird that morning and now Scott knew why.

"*Fuck.* What do you mean you thought about it when we left?"

"I wondered why I was even coming back here…that's all."

Four times! He doubted if it were really only four times. He wondered if Ryan was being truthful about things, even now. His preoccupation with suicide was starting to become disturbing to Scott.

Ryan turned toward the car. "Come on." He opened the passenger door while Scott stood at the railing just looking at him. *I'm the stupid-fuck*, Scott thought. Ryan stood by the Jeep with the door open, looking back at him. Scott shook his head and went to the driver's side. Only the wind and the crunching of gravel underfoot at the shoulder broke the silence.

Scott started the Jeep and pulled back out onto the blacktop. Before they reached the end of the bridge, Scott could just barely see the ocean on the left as the river spilled into it. Scott didn't want to keep harping on Ryan's anxieties but had to get some more information.

"Ever thought about talking to a psychologist?"

"I don't need a fucking shrink!"

"All right, all right." Scott only knew anecdotally what psychologists did and immediately thought about Kyle Sorenson. He was sure he'd have to come out to Kyle if he talked about the situation. He wondered if he was up to that. To put a cap on Ryan's clearly deteriorated mood, he changed the subject.

"Won't the neighbors complain if Adina's parents are away and we party there?"

"Nah, her neighbors have kids our age on both sides. They'll cover for her. By the way, she told me you were cute."

Scott remembered the whispering and the grin he saw on the back porch. "So that's what she said."

"I told her you thought she was cute."

"You didn't."

"She'll probably try to hit on you."

"If she tries to I'll tell her I'm your boyfriend."

Ryan couldn't tell if Scott was serious or not. "I don't *think* so."

"You set it up. But I'll tell her I'm not about to fuck anyone else except you."

"Dickhole."

"I'm just kidding. Dude, you're just gonna *have* to get used to my style."

Ryan was silent for a moment, trying to sort out why he constantly overreacted to him. Sometimes he could tell when Scott was playing mind games, but most of the time he couldn't. There was no easy answer. *Maybe it was the years of hanging around my stupid friends,* he thought. *They never made idle threats. They always carried out everything they said they'd do.*

They continued along the winding road through the hills and eventually reached Del Norte Pass Road north of the park.

"If we go left here and up the road about four or so miles, we'll reach Frank Gaviota's house. I'll take you there tomorrow. I'm sure he'll be home. But take a right for now. We're only a little way from the house.

Scott turned right and went slower so he wouldn't miss the turnoff. The one-story ranger station was the landmark he was looking for and he made the turn. It was early afternoon now and Scott's stomach was rumbling.

A light haze had settled over the property from the smokehouse, concentrating the aroma of the salmon. Ryan took a deep breath. "Mmm. Can't wait to eat that fish!"

They entered through the side door and went into Ryan's bedroom. Scott shut the bedroom door as Ryan dropped to the bed on his back.

Scott stood at the door and leaned against it. Mixed emotions swept through him. The revelation of Ryan's suicide attempts was weighing on him. He still thought Ryan was the cutest guy he'd ever known. He'd get naked with him in a second, even now. That in itself was reason enough to keep hanging with him. But a nagging feeling of death haunted him now. It wasn't something he was used to, or could get used to.

Ryan beckoned him with his forefinger. His wide smile drew Scott from his momentary reflection and he crawled onto the bed next to him. "Kiss me," he said.

"How many times?"

"You mean how long."

"I know how long it is."

Ryan chuckled, then took Scott in his arms and lightly pressed his lips against his. Scott felt what he could only describe as an electric charge as he did so. Ryan started running his fingers through Scott's hair. Scott's heart pounded as Ryan then passionately pulled him down and embraced him.

Scott pulled back and looked in his eyes. "Promise me something?"

"What?"

"Promise me you won't try it again."

Ryan noticeably tensed up. "I told you I only thought about it when we left."

But Scott was worried that he refused to promise. Ryan's stomach rumbled, and as if on cue, they got up at the same time. Ryan unlocked the bedroom door.

Scott pointed to the bulge in his pants. "Wait up."

Much later, after lunch, Ryan's mood shifted back to the mostly happy demeanor Scott was more used to.

Chris brought Teresa home that night while they watched TV with Muh. *Thank God*, Scott thought. The two of them were the diversion he was looking for. Muh had been talking so much it was hard to follow the newscaster as he had talked about an impending attack by Iraq on a neighboring country. It sounded like the US was going to be involved in some way or another. He hoped that whatever was up that it wouldn't keep the band from being able to play on the Marine Base later. He stopped his ruminating and checked his watch. Adina would be off work soon and he wanted to get away again to talk with people their own age.

Chris and Teresa hung onto each other despite the audience. Muh seemed to ignore them. *Ryan's right,* Scott thought, *Teresa looks trashier than Stacey from the trailer park back home.* Scott figured the relationship was just something for her to tell her friends about when school started again in a couple of weeks. *He's probably getting his share while she allows him to be around,* he thought.

They munched from a bowl of popcorn that Ryan had placed between them as they leaned back on the couch. Scott watched as Ryan unconsciously curled and uncurled his toes against the coffee table. He was so close he could count the number of hairs on his big toe. He couldn't believe that just looking at his toes was sexy. *I guess he's right,* Scott thought. *Everything is sexual to me.*

"You guys coming to the party?" Ryan asked his brother.

Muh interjected before Chris could answer. "Where did you decide to have it, Ryan?"

"Uh, one of Adina's friend's houses."

Scott knew why Ryan was lying, and Chris was in on the secret already.

"Heck yeah, we're going."

"None of your sophomore friends are invited though."

Chris mouthed 'fuck you' while Muh wasn't looking, then tickled Teresa and stood up. They went off to his bedroom. Scott wondered if it was to get high or to have sex or both. Probably both, he figured.

Later Scott and Ryan took off to meet the girls at the *Redwood Cafe.* They ordered and the girls gossiped about one of the customers they had at work until Ryan changed the subject. "What should we bring to the party?"

"Nothing. Just your bods. I said I took care of everything," Adina answered.

They talked for a little longer and Scott went to the bathroom. Just as he left, Adina asked the question she had in mind all day.

"Good God, Ryan. You should really warn me when you're bringing a cute guy to my house."

"Yeah," Kathy agreed, wide-eyed.

Ryan was flattered and embarrassed at the same time. "I don't usually tell girls whether my friends are cute or not."

"Well, you should. It's embarrassing to be attracted to someone and not be warned."

Ryan mulled over her comment for a moment. He felt a twinge of despair pass through him. *She doesn't have a clue what that feeling is like,* he thought. *How about being attracted to a guy and never getting to say a word to anyone—ever? How about not knowing if that guy felt the same and feeling awful because you not only didn't know, but you didn't dare ask him?* Despite her complaint she had it made. With everyone assumed to be straight, the whole issue was a breeze for her. No, she could never know the agony or the misery he understood so well.

"Where did you meet him?" Adina asked, breaking his reverie.

"His parents own the restaurant me and Uncle Howie eat at a lot. He's a host there and we got to be friends."

"Oh. Oh, Zirk said he wanted to talk to you."

He knitted his brow. "About what?"

She noticed his reaction but didn't comment on it. "He didn't say."

Ryan didn't want to talk to any one of his old friends anytime soon. Now that he was around Scott, he was beginning to realize how much better he felt not having to experience the straitjacket of their homophobia, much less any of their other narrow-minded attitudes. He didn't want Scott to be exposed to them either. He decided he'd completely avoid them unless they came to the party.

"I'll call him this week," he lied. "Anyway, I guess I'll see him and the rest of the guys at the party."

Adina started playing with her spoon. "He said they're coming. I hope Dolf doesn't get too wasted though. He gets stupid sometimes."

Maybe they won't actually come by, Ryan thought.

Scott came back, his smile giving away something.

"What's so funny?" Kathy asked.

"Some graffiti in the men's room. *'Nuclear power is your friend'*. It just sounded funny."

They stayed and talked some more until the girls were done eating and left soon afterward.

It was a cloudless night and the stars shone through the narrow stretch of sky above the road as they drove back to the house. As they pulled up the long gravel drive and parked, Scott could still only see a somewhat rectangular stretch of open sky above them. *How strange to only see a small portion of sky at night*, he thought.

Ryan opened the side entrance and put a finger to his lips as he tiptoed to Chris's bedroom door. They heard the stereo going and Teresa was saying something they couldn't quite hear. Ryan raised his eyebrows, then pointed to his bedroom. They tiptoed back and Ryan shut the door. "I can't believe he's going out with her," he said.

"You're jealous."

"Yeah, of her."

They sat side by side on the bed and Ryan inserted a tape into a tape player that sat on the nightstand. He pressed the play button. "I guess I am jealous. I don't know why. I guess it's just that…oh, I don't know."

He got up, securely shut the door, and turned the key. Scott got off the bed, pushed the pile of blankets onto the floor, and sat down on them. He patted them while looking up at him. Ryan kicked off his shoes and dropped down to kiss him.

Scott pulled off his shirt, then pulled Ryan's arms up so he could pull his off as well. They embraced, pausing only long enough to give each other deep French kisses.

Scott suddenly realized their time together up here wouldn't last forever, and it made him feel glum. Already he decided he wanted as much of Ryan's time as he could to hug and kiss him. What incredible luck to have this quality time despite Ryan's strange mood swings which made him recoil at the oddest moments. And the newest revelations about his attempted suicides simply melted into the background as he held him. If he could only help Ryan to just come completely out, to help him quit playing his 'I'm not really one-hundred percent gay' game. How to do it still nagged at him. It was more of a job for his aunt. She was the expert at things like that.

As much as he wanted to kiss Ryan all night, he equally craved at least a few hours of sleep. Scott got up onto the bed and Ryan followed. He lightly caressed Scott's stomach until he fell asleep.

Scott was surprised he slept soundly through the entire night. The next morning, the sound of the door shutting woke him when Ryan returned from the bathroom. His hair was wet and he was wearing only his underwear.

He dropped onto the bed. "I guess Chris got some last night."

Scott yawned and stretched before answering. "How do you know?"

"I asked him."

"You told the same lies when you were fifteen. By the way, how can he drive by himself if he's not sixteen?"

"Hardship license."

"Oh."

"And he showed me the condom. So I know he did."

Scott made a face. "Ugh, I can't imagine my brother showing me his used condom."

Ryan stood now and combed his hair in the mirror by the door. "It was in the trashcan. And you were crashed out heavily when I woke up or I would've fucked you 'til you were blind."

Scott pulled away the covers. He rolled over, sticking his butt in the air. Looking through his spread legs, his head upside down, he whispered. "What're you waiting for?"

Ryan looked at his upturned rear end, then to the door. He quickly locked it. It took him only a second to step out of his underwear. Ryan was hard in a second. Scott didn't really think Ryan would respond so quickly. He came to the bed and ran his hand over the downy hair on Scott's buttocks. He caressed the hard hump at the base of Scott's penis and kneaded his balls for a moment. He reached down into his pack and rummaged for a condom, which he tore open and quickly unrolled onto his shaft. Spitting onto his hand he worked it all over the condom, then applied his aloe gel onto Scott's anus. He seemed to be wasting no time. Scott was a little concerned, since he had to pee. But he knew how intense it would feel when he had to hold it.

Scott had to clamp his teeth tightly together so he wouldn't moan as Ryan slowly worked himself in. It made him even stiffer as Ryan pushed until he could go no further. As Ryan thrust slowly at first, then faster, Scott kept time with his rhythm by sucking in quick breaths. The bed squeaked a little as he bucked back and forth, then squeaked more as he pumped up and down when Scott slid down a bit. Ryan ran his hands up and down Scott's back and lats as he pumped, lingering to play with Scott's nipples ever so often.

Scott hoped it would last a lot longer than it did, but Ryan was ready to shoot right away. A few more pumps and he felt him stiffen as he emitted a low moan. He fell over Scott's back, tensing his abs as his penis twitched inside him. Scott jerked off as best as he could from his bent over position. The pressure quickly rose in his loins. He started straightening upright and Ryan helped pull him up. He held Scott around the chest for support as it landed on one of the pillows. Scott felt he would never get his eyeballs back into their correct position as his body numbed deliciously.

Neither of them expected Chris to knock on the door.

"Hey, you guys," he said from the other side.

Ryan tightened his grip around Scott. Just as Scott's sphincter quit its rhythmic tightening, he pulled out with a quick motion.

"Ow!" Scott exclaimed.

They heard Chris' muffled voice. "You got a girl in there?"

"Go away. We'll be out in a minute," Ryan responded angrily.

There was no response from Chris. Maybe he left. His intrusive arrival freaked them both out. It was one of those rare times when Scott lost his erection almost instantly. That surprised even him. Ryan scooted off the bed and started pulling the condom off as he put an ear to the door. Scott grabbed a towel from the dresser and wiped up the pillow and his butt as he listened, too. Still nothing. Chris must have gone away after all.

Ryan rested a knee on the bed as he finished wiping himself off. "Fuck, I'm sorry," he whispered.

Scott laughed, then whispered back. "I've been having sex for what, a few weeks now? And I almost get caught? If you ask me, it was pretty funny."

Ryan dressed and unlocked the door as Scott donned his underwear. "You coming? Breakfast is ready."

"Not 'til I shower. And I have some more fantasizing to do." Scott rubbed his genitals through the fabric. Ryan gave him a face, then turned to go to the kitchen.

Later that morning Scott found his Frisbee. He'd been wanting to use the huge clearing next to the house as a practice area and the gravely driveway with its adjacent flat treeless area would be perfect. Once outside he tossed it to Ryan.

"How did you explain this morning to Chris?" Scott asked.

"I told him I was showing you what he was doing with Teresa last night. He thought I was razzing him and shut up."

"Good save. But you'll have to tell him sooner or later."

"Yeah, like I'm gonna." He pointed at Scott. "And don't you go blabbing anything to him either," he said sternly.

They tossed the Frisbee back and forth, testing the length of the unobstructed yard. Chris joined them a little later and surprised Scott again. He didn't seem the type who would lift his little finger unless he absolutely had to, much less throw a Frisbee with any accuracy. But he seemed in good practice.

Scott caught it behind his back again. "Hey, Chris."

"Hey, what?"

"What'd Muh say about Teresa being here at night?"

"Nothin'."

"She must've said something."

"She never does. Believe it or not, we talk most of the time."

"Yeah, sure."

"Who could fuck all the time anyway?"

Scott and Ryan looked at each other. They said it at the same time. "I could."

He give both of them his middle finger.

Soon insects were buzzing around and the sun started to make them sweat in the somewhat cool humid air. Ryan snatched a perfect hover toss from the air. "Time out. I'm gonna call Frank to see if he's home." He tossed the Frisbee back to Scott, then went inside to make his call. Scott fanned himself with it while Chris looked on. He seemed full of questions.

Chris approached him. "How'd you really meet my brother?"

"At the restaurant."

"You really own a restaurant?"

"Well, it's not mine, it's my parent's. My dad built it from nothing and turned it into the best restaurant in the high desert."

"I guess you'll inherit it, huh?"

"Yeah. I guess." There it was again. He was still faced with his parent's decision about school. And that reminded him about Ryan leaving for L.A. again. Strangely enough, he suddenly felt sad thinking about it. *Uh oh, I'm letting Ryan's moods get to me,* he thought.

"You really like my brother?"

No way. He couldn't know about us, he thought. "Whadda ya mean?"

"He's usually weird."

"Yeah, don't I know."

"He hasn't been as weird since he's been back though. Muh said it's 'cause of you."

Scott grinned. "I guess he needed a change of atmosphere."

"She says he should have left earlier so he coulda met you a long time ago."

Hearing that, Scott felt particularly proud all of a sudden.

Ryan appeared again, with a wide grin on his face. "Hey, Frank's home! He was pretty excited about us coming over. I guess he wants to find out if I'm okay and all."

"Totally. Let's go."

They first went inside and drank all the cold water remaining in the pitcher in the refrigerator. Scott retrieved his keys and they took off up north to Frank's place in Prieto Canyon.

CHAPTER 22

The two-lane road twisted and turned through narrow stretches that had long ago been blasted out from the hillsides. It was slow going, with yellow and black signs warning of hairpin curves all along the way. Ryan pointed to the place where he wrecked the car but the foliage was so thick it was difficult to see where it might have gone over the side. Scott had no intention of stopping for a better look, since it would only serve to get Ryan in the wrong frame of mind for the day.

As usual, traffic was only incidental as they made their way uphill, then along level areas, downhill for a way, then back up. They finally reached a turnoff to a narrow canyon with a wide unmarked lane. The two-block long lane was perfectly straight along a shallow rocky tributary which became visible along the right side. There was a single row of houses on a flat stretch along one bank. The homes were rustic in appearance, but Scott could tell they were expensive since they all appeared to be solidly built as well as quite large.

Ryan pointed, showing him several lines of parallel rapids through clear chilly water. "I've kayaked with him right here when the water was higher."

"Frank seems like my kinda guy."

"Yeah, but he tries to get into your head sometimes."

Scott wondered if that meant Ryan felt invaded by him. Maybe it really means that he's more perceptive than most. *Probably,* he thought.

The sun filtered down onto them through the trees, filling the air with shafts of brilliant sunlight. Even from the road they could hear the water against rocks beyond the houses. Scott drove slowly as he took in the big homes separated by huge oaks, hickories and the occasional blue spruce.

Ryan tapped on the windshield. "It's the next one."

The Gaviota home was perched on a level stretch right up against, but higher than, the bank of the river. Out front was a mailbox on a wooden pole. A painted silhouette of a seagull had the names *Frank and Carol Gaviota* engraved on it. The back end of the house rested atop a high stone wall that ran vertical to the water below.

A short asphalt drive led to a spacious wood-frame workshop at the side of the house. The double doors were wide open and Scott saw all kinds of tools hanging on a finished wall, the floor, and scattered on a workbench. A tall iron rack just inside the doors held three brightly colored kayaks.

A nondescript gray van parked in the drive had a bumper sticker on it, which read '*Have You Hugged Your Kayak Today?*' Scott parked behind the van. Ryan was quite animated now and quickly got out as Scott came to a stop.

Frank met them as they approached the entrance of the workshop. He was wiping his hands on a rag. Scott was immediately captured by his rugged looks. He had almost-shoulder-length unruly dark hair, and a full neatly trimmed black beard and mustache. His green v-neck t-shirt revealed a trail of sweat down the middle and a chest of dark hair. He had a well-developed upper body, wore baggy khaki shorts, and had on old tennis shoes with no socks.

He removed his safety glasses, whereupon bright eyes showed his delight. "Ryan!" Frank took Ryan's outstretched hand, then pulled him toward him to give him a bear hug. "Sorry about the sweat. Good to see you again! The arm's better?"

"It was only in the sling for about a week. This is my friend, Scott."

"Faraday," Scott said.

Frank took his hand and gripped it in a firm handshake. Already Scott liked him. Something about his handshake, the deep rich tone of his voice, the way he held himself. Everything spoke of a man who was confident and, well, happy with himself.

Frank showed Scott his workspace. On a platform in the center of it, he had just C-clamped several layers of plywood against a support beam. An open bottle of wood glue was on the floor. A yellowish drop of the glue slowly oozed down its side. Fiberglass molds and finishing sanders were in one corner. Woodworking equipment was along one wall while sawdust was swept into a pile to one side. The smell of fiberglass resin, glue, and wood greeted their noses. Scott studied the brightly colored finished kayaks gleaming on the rack.

"So, you're gonna sell these?" Scott asked.

"They're already sold," he answered. "I only make to order."

"His only advertising is word-of-mouth," Ryan offered.

They heard footsteps come up the walk from the house behind them and all turned to look. "Carol, you know Ryan. And this is Scott, his friend from down south."

Scott noticed that Carol had a vague resemblance to Kyle Sorenson's wife, only Carol was at least ten years older. Her hair was much shorter, but she wore similar style glasses. Seeing her reminded Scott again to make a mental note again to talk to Kyle later after they returned.

She hugged Ryan warmly. "Frank said you called. How are you? You just disappeared."

"Yeah, to a Podunk town in the desert."

"Podunk?" Scott said defensively. He stuck his hand out, shook hers, and introduced himself.

She turned to Frank. "Honey, you can take a break, can't you?"

He looked at his watch, then capped the glue. "Sure, but only until my paying customers get here." He said that more for the boys than for her.

"Good, I'll get some water for tea."

She led them into the house. Scott felt right at home. The interior was a curious mixture of high tech and backwoods. The huge over-stuffed sofa sectional in the den looked very expensive, as did the vast array of what looked like brand new stereo equipment on one wall. All the floors were carpeted and it seemed to muffle their voices. The house was also well insulated from the sound of the rapids outside. Books on shelves that covered two other walls briefly caught Scott's attention as he glanced at some of the titles.

A wooden flute, with beautiful eagle feathers tied to it, rested in a framed glass case on a wall in the dining room. Above it hung a plaque that read, "*A man's worth can only be measured by the happiness in his heart.*" Other Native American artifacts were hung on the stone chimney above the mantel. Scott examined the relics in detail.

"I collected all the Native American stuff myself," Frank offered, as he watched Scott study the pieces.

Down a short hallway to the back bedroom hung photos of karate tournaments from Frank's younger days. His hair was much shorter then, and he didn't have a beard. Scott noted that Frank had been strikingly handsome. Along with the photos, trophies were perched high atop shelves on both sides of the hall, almost as if they were hidden. Scott wondered why they weren't displayed more prominently.

Scott finally made it to the kitchen and leaned against the counter with the others as they talked. Ryan explained to the couple that his grandmother had made him move to Yucca Valley with his uncle and he hadn't had much time to say goodbye to anyone. He left out most of the significant details, which slightly angered Scott. He explained that they were back for only a week due to their double birthday party. Frank and Carol both said happy birthday to the boys.

Carol filled a pitcher with hot water from a separate tap at the sink, then removed the lid from a large hand-thrown pottery jar. She offered the opened container to Scott. It was full of different tea bags. The aromas of cinnamon and oranges were the strongest as he sniffed the pile. He wasn't sure what he was choosing and just pulled one out at random.

She pointed to a mug and he dropped the bag in. They all went out onto the back patio and sat at a circular wrought iron table. The railings of the deck were made of thick roughhewn beams spaced widely enough that they could see the rushing water below. The sound of the rapids just upstream from the house wasn't overpowering at all. In fact, the sound was so soothing Scott felt he could be lulled to sleep in a moment if given half a chance. He poured steaming water from the pitcher Carol had brought out into his mug and watched it turn green-brown as it steeped.

He was only half-listening to Ryan's continued explanation of his abrupt disappearance when a long, narrow, still-green pinecone landed with a thud on the deck. Scott retrieved it and idly examined it as the conversation continued. Twenty minutes later they heard a van door slide open, then a car door shut.

Frank stood and placed his mug on the table. "Business calls," he announced.

Scott downed the last of his lemony tasting tea, set the mug on the tabletop, and followed everyone back inside.

"I hope you guys can come back soon," Frank said. "Sorry this was such a short visit."

Next to his gray van was a big blue one with a canoe rack on top. Another car had pulled up behind it. Two tall men and a young boy were standing at the workshop entrance. Frank waved and smiled. "Be right there."

The boys waved good-bye and jumped into the Jeep. While they drove away, Scott thought about what Frank said about coming back. With or without Ryan Scott needed to talk with him. It seemed Frank knew his boyfriend pretty well, more so than Ryan admitted. He licked his lips of the lingering taste of lemon as he considered how to meet up with him again.

Now it was Ryan's turn. "Need some help there?"

"Help?"

"An extra tongue maybe?"

Scott surely wasn't going to fend him off. "If it's *your* tongue."

Ryan squeezed his knee, making it tickle.

"That Frank guy is cool," Scott said.

"Yeah. He didn't try to get into my head today. I don't like it when he does that. Otherwise, he's the coolest guy I know."

Scott abruptly changed the subject. "Hey, when are you gonna start that poster for the band?"

"Oh shit," he said as he remembered his promise. "Uh, we need to head into town. Go back down Del Norte Pass Road and I'll show you how to get to the strip mall. I need some poster boards and some other stuff."

The mall had the largest collection of stores in the area and was located in an unusually flat area atop a high cliff south of town. The lot was packed and they had to park toward the back. A thick stone wall ran along the edge of the cliff three car rows from them. They could see the open ocean at the horizon from there. If the mall hadn't been in this location, another scenic overlook surely would have been, Scott thought. After they parked he headed for the wall to take a look at the waves crashing below.

Ryan jerked his head. "Where're you going? The store's this way."

"I'm checkin' out the view."

Ryan pointed. "I'll be at that art supply store." He headed to the mall through the parked cars. A thermal coming up the side of the cliff breezed along the edge of the wall. Scott stuck his arm out as far as he could reach to feel the breeze coming up from below. He figured it would be a perfect place to hang glide. A hang glider, a good thermal to get up over the ocean, and a large parking lot for touch down. What more could one want? *There's probably a sign somewhere though,* he thought, *that says 'No hang gliding'. It would be one hell of a rappel down to the water below.* He wondered if Kyle had ever ascended anything like it before. His curiosity satisfied, he turned and almost immediately saw the sign on one of the light poles. It said "*No Hang Gliding Allowed.*" *Whoa, am I psychic or what?* He scanned the signs that hung above the mall walkway across the lot and looked for the art supply store. The facades all looked brand new. At regular intervals short triangular peaks, each with a hole through the middle graced the roofline.

A broad sidewalk stretched in front of the shops, allowing for a wide stream of pedestrian traffic. There was plenty of foot traffic today. As Scott scanned along the walkway he saw the sign marked "*Donovan's Art Supply Hut*" as it swung back and forth slightly in the breeze.

Ryan was standing outside the store looking agitated as he spoke to a man just a little taller than he. As Scott got closer he saw more of the man's features. Short dark hair with sunglasses on top of his head, slightly receding hairline, nicely developed muscular body, wide lips. *It couldn't be,* he thought, as he bolted through the traffic and onto the sidewalk.

"...you didn't say good-bye," said the good-looking man.

"I..," Ryan started, but his heart felt as though it was in his throat. He had no idea he would see Crawford and was completely unprepared for this moment. He couldn't decide whether to walk away or say some-thing nasty.

Scott's heart raced. From just that one word, he could hear the unevenness of Ryan's voice. In a second, everything bad he'd said about Crawford flooded his mind. Not thinking, but rather acting on impulse, he immediately intervened.

"Crawford!" he said in the roughest voice he could manage.

That caught the man off guard and he shaded his eyes as Scott approached. "Who are you?

Scott threw back his shoulders, trying to look formidable, but knowing it probably looked ridiculous. Crawford was a good four inches
taller and at least forty pounds heavier than he was, and he wasn't sure
if his act would take. "Someone who knows enough about you," Scott
stated.

Crawford issued a short laugh, more of a grunt actually. "Like I said.
Who the hell are you?"

"Look…," Scott began.

Ryan finally found his voice and glanced at Scott. "I can defend
myself," he interjected. His heart was racing now. His mixed feelings
about Crawford were overwhelming him, and with Scott there as well,
he felt completely confused.

Crawford quickly looked back to Ryan. "Defend yourself…from
what?"

Scott took a step closer, not believing how bold he was. What a contrast Ryan was now from his usual impetuous self. He was doing nothing!

"I know all about you, Crawford Grant. And I know about you and
him. If he says he doesn't want to talk to you, then listen up."

"Oh, I get it," Crawford said. He looked back at Ryan and lowered his
voice. "So, you went and got a queer buddy?"

Crawford had taken the bait. *Good*, Scott thought, but he was fighting to keep his breath steady.

There it is again, Ryan thought, *that word*. Crawford always kept him
under his control by the simple use of that word. In a way, a part of
Ryan found it humorous that he ever thought Crawford had any control over him. It was the simple use of the right inflection, the right tone
of voice. Crawford had easily pierced through all of his fears, his anxieties, and all of his naiveté, by using that one word. But time away from
him, and his relationship with Scott now, showed him something he
didn't quite understand before: Crawford simply used him.

Scott mustered more bravado. "He doesn't need you. And for the record, the word is *gay*." He made sure Crawford understood him by pointing at him, then just barely touched him on the chest.

No crowd had gathered since they hadn't raised their voices, and so far, pedestrians showed only incidental interest in the three as they stepped out of their way.

Finally, Scott's unexpected identification of him, and his audacity, made him decide to go. Crawford started to steadily flip his key ring around his forefinger. The keys jingled steadily as he did so. He looked back and forth to each boy. "I see what's going on," he said nodding. "But I know it won't last." He looked steadily at Ryan. "You can come over and talk about it anytime you like after it's over between you two."

Like hell! Ryan thought. *I played your game too long.* "Fat fuckin' chance," he finally said, this time without any hesitation. Yet, his voice cracked when he said it.

Thank God he said something, Scott thought.

"Pu-leez. Don't be mean," Crawford huffed almost pitifully. "I hope you haven't forgotten all our good times." Without another word, he flashed a quick smile, slipped the sunglasses over his eyes, and headed toward the parking lot. He looked back at the boys only once as he crossed the first row of parked cars.

Ryan went to the other side of a pillar out of view while Scott stood with his hands on his hips and watched Crawford go further and further into the lot. People continued to pass by, not knowing anything had happened. Scott watched Crawford's every move until he started unlocking a large black pickup truck.

Satisfied that Crawford was indeed gone, he returned his attention to Ryan. He looked quite shaken up. "You okay?"

Ryan swallowed once. "Fuck," was all he could muster.

Scott wanted to hug him right there. He didn't know what the conversation had been about before he got there, but he still felt he'd done the right thing.

Scott looked through the crowd. "Come on. Let's get outta here."

They reached the end of the walk and went around the side of the mall. They didn't stop until they had rounded the corner and were in back between two green dumpsters.

Ryan sat on a cockeyed cement parking block and put his head in his hands. A gentle breeze blew his hair as Scott sat next to him. "I'm sorry," Scott said. "I figured it was Crawford and didn't know what else to do. I-I just had to say something. I could tell…" He stopped in mid-sentence as Ryan raised his head up.

His eyes were red and the look on his face said he was a lost little boy. It was a moment before he found the right words to say. "When I saw him, my heart, like, fucking jumped out of my chest. It was like I was looking at someone I…loved a long time ago. He started smooth talking me again. I was praying you'd show up and do something."

"*Do* something? Why didn't you tell him to get fucking *lost*? Hell, I should probably call the police."

Ryan looked away as he shook his head. "I don't know why I didn't say anything," he said angrily. "Tell me why I kept seeing him all that time."

"He blackmailed you. But you could've just told him to hit the road back there. You don't live here anymore."

"I-I couldn't. I saw his face and I-I just lost it."

Scott stood and looked up and down the alleyway. He then pulled Ryan up by the hand. "Look. You don't *live* here anymore."

"But…"

"He's in your past," Scott said slowly. "Just like *you* said before."

He fished in his pocket for some bills. "Come on. Let's get some ice cream at that place around the corner." Ryan carefully studied Scott's face. Scott let his five-dollar bill wave in the breeze and feigned a French accent. "Thees eez for you, ay for moi."

Ryan grabbed the hem of Scott's t-shirt. "Please don't ever leave me."

Ryan's tone worried him for a moment. But thoughts of a dish of Rocky Road had already made his mouth water. He dismissed his worry as they entered the store. Ryan could buy the art supplies after he was filled with ice cream.

*   *   *

They lay in bed that night with the door securely locked. Earlier they were talking, but Ryan had been quiet for a while now and Scott could tell he was thinking. It was strange. He had been unusually quiet for most of the evening. He even let Muh continue to talk incessantly without once cutting her off or making stupid remarks. Only crickets through the slightly open window broke the calm. Scott wanted to touch him, but Ryan had rolled over almost as far away from him as he could get.

"Ryan?" Scott whispered.

"Yeah," he said slowly.

"Are you okay?"

"I don't...feel so good."

Scott thought he would be able to understand the issue better if Crawford had been fat or ugly or even old looking. He had turned out to be nothing of the sort. Then again, Scott could only imagine how complex their relationship really had been after all.

"Wanna do something?" He half-hoped Ryan would want him to caress him, stroke him, and kiss him. Maybe that would make him forget about Crawford, at least for a little while.

"Whenever I feel this way I go out to the big rock on the river and think."

"What big rock?"

"It's a little closer than where we went yesterday."

"Well, what're you waiting for?" He wanted to do whatever would make Ryan feel better. And going to the river in the dark was another adventure waiting to happen.

Ryan stirred and raised his head a little. "Really?"

"Sure."

Ryan pushed off the covers and stood at the side of the bed. Scott could just make out the outline of his body in the dark. Ryan grabbed a t-shirt. "Come on. Get some clothes on."

Scott got up and slipped into some shorts. Ryan pulled on some shorts and Scott found a tank top. They donned their tennis shoes and Ryan flipped his painter's cap on. "I got the flashlight." They quietly slipped out of the side entrance and headed across the wide expanse of the yard to the woods.

"You know the way in the dark, huh?"

"I've only been there a hundred times."

When they reached the trees he took Scott's hand and led him down a narrow footpath, only every once in a while flashing on the light to see.

The rush of the river slowly became louder as they continued their trek. Soon the woods broke open and Ryan shined his light on the slope ahead of them. "It's kinda treacherous here, so watch out." He wasn't kidding. There was just enough light from the stars overhead to make out how steep the slope was. Ryan played his flashlight down toward the water so Scott could see.

Now they were out on a narrow peninsula of rocks. Up ahead loomed a huge well-rounded boulder. Ryan carefully walked across the rocks and went to the left side of the boulder. He shined his light back so Scott could keep his footing.

"It's right around the corner." He pointed his light ahead of him as Scott came near. The boulder turned out to be shaped like a hollowed out boiled egg that was tilted slightly to one side. Facing toward the river, a concave space went back a good six feet and had an almost perfectly flat floor-like space that rose about a foot above the current waterline. The hollow was a perfect shelter for perhaps three people. The ceiling was only an inch higher than the top of Ryan's head. When they stepped in, the sound of the river resonated in a curious way.

Ryan sat down cross-legged. Scott sat next to him and took his hand. "Wow, all you see is water and trees. Like a TV screen."

They sat and listened to the soothing sound for many long moments. Scott occasionally brushed the back of Ryan's hand against his face and kissed his knuckles.

"Somehow this place always makes me feel empty. A good kinda empty, you know?"

Scott could feel it, too. But it wasn't an empty feeling to him. More like peaceful. It was as if he were being mesmerized, since all he could see was the constant movement of water. He realized he hadn't worn his watch and had no idea what time it was. Ryan moved his legs, and shifted a little, so he could lay his head on Scott's lap.

"Don't press down. It'll give me a hard-on."

"That always happens to me when I come here. I nearly always ended up jerking off."

Scott feigned disgust. "You mean we're sitting on your dried...?"

Ryan motioned with his hands. "Lots of little dried up sorta-babies are all over the place in here."

Scott felt a bit punchy from the late hour and started laughing. Somehow, the way Ryan said it was so funny he couldn't stop.

That made Ryan laugh, too. He couldn't quite catch his breath and finally had to sit up. "Aw...*hic*...shit...*hic*...you gave me...*hic*...the hic-cups."

"You started it."

"Maybe I could finish it...*hic*..., too." He pulled off his cap and his t-shirt. He tugged on Scott's tank top and Scott pulled it up and off. Ryan stood and dropped his shorts then stepped out of them. He unsnapped

Scott's shorts and unzipped them. Scott looked over at Ryan, then stepped out of his own shorts and underwear.

Ryan sat on his heels, looking out over the water. Scott did the same. Both were only clad in their tennis shoes. Ryan's shoulder brushed against Scott's. "Doesn't it feel great?...*hic*...Just sitting here, looking...*hic*...at the water?....No one to bother you?" He burped and his hiccups stopped.

Scott reached his arm back, and ran his fingers down the middle of Ryan's buttocks. He stopped when he reached his balls hanging loosely between his legs. At his touch, his scrotum started to tighten. "Except your boyfriend's hands, you mean. I have a place like this back home, too. I'd bring my flute and make up my best tunes up there. But there's no water in sight and...I've pounded out quite a few up there, too." He grinned as his penis stiffened even more than it already was.

Ryan turned his head and kissed him. Scott tossed a small stone out into the water, then kissed back. Ryan stood and touched Scott's shoulder to pull him back away from the water's edge. Scott stood, and rubbed his groin into Ryan's until he could feel the moisture from Ryan's pre-come. He had been hard the whole time they were sitting there.

Scott could smell the water and the faint scent of both their bodies as he nuzzled Ryan's neck. What a great sensation it was being naked outside in the dark, hearing the sound of Ryan's breathing and the river softly lapping the bank nearby. Blood rushed in his ears as his heart pounded. He had an overwhelming urge to watch Ryan's face so pulled back and dropped to his knees. Ryan raised his arms up and braced himself against the curved roof as Scott sucked. It was almost animal the way Scott felt as he allowed himself to grunt and slurp without suppressing any noise. Ryan's rhythmic groaning and moaning encouraged him to continue as he clutched Ryan's firm buttocks and pushed his hips back and forth, taking Ryan's full length into his mouth. Ryan took over and started thrusting as more and more pre-come oozed into

Scott's mouth. Ryan's body tensed while his moaning reached a crescendo.

Scott pulled away so he could see it. He took Ryan's penis in hand and jerked on it a few times as glistening strands landed on Scott's arm and hand.

He flung off most of it, stood, and put an arm around Ryan's waist while he beat off with the other hand. Ryan slowly grew softer. He leaned down to lick Scott's nipple. Scott didn't care how loud he moaned as he launched out and onto the stone floor.

When he finally caught his breath, he dipped his hand in the cold water and washed off. They rubbed against each other until the remaining wetness from their penises smeared, then dried.

They shook off their scant clothing and dressed. Ryan put a finger to Scott's lips as if to tell him to be quiet, and they kissed for a few moments before heading back with big yawns and wide smiles to the big comfortable bed.

CHAPTER 23

"**W**ell, *I'm* getting up," Ryan said.

Scott opened on eye and felt between Ryan's legs again. "You've been up for at least half an hour." He lay on his side and watched Ryan's arm muscles as he stretched. He lightly touched Ryan's armpit then ran his hand down his lats. Ryan kissed him and got up to don his underwear.

"Leave some food for me," Scott announced in a sleepy voice.

Ryan unlocked the door. "I don't usually eat in the shower."

The noise Ryan made coming back woke Scott up again. He combed his hair as Scott sat on the edge of the bed. A corner of the sheet over his lap was the only thing that covered him. "How late do you think we stayed out?"

Ryan put the comb down on the dresser. "I don't know, I didn't look at the clock before we crashed. Chris was done before me. You can get in the bathroom now."

"Yeah, yeah." He washed up and ate with Ryan and Chris. Muh talked incessantly as usual, as she put out plates, silverware, and the food. At one point, she told them the salmon was almost done and that she would have it ready for them for the trip back. Scott couldn't think about eating fish this early in the morning and finally ignored the thought. After breakfast they went back into the bedroom and Ryan took one of the blank poster boards from the corner.

"I'm gonna start on this today. And I'll probably be a boring dude because of it."

"Whadda ya mean?"

"I get pretty concentrated when I start drawing. And for it to look really good I have to have time and quiet."

Scott thought about that. It was neat that Ryan would bother to sit still long enough to really get into making the poster. "That's okay. It'll give me some time to hang out or drive around and see stuff."

"You don't care that I'm gonna be ignoring you?"

"No. I'll find something to do." Scott looked to his left and right, although there was no one there, and whispered. "But first you have to hug me."

Ryan laid the poster on the bed, which curled up by itself again, and waited. Scott didn't move and waited for Ryan to come forward. Ryan planted a kiss on Scott's lips and hugged him. He took a step back and looked at Ryan's face. "God, you kiss good."

Ryan pointed to his crotch. "And every time you kiss me this starts to crawl around."

"It's my intense good looks. Does it every time."

Ryan picked up the poster. "I know," he said to himself, but it was loud enough for Scott to hear.

The property was still in the shadow of the tree-covered hills when Scott went outside. Somewhere out back he heard a rooster crow several times. Otherwise, it was peaceful and quiet. He wondered if they'd have time to see Frank again after all. *What the hell, why not just stop by now,* he thought. *The drive would be interesting, even if Frank weren't home.* Jingling his keys, he quickly stepped into the Jeep. As he rolled past the ranger station, he saw two men standing outside in the back fenced area. It was the first time he'd seen anyone there since they'd arrived. One of the men wearing a park service uniform was using his hands to describe something. *That's probably 'Ranger Rick',* Scott surmised, with a smile. But as he reached the highway, he again focused his attention on seeing Frank.

He was sure Frank knew some things about Ryan that might be useful if they were going to have a meaningful relationship. He could have just asked Chris, but Scott was sure he was both too biased and not at all well informed. Muh wouldn't give him the picture he was looking for, since she didn't really know him the way he needed. Adina didn't know Ryan was gay, nor about the two of them, so that was out, too. And of his friends, Dolf and the others were completely out of the picture, and Ryan wasn't volunteering to see them until the party anyway. Frank was the only one, Scott was sure.

A sudden thought came to mind about what Frank might say regarding Scott's questions. In fact, he was sneaking around behind Ryan's back. But he surmised that Frank wasn't the type of person to lay a heavy judgment on him.

Satisfied that Frank would be fine with it, Scott took off. The closer he got to Frank's house, the more intrigued he was. He and his wife seemed to be living the perfect lifestyle. What a way to make a living, too. All he had to do was turn out one kayak a week and he'd have thirty-two hundred dollars in his hands every month. He knew it must be the guy's passion, but he couldn't imagine spending all his time in a little workshop, slaving over wood and fiberglass.

The turnoff to Prieto Canyon Road came up faster than he remembered. He slowed and waited until a newer model Jeep than his turned in front of him, then took the trek up the winding road. As he went up the switchbacks, Scott still avoided looking for the spot where Ryan had wrecked his car.

The road reached its highest elevation and came back down toward the small isolated canyon neighborhood. The quiet straightaway next to the river was the same as yesterday. No one seemed to be around, but he was sure most activity took place on people's back porches since they all faced the water. The doors to the workshop were open again and

Frank's van was in the driveway just like yesterday. Scott pulled up behind it and parked. Frank was inside, hunched over the same kayak on the platform in the center of the workspace. He saw Scott and waved. His big grin was infectious and made Scott smile back.

"Hi," Scott called out as he entered. He stood, hands in his pockets, with the kayak between him and Frank.

"Hey, guy." Frank furrowed his brow. "I don't see Ryan."

"He's working on a project for me. Mind if I visit for a while?"

"Not at all. In fact, I was just thinking how extra quiet it is here today. Carol's in town with our next-door neighbor 'til late and my customer won't be coming by until later today. So I don't have to run you off. He's working on a project?"

"It's a poster. I'm in a band back home. He's a great artist and offered to draw up a promo poster for us. He's gonna be busy for a few hours so I started driving around."

"I see. So, what's the name of the band?"

"Centauri."

"Like the star?"

"We thought about that and decided to stick with the mythology idea instead 'cause hardly anyone knows what Alpha Centauri is."

"So, like a Centaur."

"Yeah, but plural. Ryan came up with this idea of drawing a series of Centaurs all with bows shooting flaming arrows at a star. Hey, I guess we could say the star is Alpha Centauri after all. We're doing a couple of out of town gigs in a few months and needed some new advertising."

"Good imagery. What do you play?"

"I don't. Not in the band, that is. I play the flute, but for the band I run the soundboard and write lyrics."

"Original tunes, huh?"

"Yeah we have about a dozen that we're known for, but we do mostly standard party and rock tunes. We've played locally for about a year and we're finally getting some good gigs."

"Doesn't sound like a run-of-the-mill garage band."

"No way, this is for real."

Frank picked up a C-clamp and started unwinding it. "So what brought you out here?" he asked as he measured its opening for the beam he'd been working on.

"You."

"Should I be flattered?"

"I guess."

Frank scratched his chin and Scott noticed the texture of his beard as he did so. Scott also noticed He seemed so easy to talk to. Yet he really didn't know how he was going to extract any information from him about Ryan, so decided to just talk about what was on his mind. "I was wondering why you moved away from New York to live in the middle of nowhere."

Frank looked up. "Now, that's a long story. You know, I could use a break. Let's take a walk and I'll give you the abbreviated version." He tightened the C-clamp around the beam, then wiped his hands with a nearby rag.

They headed out of the shed and down the road. Frank gathered his thoughts for a moment before he started talking. "Once upon a time I was a stockbroker," he said, then chuckled. "Carol and I had it all— money, a condo *and* a house, lots of friends, everything. But I also had this nagging feeling that something was missing."

Scott's imagination went into high gear. From the sound of it, how could that have been true? One of his eyebrows went up. "Missing?"

"It's the age-old problem. I don't suppose you'd know about it yet. You get everything you could possibly want and still find something missing. It took a good long time but what finally became obvious was that what was missing was inside, not outside. I was so busy acquiring *stuff* I had forgotten to stop and listen to what I really needed. It's easy to do that when you live a high-powered lifestyle. Don't get me wrong, though. We were pretty comfortable." He chuckled. "One time I even woke Carol up in the middle of the night and asked her what we should buy next. I didn't have a clue what we wanted. I just knew that we had to spend some more money. What we really needed was a permanent vacation."

"So, you're from here?"

"No, I'm originally from BC but I've been a citizen since I was about your age. Carol and I dated in college and lived in New York for the same reason, to live an exciting urban life. It turned out that the life we really wanted was entirely different from what we thought. I sure am lucky to have married her. She's been with me through all the wild transitions."

Scott listened with great interest. He gave everything up to live in the woods?

He saw the questioning look on Scott's face and continued. "It's funny how we think life works a certain way because of TV and movies. Most people don't really think about how scripts are edited and how people get to practice their lines and rehearse. If one doesn't get it right, you get to redo the scene until you do. In real life, what's missing or not working only comes up when we're going along full blast. We end up being the editors of our lives only while we're running in real time."

Scott wasn't quite sure what he was driving at just yet despite recalling the rehearsals he'd done for the two plays he was in during junior year. He remembered Frank's hallway and the half-hidden trophies. "What about those karate trophies?"

"Oh, those. I was into Tae Kwon Do for about ten years. Winning was the only answer. And, to a *certain* extent, it is. But I ignored the finer elements of martial arts philosophy. It's odd how that happened. I was really good at it, but didn't fully appreciate the foundational training I received. And you know, you can only feel quiet and still inside when you're focused on making it that way. So, as time passed, I found myself focused only on acquisition and winning. My career reinforced that notion big time. I eventually completely forgot how to focus inside."

"So, how did you find this place if you were in New York?"

"Believe it or not, an ad in a newspaper. I worked near the New York Public Library, and every once in a while I'd stop in and check out newspapers from all over the country for real estate deals. I came across the ad describing this property and it was perfect timing. I was just about fed up with not knowing what I needed, and somehow, and to this day I don't know how it happened, I just knew moving out here was the right thing to do. After seeing it, I made an offer right away. We closed a month and a half later.

"I quit my job, sold off a lot of the useless stuff we owned, a *lot* of stuff. We gave a lot away, too. I knew I had to chuck everything as fast as I could before I backed out. Carol had a great job. At least it paid well. But it was high pressure and she wanted to quit anyway. It was the scariest thing we ever did. But it was the most important change of our lives."

Frank was hitting on something Scott could relate to now. "A transformation?"

"Yeah, that's the word," Frank answered, raising an eyebrow and looking at him.

"I know what you mean. I wish you could meet my Aunt Cinnamon. She's kinda like you, except for the New York part. She really knows how to talk to me. And she taught me how to meditate and look inside my head and stuff."

Frank cocked his head and looked at him. "Hmm. When I first came across meditation in my martial arts training, I thought it was such a waste. Amazing what being ignorant does to you. My whole day is a meditation now, almost like a song even. You play the flute, you said?"

"Yeah."

"You know the legend of the flute, don't you?"

"Legend? Does it have something to do with that one in your house?"

"Sure does."

"I've never heard of a 'flute legend.'"

"Well, my boy, the flute was originally an instrument of love."

"Love?"

"According to Lakota Sioux mythology, the flute was supposed to do your talking when you were in love but were too shy to let the girl know. It was always made of cedar and had a head on it shaped like a bird. According to the legend, the first flute was shown to a hunter by this bird that turned himself into a man. The bird, who was the man now, showed the hunter how to play. The hunter got the chief's daughter because of the music from the beautiful new instrument." He cleared his throat. "Now that's the extremely condensed version and leaves out the best parts, but mostly that's the story."

As they walked, a tuft of bird down drifted across the road and swirled at their feet before moving on. Scott watched it for a second before he said it. "Hmm, I played my flute for him at the VFW. Maybe that's how it started."

Frank studied the expression on Scott's face, not sure what he was talking about.

Scott couldn't contain himself anymore. He hoped Ryan would forgive him if it got back to him. He felt his heart ramping up. "I didn't just happen by," he said. "I wanted to talk to you about Ryan. This is kinda embarrassing, since I hardly know you, but I'm…gay. And we're, well, we're, like, going out."

Frank's face showed a wide grin and he stopped in mid-stride. "Well, well, well. That explains everything."

Scott stopped with him, his pulse still racing. "Explains what?"

"The missing part."

"Huh?"

"He *was* trying to tell me something that night."

Scott's face light up now that Frank had hit on it. And he was still surprised that Frank hadn't freaked out.

"You know, Carol's younger brother is gay and lived with us for a while back in Manhattan. I knew his partner and met plenty of his friends. I've known gay people all my life." Frank chuckled. "And now that includes Ryan."

"He's really the reason I'm here," Scott said excitedly, as they resumed walking. And immediately he told Frank everything. He told him all about how they had met and how the relationship started but left out all the sexual details, of course. He went into as much detail about Crawford as he felt comfortable with, then finished up with what he knew about Ryan's friends, his relationship with his grandmother, and then about his parents. Most importantly, he wanted Frank to provide some insight into what seemed to be really bothering Ryan. All during his narrative Frank noticed the intense interest with which Scott spoke.

He let Scott ramble on, not interrupting once during the monologue, but finally he spoke up. "His parents. That's the key."

"My aunt told me the same thing. Why do you think so?"

"The past only has power over you when it's forgotten or, in Ryan's case, ignored or repressed."

"What?"

"Psych 101. You know, we have available to us a full range of emotions. Some of us get caught in a whirlpool of the more powerful ones like hate or anger and then get stuck in them. Ryan got stuck in one of the whirlpools called grief and can't seem to get out. So it colors everything he does."

Scott tried to absorb what Frank was saying, but didn't fully understand. "I don't quite get it."

"Sometimes people are unhappy because they don't or can't change their minds. They don't allow themselves to make new decisions about old thoughts or experiences so that they can make themselves happy. Maybe it's human nature, but sometimes we generate grand, sweeping illusions of reality, then try desperately to get agreement about the illusions, just to be right. We sometimes end up getting ourselves into situations or relationships that keep us locked into the illusion. Sounds like he's pretending he's not hurting while he struggles with the hurt. He's so busy struggling he can't find freedom. It's a vicious circle. Based on what you said, he was struggling with grief *long* before he met Crawford. He let that guy fulfill his need to feel connected to a parental figure."

Scott wondered if it might be true. That Crawford might have actually provided something Ryan needed at the time, despite the result.

Frank continued. "It's unfortunate when we unconsciously follow certain destructive patterns. Sounds like Ryan acquired the pattern called 'getting hurt by someone you love.'"

Scott listened intently. The only person he'd ever remotely even heard talk like this was his aunt. But Frank was much more direct.

"Do you think he was in love? And how could it explain where we are now? I don't want to hurt him."

"Well, Crawford was clearly meeting some very powerful needs. Why else would Ryan have kept going back despite the secrets he had to keep, the lies he had to tell, or the abuse he endured? As for you? I don't know, really. Maybe he just likes you. Could be that things are finally changing for him. Maybe he's coming up for air."

"God, I hope so. He once told me he sometimes felt like he was drowning and I was like a life vest or something. I hope I don't get too waterlogged."

Frank chuckled at Scott's imagery. "I'm sure you've noticed that he has a rough time expressing his feelings," he explained. "That's typical for us guys anyway, you know. Especially if you're isolated from more, how should I put it, refined aspects of civilization. He needs to completely trust someone before he lets go. Maybe you're that someone. He only started opening up to me just before he had to leave town."

"You know, from the way he described you, you seemed like someone anyone could trust. I asked him why he didn't just tell you. He said he wanted to. But he just couldn't."

"I wish I had known him a little longer myself." It was almost as if Frank were genuinely hurt, the way he said it. "If only he had. He could have avoided wrecking his car and ending up in the hospital."

"And losing his license."

Frank stopped walking and turned around to go back toward the house. "I have a question for you."

"What's that?"

"What's eating *you*?"

"Eating *me*?" Scott had no idea what he meant.

"It's an ancient Inuit expression. It's something like, '*You eat life, or life eats you*'. I'm sure it originally dealt with their culture's observations of nature, but it has quite a deeper level to it, if you look at it just right." And with that Frank looked directly at Scott.

Scott repeated the expression several times but it didn't make much sense.

Frank prompted him. "What lessons are you learning with him?"

"Lessons? I don't know."

"Think about it. All of our experiences in life ultimately teach us something."

Scott was there to get insight into Ryan, not about himself. "All I can think of is how stuck he is."

Frank was fully aware that Scott thought Ryan was the only enigma here. What Scott didn't know was that Frank had been studying Scott's reactions and comments with great interest as well.

"No. The lessons *you're* learning. *Your* deepest fears that you have to confront anyway. Things *you're* avoiding that you know you can't. What is it that *you* don't want to face? What's *eating* you?" At that point Frank stared at him longer than Scott was used to.

Scott looked away as his dad immediately came to mind. *His dad was eating him.* Funny how they had a fully stocked restaurant and all this time his dad was eating *him*. The thought made him laugh.

"What's so funny?"

Scott sighed. "It's my dad. He's been on my case to be his partner. It...freaks me out to think I'd be stuck in a business I really don't have all that much interest in. And he doesn't know about me being...you know...gay."

"You live with your dad?"

"My mom and dad."

"You think he'd throw you out or something?"

"No. I don't think so. I guess it's just that we aren't that close actually. Besides, I don't live *in* the house. My bedroom's the guesthouse in the backyard. He seems to think I should follow his example or something. But music is my real interest." He kicked a rock and watched it skip into the ditch to his right. "I've tried to explain it to him but I don't think he hears me. He thinks pursuing music is a waste of time and money. And the only way I can go to college is if my parents pay for it. Since the only job I have is working at the restaurant, and they pay me, I'm kinda in a bind. Dad said he'd only pay for school if I go to college in town and take business courses. Do you think that's fair?"

"I can't judge your parents. And your father may seem angry, or act upset at some of the things you are or do, but in the long run, your parents will always love you no matter what. I can only remind you that it's important to remember that saying. And know this, there are plenty of ways to pay for college. Your parents don't have to provide the up front cash or even pay for it at all."

Scott repeated the phrase again. Maybe if he thought about it hard enough it would sink in just right and provide an answer to his dilemma. And what was that that Frank had just said? That his parents didn't have to pay for college? He hadn't seriously thought about other options and it suddenly struck him as odd that he had thought there was only one way to do it. He wondered why he hadn't ever talked to Colleen or Barry about how they paid for college. Maybe it was because he just assumed that since his folks had paid for his brother's schooling, that that was the way everyone did it. It dawned on him that he might be brainwashed and not even know it!

They eventually reached the workshop again and Frank immediately checked the tightness of the C-clamp by wiggling it slightly. He took one of the adzes and a wooden mallet in his hands and knocked a rough spot off a support beam with a quick tap.

Scott's eyes sparkled as the conversation lingered in his mind. "Dude, you are just awesome."

"I admire *you*. I know it takes guts to come out. And I have to say, to bother this much about a relationship? Are you sure you're only seventeen?"

"Just turned it."

Frank shook his head and grinned, then rechecked the spot he just shaved down with his thumb. "I'd be careful if you talk to Ryan about our conversation. He needs to know he has your total trust."

Scott held up his hands. "I was never here."

Frank laughed heartily. "And *I* never said a word."

Scott said goodbye and took off with a warm feeling spreading through his body. What a find! Frank was like a teacher, only it wasn't like in school. It was as if he spoke directly to Scott's mind. He came to get some insight into Ryan, and instead, discovered something he'd never heard before, 'You eat life or life eats you'. How powerful it sounded and yet how elusive it was. What else have I not been eating? Is life eating Ryan? What's eating us both? And now that some more of the clues were in hand, how to act on them was the problem. Ryan was certainly being closed-mouthed about the real problems that seemed to plague him. Scott knew he was nowhere near as perceptive as Frank, so getting Ryan to try to change his mind about things was going to be a serious issue.

Scott started a dialogue with himself as he drove back to the house. Shifting voices, he acted as if he were Frank, trying to get it just the right tone and resonance to sound like him. Somehow, he felt that if he could emulate Frank, he could assimilate his persona.

"*You and Ryan are in a play, Scott,*" he said aloud.

"A play?" he answered in his own voice.

"*You're acting, only neither of you know the script.*"

He stopped there and thought a moment about what he'd just said as Frank. "So that's why he's so confused?"

"*What makes you think you're not confused, too?*"

"I don't know, *he* seems confused."

"*But you're going to that stupid school...*" He stopped again. Frank wouldn't say 'stupid'. He'd say something a little different, he decided. "*You're going off to college and majoring in something you have no interest in...and you still haven't told your dad who you really are.*"

He quit the back and forth volleying with the imaginary Frank. There were two issues he had been avoiding, not one! *Whoa, I've been thinking they're the same thing,* he thought.

Now back in his own voice only, he spoke aloud his thoughts as they came up. "Just because I'm not out to him doesn't mean that I can't say absolutely 'no' to High Desert College. I've been going along with him with hardly an argument. Is that stupid, or what?" He smacked his palm against the steering wheel, feeling angry for letting himself be snowed over. "Fuck! I can't believe this. I'm going to let him tell me what I *have* to study? And I avoided arguing too much about it because I haven't told him I'm gay?" He took a deep breath. The heavy pine scent in the air cleared his head. This was the first time he ever seriously thought about these particular issues in this way. Here he was, as bold as his brother was and in some respects more so. But he was doing himself a serious disservice. He was feeling angry now, truly angry at the thought. And he was letting them dictate to him because he had been avoiding the most important issue of his own life. As he let the knowledge swirl around in his head, he realized he wasn't angry with his parents, but rather with himself. He felt like kicking himself over and over.

As usual though, Scott's thoughts drifted back to Ryan as he pulled up to the house. As he came in the side entrance he saw Ryan coming out of the bathroom. Ryan raced back to the bedroom door to block Scott's way.

"What's the deal?"

"I'm not done yet."

"So?"

"Go out and play for about another hour, then you can come back in."

"Go out and *play*?"

"You know what I mean."

Scott grinned and poked Ryan in the stomach with a finger. "I'll be outside." He turned back around and went back outside.

He shoved his hands into his pockets, then went to the Jeep. He looked at the Frisbee in the back seat for a moment, then took it out. Chris's truck was gone or Scott would have asked him to toss it around. Instead, he tossed it up as high as he could and caught it by himself. His progress against a light breeze led him across the clearing, then onto the tall grass along the edge of the yard. Now he was at the side of a steep hill covered in tall majestic firs. Walking a few yards up the slope, he spied a particularly thick trunk. Ducking under the lower foliage he looked up to the sky through the profusion of branches. The trunk was perfectly straight and the branches were regularly spaced. It seemed the perfect climbing tree. How long had it been since he'd climbed a tree? Not since he was eleven, he figured. He let the Frisbee drop to the bed of needles, climbed up about twenty feet, and looked out through the branches toward the clearing and the house. What a view! And there were at least another eighty or more feet to go.

A glob of sap on one of the branches got on two of his fingers, making them sticky. He rubbed them on the bark, which flaked off in paper-thin pieces. *To be up here with my boyfriend*, he thought. *What could be more romantic than kissing him while enjoying a view like this?*

He started back down, and, at the lowest branch, jumped to the ground and landed on the soft mat of needles underneath. Retrieving the Frisbee, he went back to the house and sat with Muh for a few minutes in the den. He spun the disc around on his finger as she talked.

As if on cue, Ryan came in. "Muh, any food around?"

The boys followed her to the kitchen where she seemed happy to fix them sandwiches right on the spot. Scott was starting to get used to the constant feasts she was so willing to make. After eating, Ryan suggested they go outside and toss the Frisbee around. Scott tossed it shot-put style as Ryan got the appropriate distance from him. "The poster's almost done?"

Ryan crouched and snatched the Frisbee from the air. "All I gotta do is fill in a little color."

"Let me see it before we boogie back."

"Maybe."

As they tossed it back and forth, Scott moved further and further toward the slope. He tapped the Frisbee five or six times into the air with his fingertips as it came down, then caught it behind his head. He stopped and shaded his eyes.

"Hey, let's climb up," he said, pointing to the tree he'd been up earlier. Thinking Ryan would think it was stupid, he didn't want to be too obvious that he wanted to kiss him in a tree.

"You climb trees?"

"Me? Not climb trees?"

"How would I know? There aren't exactly a hell of a lot where you live."

"It's been a while, but I still remember how."

He led the way to the one he had checked out earlier. They picked their way through the low branches and reached the trunk from opposite directions. He dropped the Frisbee and they started up.

A perfect open spot between branch levels gave them an awesome panorama of the valley some eighty feet below. Even this high up, the branches were still quite sturdy and they leaned back, resting their feet below on other thick ones.

Scott leaned over and kissed him. Ryan leaned and kissed him back. The branches they were touching shook. Scott felt they were in plain sight of anyone looking from below. *Hmm, who could possibly see us through all this greenery?* For long moments, they didn't speak as they took in the magnificent vista.

The conversation with Frank popped into Scott's head again. It seemed like there were a million things he could ask Ryan now. He chuckled as the word 'can opener' came to mind. Frank was a can opener. Frank had opened him to amazing new discoveries.

"What are you laughing at?" Ryan asked.

"A can opener," he said, knowing Ryan wouldn't know what he was talking about.

An unusual idea came to Scott's mind. A can opener? No script? He was going to make up some lines right now.

"Say, Ryan?"

"Yeah?"

"Tell me everything about your parents."

Ryan studied his face for a moment. "Why?"

"I just wanna know. What was your dad like?"

Ryan looked away. "He was an asshole."

"An asshole?"

Ryan's wouldn't look at him. "I hate him."

"How could you hate him? He's dead."

"Hated, okay?" There was touch of anger in his voice.

"Even after all this time?"

"Seems like it was yesterday."

Hmm, that's not getting anywhere, Scott thought. *Perhaps a different tack's necessary.* "What about your mother?"

"I hate her, too."

"Yeah, you hate 'em both."

Scott hadn't noticed it yet, but Ryan's eyes were fast filling with tears. They were impossible to hide now, since they started rolling down his cheeks. He gripped the branch in front of him as his knuckles turned white. His chin quivered and before Scott knew it, Ryan was all out crying.

For so long Ryan had managed to hold it inside. All it took was for Scott to ask him a few simple questions to make him cry like he was ten years old again. How in the hell did he do that?

"Mom said she was...gonna be home...before Christmas. She...never came home," Ryan said as he sobbed.

Alarm rang in Scott's head. *Oh, fuck* he thought, *what the hell did I do?* He wasn't sure how to handle what was happening. He had no idea Ryan was going to outright bawl up here. He just wanted a short romantic interlude and to get some stuff aired out about his parents.

"I was scared...of what dad would do to us...'cause she was dead and couldn't protect us. I was so scared and numb...I don't even remember being...at the funeral, God damn it!"

Scott put an arm around Ryan's back, keeping his other hand on the branch in front of him. He was getting really freaked now since things were rapidly getting out of control and they were precariously perched on the branch.

"I wanted him to tell me everything was okay, but he kept drinking more and more and not saying anything to us. I wanted him to hug me and tell me he...loved me." Ryan's nose was running now and he could barely speak coherently.

Scott became more and more frightened. As weird as what Ryan had told him about how Crawford was, it didn't have this kind of intensity. Ryan didn't bawl about him. This was completely different.

"But he didn't. He didn't tell me he loved me, or that things would be okay. Then, I found him dead."

Now Scott had to wipe tears out of his own eyes while he listened. Ryan was crying so hard that it was wrenching Scott's heart to pieces.

It took a few minutes, but Ryan's crying died down to what amounted to a whimper. Finally, he brushed tears from his face and just sniffled.

Scott fought for the right thing to say. "I know you loved them. I just know it." *It has to be true*, he thought, *or he wouldn't cried so hard.*

His mood shifted now. Resentment sounded in his words. "I hate that they left me alone. I hated finding my Dad's fucking dead body. But I…I never got to say I loved them before they…" Ryan's angry tone took Scott aback. *Where in the hell did that come from*, he wondered.

Ryan didn't finish his sentence and started crying again. Scott wondered why he ever suggested they climb the stupid tree. What if he kept crying all day? What if Ryan hated him for doing this to him? *No script*, he thought. *Fuck, that's why there* are *scripts!*

Ryan spoke again. His voice was only a whisper. His eyes were tightly closed and tears still dripped from his lashes onto his cheeks. "I…love you Mom. I love you…Dad."

Ryan's hands were firmly gripping the branch in front of him. He rested his forehead on them as his body shook. Tears ran down to his wrists and dripped off, sailing downward, downward to the ground far below. He barely made a sound as he shook against the branch. It was a long while before he stopped.

"My hands are tingling and I-I can't feel my lips," he said finally, as he straightened up.

"Breathe," Scott said. *Breathe*, he said to himself, too.

Ryan rested his forehead on his hands again and breathed deeply as Scott ran his palm up and down Ryan's back. He was hot and his shirt along his spine was wet from sweat. Ryan wiped tears every once in a while then finally sat upright again.

"I…I always loved them. I just never knew it 'cause I was so busy hating them."

Scott laughed as he wiped his eyes, too. "That sounds funny."

"It seems funny to me, too," he said through a sad smile.

"I still like you, in case you're wondering," Scott said, feeling apprehensive. He was sure Ryan would hate him now.

Ryan looked long and hard at him. "You're sure?"

"Yeah."

The branch shook as Ryan rubbed his hands together. "This is weird. My arms are tingling, too. I-I feel stupid...crying in front of you."

"*You* feel stupid? I'm sorry I *asked* about it."

Ryan looked out in the distance. "Sometimes I'd wake up in the middle of the night, even up to last year, and I'd think she was still alive. I woke up at Crawford's in the middle of the night once and went into the kitchen 'cause I dreamed she was there. He thought I was stupid when I told him."

"What an asshole from the start."

Ryan clamped his lips together and closed his eyes tightly. Tears sprang out again. His face contorted and he started to weep again, this time quietly and a lot more softly. "I'm sorry," he said as he wept.

Scott held onto his forearm. He had to brush more tears from his eyes as he waited for him to stop. He had never been in the presence of anyone who had cried like this before, and it was truly an emotional experience.

"I'm sorry. I was thinking about how much I loved her. I don't remember telling her. It feels like a knife going through my chest." It was hard for him to find a dry spot on the front of his shirt to wipe his face. Finally, the tears completely subsided and he was able to speak somewhat normally. "I'm thirsty," was all he said.

"There's only so much scenery I can take," Scott told him. He was relieved that Ryan was more composed. He was hoping they'd be able to start down soon. It was beginning to be extremely uncomfortable trying to keep his balance, watching to make sure Ryan didn't fall, and keep his own emotions in check, all at the same time.

Ryan was stiff from his awkward posture on the branch, and felt emotionally drained from the turbulent swirl of grief. They slowly and carefully climbed down. They jumped the last several feet and Scott sat motionless in the soft pile of needles looking at him.

"What are you looking at?"

"I'm waiting for you."

"Does it look like I'm still up there?"

"Your face. It looks like you were crying."

"I *was*."

"I could just imagine what Muh would say if she saw you."

Ryan looked down at his shirt. "I'll tell her my boyfriend made me cry."

'*Boyfriend*', Scott thought. He loved Ryan saying that. He raised his eyebrows and grinned. "No, say I spanked you!"

Ryan pulled off his shirt. "Don't get any ideas." He bunched it up and wiped his face. Scott didn't do anything except marvel at the contours of his deltoids, the sparse dark hairs that spread across the middle of his chest and the cute rolls of his abdominal muscles. Ryan continued to sit on his knees while taking deep breaths. Scott spun the Frisbee around on his index finger as he waited

Ryan stuck his chin out a moment later. "How do I look now?"

"Your eyes are red and puffy. You look like shit. We had better stay here for a while longer. I can slap you around a little to make it look good."

"You must want me to punch you out." He looked a lot more composed now.

Scott pushed him, not very hard, but with an ever so slight grin. Ryan pushed back, with the same playful smile, and they scooted out from under the branches of the sturdy tall fir tree and into the sunlight of the clearing.

*   *   *

That night in bed, Ryan lay on his back as Scott clasped his fingers. They had the window open, the ceiling fan going, and the sheet up to their waists.

"Ryan?" Scott whispered.

Ryan answered a few seconds later. "Yeah?"

"Whatcha thinkin'?"

"About her smile. I remember it now. I couldn't ever see it before. I remember the night she surprised me on my birthday the summer before she died. She bought me that hockey stick in the closet," he said, pointing in the dark. "I knew what it was but pretended I didn't. She thought it was funny when I played like it was a surprise."

Ryan clasped his fingers tightly with Scott's. With his other hand, he lightly stroked the hairs on Scott's forearm. He turned to his side and shifted so he could lay his head on Scott's bare chest. Listening to Scott's heartbeat, Ryan realized that although his mom was dead, she wasn't really gone. He was the one who had created the distance between him and everyone else who was left. Muh was always there when he needed her. Chris was always there, too, although he fought with him like any brother would. All that so he could hide his anger and sadness over his mom and dad. Scott hadn't laughed at him at all through the whole catharsis. Scott seemed able to withstand anything. Ryan was sure he would fall apart if he didn't stay on the alert for the next blow to his still bruised emotions. He had a long road ahead of him. Ryan reached his hand over Scott's chest and held tightly for a moment before letting go.

Scott ran his fingertips lightly over Ryan's upper arm, plucking at a hair now and then. How many nights had he longed to simply lay in bed with a boy and just touch him? To be with someone he could call his boyfriend? But this deal came with more than he had bargained for. He had discovered more than just a sexual outlet. He found someone who had an entirely different kind of life. One full of turmoil, sadness, and even suicide attempts. *Whew, who woulda guessed,* he thought.

And which was worse? Not having a father, or having one and not being close to him? Despite all of that, Scott stared at the ceiling and smiled as he thought how wonderful it felt to be with Ryan. It seemed he was on a wild roller coaster ride, but at least he was securely strapped in.

CHAPTER 24

The next evening, when Scott came out of the shower with a towel around his waist, his pulse quickened as he thought about the party. He was even envisioning the band, his band, setting up and playing in Adina's backyard, which would easily hold over one hundred people and would be a pretty decent venue for them. But that was just his imagination going.

Ryan was standing in front of the closet with a funny look on his face. Scott shut the bedroom door, then came forward in an attempt to see what Ryan was obviously trying to hide. "Close your eyes." Ryan said.

"What for?"

"You don't have to really, but I want you to be surprised."

"Just show me."

Ryan pulled out the rolled up poster that was bound by a large rubber band. The zipping sound as he pushed it off with several quick motions filled the quiet room. He held two corners and presented it to him.

The poster board had originally been white. Now it was adorned with a brilliant red border. A bright yellow eight-pointed star was in the upper right hand side. Below it, several Centaurs in a row were aiming flaming arrows at the star. In the background were the Little San Bernardino Mountains near Yucca Valley. A highly ornate single Joshua Tree was at the base of one of them. Beautiful calligraphic letters spelling Centauri flowed from the lower left to the upper right. The sky was a perfect gradient of cerulean blue at the top to a light sky blue at the horizon. The entire design had a unique surreal three-dimensional look to it.

"Wow! You drew that? It looks like a computer did it."

"Think the guys and Colleen will like it, too?"

He examined it in more detail. "If they don't, I'll personally kill every one of them."

Ryan rolled it back up and put the rubber band around it again. "It's staying safe in the closet 'til we leave."

Scott looked at the time as he put on his watch. "You should be getting ready."

"Not to worry. I'm showering now." Ryan quickly showered and came back to the room.

Scott had put on a pair of white button-fly jeans and a thin gray t-shirt with a single black silk-screen Joshua Tree on it. Ryan could just barely make out the tiny bumps of Scott's nipples through the thin material. Scott pulled a green and white vinyl jacket from his bag on the floor.

"Hey, I didn't know you had a letter jacket."

"It's too hot to wear during the summer back home. You said it might be chilly up here so I brought it."

"Jeez, my boyfriend has a letter jacket," he said in a low voice. Then louder, "Let me try it on, jock boy."

Scott handed it to him and Ryan dropped his towel. He donned the jacket over his naked body and stood in front of the mirror. "It's almost a perfect fit." His arms were an inch too long for the sleeves.

He checked out Ryan's rear. "I think you should go to the party like that."

He turned around and acted as if he was modeling a new fashion. "Not even tennis shoes?"

"Nothing except the jacket."

"Then you can't wear underwear."

With a grin, Scott kicked off his shoes then peeled off his pants. He shed his underwear and, aiming at Ryan's face, flipped them with a thumb and finger. They veered off to the right, missing him altogether. "You said no underwear," he said as he pulled his jeans back on and buttoned the fly.

Ryan inspected Scott's butt. It was obvious from the way his jeans rode up on him that he wasn't wearing them. "I was kidding."

"I wasn't."

"You're gonna turn on every girl at that party."

"Maybe even some of the guys."

Ryan took off the jacket and started putting on his underwear. "Maybe."

The doorknob rattled and the hinges creaked as the door slowly opened. It was Chris.

Ryan pulled his underwear up. "Don't you knock?"

"Who knocks around here? I'm going to Teresa's. I'll see you guys at the party later." He turned and left, shutting the door behind him. Ryan turned a dark green sweatshirt inside out, donned it, and then pulled on some blue jeans. Scott picked his bag off the floor and searched it a moment.

"Oh, birthday boy?"

"Yeah?" Ryan answered, as he combed the hair up off his forehead.

"I found this in my bag earlier. It had your name on it, so I figured it was yours."

Ryan snatched the envelope out of his hand. "What're you doing with my stuff in your bag?" he asked playfully.

Scott shrugged and grinned as Ryan opened it. On the outside was a little yellow chick. Ryan looked up at Scott for a second wondering what to make of it. On the inside it said "*Peep, peep, peep. Happy Birthday, your boyfriend, Scott.*"

Ryan snorted and gave him a quick hug. "Thanks. Come on, let's get outta here."

Scott stuffed his wallet into his back pocket, then pulled it back out, not happy with the bulge it made. He retrieved a twenty-dollar bill and his license from it, and stuffed them in a front pocket instead. He threw the wallet into his bag. "We're outta here," he said as he picked up his keys.

The driveway at Adina's place was already full of cars so Scott parked the Jeep several doors down the street. Once up the front walk, Ryan didn't knock when they reached the front door but rather just let himself and Scott in.

The family room was lit with candles placed on nearly every available surface. The undercounter lights from the adjacent kitchen added more illumination. Music emanated from the living room. It was also channeled into several rooms with different sets of wall-mounted speakers. About a dozen or so people were already there, only one of which Ryan recognized. They found Adina and Kathy in the kitchen shoveling ice from a bag into a big white bucket.

"Hey, guys!" Adina put down the bucket and grabbed Ryan around the neck to hug him. It caught him by surprise and he steadied himself with a hand against the wall. "I didn't hear the doorbell."

"We just walked in."

Kathy smiled at them, said hello, and took the ice bucket out back.

"Come here," Adina commanded Ryan. She took him by the hand briefly as they headed to the patio. Three more people were leaning against the railing near a keg of beer. Eighteen helium balloons were evenly spaced and tied to the rails around the perimeter of the deck. Each was a different color. On them was written *Happy Birthday* in black letters. In the middle of the patio below was a folding table with bowls of munchies on it. "I hope you're not embarrassed about the balloons."

Ryan glanced at Scott, then shrugged. "Not at all."

She pointed to the keg. "There's beer in the corner, and munchies here, down there," she pointed to the patio, "and inside. Tons of people are coming. It's gonna really kick!"

More and more people arrived, and with Scott in tow, Ryan mingled with several groups of people, and introduced him. Scott thought that Kathy would come on to him, but she seemed to be interested in another guy who was already there when they arrived. Later, back on the patio, he saw Adina pull back the insulation pads from the hot tub up on the enclosed gazebo. She pulled up the thermometer and checked the temperature. No one seemed particularly interested in an evening soak so far and he wondered if it was because it was too separated in its gazebo enclosure from the main activities on the deck and back in the house.

As it grew later and the party started to pick up even more steam, the boys split up and mingled in different directions. Oddly enough, Scott felt a little put off. It was almost as though Ryan seemed to be deliberately trying to keep his distance.

Three girls, whom Scott hadn't seen before, walked up the steps to the patio from the side of the house. He watched as they talked amongst themselves. The one with the darkest skin and long black hair had somewhat Asian features. Scott figured right away that it was Little Trout. A few minutes later he saw her make a beeline to Ryan when she saw him. He was talking to a group of guys in the living room. *It must be her after all*, he thought.

A guy about Scott's height came up to him just as he was watching her leave the patio. "Hey, I'm Craig." He swapped his beer cup to his left hand.

"Scott," he said as they shook. He had noticed Craig before but hadn't met him yet. He did notice, though, that he was one of the cuter guys, and it intrigued him that he had initiated the conversation.

"I see you noticed the arrival of the Elite Women's Club," he said, feigning a look at them.

"The what?"

Craig pointed with his beer hand. His plastic cup had his name crudely emblazoned on it in red magic marker. "The Bevy of Bitches," he said acidly.

"Oh, you know 'em?"

"Who doesn't?"

"I'm not from around here."

He scanned Scott's jacket again. "I thought I didn't recognize those colors."

"Yucca Valley Regional High. Southern California."

"*Southern* California? Who are you with?"

"I'm a friend of Ryan's."

"Oh. Little Trout used to go out with him."

"Yeah, I know. So tell me more about the 'Women's Club'."

"What's to tell?" He pointed to the two remaining girls. "Janice and her snotty friends think they're too hot for most of us."

Scott figured out the translation. "You must have been after her."

Craig nodded. "Janice is the one on the left."

The thought occurred to him that he didn't need Craig for any information. He had nothing to lose by talking to them himself. He could coyly ask them questions and get a completely different perspective on her and Ryan's old relationship. He watched the two girls. "Maybe they need someone from SoCal to help 'em out."

"Huh! You're wasting your time."

"I'll give it a try anyway," Scott lied.

"Don't say I didn't warn you." Craig downed the last gulp of his beer, licked the foam off his upper lip in one quick motion, and headed for the keg. Scott took another sip from his still half-full cup and wandered through the crowd toward them.

"Hi, name's Scott," he said as he introduced himself with the biggest smile he could muster.

The girls looked at him, then at the letter jacket, almost in unison. He was glad he'd worn it. It had been the perfect icebreaker all evening and now was no exception. Nonetheless, Janice eyed him suspiciously as he tried to make small talk.

There was a lull in the conversation almost right away. "Nice party, huh?" he asked.

"Yeah. Adina knows how to have a good time."

"So, you girls been to L.A.?" he asked, trying to maneuver himself to the question he really wanted to ask.

Janice's friend, Darlene, spoke this time. "My sister and her husband live near Disneyland. I've been there a lot actually," she replied with a great air of importance. With that, she pulled out a cigarette from her purse and lit it.

Scott continued his questions, avoiding trying to sound like he was coming on to either of them. He was careful not to let them know he knew Ryan either.

The girls were difficult at best. Figuring that no matter how he phrased any of the questions they would be interpreted as flirting, he quit playing around and came to the point. "I thought I saw another girl standing with you a few minutes ago. She looked Indian. I don't see her now."

Janice corrected him. "You mean Little Trout. She's Choctaw, not Indian. She went to talk to her ex," she offered, making sure Scott understood her meaning.

As the minutes wore on, Scott tried to get them to divulge more about Little Trout, still without being too intrusive. But both girls were becoming more standoffish and he felt like he was getting nowhere. He was sure they both knew a lot about Ryan because of her. Why were they being so aloof? Maybe Craig was right. They didn't seem to want to talk about anything, much less about Little Trout or Ryan.

He eyed the crowd for Craig but he wasn't near the keg anymore and too many people were in his line of sight to see him nearby. He scanned in the house for Ryan again, but couldn't find him either. Ryan and Little Trout seemed to have disappeared. *Maybe he's at the front of the house explaining me to her*, he thought.

Adina stopped by the girls to talk and immediately they were much more animated. Craig appeared at Scott's shoulder and motioned for him to go with him.

Once out of earshot, Scott spoke as they went into the house. "Those girls are ridiculous."

"I warned you, but you seemed determined. Not to worry though. I met some other hot babes. There's two of 'em and they're by themselves. We'll have our pick."

The fact that Craig seemed to have latched onto him seemed odd. He wasn't going to just tell Craig he was gay and make him go away though. Getting attention from someone he thought was cute was sort of a turn on, actually. As they went into the den Scott looked everywhere but still didn't see Ryan.

Pouring on the charm, Craig introduced Scott to the girls. "I told you I'd be back. This is the friend I was telling you about." Craig gave him a 'follow my lead' look.

Friend, Scott thought. *We just met*. Nonetheless, he decided to play the game, wondering where it would end up. "I'm Scott," he said, introducing himself.

The girls were indeed some of the cuter ones, he noted. They introduced themselves as Vicki and Lori. Craig seemed to be taken by Vicki and kept her occupied as he sat next to her on the couch. It occurred to Scott that his presence was simply to give Craig moral support to talk with her. Luckily, these girls weren't at all uptight like Little Trout's friends. Lori wanted to know all about the band, Yucca Valley, and how he got the letter jacket.

He wondered if he would feel something while talking to Lori and kept watching how Craig was reacting while talking with Vicki. At one point, he was sure Craig had a partial erection. *Could it be that merely* talking *to a girl could make him hard? Is it that easy with straight guys*, he wondered. *Maybe it is*, he thought. *I can listen to Ryan breathing sometimes and it can make me hard.* He noticed he was starting to catch a buzz from constantly sipping his beer.

A moment later, Adina came by and Craig caught her sleeve. "Hey, is that hot tub ready?"

"It's been ready," she said as she leaned on the back of the couch.

"Anybody in it yet?"

"I don't think anyone brought swimwear."

Hearing that, Craig raised an eyebrow and looked first at Vicki, then Scott. He could see it coming. "Who needs swimwear?"

"It's up to you." She grinned, then left.

Scott hoped he'd be spared the inevitable invitation by Craig to hop into a Jacuzzi with a bunch of naked girls, but suddenly found the idea intriguing. *It must be the beer*, he thought as he looked at his cup.

He scanned the crowd for Ryan again and still didn't see him. *Where is he*, he wondered. It was beginning to bother him that he hadn't seen him anywhere.

Craig turned to him. "Let's get a refill." Then to the girls, "You ladies need a refresher?"

They gave him their cups and Craig handed Lori's to Scott. He followed Craig through the crowd, then to the patio. "Hot babes and a hot Jacuzzi. Good thing I have you with me," Craig told him.

"Why do you need *me*?"

"I wouldn't have gotten this far unless you were here."

He rolled his eyes. He had been right after all about the moral support. No, it was the letter jacket. That had been his ticket to meeting people all evening. He should have known. But he figured he could just ride out the situation until he was bored.

Craig pumped Scott and himself each a cup, then filled the girls' empties. Scott did a scan of the back yard and still didn't see Ryan. Now he was becoming irritated about his absence.

They went up the couple of stairs of the gazebo to the hot tub. A switch next to one of the rails was labeled *Bubbles*. Craig flipped the switch on and the water rumbled as bubbles broke the surface. He watched the water swirl around for a moment, then flipped the switch off.

"This is perfect. They don't have suits, we don't have suits, and the bubbles'll keep 'em from being embarrassed. You seem pretty hot for Lori. This is your chance, buddy."

In a way, Scott was annoyed with Craig's typical heterosexual response, yet he was also interested. Was there a better way to see what Craig looked like naked? He already looked decent with clothes on. Scott would have to pretend he was interested in Lori. Yet, it was a small price to pay to see Craig with all his clothes off, he decided. And where the hell was Ryan? Scott looked over the railing to the backyard where a couple of people had just gathered, but he wasn't in that crowd either.

They quickly returned to the girls and Craig somehow persuaded them to go with them after all. Scott figured they wanted to get in the hot tub all along. In fact, Lori was paying way too much attention to him. He hoped he hadn't gotten himself into something he wouldn't be able to follow through with.

By now, most of the partiers were either inside the house or next to the keg. No one else was near the gazebo. Craig took the lead when they reached it and pulled off his shirt. *Well, that's a good start*, Scott thought. *He's especially cute without the shirt.* Scott laid his jacket over the railing and untied his shoes. It was so weird to just be shedding his clothes around people he just met. Luckily, the gazebo was enclosed and far enough off the patio to be somewhat private. Craig reached over and flipped on the switch again. Bubbles swirled around as before.

"You guys get in first," Vicki said.

Craig unbuckled his belt with much gusto, then paused. "Hey, I ain't gettin' in there with just a guy. You have to get in, too."

Scott figured Craig was buzzed enough to do anything, despite his protest. He scouted a cabinet behind him, opened it, and found a stack of towels. "Here." He held them out and the girls each took one. They gave each other a knowing look, which Scott noticed, as they started to shed their clothes.

Scott waited for Craig to get down to his underwear before he kicked off his shoes and stuffed his socks into them. Not wearing any underwear made it so that he had only his shirt and pants left to take off and he didn't want to be completely naked while they were still mostly dressed.

Craig turned around and shed his underwear while Scott pulled off his t-shirt and dropped his pants. They both slid into the bubbly water and sucked in their breath as the hot water hit them. "Come on in, the water's g-g-reat."

Just before Craig turned around, he flipped off the overhead light. Scott was disappointed that he didn't get to see anything more of his crotch except for a dark patch of pubes. Despite that, he saw that everyone was noticeably pale. Not a tan in the crowd except his.

The girls were sly. They had on bikinis under their clothes, which they conveniently didn't mention before. *So, that's what the look was all about*, Scott thought. But Craig was completely nude and that's all Scott wanted to see anyway. The girls stepped down into the water, then slid down to the underwater seats until the bubbles were up to their necks.

It was obvious that Craig was playing footsie with Vicki right away. Scott wanted to slip his hand onto his crotch and see if he was hard. Just thinking about it started making him hard and he tried to stifle the thought. Lori seemed to have the same thought, but about Scott. The quick brush of her hand and the furtive look she gave him almost paralyzed him. It was a good second before he figured out that she couldn't read minds and had no idea he was thinking about Craig. Her interest made him nervous despite his buzz. And for sure, she had felt him partially hard. It wasn't the first time a girl had touched him there, but it was the first time one had ever touched him while he was completely naked.

Craig's fantasy scenario didn't pan out at all because some of the people on the back porch discovered them. Some razzed them while the rest just took casual notice and continued to talk amongst themselves. Craig told the hecklers they were jealous and made a poor attempt at splashing them as a couple of them came up the stairs.

Adina stopped by, flipped on the overhead light, and knelt down to check the thermometer again. "I can't believe you guys are in there with nothing on."

Vicki rose up just enough to show Adina the straps across her shoulders. Adina saw them and grinned. Vicki smiled back at her before the boys in the hot tub noticed their quick interaction.

Craig raised his beer in a mock toast to her. "What are you waiting for? Come on in."

"Sorry, the hostess has to keep her clothes on at all times."

Craig turned to Vicki and made goo-goo eyes with her as Scott motioned for Adina. She knelt down by him. "Have you seen Ryan?"

"Yeah. They just came down."

"Down?"

She cupped her mouth and whispered to him. "I told him and Little Trout that they could use the guest bedroom."

Scott's body stiffened a little and a look of alarm crossed his face. "For what?"

She giggled. "What do you think?" She paused while studying the look on his face, not realizing the implication of what she said, and left. She switched off the lights as she went down the steps.

Scott was furious at the images going around in his head. *What do I think?! What do I think? I think he's an asshole, that's what I think! I'm his boyfriend!*

Adina explained it clearly enough. They had disappeared for the longest time and she'd even let them use a bedroom. *That's what straight people do. Ryan's not straight! And what about Little Trout? If she were so hot, why is she still pursuing my boyfriend? Why doesn't she have another boyfriend already? What the fuck is going on here?*

Lori noticed him being distracted about something. "Hey, what's wrong?"

"Nothing," Scott spat. "It's…too hot. I'm gettin' out."

Lori and Vicki looked at each other. "I need some water," Vicki said.

Craig wasn't exactly being obnoxious, just too tipsy to care. "No, no, no. You ladies have to stay. *He* can go."

Lori finished her beer and put her cup down in a wet footprint. "I'm thirsty, too."

Craig gave in without further protest. As he exited the water, Scott was able to see Craig fully naked now since he had turned toward the porch and its lighting illuminated his crotch. He saw what he wanted to see this time, but the thrill of it was dashed by what he had just learned. Scott quickly dried off and put his clothes back on, except for his jacket, which he clutched tightly in his fist. They all stood on the patio for a few moments, after drying off, to cool down in the light breeze. Finally, he excused himself so he could look for Ryan.

He and Little Trout were in the corner of the living room on a pile of huge throw pillows. Scott stood in front of him, tossed his jacket over the back of a chair, and crossed his arms. "You!"

Ryan looked up, surprised at the sudden outburst. "What?"

Scott jerked a thumb in the direction of the patio and motioned with his head at the same time.

Little Trout touched Ryan's shoulder and whispered something in his ear.

"I'll be right back," he said loud enough for Scott to hear. He followed right behind as Scott led them to the dark of the backyard.

Craig and the girls were talking in the gazebo with a couple of other people. Scott didn't look at them as they went past. The two boys stopped behind the branches of a wide Blue Spruce at the end of the yard. He wanted to hear it from Ryan's mouth. "Where the hell have you been?" Anger was resonating in his voice.

Scott's tone didn't sit at all well with him. "With Little Trout."

"I hope you don't think she's still your girlfriend or something." He couldn't believe he felt so angry. He was really jealous! His emotions were getting the best of him and he was still feeling overheated.

"What the hell does that mean?"

Scott pointed behind himself to an upstairs window. "You were up there for a good hour."

Ryan glanced up to the window then back to him. He started walking in a tight circle around Scott. "It took us that long…"

Scott cut him off. "An hour?!"

"We would've been in there longer if someone hadn't knocked!"

Scott threw his hands up in disbelief. "You fucked her, didn't you?"

Ryan was pissed now. "Yeah, I fucked her," he said, now much louder, but not caring that he had Scott going now.

"How could you *do* that?!"

Ryan looked back at the patio to see if anyone was watching or listening. Scott had said it pretty loudly. "You don't tell me what I can and can't do!" he shot back.

Scott lowered his voice. "Well, you don't go around fucking *girls* while you're boyfriends with someone."

Ryan pointed a finger at him, angry as well, and directed all his focus at him. He deliberately kept his voice low though. "What the fuck do you know about girls? You wouldn't know what to do with one."

Scott's mind was reeling. The annoying suspicion he had had earlier was, in fact, a worse reality. Ryan was even arguing his case!

From his vantage, now that they had circled each other a few times, Scott saw Craig peering at them from the gazebo. They must have heard them shouting.

Craig pointed and his entourage joined them, all with cups in their hands. It was poor timing, to say the least. "Hey, what're you guys doing back here?" he asked innocently, once he was within earshot.

"Nothing," Scott spat as he glared at Ryan. "He was just leaving."

"That's right," Ryan agreed. Without another word, he turned around, stomped back across the backyard, and went into the house.

Scott stayed put for now. He was angry, and glad he'd gotten Ryan out of his face. But he couldn't keep his mind off what Ryan had done with Little Trout. *How could he? He hadn't seen Little Trout in months and he just up and fucked her!*

Now that Ryan was acting so weird, so completely unlike the last week, Scott felt a queasiness that cut through what little beer buzz he had left. He made up an excuse and left the group to head back into the house. As he approached the sliding doors, he saw Ryan in the foyer talking to a tall thin guy with foppish, dirty-blonde hair. The tall guy wore a black t-shirt and jeans with holes in the knees. As he watched, he saw that they, too, were arguing. The guy was pointing at Ryan and making all sorts of threatening gestures.

Scott turned away and went to the railing on the edge of the patio, not quite knowing what to do. *Jeez, how things change in just ten minutes,* he thought. He took one of the balloons and squeezed until it popped. No one noticed. After long minutes, he was still feeling that unaccustomed mixture of anger and jealousy, and had no idea what he should do or say. In frustration, he sighed as he crossed his arms, and glanced down at his watch. It was nearing one o'clock. Somehow, he'd have to contain his anger so he wouldn't completely ruin the party.

By the time he made it back inside, Ryan was again nowhere to be seen. The tall blond was standing with two other guys now, both of who had noticeably longer hair than anyone else at the party. One wore a black leather jacket and jeans that were ripped at both knees, the other a heavy metal band t-shirt and black riding boots along with jeans with only one knee ripped. Scott was immediately not impressed with any of them.

He wondered if Ryan was with Little Trout again. When he found her, she was in the den with her two friends now. Ryan wasn't with them. *Damn it!* he thought. *I can't let something like this get in our way.* Adina came down the stairs from the second floor as he pondered what to do. "Hey, is Ryan up there again?"

"No. He just left."

"He left?"

"Yeah, I saw him when I looked out the bathroom window."

"Which way did he go?"

"He was getting into Chris's truck."

Before she could say anything else, he whirled around to look for Chris. Why would Chris give him his keys? Chris knew Ryan didn't have a license and he hadn't seemed to want to do him any grand favors so far this week. Where would he have gone anyway, back home? And, why? To pout?

Adina spoke as he turned around. "What's wrong?"

He turned his head and answered curtly. "Nothing." When he turned back, he spied Chris nearby. Teresa was on his lap by one of the speakers in the living room. Scott went over and sat down next to them, wearied by the intensity of the last few minutes.

"Hey, Adina said Ryan left in your truck."

"Yeah. He said he needed some air."

"Some *air*?"

"Yeah, he and Dolf were bitching each other out about something."

So the dirty blonde's the infamous Dolf. He eyed Dolf still standing there with his buddies. "Did he say where he was going?"

Teresa leaned forward. "He was just going to the bridge, you know, the one out on the main road? It was weird too. It looked like he was about to cry or something."

I hope he was crying.

Chris and Teresa both were wide-eyed at the sudden look on Scott's face. The bridge. *Not the bridge!* The worst thoughts of his life flashed through his mind as he leaped up, found his jacket, grabbed it, and dashed outside.

The relative quiet of the front porch was startling as Scott stopped for a moment to catch his breath and pull on the jacket. All he could think of was their argument, then whatever it was Ryan was arguing about with Dolf. Pissed off or not, Scott wouldn't let him do it. He closed his eyes and made fists. "Please don't," he said aloud. He fought to compose himself, then dashed to the Jeep. As quickly as he could he started it and headed toward the main road.

"Down and to the left," he said to himself as he turned off the tape player. "Then about a half-mile." He said it aloud only to hear a voice to soothe his fear. "He's gotta be there already. *Fuck*, why didn't I look for him sooner?" *I didn't because I was angry*, Scott thought. And he still was, but it was mixed with certain fear now. *Is he completely fucking crazy? It's his birthday!*

Scott was doing seventy-five mph after he sped out of the neighborhood. The bridge's arches shined in the light of the half-moon as it loomed ahead of him. He saw Chris's step-side truck parked on the shoulder where the asphalt ended and the concrete bridgeway began, and pulled to a stop behind it. He bolted out and looked in the bed, then the cab. No Ryan. He whirled around and scanned the length of the bridge. No movement, no one hiding, no one crouching. Still, no Ryan. The only sounds he heard were crickets at the edge of the bridge and running water below. Without hesitation he ran out onto the middle of the lanes on the bridge and looked all around. He couldn't see anything moving from there either. He yelled Ryan's name once but only heard an echo of his own voice. He dashed to one of the shoulders.

If Ryan had jumped, Scott surmised, he would have had to climb up a short way, step over a couple of cross girders, then a short chain link fence. It would be difficult, but it could be done.

It was impossible to see much directly below in the dark from his vantage. He was terrified of what he might find, but he figured he'd have to climb down to the riverbank. Adrenaline surged through his bloodstream. His breath was hard to catch. He could feel his hands shaking. Every horror movie he'd ever seen before seemed to be playing in his head at that moment.

He sprinted back toward the truck. The dirt at the shoulder where the asphalt ended and the concrete began was cut into by years of runoff. Its slope would be somewhat manageable if he slid down it. He remembered earlier in the week the peninsula of rocky ground under the bridge and what seemed to be easy access to the river's edge. If he could just maneuver down the embankment, he'd get there. It didn't matter that he had on white pants or if his prized jacket got dirty. Finding Ryan was much more important. That is, if he wasn't already carried away by the swift current. The thought of it stung him in a way he'd never felt before and made him tremble all over.

The moon, high in the sky, lit the area with an eerie glow as it reflected off the girders and leafy foliage. He crouched down and slid flat-footed down the embankment on the soles of his tennis shoes. What sounded like thousands of crickets assaulted his ears as he descended. The stark girders of the bridge looked ghostly as he became swallowed up in the darkness below. The murky water ahead of him contrasted with the gray rocky shoal in the pale light. He grabbed onto grasses that grew along the ravine to keep his balance as he finally reached bottom. He stood up, trying to get his bearings in the silvery darkness. A lump was caught in his throat as he slowly approached the mired log in the middle of the shoal. Ryan was on it and he was perfectly still.

He approached slowly. He had a hard time keeping any semblance of composure. It was another second before he realized that Ryan was just sitting there, very much alive. He was facing away from him, his head down.

"Son of a *bitch*! What the *hell* are you doing?" Scott put his hands on his hips and stopped about five feet from him, waiting for an explanation.

Ryan looked back briefly, swiveled around, slid off the log, and leaned back against it. He wasn't at all composed, yet didn't seem startled to see him. Even in the relative darkness, Scott could see his cheeks were wet.

"I'm sorry," Ryan said. Scott didn't reply. "I'm *sorry!*"

"What the hell are you doing here? You scared the *fuck* out of me!" He was still trembling.

Ryan continued to apologize. "I'm sorry I yelled at you back there. I was stupid. Stupid like I've been my whole *fucking* life."

"What the fuck *are* you doing?" Scott demanded again, this time not yelling as loudly.

"I had to get away from Dolf. I was so embarrassed I had to leave."

"How do you think I felt?" He raised his arm and pointed upward. "You went off and fucked Little Trout, *you dick!*"

"Please, I can explain."

All Scott wanted to do right now was pummel him. Nonetheless, he answered. "Start," he commanded as he crossed his arms. But even as he was feeling angry, he could see that Ryan was somehow feeling deeply hurt about something.

Ryan held his hands up and gestured wildly. "I'm sorry about her. I'm sorry about Crawford. Fuck Dolf and his dickhead friends. They're all assholes. I'm-I'm trying to tell you I figured this mess out."

Scott heard him at last and took a few steps forward. "Whadda ya mean?"

He turned slightly so he wouldn't have to face him. "I fucking snapped to what I've been doing. With Dolf and Crawford, to Chris, and Muh, and Frank, and especially...*y-you*. Fuck, fuck, *fuck!* It hit me when Dolf...laid into me." He shook his head. He turned around and pounded the smooth log surface with both fists. "I've been such an ass-hole to everyone I-I care about."

"Asshole isn't the word for it," Scott said sternly, pointing at the huge steel structure overhead. "I thought you *jumped*!"

Ryan looked up at the cold metal, then faced him. "I can't even believe I ever tried to do that."

Scott followed as Ryan walked around in a random pattern on the sand. "I'm sorry about Little Trout. I didn't expect to go upstairs with her. But she wanted to talk and I *had* to. She wanted to know why I left without saying anything—so I told her what happened. She started kissing me and telling me she was sorry. Then she wanted me to take off her bra. But I held her off."

"What? You *didn't* fuck her?"

"No. I didn't."

"Then why did you say you *did*?"

"Because! You were bitching me out and I wanted you to shut up."

"But to say something like *that*?"

"I wanted you to feel *hurt*."

"Well, you *asshole*. It *worked*!" He was yelling again because he was still feeling the adrenaline. The fear he had felt hadn't completely faded either. He found the lump in his throat again, too.

Ryan stopped talking as tears streamed down his cheeks. He wiped them with the back of his hand and sniffled. He was completely vulner-able. It was a different situation from just a half hour ago.

"Scott, I'm sorry I ever called you a fag. I'm sorry I led you on about what we did upstairs. Now Dolf! The only reason I ever hung out with him is 'cause I thought he was good looking. And his buddies, too. But I couldn't ever admit it. I knew he was an asshole, but his attitude rubbed off on me before I knew it. Then I was hanging out with him so much I-I just couldn't up and say 'fuck you guys.'"

"What did you do, come out to him?"

"No. You wouldn't fuckin' believe it. Crawford came to the lumber store looking for me a week after I left. He asked Dolf where I was. Dolf asked him why he didn't know if he was such a close uncle. Then the asshole came on to *Dolf!* Dolf told me that he had figured the whole thing out then and knew what was really going on between Crawford and me."

"You gotta be kiddin.'"

"I'm not. Dolf wanted to know why I was hanging out with *him* if I was really a...fag. He wanted to fight about it and I...I just snapped. It hit me all at once. It was like I'd been setting myself up for disaster from the first minute I talked to Crawford....But I did it only because he was the first person who was ever interested in me." He coughed and stopped to clear his throat. "I couldn't say no to him because I just wanted someone to hug me."

He fell silent for a moment and sniffed back more tears. "But I only want *you* to hug me. I don't want to fuck girls, I don't want Dolf as my friend. I don't want to see Crawford ever again. I just want you as my boyfriend and that's all I want. I've just been *completely* stupid."

That finally did it. Scott melted. Any lingering doubts he may have had disappeared. He came forward in a lunge, grabbed him, and hugged him as hard as he could as he listened to Ryan's ragged breathing. It was if he were hugging a small boy who had just scraped his knee, who felt more frightened than anything else.

Ryan talked over Scott's shoulder. "I came here to sort it out. Damn it, I'm *eighteen,* but I feel like my life didn't even start until I-I met you. You don't know. You just don't know. Please don't say you hate me."

Scott hugged even tighter now, feeling tears in his own eyes. "I don't, I don't."

Ryan pulled back and leaned on the log again. "When we were in Parker I was scared it was happening again. I'd had this perfect chance to get away from him and it seemed I was just going right back into the same situation. But you-you were different." He reached up and caressed Scott's face. "And after you just about demanded I be your boyfriend I wanted to tell someone I had a *real* boyfriend this time, but there was no one to tell. You aren't at all like him. And you didn't know how much of an asshole I was then."

"Yes I did."

Ryan ignored his jab and continued, although his voice was racked with sadness. "But you changed me. Damn it, after I met you I was happy for the first time I can remember. You didn't know it, but you did something to me. When we went camping in the Monument, I wanted to tell you that you were the only person I ever thought was worth anything. But I just couldn't then 'cause I was hurting so much.

"I know I'm not the best person to hang out with. But please, please, *please* believe me: I want you to keep being my boyfriend."

Scott grabbed him again and hugged, not believing what he was hearing. Soon enough Ryan's sad face was awash in smiles and he finally laughed. His laughter was different. It was full and with a new tone that Scott didn't know was in him.

They spent long moments kissing until a vehicle stopped above them. A bright flashlight panned down on them. Turned out it was a cop. He ordered them to come up and wanted to know why they were stupid enough to park their cars on the bridge. Ryan made up an excuse the officer bought about why they were down there but the cop checked out the Jeep and the glove box in Chris's truck for anything suspicious. They knew the cop was looking for drugs, but also knew he wouldn't find any. Luckily, he only asked for Scott's license, made small talk about Southern California for a few minutes, then let them go with a warning. Ryan was lucky this time. His license was still suspended.

"Don't let me catch you parking your vehicles on a bridge again. Even on the shoulder of one," the cop said before he took off.

When they arrived back at Adina's house, Scott went in to give the keys to Chris. He avoided Dolf, who was still there. They went home and spent the next couple of hours talking and making out on Ryan's high soft bed. Eventually Scott started to feel the day's fatigue. He settled in next to his boyfriend. He didn't want to, but sleep started taking him away. He rested his hand on top of Ryan's arm, placing it in such a way that he would be woken up if Ryan moved. It was just past 4 a.m. when they both fell asleep.

CHAPTER 25

A thin silent stream of fog was flowing down the mountainside along
the edge of the clearing outside the window when they awoke only
a few hours later. Bleary eyed, Scott rose up and peered through the curtain momentarily to see what it was like outside. He woke Ryan and
pinned his arms above his head as he straddled him. He slid his butt
back and forth across Ryan's crotch, then leaned down to kiss him. He
knew his breath must smell really bad but didn't care. Ryan's smile
showed he was still in good spirits.

"You still like me," Ryan asked.

To Scott, it was if nothing else mattered except for the fact that Ryan
was still alive. Never in his wildest dreams would he have ever concluded that the week's events would have transpired. There was no way
he could possibly have known that Ryan would have burst open like he
had, spilling his secret life out, shedding layers of emotional pain in
waves of tears, and being himself like no time before, at least no time
that Scott had known him. Nonetheless, he knew Ryan would have a lot
more opening up to do before he was completely alright. Then, it just
came out before he could think about it. "No. I love you."

Ryan loosened his arms from Scott's grip. "No, you don't."

"I do, too." He dropped to Ryan's side. He stared up at the ceiling,
then turned his head to look at him.

Ryan studied his face then looked down at Scott's body. Yes, the hard-on he could definitely understand. Scott's race to find him last night, he could also understand. Now Scott was saying the words he never understood. He thought about what he really meant. "You're just saying that."

"Do you love *me*?"

"How could you love me?"

"Quit trying to figure it out!" Scott reached behind his head, picked up his pillow, and hit him with it. Hard.

Ryan pushed the pillow back and turned away from him. "It doesn't make any sense after what I did to you last night."

"Idiot, it's *because* of last night."

Ryan faced him again. Scott laid on the pillow at Ryan's side. His eyes darted back and forth to both of Ryan's. "Every time I look at you. Every time you touch me. Last night, when I hugged you before I fell asleep, just a minute ago when I kissed you. It's this funny feeling I have, like we're supposed to be together." He dropped his eyes away as he thought of school starting in only a few weeks. The intense amount of time they'd been spending together would soon be cut to almost nothing and he wasn't sure how he was going to handle that. He looked back at him. "At least for now."

An alarm went off in Ryan's head but he didn't suppress the feeling this time. Scott was the only real friend he had. Well, maybe friend wasn't the right word. And it was impossible to deny the momentum of the last several months. He reached over and hugged Scott as hard as he could, shutting his eyes tightly as he did so. He didn't want to say it too loud in case it come out wrong, so he whispered in Scott's ear. "I love you." It was the third time he'd said that this week, but the first time in years he had said it to anyone who was alive.

An insect outside hit one of the windowpanes with a dull thump and broke the intensity of the moment. Scott crawled off the bed but kept his eyes on Ryan, wondering if he was being truthful, even now. "I'm first in the bathroom this morning," he said as he left the room.

After breakfast, Scott put the last bag in the Jeep and went back to the bedroom to make a final search for anything he might have missed. Ryan was just getting off the phone when he came into the kitchen. He played with the long black tangled cord for a moment. "That was Adina. She wanted to know why we left so early."

"What'd you tell her?"

"That we had some things to talk about," he said, and left it at that. Scott ran his eyes down the front of Ryan's shirt and reached his crotch just as he heard footsteps behind him.

Muh had two shoeboxes which she laid on the kitchen table. She opened one of the lids for a moment to show them succulent strips of smoked salmon laying in waxed paper. Funny how they smelled good this morning, even this early, and Scott couldn't wait to be hungry again once they were on the road. She tied some string around them, then held her arms out to hug Ryan. She hugged Scott with equal affection. "I'm so glad you two are friends. It's nice to have so many handsome men in my house. Please come back sometime," she said to Scott.

"I have a feeling you might see me again."

Ryan was standing across from him and made a face at him behind Muh's back as he picked up the shoeboxes. Chris came in to the kitchen and half-heartedly hugged his brother. Scott shook his hand and they all went outside.

The sun was just now making its way up over the forest. The fog, which was earlier confined to only a part of the property, was now disbursed all over the place. Large patches of blue here and there above them indicated that it was rapidly burning off. Muh continued to talk to Ryan from the passenger side as Scott started up the engine. He turned his head to check their stuff stowed in the back seats. The glass globe he found on the beach was carefully wrapped up in an old towel on the floor behind him. Next to it was the rolled up poster. He couldn't wait to show it to the band and later place it on an easel at the Marine base outside the auditorium.

Almost as an intrusion, the discussion that he had had with his parents about college went through his mind. His dad had told him that no seventeen-year old boy could possibly know what was best for him. Well, he was seventeen now and knew *exactly* what was best for him. That was something he was extra sure of now. If he wanted to major in music or work in a music studio, he had every right to pursue it. He had seen, vicariously through Ryan, what happens when one does things against one's will. It seemed vastly more important that he do just as he wished than to go through life pleasing everyone else. He took a deep breath and slowly let it out. He expected further heated discussions with his parents on the subject. UCLA seemed like a good place to start. Scott just realized they'd both be freshman at the same time. That is, if Ryan actually ended up there after all. Scott made a mental note to check their catalog to see if they had a decent music school. Just the thought of it made his pulse race.

He still had his promise to keep with his brother about telling his dad. He had a lot to talk about with him. Things were going to be a lot different after he returned. In fact, it seemed that senior year was going to be quite a bit different than he ever suspected. *I'll* be eating life from now on, he resolved. "Thanks, Frank," he said under his breath.

Muh said good-bye for the thirty-ninth time and waved at them as Scott turned the Jeep around and headed down to the end of the drive. He stopped and hesitated longer than seemed necessary. Ryan gave him a questioning look since there were no cars coming in either direction. Scott opened the glove box and pulled out the 5 x 7 photo that he had put there earlier. He looked at it briefly, then at Ryan sitting next to him. He shut the glove box, reached out to take Ryan's cap off him, and stuck it on his own head. Grinning, he stuck the photo above his visor, adjusting it so that he could just see Ryan's face looking out at him. He shifted into first, pulled out onto the road, and headed south.

About the Author

Mark Ian Kendrick is the author of five novels.

Desert Sons is the first of two stories that trace the relationship between Scott and Ryan.

Scott Faraday, sixteen, has no idea that his world is about to radically change. Scott is in a small-town rock band, is fun loving, and out—but only to a select few. When Ryan St. Charles comes to live with his uncle in Scott's hometown of Yucca Valley, CA, they meet and form a tentative friendship. Ryan is a brash seventeen-year old who has just severed a long relationship with a man, but still considers himself straight. As Scott and Ryan's friendship develops, Scott begins to suspect that Ryan might be covering up that he's gay. Scott is sure Ryan has no idea that Scott is gay, so he comes out to him. The result is that Scott transforms their friendship into his first real relationship. Then, Ryan's hidden past comes into view. Scott is not at all prepared for what he discovers. Despite their vast differences, Scott sticks with him, and learns more about himself and relationships than he ever thought possible. This novel spans the summer that forever changed them both.

Into This World We're Thrown is the sequel to *Desert Sons.*

In this dramatic conclusion to *Desert Sons*, Scott and Ryan's relationship takes on new twists and turns. They both come out to those they love and have to confront their responses. Ryan's grandmother, his long-time caregiver, dies, which causes Ryan to re-evaluate his entire life. The band Scott is in might break up. Scott discovers he has secret allies, a schoolmate who's bent on having Scott be his no matter what, and a twisted foe. Will his secret admirer permanently ruin his now tenuous relationship with Ryan? Will Scott's foe turn his life into a living hell? Will Ryan pull himself from the depths of his emotional turmoil? Can the boys remove the bitterness that develops as a rift opens and widens between them? Can they uncover and express their love for one another before it's too late? All of this and much more is revealed, explored, and concluded in this exciting sequel.

Stealing Some Time is a gay science fiction adventure story. Told as a trilogy, this series follows Kallen and Aaric and the two time periods they come from.

Book I: World Without You

It is 2477 CE. Much of the world has long since become desert due to the unchecked use of fossil fuels in centuries past. But the world of the 25th century is an advanced one, where technology rules, where ruthless leaders have the upper hand, and where water is the limiting factor for all of civilization. Eighteen-year old Kallen Deshara is entering his obligatory 5-year stint in the North American Alliance's Air Defense Force. While in boot camp, Kallen comes to terms with the fact that he's gay. He even finds his first gay relationship with a fellow graduate recruit, but is dumped shortly after it starts. While nursing his wounds, he finds his second relationship in a fellow student while in the ADF's Schools Division. After being dumped again, Kallen is shipped off to his first duty station in the mountains at the edge of North America's Great Central Desert. There, Kallen becomes a force to be reckoned with as his natural talent in photronics, the 25th century form of software, comes to the fore. Another relationship follows. This time with an officer. But it falls short again. When called to Central Security, he's sure he's walking into a court-martial due to being found out since gay activity in the ADF is a serious breach of military law. Instead, he finds that he's been called for a secret mission to 1820. *Time travel!* He and a hastily assembled team have been called to rectify a problem caused by the very device that opened the portal to the past. Not expecting more than to do his duty, Kallen isn't prepared for what awaits him.

Book II: Chance Encounter

Sergeant Technician Kallen Deshara's mission to 1820 Kentucky hasn't prepared him to meet young handsome Aaric Utzman, whom he literally and figuratively falls head over heels for. And, while on the mission, one of the scientists who invented the device that opened the time portal, uploads to him the real history of how the world became burning hot. Kallen couldn't be any more ill-prepared for that long-suppressed truth. In addition, before he left, he hacked into the base commander's personal files. Once he goes through them it brings him face-to-face with the awful truth about the commander, his country's President, and a long abided-by water treaty. Everything he thought he knew about the past, his present, and his allegiance is put to the test. In fact, he's forced to challenge the limit of his sanity as he tries to absorb the truth of the world and of his heart.

Book III: Journey's End

Kallen Deshara now knows his world's origin, nature, and destiny; and has fallen madly in love with young Aaric Utzman. His decision to stay with Aaric, knowing full well that his presence might change all of history, brings him to the very edge of reality. But his colleagues who have returned to the 25th century have other plans. They intend to bring him back before he changes anything, even if it means killing him. But first they have to find him. Traveling along the Wilderness Trail with his new companion, Kallen is totally unaware he's being stalked. In the meantime, he realizes what had been missing his whole life, deepens his love with Aaric, and sees more water than he thought possible. Slowly but surely, he recognizes that he has more to offer than he ever knew. In fact, he may even be able to shape the future that should have been! But he learns an even more important lesson. He discovers that love knows no boundaries—not even of time itself.

Mark's website is www.mark-kendrick.com.

Printed in the United States
937100002B

9 780595 191307

0-595-19130-4